"You will do it for love of me..."

he told her in a rich low voice that throbbed in her ears. "Because you know my only purpose is to keep you safe."

It was a hard argument to combat—especially with van Ryker holding her so breathlessly close. Against her will, her passion flared again, seeming to light the room with its fire. His warm mouth pressed down on hers, his lips moved over hers sensuously, his tongue probed deeply, ardently, past her lips—and her resolve, so strong a moment ago, weakened. His hair spilled over her shoulder to tangle with her own and his strong hands encircled and lifted her. A soft moan caught in her throat as her body waked anew to this magical lover who could always take her with him on voyages of delight—and discovery...

Novels by
VALERIE SHERWOOD

This Loving Torment
These Golden Pleasures
This Towering Passion
Her Shining Splendor
Bold Breathless Love
Rash Reckless Love
Wild Willful Love

Published by
WARNER BOOKS

Valerie Sherwood

Wild Willful Love

WARNER BOOKS

A Warner Communications Company

WARNING

Readers are hereby specifically warned not to use any of the medications or cosmetics or exotic food or drink mentioned herein without first consulting a doctor. For example, the popular seventeenth-century cosmetic ceruse contained white lead, which is lethal; other concoctions of the day were often as bad.

WARNER BOOKS EDITION

Copyright © 1982 by Valerie Sherwood
All rights reserved.

Cover design by Gene Light

Cover art by Elaine Duillo

Warner Books, Inc.,
75 Rockefeller Plaza,
New York, N.Y. 10019

 A Warner Communications Company

Printed in the United States of America

First Printing: November, 1982

10 9 8 7 6 5 4 3 2 1

Dedication

To Fancy, my remarkable long-haired black and white tomcat and sire of Spicy's kittens—Fancy with his unbelievable beauty, a real "puss in boots" with paws like white gauntlet gloves, broad white boots, a gigantic waving plumelike black tail carried proudly aloft, big expressive green eyes, a huge burst of white fur ruff at his throat, an ethereal white curl in each silky black ear and the widest wingspread of white whiskers I have ever beheld—dear gentle Fancy with his sweet melodious voice, always magnanimous toward the other cats, always tender with his lady—to Fancy, as chivalrous and dashing as any of my heroes, this book is dedicated.

Author's Note

The past with all its mystery and glory will ever haunt us, and perhaps never more so than in the dashing seventeenth century, when events outstripped men's efforts to record them. Wild buccaneer Tortuga with its scalding intrigues and daring exploits is gone forever, of course—and let me say that it was that valiant Dutchman Piet Pieterzoon Heyne who took the Spanish treasure fleet intact and not van Ryker, and that Tortuga had indeed a French governor who sold letters of marque—but it was not Gauthier Touraille whose wife browbeat him and whose daughters scandalized him.

There are "huers" still in the Scillies; and on St. Mary's the remnants of Ennor Castle's crumbling stones; and history does record that rugged St. Agnes Isle, set in the cauldron of the sea, was notorious for its wreckers—but none were quite like Melisande, "Queen of the Wreckers," and her Harry; no legend perhaps so glowing as that of the tall buccaneer van Ryker and Imogene, his golden bride. As for Veronique and her Diego—their story has a terrible reality, for in Spain an aristocratic lady was once stabbed by her husband for inadvertently showing a bit of ankle on a Madrid street, and Veronique's punishment for shocking the queen with a dress cut a shade too low could well have happened.

In this saga of a fiery woman and her buccaneer, and those who loved and envied her, we will sail again the Spanish Main of romance and legend, and I will take you with me—in fiction of course, for this novel is entirely a product of my imagination—from blazing tropical Tortuga to those "Fortunate Isles" of the ancients, the storm-tossed, flower-strewn Scillies, a vivid journey through a fabulous and now but half-remembered world of gallantry and glory—and endless, endless love.

> *Across the long forgotten years*
> *I sing of reckless men*
> *And reckless women with their tears*
> *Sigh with me once again....*
>
> Valerie Sherwood

Contents

Wild Willful Love

An old love's fitful shadow
Flickers back into her life
And makes her now remember him
Who took her not to wife....

Prologue
Cornwall, England, 1661

The courtroom was packed. Lords and ladies in silks and plumed hats jostled chambermaids and hostlers and innkeepers for a better view. For the reckless beauty on trial for her life was not only a buccaneer's bride—four years earlier she had been Imogene Wells, bred on these very Scilly Isles at the southern tip of England, and even then scandal had swirled round her golden head.

"D'ye think she did it? Helped that no-good Linnington fellow murder young Giles Avery?" a plump dairymaid whispered to her gaunt fishwife friend. "I mean, after all, Avery *was* her betrothed."

"That's why she done it!" Triumphantly. "She wanted to get rid of him so's she could run away with her lover—Linnington. All the world knows *that*!" The fishwife touched her unfashionable yellow-starched collar and sighed. "See that dress she's wearin'? Blue as the sky—and they say sin don't pay!''

"Yes, but she didn't *know* she'd been betrothed to Giles Avery,'' insisted the dairymaid softly. She craned her neck to see better, for it was difficult to get a good view of the pale composed accused from the back of the courtroom. "Her guardian did it without her knowledge, they do say. So who's to say what's the right of it?''

"Who's to care?'' retorted yellow-starch impatiently. '' 'Tis the richest man in Cornwall's son was done in, and Mortimer Avery is a man to have his vengeance. 'Twill make a fine hanging, it will, and folks will be coming from miles around to see it. I don't plan to go back to Plymouth till it's over, I don't—I'm going to stay and watch Imogene Wells dance on the gibbet!''

"But the jury ain't decided nothing yet!'' cried the dairymaid, shocked.

"They'll find her guilty, you'll see.'' Yellow-starch nodded her angular head wisely. "The cards are stacked against her, as they say. Look at her, not one bit penitent, just standing up there in the dock as proud as you please!''

"I wonder what really happened?'' murmured the dairymaid. She was gazing half in sympathy at that slender aristocratic figure in blue velvet. "All those years ago . . .'' Her voice trailed off as the periwigged judge rapped for order.

"We've heard all the evidence, have we not? Have ye more to say on this matter, Mr. Allgood?'' he demanded in a bored voice of the barrister he had appointed to defend the intractable accused.

"Yes, Your Honor.'' Allgood straightened a wig that was

slightly askew, heaved his great girth out of his chair with some difficulty and moved forward ponderously. He cleared his throat and toyed with his gold snuffbox. He was trying to keep his eyes from straying toward the prisoner's shimmering golden hair, haloed by the light pouring down from a high window in the courtroom's thick stone walls. Lord, she looked a very madonna! He was already half in love with her and he had known her less than forty-eight hours.

"I suggest to you gentlemen," he told the jury impressively, swinging his bewigged head toward the twelve solemn fellows who stared back at him from the jury box, "that the accused was but sixteen at the time of Giles Avery's untimely death—she is now but twenty. I suggest to you, sirs, that Imogene Wells's only crime was to choose one man—while being *chosen* by another. I suggest to you that she is on trial not for her crimes but for her beauty, which beggars all description." Judge Hoskins cocked a cynical eye at him but Allgood rushed on. *"Look at her."* Allgood's voice rang out and as one man the entire courtroom turned to consider the blazing beauty standing so defiantly in the dock. Her delicate chin lifted and her delft blue eyes flung them back a challenge. She took a deep breath and the sky blue velvet of her tight, low-cut bodice strained with that breath, causing every man present to breathe an inward sigh, for the body encased in that modish gown was of an elegance that courtesans might well envy and the face above it was unforgettable. She was Eve, she was Temptress, she was Woman.

"Look at her," he repeated raptly, his own hazel eyes kindling at the sight. "Could any man *not* desire her?"

The beauty of lustrous Imogene had scarcely escaped the

notice of a man like Judge Hoskins. A slight tremor went through his back muscles as he thought what it would be like to brush his fingers over the silky skin of that snowy bosom, so impudently highlighted by the prisoner's rapid breathing. He brought his thoughts sternly to heel. He was not here to admire this glowing wench but to see her convicted and decently executed: the jury, all local fellows, some of whom had known young Avery—though it was hardly likely they had admired him—would see to the first; he, Hoskins, would personally arrange for the second. And that execution was indeed essential to the judge's personal well-being, for Mortimer Avery had not hesitated to remind him just before the trial of the large sums of money the judge owed him, moneys that had been due and callable these six months past. Judge Hoskins kept before him the frightening fact that everything of consequence he owned was mortgaged to Mortimer Avery; it made it easier to turn his face stonily away from the woman in the dock.

"Is that all? Have you anything else to say, Counselor?" he asked crisply.

"That is all I have, Your Honor." Ponderously, Allgood sat down.

"I have something to say if he has not!" Aristocratic and indignant, the prisoner's clear voice rang out.

"Prisoner at the bar, be silent," began the judge impatiently. "Your counselor has already spoken for you."

"Spoken for me? Ha, that he has not!"

"Be still. Your sex does not excuse these outbursts."

"My sex?" Imogene gave an angry laugh. "I would have

expected somewhat more of a notorious wencher,'' she said bitterly.

A ripple of indrawn breaths went through the courtroom at this temerity but Judge Hoskins, his color heightened a bit beneath his powdered periwig, now favored her with a genial smile. It was the same smile he had cast upon poor Turner and other culprits long since beneath the sod, just before he pronounced sentence on them. His clerk called it his ''hanging smile'' and gave the rebellious Imogene a frightened look.

''We will overlook this outburst, Mistress Wells,'' said Judge Hoskins cheerfully.

''Not 'Mistress Wells'—I am Madame van Ryker,'' Imogene corrected him through clenched teeth. ''And as a prisoner at the bar who is being given short shrift to the gallows, I insist on being heard!''

Judge Hoskins would have blithely disregarded the accused's wishes in the matter, but Imogene in her fury had grasped the low railing behind which she stood and leaned forward in a way that, in her low-cut gown, all but exposed her nipples. That sudden expanse of pearly skin was breathtaking, for four years ago young Mistress Wells had been referred to in whispers as ''the girl with the whisk,'' meaning she was always lightheartedly tossing away the lawn whisk, or ''pinner,'' that women wore across their bosoms for modesty to fill in the space above their fashionably low-cut dresses, and baring her bosom to the nipples in the fashion of court ladies at Whitehall.

Now faced with this delectable view, Judge Hoskins told himself that because Imogene was talking did not mean necessarily that he must listen. He could stare at her as much as he pleased and no one would think less of him for it—after all, he was giving an impudent prisoner enough rope to hang herself. Who could ask more of a judge than that?

He leaned upon his arm in what he considered a nonchalant fashion and resisted the urge to scratch beneath his great powdered periwig where some small insect—a louse, he'd no doubt, contracted from this stenchy rabble about him—was biting. His small shrewd eyes narrowed as he considered Mistress Wells's angry countenance.

A luscious piece this one, he was thinking. He remembered when she had been among the crowd at—whose was it, Turner's hanging? He had viewed that pert bottom in those blowing calico skirts and edged forward through the crowd, jostling bold fellows aside to stand behind her. She couldn't have been more than fourteen at the time, he judged, and he remembered that she had been fiercely partisan to poor Turner, who it turned out later had been innocent of stealing the money—some fellow named Warren had fled to France with it and never been heard of again. Indeed young Mistress Wells had attracted Hoskins's attention by jumping up and down shouting "No, no!" as the crowd roared its satisfaction when the rope snapped taut and Turner, with his horrified eyes bulging, found himself dancing on air.

It had been too good an opportunity for Judge Hoskins to miss. With his gaze fixed tranquilly on the gibbet, he had eased one ringed hand forward toward those calico folds and under cover of all the excitement, with everyone's attention fixed on Turner, he had given Imogene's round bottom a squeeze with his big spatulate fingers.

The girl's reaction had been immediate, he remembered with an inward chuckle. She had turned on Tom Cobb, who was standing beside her, and given him an indignant slap across the face. Tom, entirely misunderstanding the basis for this assault, had turned upon Mistress Wells with an indignation that matched her own, exclaiming that he was as entitled to shout "Good riddance!" as she was to shout "No, no, don't kill him!" for wasn't it his own uncle that had been bilked of the money?

Judge Hoskins had not stayed to see how Tom and Imogene resolved it; he had melted away into the crowd. But his fingers had continued to tingle appreciatively with the soft springy feel of the cheek of her youthful bottom and after that he had observed young Mistress Wells at every opportunity.

His chance to fondle her again had come the next year at a ball given by Mortimer Avery, whose son Giles was even then enamored of the fifteen-year-old beauty. Judge Hoskins, taking a breath of air in the Averys' Cornish garden—actually he was frowning over how to separate the Averys' visiting London cousin from her elderly husband and try out her charms in the darkness of the box hedge—had chanced upon Mistress Wells.

It was an interesting moment.

As Judge Hoskins rounded a corner of the old boxwood hedge, Imogene was in the act of saying "No!" in a violent tone to young Giles Avery, who had just seized her fiercely around the middle. Giles ducked and lost his grip as Imogene swung at him wildly and her slight body spun away from him.

Judge Hoskins could easily have stepped aside and let the

girl right herself but he chose not to. Instead he stuck out his satin-breeched leg and allowed her to trip over it, so that she lost her footing. In the scramble as she went down, one of Judge Hoskins's practiced spatulate hands somehow managed to rove quickly over her young breasts while the other, in the guise of helping her up, explored the silky smoothness of her trim thighs.

Sputtering, Imogene gained her feet and gave her "rescuer" a sharp kick in the shins.

"Lecher!" she flung at him.

Judge Hoskins's brows rose in feigned wonderment and he turned to look quizzically at young Giles, who had paled at this verbal attack on a magistrate. "What ails the child?" he had demanded of Giles in a puzzled voice.

"I—I don't know, sir," gulped Giles, who had not noticed the old debaucher's roving fingers and believed the judge only to have broken Imogene's fall. "I apologize for her, sir—she don't know what she's saying." He hurried away after Imogene's flying skirts while Judge Hoskins bent down to rub his stinging shin and chuckled. The kick had been well worth it, for the silkiness of the girl's skin had been delightful; it had fired his veins and he had set off in pursuit of the Averys' London cousin with a jauntiness that brought her to earth in record time.

The handsome judge was indeed a notorious wencher and almost invariably successful with women. Many a ripe young beauty had lain in his arms since that night in the garden when he had tripped young Mistress Wells, but her memory had remained green. Even now he could recall her soft resilient flesh beneath his roving spatulate fingertips, her instantaneous and spirited response—imagine what that response would be like were it willing!

He delivered himself of a sigh—quite appropriate under the circumstances in the opinion of the audience. How could they know he sighed only because he dared give the accused nothing but speedy justice and not the slow wait in jail and little "visits" in the night that would have pleased him better?

He caught at that moment the evil expression on Mortimer Avery's stern countenance, as he sat with taupe satin legs crossed beside his pale wife, who clutched her smelling salts in the front row. Mortimer wished to have done with it, of course, get Mistress Wells hanged quickly. And he had better do it. Quickly.

His gaze went back to the accused. Proud and passionate, she stared back at him. His contemptuous gaze flicked over her, from her shimmering golden head to the toe of her satin slipper—then came back to linger on that heaving blue velvet bodice. The flesh above, pale as watered silk, still tempted him. His eyelids fell hoodlike as he let his cold eyes range over that wondrous white expanse that seemed to beckon him. And what real harm, he asked himself lazily, to let her speak—nay, it would be best to let her do so. It would make a better impression on the citizenry, especially since the conclusion was foregone. Then no one could say later that he had muzzled her, denied her a fair trial—not even if his heavy debts to Mortimer Avery should somehow be brought to light. Far better to let her speak now, then let her make the usual confession and plea for redemption on the scaffold; none of it mattered anyway.

"Speak," he said indifferently. "This is a just court. We will hear you out."

Imogene cast a sweeping glance over the crowd. In the forefront Mortimer Avery and his wife, wishing her dead. Around them, supporting them, a bevy of plume-hatted gentry, the periwigged men—some of them remembering her rebuffs—taking snuff, the embroidered, satin-clad women—glad to see her brought low—idly wafting ivory fans. Somewhere in there was a friendly face—Bess Duveen's—but at the moment Imogene could not find it. She could tell them the truth, of course—that Giles had found her and Stephen clasped naked on the beach in scalding embrace with the onrushing surf licking lazily at their toes—and died when he plunged forward, tripped and impaled himself on Stephen's hastily drawn defensive sword. It was accident, death by misadventure—but never murder. She could tell them, but would this crowd of fishermen and farmers and tenants on Avery land and riffraff from the towns roundabout—tavern wenches and harlots and their ilk—believe that? Surely they'd prefer the excitement of a hanging?

Her gaze left them for the jury. Twelve solid-looking men clad in their Sunday best; wearing stiff uncomfortable white collars that their wives had no doubt fresh-starched and ironed for the occasion. She looked into their stolid faces and knew that they would never understand what had lured a golden-haired aristocrat and a copper-haired adventurer to chance it all for love. Not these dull-faced men who worked dawn to dark and trudged home of nights to fat complaining wives and houses full of clamoring children—they never knew what it was to wing it to the stars, or look up at a

22

mocking moon and curse their fate. She would never get through to them—never. They would shake their heads and mutter, and then they would hang her high. . . .

As she stood there, poised on the brink, she seemed to hear again the wild surf ringing in her ears and see Stephen's wicked laughing face as he pulled her, naked and protesting, from the sea to claim her body and her soul upon a warm sunlit dune on St. Agnes Isle. She had danced with him beside the parapet of Star Castle, he had fought a duel for her, and beneath blazing stars flashing from a black velvet sky they had plighted their troth. How she had loved him . . . and he had proved false. He had gone away and left her to all that had happened later. But just for the moment an old love's enchanting shadow had drifted over the courtroom and she had seen through the mists of yesterday another time, another place.

The vision left her and she was standing squarely in the dock in the stark light of day, facing her accusers. Men had called her rash and reckless and wild and willful—and she was all of those things. But no one anywhere had ever doubted her courage. For Imogene was not only a beauty—she had a fighting heart.

If the truth would not save her, *something else would*!

The jury listened raptly as her lovely voice rang out. They were waiting for that cool mask of challenge to break up, waiting for her to plead for her life, to throw herself on their mercy, waiting for her to weep.

They would wait a long time for that, for the dazzling

woman in the dock was cast in a different mold, and what she had to say left them startled, set them back on their heels casting uneasy glances at each other.

It was a day nobody in Cornwall would soon forget.

BOOK I
Trouble in Paradise

This bright moment filled with joy,
Will it warn the girl and boy
Of the earthly paradise they well might lose?
Will they realize its worth?
Hold it dearest on this earth?
Will they choose aright, or will they even choose?

PART ONE
Veronique

Silk skirts and mended petticoats
Blow in the same light breeze,
And duchesses and chambermaids
Are sisters beneath the chemise!

The Island of Tortuga, 1661

CHAPTER 1

Like a hot golden ball, the sun rose over the buccaneer island of Tortuga. It sent its fierce rays impartially over Cayona's busy quay, the harbor alive with ships, and above them the frowning gray Mountain Fort whose guns gave them safe harbor, and—more caressingly perhaps—through the open bedroom windows of an imposing white-stuccoed stone house where a golden woman, lying late abed, awoke to find her lover gone.

It was those burning rays that had awakened her, shafting a scorching path through the wooden lattice into her bedchamber to sear her long tapering white legs and slender body naked to the heat, and pour its molten light over her long golden hair, turning it to leaping flame.

Now Imogene's delft blue eyes blinked into the tropical sunlight and she woke confused, and realized that it was only a bolster her slender white arms were clutching—and not the lean hard body of Tortuga's most celebrated buccaneer.

For a moment she sighed and relaxed, letting her smooth breasts scrape sensuously against the feather bolster. It seemed but moments before that van Ryker had been making love to her, her slender nakedness locked in his strong, sun-bronzed arms, her whole female body alight with the fire of his passion. She had felt herself swept up by that passion, driven before his ardor like a leaf before a hurricane, and the whole night had been one long conflagration of touching and sighs, of tangled limbs and soft murmurs and little bursts of shared laughter over secret things of the heart. And as their passions rose and towered, lingering expectation gave way to soul-shattering excitement and they were tossed aloft and crested into a glittering unreal world of magical splendor and exotic delights, until with mingled hearts and minds they had drifted softly downward to lie together in utter content, with van Ryker's lean form lying relaxed beside her, lazily caressing her tingling nakedness in the afterglow.

With a little shudder of regret, Imogene pushed away the bolster but it left her fingers reluctantly. Her blue eyes gleamed with pride as she thought of the man whose head had so lately reposed on that bolster: tall and dark and arresting, accounted the best blade in all the Caribbean.

But it was not the intrepid buccaneer who swept Spanish decks clean with broadsides from the *Sea Rover* that Imogene loved—nor yet the genial freebooter who rested his booted heels upon a tavern table, leaned back and matched the sturdiest rogues drink for drink.

She knew the man behind the mask, knew that he fought

under a name and a flag not even his own. She knew him for what he was—an Englishman hiding from the law for a crime he had not committed, who had taken a Dutch name not only for concealment (for he spoke Dutch fluently) but for the convenience of trading his captured Spanish goods for higher prices in Dutch New Amsterdam than they would bring in overstocked Tortuga or Port Royal.

And Esthonie Touraille, wife of Tortuga's French governor, had dared to suggest that his affections might wander—indeed, might have wandered already!

The thought gave her energy, even in this oppressive heat that hung over the island. She sat up, tossed her long legs over the side of the bed and stretched her white arms above her head. Her bare toe caught in something and she smiled down at the little mound of lace-trimmed white cambric on the floor—her night rail, hastily shed and somehow fallen from the bed. She rose, snatched up a sheer lacy chemise and felt it slither luxuriously down over her sleek hips and firm thighs. Its light skirts billowed around her ankles as she strode across the room and flung wide the shutters that an errant breeze was just blowing shut.

The town of Cayona stretched before her, with its maze of crooked streets. And beyond the sprawl of taverns and brothels and inns, the quay where heaped-up Spanish loot was being sold. And beyond that the ships. A smile curved her soft lips as she saw the *Sea Rover*'s golden hull gleaming in the sunlight—van Ryker's vessel. Of course, those other captured galleons lying alongside were his too, a whole covey of them, for Captain van Ryker had done the impossible—he

31

had captured an entire Spanish treasure *flota* and the buccaneers were still tallying up his wealth.

But now her delft blue gaze glimpsed something else: a raven-haired woman, riding by, cast an upward look at the house. An arrogant woman with smooth olive skin and long, wickedly shaped amber eyes, and a haughty tilt to her head. Involuntarily Imogene drew in her breath and stepped back from that hard predatory gaze that raked the building. Her mouth hardened.

Veronique Fondage (according to the governor's wife) had sworn she would wrest van Ryker from his golden English bride. And while the bride had lain asleep, Veronique was on the prowl and looking far too beautiful in her sleek black taffeta riding habit. And that rankled too because Veronique, who had been rescued from one of the galleons of the Spanish treasure *flota*, had been lent that very riding habit by Esthonie Touraille, the governor's wife, who had had the fabric as a gift from van Ryker.

Imogene closed the shutters with a slam. Sight of that woman with her flaunting beauty had brought to mind her conversation of yesterday afternoon with Esthonie Touraille.

"Ah, you will have to take second place to Veronique, I fear, *ma chère*," Esthonie had purred. They'd been seated in the garden courtyard of the green-shuttered white house that served as a "governor's palace" for Tortuga. "Even her name, Fondage, means 'melting.'" She waved her ivory-paneled fan meaningfully. "And how appropriate! Have you looked into her eyes? Amber—with little leaping yellow flames in them!"

Imogene had resettled her lettuce green silk skirts on the

white marble bench and bent down and stroked Malcolm, the Tourailles' cat, before answering. Malcolm stretched his white and orange body and purred appreciatively. She replied without looking up. "Van Ryker has sympathy for the lost," she told Esthonie shortly. "And"—this to remind Esthonie that Veronique had recently been a prisoner of the Spanish—"for the trapped."

"Lost? Trapped?" Esthonie's expressive French brows shot up. "I doubt Veronique has ever been lost in her life—*or* trapped. She would have had those Spaniards wrapped around her little finger long before their ship ever saw the Spanish coast! Ah, it is too bad she speaks no English and you no French. Van Ryker"—this to remind Imogene that van Ryker spoke French fluently—"conversed with her for perhaps two hours in my salon after he brought her to me. Is that a new gown? I don't recall having seen it before."

Imogene, nettled at being reminded that Veronique, as a rescued French aristocrat, was now a houseguest of Tortuga's French governor, shrugged that off. "Van Ryker was only being polite, Esthonie. And yes, it is a new gown. From Paris." She knew that would irritate the governor's envious lady.

"Polite? *Polite?* You think that was his reason?" Esthonie rolled her eyes at the cascading bougainvillaea. "Ah, you English, you must be made of ice. *I* would be yearning to pull out every hair of Veronique's so lovely head if she spent so much time with *my* husband!" Her gaze raked over the delicate pale green silk flounces of Imogene's wide skirts, wandered with annoyance over the delicate silver embroidery of the bodice that gave it an icy look, cool and tempting below the smooth white skin of her breast tops, so tauntingly displayed by the gown's low-cut neckline. "I have not seen that petticoat, either," she grumbled.

"No?" Imogene moved her green satin slippers artfully so that the thin moss-green taffeta of her frostily embroidered petticoat rustled to advantage. She fixed her tormentor with a sweet smile. "But this petticoat is quite *old*, Esthonie. I have had it for at least two months! And"— she leaned forward to give her opponent the *coup de grâce* because Esthonie's sly barbs had upset her— "I imagine Veronique has probably spent *at least* as much time with Gauthier, since she is a guest in your house!"

Esthonie's dark eyes left the petticoat and traveled to Imogene's slightly malicious smile. She meant to wipe that smile off the English beauty's face.

"Ah, but no so *intimately*! With Veronique stretched out at her ease on the red velvet divan in my drawing room and Captain van Ryker lounging there with his long legs crossed, observing her as he sipped his Malaga." Having sent her barb home, Esthonie leaned back and fanned her plump face vigorously and resettled her black brocade skirts. "Tell me, do you think I should redo the walls now that I have the red velvet divan? The green walls seem to clash with it."

"Esthonie," laughed Imogene, "in the time that I have known you, you have already redecorated that room three times. It was gold and you changed it to 'ashes of roses,' then to ivory and lastly to green. Don't you tire of having the place torn up?"

"I was thinking perhaps a soft red—not quite a puce but nearly so. In time for my next party."

Imogene felt sympathy for the short, voluble little French governor, who needs must live in a house in which the furniture was constantly being whisked in and out to make way for the painters. She reminded herself that Esthonie, when not eaten up with envy, had been very kind to her since her arrival in this buccaneers' stronghold, and that Esthonie's parties were almost the only social life the island afforded. "The red velvet divan does dominate the room," she agreed. "So perhaps you are right to change the walls." Though not to *puce*, surely!

Mention of the divan brought Esthonie back to her guest, Veronique. Her jet-spangled bodice shook as she leaned forward. "I can tell you she had a lot to say to him!"

"Say to who?" asked Imogene with feigned innocence.

"To your husband, of course!" Esthonie's fan fluttered indignantly. "She talked and talked while he interposed questions to draw her out."

The shadow of a frown passed over Imogene's usually tranquil countenance. She could see the scene as Esthonie must have seen it—a lustrous woman, elegantly displayed in black satin and pearls (for Veronique usually affected black satin in the evening), with her heavy black hair swept up in that unique coiffure and cascading down in shiny ringlets. She could see those amber eyes with their flickering little yellow flames playing over van Ryker's sardonic face, *challenging* him to desire her. And she could see her lean buccaneer, elegant in the dove gray silk breeches and silver-shot doublet and wide-topped polished black boots he would no doubt have worn to call at the "governor's palace," could see him lean forward, debonair as always, with the frosty lace of his cuffs spilling over his fine hands as he refilled a Venetian goblet with wine for the lady, could see him leaning back considering her from those saturnine features, the gray eyes hooded, contemplative.

What would he have been thinking? That she was desirable forbidden fruit? And would that not make her all the more attractive?

It also rankled that when she had been introduced to Veronique at Esthonie's house, Veronique had met her polite nod with a burst of French in which the words *El Cruzado* came through plainly.

"What is she saying?" Imogene, who spoke no French, had asked Esthonie.

"She is telling you how much she enjoyed her voyage here aboard the *Sea Rover*."

"I've no doubt she enjoyed it!" A woman like Veronique must always enjoy being the sole woman amid a shipload of lusty men. "But I heard her mention *El Cruzado*."

"That is what she calls the *Sea Rover*," supplied Esthonie. "She says it was once Don Luis Alvarez's flagship."

Imogene was well aware the great golden-hulled *Sea Rover* had been called *El Cruzado* when van Ryker had seized her from the Spanish. But even she had not known that it had been flagship of the fleet of Don Luis, grandee of Spain, a man in the confidence of kings. It nettled her that van Ryker—who must be Veronique's source for this information— had told Veronique and not herself the great ship's history.

"Ask her how she knows that," she had demanded bluntly.

A rapid conversation in French ensued and Imogene had seen a hunted look appear suddenly in Veronique's amber eyes. "She says," reported Esthonie, "that she once saw *El Cruzado* in a French port and recognized her by the magnificent golden figurehead."

It sounded reasonable, but Imogene had only to look into that beautiful predatory face to know that Veronique was lying. Van Ryker had undoubtedly told her the ship's history . . . something he had not deigned to tell his wife.

She roused herself with a start. Esthonie was speaking again.

"Of course I realized they must have come to know each other rather well during all that time the salvageable ships of the treasure *flota* were being refloated and the gold and bullion from the broken ones taken off and loaded onto the *Sea Rover* and the *Hawk* and the *Heron. Ma chère,* you should have been here the day they sailed Cayona Bay, laden so heavy with booty that they rode low in the water. They used gold and silver for ballast! The town went wild to see them."

Cayona was wild enough at best, and it was still enjoying one long holiday over that event, which had happened months ago. "Busy as he was, I doubt van Ryker had much time for Veronique," she told Esthonie airily.

"On the contrary! Veronique tells me he was very gallant with her. She slept in the great cabin. *Ma chère,* those colors do not become you. Your skirt seems made of lettuce leaves on an icy bed of watercress for a petticoat. All you need is to powder your hair and you would look like a salad!"

Imogene ignored the jibe—and ignored Malcolm too, who had sat down on the toe of one of her green slippers and was nuzzling her ankle in an open invitation to have his fur stroked again. She leaned forward. "You say Veronique *slept*—?" she demanded incredulously.

"In the *Sea Rover*'s great cabin? Yes, she told me that. Of course, it was all very innocent, Captain van Ryker bunked in with Dr. de Rochemont the whole time!" She tittered. "If one can believe Veronique!"

Wild unbidden jealousy pounded through Imogene's veins. The *Sea Rover* was very special to her. Van Ryker had pursued her across half an ocean in that ship, had carried her unconscious to the great cabin and there she had waked to hate him, to fight him—and eventually to love him. So many memories of her deep abiding love for van Ryker were inextricably intertwined with the golden-hulled *Sea Rover*'s proud voyaging. How often had she stood beside van Ryker at the taffrail with the trade winds blowing her golden hair and a red sunset in the west crimsoning the big white sails and turning the sea to blood. That first time he had taken her—against her will although subconsciously she had always wanted him—had been in the great cabin of the *Sea Rover* with the mighty ship creaking about them and a wisp of song from some lonesome buccaneer floating down to them from the rigging. In that very bunk the storms of unending passion had been roused in her female breast : . . it was there van Ryker had tried to comfort her for the loss of her daughter when she had wanted so much to die. She had been lying in that very bunk when van Ryker had willed her to live, and made her strong and whole again against her will.

And now another woman had slept in it! And . . . perhaps . . . with him? Certainly Esthonie was implying it, going on and on about Veronique's classic beauty spread out on the divan and van Ryker drinking goblet on goblet of wine as she talked.

"What did they talk about?" she asked mechanically.

"Ah, but I was not in the room with them!" The jet on Esthonie's bodice shook complacently; she had Imogene's attention at last.

"But you could see them? The door was open?"

"Of course! Ah, you are not to fear—nothing happened in *my* house! But I made a point of telling you that she sailed back with him on the *Sea Rover* because their conversation astonished me."

You made a point of telling me that she sailed with him on the Sea Rover *because you wished me to understand that van Ryker had spent weeks in Veronique's company—and had every opportunity to make love to her. It is your passion to probe and poke into other people's lives!* Aloud she said, "Astonished you? How so?"

Esthonie leaned forward, jet shaking, and aimed her fan pointedly at Imogene. "I passed the door frequently to see what they were up to—in your interests, of course," she added hastily. "And Veronique was telling him all her troubles. Is it not strange that she chose my drawing room for her revelations? When she could have had the intimacy of the ship?"

Imogene felt a little knife turning in her breast. Her unease communicated itself to Malcolm, who got up, leaving her slipper, and strolled in orange and white luxury toward a green chameleon that darted into the bushes at his approach. Malcolm followed.

"Troubles? What troubles?" Imogene asked in a strangled voice.

"Well, there is the small trouble and the larger trouble," confided Esthonie. "The small trouble is that the Spanish seized her jewel case when they sank the *Fleur-de-Lis* and massacred everyone aboard."

"I hadn't heard that!"

"Oh, yes, Veronique tells me she was the only survivor."

"She and her jewel case," said Imogene ironically.

"That's right. The jewel case disappeared. When last seen, it was in the hands of the Spanish captain, who spirited it away, probably for his private trove—and then was killed in the storm. She insists that her jewels are very valuable—which brings me to another point, Imogene. With that frosted lettuce concoction you are wearing, why are you not wearing another frosting of diamonds? Why no jewels? I remember when first you came to Tortuga you brought with you a marvelous collection of jewels—that diamond necklace and earrings you wore to the first party you attended here quite took my breath away. I have not seen you wear them lately."

The van Rappard diamonds. . . . A shadow passed over Imogene's face. She had worn those diamonds when she first arrived, to spite van Ryker, to flaunt before him that she was no penniless wench but a woman of wealth, in her own right heiress to a vast fortune in New Netherland if she cared to claim it. But after she had come to love him, after the golden Tortuga sun had melted her heart and she had realized how much he meant to her, she had put away the van Rappard diamonds. Forever. To her they symbolized, like frozen tears, the snows of far Wey Gat, and the proud young patroon she had married in haste and lived to regret. A dark, slender, prideful man who had loved her eerily, frenziedly—and far too well. An unbalanced man whom grief had driven mad. . . . She had fled from him on a terrible moonlit night across the frozen wastes of the North River. The iceboat's roar and chatter washed over her now in a great remembered wave, enveloping her senses as it swept toward her out of the violent past. Elise, her old nurse, was on that iceboat and Stephen, her copper-haired lover of the Scillies when she was but sixteen—and baby Georgiana, the daughter she had borne him. It was the last time she had seen Georgiana, the last time she had seen Elise, and when on board the *Sea Rover* she had learned how the ship *Wilhelmina* had gone down with them aboard, she had sought death—and found life in van Ryker's arms.

"I never wear the diamonds anymore," she said in a choked voice. *They bring back too much.*

"Anyway, van Ryker was telling Veronique that he would turn her jewel case over to her if he found it." A self-satisfied smile spread over Esthonie's features, for in Imogene's place she would have been furious, believing any jewels found should end up in *her* jewel case!

To her annoyance, Imogene shrugged and said, "Of course he would return it! Did they not find it?"

"No, and van Ryker was urging her to try to discover its location through the surviving Spaniards. Perhaps the officers could help her. Veronique thought a certain Spanish officer might know where it was secreted in the galleon. Van Ryker told her to seek him out."

"Which Spanish officer?" Imogene had visited the captured Spanish officers' quarters several times with great baskets of fruit—bananas, mangoes, plantains. Terrible those Spaniards might have been on the seas, but the remnant of them here on Tortuga seemed to her a pitiful lot, waiting forlornly for their families back in Spain to ransom them. She had asked van Ryker if he could not just let them go but he had explained it was established custom to pay ransom or work it out as an indentured servant for three or four years—and that was what gave Tortuga its style and elegance, for some of the captives turned out to be master masons and ironworkers and carpenters.

"Which officer?" Esthonie frowned. "Oh, Navarro, I think his name is. Don Diego Navarro."

"Yes, I remember him," murmured Imogene, her mind conjuring up a tall, indolent-appearing fellow of impeccable manners who had always risen—albeit painfully—to his feet at sight of her and swept her a bow that must have cost him a deal, for his olive face was always a shade whiter when he straightened up. Imogene, who spoke no Spanish, had been unable to converse with him. "He is the one with the leg injury," she supplemented. "The one Raoul is always visiting. Raoul told me he is the sole surviving officer of the galleon he sailed on. A gallant officer, according to Raoul."

Esthonie nodded energetically. "The same. It seems he was one of the few who sprang up from the beach to fight the onrushing buccaneers and his leg was seriously injured in a sword thrust from van Ryker. Your husband admired his courage and so he has arranged for Dr. de Rochemont—Raoul, as you call him—" (Esthonie's sniff told of a recent tiff with the *Sea Rover*'s French doctor) "to pamper this Spaniard. Veronique was eager to question him."

"And has her inquiry borne fruit?"

"Not yet," shrugged Esthonie. "Although she has been to see him several times and has entreated him at length to tell her where the jewels are hidden. Navarro claims a head injury suffered at the time his ship was driven onto the beach and broke up during the storm. He claims a mast fell on him. Anyway, it seems to have damaged his memory."

"Perhaps he is lying and knows where the jewels are. Wasn't his ship one of those refloated and brought back here to Tortuga?"

Esthonie nodded. "I suggested that to Veronique but she is very sure that when Navarro remembers anything, he will tell her."

Veronique's smile of utter confidence flashed before Imogene—confidence in her sex and in her allure. Veronique was undoubtedly sure she could twist any man around her finger—even a former Spanish captor.

"So that is Veronique's minor problem," said Imogene ironically. "What of her major one?"

"Men," said Esthonie significantly. "She is troubled by a surfeit of lovers. They fight and brawl over her, it seems. I heard her tell van Ryker it was for that reason she fled her native France aboard the *Fleur-de-Lis*—and had already entered into a liaison with the captain before the ship was captured by the Spanish. I don't doubt she would have had a liaison with the Spanish captain too, save that he was occupied by a gale and then van Ryker seized his ship along with the rest of the *flota*. But *he* would have been next, I'll warrant!"

And now van Ryker was next in line. The implication was clear. Imogene fought to keep down the flush that rose to her cheeks and was furious that she could not.

Esthonie was smiling mischievously at her and Imogene could well guess what the wife of Tortuga's French governor was thinking: *About time someone brought down that proud English wench who has snatched up the catch of Tortuga! And raven-haired Veronique with her insatiable lust for men is just the one to do it!*

Esthonie smiled and played her trump card.

"I thought I saw Captain van Ryker with Veronique yesterday afternoon," she purred. "It was near the church, where the road disappears into a grove of pimento trees—so sylvan, a perfect trysting place."

It was too much. Van Ryker had told Imogene he'd spent all of yesterday supervising repairs to the captured galleons. *And she believed him!*

CHAPTER 2

Imogene's back stiffened ever so slightly. It was a warning sign and Esthonie should have seen it, but she did not for Malcolm had tried of chasing the chameleon and Esthonie was busy trying to push him away before he could shed any orange and white hairs on her dark skirts.

"I just realized my feet are in the sun, Esthonie," Imogene said sweetly, glancing casually behind her at the huge trunk of a giant pepper tree that shaded the courtyard. Her gaze focused on a raw gash where a large limb had been sawed off. "Tell me, whatever happened to the limb that used to shade this bench so effectively?"

Esthonie's smile became rather fixed. She forgot all about Malcolm and straightened up. "It scraped the house," she said vaguely. "And frightened Virginie by making noises in the night. Some more limeade? It's very cooling."

"No, thank you." Imogene toyed with her half-empty glass, considering her hostess through narrowed eyes. "Where *is* Virginie?"

Esthonie cast a hunted look around her. At her feet Malcolm, unnoticed now, was rubbing and purring and covering one side of her dark skirt with cat hair for he was shedding in the heat. "I am not sure it was van Ryker I saw," she amended hastily. "I only said it *looked* like him."

"And I'm sure you have excellent vision, Esthonie."

"Oh, perhaps not!" A flight of seabirds wheeled by overhead. Esthonie looked up in exasperation. "Oh, those birds! They make so much noise." She was suddenly aware that Malcolm was rubbing against her leg. "Go away, Malcolm!" She kicked at him and the cat gave her an injured look and strolled away disdainfully.

Imogene had watched all this calmly.

"Let us forget van Ryker, *and* the cat, *and* the seabirds for the moment, Esthonie. I asked you a simple enough question. Where is your eldest daughter?"

Everybody on Tortuga knew where Virginie was: locked in her room above them by a hysterical mother. Everybody knew how the pepper tree had lost its limb—and why. Esthonie's plump hand shook as she busied herself pouring limeade from a silver pitcher.

"It was so clever of you to build a room on top of your house so Virginie could have a view," Imogene continued. *A view of the pepper tree. With the wall scraped by a limb sturdy enough for a man to climb.* "I thought your explanation of why Virginie had left the first floor so amusing," she added mercilessly.

46

"Well, as I told you, Gauthier had a sister who eloped—so unfortunate, the man was a gamester and they ended in *ruin*. Now that Virginie has reached marriageable age, it was Gauthier's idea that we should build a room atop the house with a stairway that led up through his own room. For Virginie's—protection." She choked on the word.

So if hotheaded young Virginie, with her precocious hour-glass figure and her bouncing black curls, decided one day to elope with one of the reckless young buccaneers with whom she flirted incessantly, Gauthier would be on hand to prevent it. How proudly Esthonie had shown Imogene the lock on Virginie's door when that room had been completed and Virginie installed in it—that lock to which she had the only key. She had completely overlooked the pepper tree.

Virginie's swains had not. Rumor had it that there had been a perpetual stream of them climbing into Virginie's window by way of the pepper tree's sturdy limb. Rumor was always rife in Tortuga, but there could be no doubting the one that had caused the tree limb to be cut down.

Last week Virginie's latest lover, one James Notley, a young buccaneer from the town, had made a tryst with her. Unfortunately he had tippled a bit too heavily before keeping that tryst. Arriving at the window he made a dizzy grasp for the sash, missed, and fell with a howl into the courtyard below, landing on a marble bench similar to that on which Imogene was now sitting—and broke his leg.

Imogene could imagine what it had been like. The house-hold, aroused by Notley's howl, had bolted outdoors into the velvet tropical night. Virginie, in her night rail, must have tearfully protested her innocence—and probably most convincingly, since both Esthonie's daughters were consummate liars. But a hysterical Esthonie had demanded the offending limb be removed. At once.

Accordingly the alarmed governor had hauled a sleepy carpenter out of bed (one of those Spanish captives working out his ransom) and ordered the limb sawed off. To the accompaniment of muttered heartfelt Spanish oaths it had been done and the limb had fallen with a crash into the courtyard.

"Esthonie," said Imogene heartlessly, "don't you think it's time you let her *out*?"

Esthonie jumped as if pricked by a hatpin. "Out?" she quavered. *"Out?"*

Imogene leaned forward earnestly. "You are causing talk by keeping her locked in. On my way over here, I met Dr. Argyll and he urged me to speak to you about it. He said too much restraint could be as bad as too little, that he had a young niece who fled the house via a rope ladder and was never seen again."

"Mamma." Virginie's plaintive voice floated down to them. "I promise you I have no ropes up here."

"Virginie, be quiet!" hissed her mother.

"Why do you not take her driving?" suggested Imogene. "So people will know she is still alive!"

"Oh, and take me too, Mamma!" A head of thick shining black curls stuck up suddenly from behind a bushy shrub.

"Georgette!" Esthonie scolded her younger daughter. "You were listening!"

"Of course, Mamma." Georgette rose to her full height. Although only thirteen, she was taller than Virginie but more coltish in appearance. "I always listen. How else am I to learn what is going on?"

Imogene hid a smile. Esthonie's tempestuous daughters, it was the general opinion, would be the death of her.

"Eavesdroppers never hear anything good about themselves!" warned Esthonie.

"And nothing much good about anyone else, either," agreed Georgette cheerfully. She came out from behind the shrub, her white dimity skirts billowing around her long slim legs. She took a mango from the silver dish beside her mother.

"Careful, you'll ruin your dress with the juice!"

"I wish I had a dress the color of this mango." Georgette held it up to the light, a globe of alternate red and gold. "I wish I had gowns like Imogene's, made in Paris. And oh, most of all, I wish I had a black satin dress like Veronique's. I'd give anything to wear black satin and pearls!"

"Disgraceful!" Esthonie's scolding voice was cut into by Virginie's disconsolate, "Oh, Mamma, *please* let me out!"

A changing play of conflicting emotions crossed Esthonie's plump face. "Well, I suppose we could. I was planning to go shopping tomorrow."

"Go both days," suggested Georgette, taking a bite of mango.

"Will you come with us?" asked Esthonie, and when Imogene nodded, she called, "You must wear something modest, Virginie. High at the neck."

"In this *heat*?" cried Virginie. And then hastily, "I am dressing, Mamma. Give Georgette the key so she can let me out." Moments later she was downstairs, dimpling at Imogene.

"What news do you bring us, Madame van Ryker? It would be good to hear, since I have been so long out of circulation!"

"Never mind asking," chided her mother. "You overheard everything we said—don't deny it. And stand straight and try not to sidle so you will look less like a *cocotte*!" She shooed her daughters into the carriage. They sat facing her, their big skirts billowing, spilling out. "Ramon," Esthonie leaned forward to give the driver her orders, "I believe we will drive by the church first."

When they reached the church, Esthonie leaned forward and peered at the grove of pimento trees behind the church where the road disappeared.

No one was in sight.

Imogene stared at that disappearing patch of road too. It wound into the pimento grove, she knew, and lost itself somewhere in a tangle of vines and sea grapes. It would have been very strange if van Ryker *had* taken Veronique into that grove.

In fact, she could think of only one reason for his doing so.

Her cheeks turned rather pink and she turned in irritation to remark to Esthonie that the walls of the solid stone church looked dingy and needed lime-washing.

"It's this terrible climate," sighed Esthonie. "The salt air devours everything—even stone. What is that out there in the road? Ramon, stop! Georgette, jump out and see what it is."

Georgette obliged, leaping down from the carriage with a young girl's agility. "What am I looking for, Mamma?"

"It looked like a gold ring with a stone in it. Pull over there in the shade of that tree, Ramon. We will give her time to look. Georgette, I think the carriage wheel struck it and knocked it away.''

And well it could be, thought Imogene. Gold coins were sometimes found in these streets, why not rings?

In shimmering heat, they waited while Georgette scrabbled about in the road. The trade winds blew softly, rustling the leaves of the big overarching live oak above their heads. Virginie resettled her flowered voile skirts and looked bored. Full twenty minutes must have passed before Esthonie called to Georgette, ''I suppose you will not find it. The wheel must have knocked it over into the bushes. Come along.''

''Oh, look, Mamma,'' exclaimed Georgette as she climbed nimbly back into the carriage.

Their eyes followed the direction in which she was looking.

Where the road disappeared behind the church, Veronique Fondage was riding out of the pimento grove. She was riding slowly, with a pensive preoccupied air. Her long black hair with its unusual coiffure was disheveled and her lips slightly parted, while her eyes seemed to glow dewily. Seeing them, she brought her horse to a sudden halt and an expression of consternation spread over her patrician face to be instantly replaced by one of lofty disdain. She nodded to them distantly.

''Veronique.'' Imperiously, Esthonie beckoned with a gloved hand.

After a moment's hesitation, Veronique rode over to them, straightening her hair surreptitiously as she did so.

''Esthonie, Madame van Ryker.'' She gave a brief nod to the daughters, dismissing them as inconsequential. How smooth and lovely her skin was, thought Imogene. Like heavy silk. And her eyelids drooped languorously so that those amber eyes peered at you like a sleepy cat. Her body was narrow and thin as Georgette's—if Veronique had a flaw, that was it, for her bustline was flat in the Spanish fashion. Somehow in Veronique's case that did not detract. Her movements were languorous and eloquent and all attention was centered on her beautiful arresting face.

Esthonie asked her something in French and Veronique shrugged and poured forth a torrent of French in answer. Completely composed now, she flashed them all a dazzling smile, nodded again to Imogene and rode away toward the quay.

"Esthonie," said Imogene, "you might have told us that you had stopped the carriage in hope of seeing your houseguest. It would have saved Georgette the fatiguing task of searching the road for a nonexistent ring for twenty minutes!"

Esthonie gave an expressive Gallic shrug. "Some people cannot be told—they must be shown."

"You have shown me nothing. Veronique comes riding out of the trees. Van Ryker is not with her, nor do I see him now."

"Who knows who is in the pimento grove? Did you see her face as she came riding out? It was the face of a woman who has just been"— Esthonie was suddenly reminded of Georgette's tender ears—"been trysting."

"No doubt you asked her what she was doing there?"

"She told me that she was exercising the horse. I refrained from asking her what else she was exercising."

Once again Imogene had had too much. With a wrathful look at Esthonie she turned her attention on that lady's eldest daughter.

"Virginie," she asked sweetly. "However did your mother come to lock you in your room?"

Esthonie gave a start. To her mind Imogene should be grateful to be warned—obviously she was not. So be it. "Poor Veronique," she cut in before a confused Virginie could form an answer, "she is as flat as Georgette!"

Georgette gave her mother a huffy look, but Virginie, glad to find the subject changed, added, "And already taller than I am!"

"Veronique is the exact same height!" snapped Georgette. "And it's fashionable to be flat! It's you and Mamma who are out of fashion—not I!"

Virginie laughed, throwing back her shoulders the better to display her well-developed breasts. Her mother frowned and tapped her smartly with her fan. "You are fortunate, both of you, that I did not put iron stays in your bodices like the Spanish—or wooden stays like the English, to keep you flat. Annoy me and I still may do it!"

Suitably cowed by this threat, both girls sank back.

Imogene realized grimly that Esthonie, by disparaging her flamboyant guest, was trying to make amends. She fell silent as they wound through the maze of crooked streets that made up the hodgepodge buccaneer town of Cayona.

"This is a terrible place to live." Esthonie grimaced. "Do you realize there are *no decent women* on this island save you and me?"

Imogene yearned to contradict her for she was still irritated with Esthonie, but she remembered van Ryker saying much the same thing. Occasional mistresses wandered in with the flamboyant rakes who appeared from nowhere and went on, usually on a downward path. But there were none the wife of a French governor wished to introduce to her daughters.

"And Veronique, of course," pointed out Imogene ironically.

Esthonie gave her a hard look. "Turn back, Ramon," she called to the driver. "We will go home now."

"But we haven't driven by the quay!" wailed Virginie.

"We will do that tomorrow when we go shopping," said Esthonie severely. "We have already driven by the houses of all the respectable people, so that they could see that you are still alive! I will *not* have you making eyes at these young pirates while the sun beats down on you, destroying your complexion!"

"Not pirates—buccaneers," corrected Imogene. For there was a world of difference: Pirates attacked anyone; they were the scourge of the seas. But Tortuga was the home base of the buccaneers, the Brethren of the Coast, and their particular quarrel was with the Spanish who had driven them from their earlier settlement on Hispaniola, destroyed all the wild herds of cattle and hogs from which they made their living "boucaning"—drying the meat and selling it to passing ships. In desperation, the remnants who were left had attacked small Spanish sailing vessels from rowboats, rowing right in under the guns and taking the ships by small arms fire. From there they had gone on to larger things and now, in captured Spanish ships, it was the buccaneers who challenged the might of Spain, while giving what protection they could to the English, French, and Dutch shipping that plied these waters and bought the goods the buccaneers wrested from the galleons.

"Yes, I should have said 'buccaneers,'" agreed Esthonie

in an altered voice. It had belatedly occurred to her that Imogene was the bride of Tortuga's leading buccaneer, and that her own husband, the governor, was amassing a fortune by selling "letters of marque" (privateering licenses for France) to these same buccaneers.

"I'm sure our drive has bored our guest," complained Virginie. "We haven't seen *anyone*," she added grumpily.

"If you mean that Notley fellow with the broken leg," warned Esthonie with a crushing look, "you can forget him. He can barely hobble around in his splints!"

Virginie had indeed been thinking of James Notley. He had such lovely curly brown hair. She loved to run her hands through it and giggle as he took liberties that would have given her mother a stroke, had she known about it. She continued to pout.

"Imogene." Esthonie turned with decision to her guest. "I do hope you will let me pick you up in the morning and take you shopping with us. These girls are too much for me to handle alone."

Imogene was about to refuse when Georgette leaned forward impulsively. "Oh, please do! You always wear something new and I love to look at your clothes—they're always so pretty!"

At this ingenuous outburst from worldly young Georgette, Imogene relented. "Very well, Esthonie—if you will refrain from keeping us sitting in the hot sun outside the church while we watch for Veronique."

A little color stained Esthonie's cheeks. "We will go directly to the quay," she promised. "Ten o'clock, then?"

"Ten o'clock," agreed Imogene.

Now in her bedchamber yesterday's outing with Esthonie and her daughters faded from Imogene's mind as she realized she must dress quickly or she would keep Esthonie waiting.

Half suffocated by having the shutters closed, she flung them open again. Veronique was gone, clattering down into the town to look for van Ryker, no doubt. Well, two could play at that game!

CHAPTER 3

Swiftly Imogene dressed, this time choosing a gown conservative enough that Esthonie could not help but approve. It was of tissue-thin French gray taffeta. The figure-hugging bodice was low cut, the deep square neckline outlined in black velvet ribands and edged in frosty white point lace. The big, fashionably detachable puffed sleeves were of the same delicate gray taffeta, but slashed to display glimpses of black velvet stitched with silver. From the elbows spilled a froth of white point lace that cascaded halfway down her forearms. Her petticoat was a miracle of heavy gunmetal satin, too warm of course, but shimmering with silver embroidery and edged in rows of black velvet ribands. Beneath it one could catch occasional glimpses of a black satin slipper or a sheer black silken ankle. She topped this off with a sweeping black wide-brimmed hat that spilled a fluttering mass of silver plumes caught by a single diamond that would flash in the sun.

Critically she studied her reflection. Perhaps—a single strand of pearls. Smiling, she clasped about her throat the short strand of big matched pearls van Ryker had given her the day she married him. If she ran across him on the quay, the pearls would be a reminder of that day. . . .

Swiftly she seized a pair of gray silk gloves. Leather might have looked better but on such a hot day she could not face the struggle of easing them over her fingers, and she knew full well that if she wore none Esthonie would rail at her for "not keeping up appearances in this Godforsaken hole."

A quick look out the window showed her that Esthonie's carriage was just drawing up and—was that Veronique in the back seat? Those massed black curls, as startling as the big black periwigs men wore in imitation of Charles II—no, the black-haired wench was clad in white. It was Georgette with her thick black curls just done up with the curling iron.

Imogene breathed a sigh of relief and ran downstairs, her wide skirts swirling about her trim black silk ankles as she swished past the tinkling fountain, through the hall past the dining room and the chart room, and found the iron grillwork front doors being dutifully opened for her by big Arne. It was bad enough that Veronique was Esthonie's houseguest but it would have been galling indeed to have to spend the day with her! Still, had not Esthonie taken Veronique in, van Ryker well might have asked Imogene to do it. She shuddered at the thought.

"*Ma chère!*" Esthonie cried effusively as Imogene greeted them. "But how divine you look!" The flash of envy that spread over her plump face on seeing Imogene's beautiful gown gave sincerity to her slightly false intonation.

"Madame van Ryker always looks wonderful," sighed Georgette, leaning forward in her delicate white dimity, elaborately stitched and tucked and trimmed in dainty point lace. Esthonie always insisted on dressing Georgette as a proper *jeune fille* as if she might be mincing down a Parisian boulevard and not winding through the streets of buccaneer Cayona, but for all her pains Georgette's worldly expression was at odds with her childish garb, thought Imogene in amusement.

"You look very handsome yourself today, Esthonie," she observed.

"La, you have seen me wear this dress all season," objected Esthonie, but she bridled and looked pleased nonetheless as she gathered up her bronze silk skirts to make room for Imogene. The motion set the jet ornamentation of her ample bodice ajingle, and the bronze plumes on her wide-brimmed hat trembled.

"Good day, Virginie." Imogene smiled at Esthonie's older daughter as she climbed lightly into the carriage and settled her light gray taffeta skirts beside Esthonie. Virginie, her hourglass figure well displayed in pastel pink organdy and sporting a matching pink parasol, gave her a pensive greeting. Her mind was obviously far away—on some strapping young buccaneer, Imogene had no doubt.

"You look very grown-up today, Georgette." Imogene smiled at the younger of the two girls seated across from her in the carriage.

"Pay her no compliments, I am furious with her," said

Esthonie. "She left her parasol behind and will be burned as black as a buccaneer before the day is out."

Personally Imogene thought Georgette's pale ivory complexion would be improved by a faint blush of sunburn on her cheeks, but to say so would only provoke an explosion from Esthonie, who would insist that ladies had complexions like creamy vellum and only peasant wenches let their skins tan nut brown. As a diversion, she said, "I was startled by the new way you are wearing your hair, Georgette. For a moment there I thought you were Veronique!"

Although now that she was closer, Imogene could see that Georgette's hairdo was a much simplified copy of the governor's houseguest's, the very mention of Veronique's name brought forth a burst of words from Georgette.

"I *could* look like Veronique if only I had the right clothes—and don't tell me I'm too flat!" Georgette turned argumentatively to her mother. "Veronique's riding habit wouldn't look *half* so good if she weren't slender as a rapier!"

Plump Esthonie rolled her eyes to heaven. "You should pray to God you get a figure as good as your sister's!" she scolded. "Rapier thin, indeed!" And to Imogene, "I hear nothing all day but Veronique, Veronique, from Georgette! Veronique dances better, she wears clothes better, she talks better, she rides better than anyone else, to hear Georgette tell it!" She sniffed.

"She does have a good seat on a horse," said Imogene in fairness to her rival. "I saw her ride past the house this morning with her back as straight as if she had swallowed a poker."

"Captain van Ryker never should have lent her that horse," said Esthonie darkly, with a frown for Georgette. "She is forever dashing about alone aboard him and she may be raped—or worse!"

"What is worse, Mamma?" Georgette was instantly alive with interest. "You told me rape was the very worst thing that could happen to a girl!"

"At your age, yes," agreed her mother with a sigh, calling to the driver to proceed. "But at my age perhaps it is worse to lose one's jewels." She patted the diamond and jet lavaliere at her neck. "Don't you think so, Imogene?"

"I would far rather lose my jewels!" Imogene shuddered.

Esthonie sniffed. "But then you have so *many* jewels," she said tartly, and Imogene was again reminded that ever since van Ryker had seized the treasure fleet, Esthonie had been burning with envy. "Sit straight, Georgette! Perhaps we will purchase a new riband for your hair."

"I'd rather have a pearl necklace," muttered rebellious Georgette.

"No doubt!" sniffed her mother. "But you cannot have one."

"Veronique says I should wear pearls," said Georgette with a spiteful look at Imogene. "She says pearls are lost on blondes—they turn to dishwater. She says pearls *glow* on necks like ours—"

"Long and too thin," supplied her sister in a calm voice.

Georgette glared at her. "*Swanlike!*" she corrected. "And against our clouds of dark hair." She paused. "Mamma, can I wear my hair like Veronique's? She has been teaching me. It is very complicated but I have almost mastered the style."

"Certainly not. It is far too elaborate for your age."

"Veronique says I would look *years* older if I wore black satin and pearls. She says I would be magnificent!"

Imogene frowned at this obvious courting of the governor's younger daughter, but Esthonie burst out impatiently, "When you are older, perhaps you shall have pearls, Georgette."

"I want them now," insisted Georgette stubbornly.

"Well, we cannot afford them now, no matter what you want," snapped her mother. "After all your father is but a poor government official and not a buccaneer!" Her tone was bitter.

Imogene gave her a glance of amusement. "But I thought you disapproved of buccaneers, Esthonie? You've said so often enough."

Esthonie's shoulders twitched irritably. "Only if they are *unsuccessful*," she said on a chiding note.

And that, thought Imogene, *was the key to Esthonie's character*. She could approve of anyone—even lustful Veronique—if they were *successful* at what they did. She made a deep internal vow that Veronique would chalk up one failure at least—she would *not* be successful with van Ryker!

"I am probably late," declared Esthonie, "because that wretched lantern clock—which is the best we can afford—is always wrong. Ah, if only I had a wonderful long-case clock like yours!"

Imogene thought wryly that Esthonie always desired everything she had. Last week it had been a length of silk as sheer as cobwebs that she had instantly desired, as soon as she saw Imogene wearing a gossamer overdress made of it. Imogene had given Esthonie a length of the gossamer fabric, but her marquetry standing clock was something else.

"I believe there are several to be found on the quay, Esthonie," she said composedly, determined not to be talked out of her marquetry long-case clock.

Esthonie's black eyes flashed her a look almost of hatred. As wife to Tortuga's French governor, she was always managing to dip her eager fingers into a pocket here, a pocket there. She was insatiable, and now as she realized Imogene was not going to surrender the clock to her whim, she was overcome with inner rage.

"Why do you think Veronique chose to ride by *your* house?" she demanded in a voice rich with innuendo.

"If you mean she hoped to hail van Ryker, he'd have had no time for her!" laughed Imogene.

"You are wrong!" corrected Esthonie on a note of triumph. "He spends a great deal of time with her."

Virginie gave her mother a surprised look—and sat back, realizing that while she was locked in anything could have been happening downstairs.

Imogene regarded her tormentor very steadily, tapping the fingers of her gray silk gloves. If the carriage had not already been in motion, she would have been tempted to hop out.

Esthonie squirmed under that level look. But now that the lie was out and spoken, she felt a need to defend it. "I shall not say more," she said impressively, "for you are still a bride. But I must warn you to look out, Imogene, *or she will take him from you*!"

"Nonsense!"

Georgette, who had a mind to gain a pearl necklace, recklessly supported her mother. "Who should know better?"

she demanded. "After all, she *is* our guest. *We* see what is going on."

Imogene gave her an uneasy look. Georgette was young and she did not as yet have Esthonie's subtlety. What did the girl know? She decided it was beneath her dignity to inquire—and, besides, she trusted van Ryker. Or did she . . . where Veronique was concerned?

"Georgette, hold your tongue," said her mother sternly. But her crushing look held more fear that her daughter would overstep and they would be caught up in their false accusations than anything else. That look was not lost on Georgette, who sat back serenely and turned her bland gaze to the blue skies above Tortuga.

The carriage, drawn by its pair of matched grays, had reached the quay. It was a breathtaking sight. Cutlassed buccaneers, many of them scarred and sporting braces of pistols, swaggered about piles of captured goods stacked up and offered for sale to buyers from half a dozen nations. Overdressed harlots and waterfront drabs vied for their favors. Behind and above them rose the imposing stone pile of the Mountain Fort, its guns pointed menacingly out to sea. And beyond the market, the forest of masts that made up the shipping, anchored in the shimmering turquoise waters of Cayona Bay.

As the carriage drew to a halt, Esthonie half rose and pointed her fat, black-gloved hand dramatically. "There!" she cried on a note of triumph. "You can see the situation for yourself!"

Imogene felt a little chill go up her spine. Slowly she turned and forced herself to look where Esthonie was pointing.

There on the quay was Veronique. She had dismounted and was standing, leaning back against her horse, gazing up at a tall buccaneer who lounged before her. Van Ryker.

" 'Tis easy to see your husband did not expect *you* at the quay this day!" sniffed Esthonie.

"Hold your peace, Esthonie," said Imogene quietly, but her mouth had tightened and her breath had shortened. For a while she sat at gaze, watching them contemplatively.

"They make a pretty picture, do they not?" said Esthonie tartly.

Imogene thought regretfully that that was so. Van Ryker, tall and tigerish and relaxed with the sun gleaming on his dark hair. Veronique, in her thin black taffeta riding habit that fit her taut slender figure so tightly through the torso and then billowed out dramatically into great skirts, was an arresting sight. How showy was that unique hairstyle she affected—upswept to a crown in front, thick curls cascading shoulder length about the ears and long long curls down the back—would any man *not* desire to run his hands through that springy hair and pull this dynamic woman toward him? From the froth of white lace at her throat to the expressive black-gloved hands that even now were gesturing as she spoke animatedly with van Ryker she was intense, almost over-poweringly female. The very heat of the climate brought an attractive flush to her cheeks and doubtless added to the sparkle of those predatory amber eyes that even now were studying van Ryker through a forest of thick dark lashes.

Even her birthmark was seductive! It was a tiny red heart placed strategically on her left forearm. Imogene couldn't see it from here, but she was sure van Ryker could as Veronique made an expressive gesture and brought her black-gloved arm up so that the cascading lace at her elbows spilled back to show it. She felt a shaft of jealousy knife through her.

"Well?" Esthonie had dug a fan out of her velvet reticule and now she tapped Imogene smartly with it. "Aren't you going to go and drag him away from that woman?"

Imogene fought back a feline desire to do exactly that. "Of course not," she said lightly. "'Tis but a chance meeting." She was determined not to give Esthonie the satisfaction of knowing she was jealous!

Unwanted thoughts crowded in around her. *This is a climate that rots men's souls*, Dr. Argyll had sighed at Esthonie's last party when the weather had been miserable. *And eats into their minds, making them forget the tie that binds*, Esthonie had rhymed tartly, with a look at Imogene.

What had that fourteen-year-old Irish girl said when she was rescued and feared she was pregnant? *I do not think the Spanish captain would have taken me to bed by force save that he had been so long at sea.* Memory of that conversation nagged at her. Van Ryker had been long at sea when he met Veronique. And Veronique with her hot amber gaze and swaying hips and peculiar floating walk was exotic—and enticing.

Suddenly Esthonie's gaze was riveted in another direction. "Virginie," she snapped. "Your eyes are better than mine. Isn't that your father over there? *There* beside all those kegs and bottles of wine?"

Virginie, who had been simpering at a young buccaneer who was standing with his arms folded, regarding her admiringly, turned hastily. "I think so," she said uncertainly.

"Who is that woman in purple with him?" wondered Georgette.

Imogene turned to hide her sudden amusement. Esthonie had been so intent on showing her van Ryker, when all the time Gauthier Touraille had been deep in conversation with one of the local madams, who, even as they watched, pinched his cheek familiarly and turned away with a laugh, blowing him a kiss from beneath the mountain of pink feathers on her hat.

"She's nobody we know," said her mother coldly. Her back was very stiff. "Virginie." She prodded her elder daughter's knee with her fan. "Go over there and tell your father he isn't to buy all that wine. We have a cellar stocked full—there'll be no place to put it!"

Imogene gave the governor's lady a droll look. It had occurred to her that Gauthier might not be purchasing the wine, for which he seemed even now to be counting out gold coins, for home consumption but for the woman in purple satin and pink plumes who was swiveling her ample hips sinuously through the crowd. Gauthier would have a lot to explain if that same thought occurred to Esthonie!

Seeking to divert Esthonie, her gaze fell on the sails of a recent arrival in Cayona's harbor, *La Belle France*, a merchantman on her way from Martinique to Paris. *La Belle France* had collided with a derelict one foggy night and her captain had of necessity put into Tortuga for repairs.

"Isn't *La Belle France* a French ship?" she asked Esthonie idly, and when Esthonie nodded, "I am surprised you have not shown more interest in those aboard her."

"Oh, we have." Georgette stuck her head up. "The

governor of Martinique's sister is aboard and Mamma called on her, but she came back very angry."

Esthonie pursed her lips and gave Georgette a quelling look. That call had been a disaster and she was still smarting from it. That wretched woman with her well-bred distant manner had shown no interest at all in the wife of Tortuga's French governor. One would have thought from her manner that she and her brother were a cut above the Tourailles. And she had firmly declined Esthonie's offer to dine, insisting—although she was at the time fully dressed, indeed *elegantly* gowned, that she was too ill to leave the ship. Esthonie had departed in confusion. And all her further invitations, sent by way of servants, had also been declined.

"*La Belle France*'s passengers are of no interest," she said with a frown at Georgette. "They are all tradesmen—except for one woman who is too ill to leave her cabin." The passengers fled from her mind as her frown played over Gauthier, who seemed about to vanish into the crowd.

Imogene wanted him to vanish. She had no intention of becoming involved in Esthonie's family squabbles here on the quay. Again she attempted a diversion.

"I thought you were going to buy Georgette some ribands," she said briskly.

"I'd rather have pearls," said Georgette distinctly.

Esthonie turned on Georgette. "See that display of ribands?" she told her daughter in a voice of controlled fury. "Go at once and select some. And stay there until I get back!"

"I may buy a trinket or two myself," Imogene murmured and dropped lightly from the carriage without assistance.

Esthonie, in her bronze silks, the bodice jingling with jet, had to be helped down. Panting with the exertion, she billowed through the dazzling sunlight in the wake of those wide sweeping gray taffeta skirts, calling out to Imogene to wait, for Imogene was heading ruthlessly away from both the governor and van Ryker.

Taking pity on Esthonie at last—for anyone with stays as tight as Esthonie's must suffer to exercise in such heat— Imogene stopped to inspect a display of clocks. Clocks fascinated her—perhaps, she told herself ruefully, because time was so fleeting. There were clocks of all kinds in her house here in Cayona: clocks from France and Germany and England, ornate gilt-brass clocks with silver dials, fat vaselike table clocks, clocks decorated with figures of centaurs and spires and minarets. In her bedroom was a fine English lantern clock with an alarm, and for traveling, a dainty French traveling clock. And in the main hall downstairs was her favorite of all, one of the fashionable new tall standing clocks with a handsome floral marquetry design—the one Esthonie so coveted.

Displayed on a barrel top like the rest of the clocks was one that caught her eye. It was a circular gilt drum clock, with its face turned upward like a sundial and etched upon that face a map of the Caribbean. Imogene picked it up in one silk-gloved hand and studied that map. There on that shiny brass face were the West Indies—and there north of Hispaniola a tiny dot indicated the island of Tortuga. Imogene sighed. She was thinking that someday all she would have of Tortuga would be memories, and wondering if she might not like to have this tangible remembrance of the island with its small shining face turned forever hopefully upward.

Esthonie was breathing hard as she caught up with her.

"I should think you would not leave your husband to that woman!" she scolded.

Imogene set the drum table clock she had just been inspecting back down rather hard. "Don't you worry about having so devastating a creature in close contact with your daughters, Esthonie?" she mocked.

Esthonie's plump shoulders quivered in an expressive Gallic shrug that set her jet jingling. "Georgette is young and innocent yet," she intoned in a low voice. "*She* will hardly catch the drift of Veronique's sallies—although she may parrot them. And, as for Virginie, she is fifteen and of marriageable age and it is time for her to observe such women as Veronique who can twist men about their fingers."

Imogene quirked an eyebrow. "You mean perhaps Virginie will learn something?"

Esthonie hesitated. Then, "Perhaps," she agreed frankly. "Nothing—indiscreet, of course. But Virginie must learn to cope with such women. For if she marries my young kinsman, Jean Claude Dumaine, whose father has written to me in hopes of arranging the match, and goes to live in Paris— heavenly city!—she will meet many such women."

A city abounding with predatory Veroniques, gliding like elegant black panthers through the streets, was hardly Imogene's idea of heaven. Personally, she found much to criticize in Veronique: all that restless moving about—even though one must admit she *did* glide, her skirts moving across the floor as if she had no feet at all. All that redundant tossing of her head just to make her heavy black curls dance! And that coiffure, while unique, was scarcely fashionable. In a day of short curls hanging in ringlets called "heartbreakers" about one's ears with a fringe across the forehead, Veronique wore her hair swept up dramatically away from her high forehead, piled up on her head and then, probably because it was so thick, she allowed big fat curls to tumble down gleaming onto her shoulders and cascade down her back—she had almost as much hair as King Charles himself, only his was an enormous black periwig and who knew how many heads had been cropped to assemble it! Imogene supposed she could not fault Veronique for that, since she had been known to sport unusual hairstyles herself, her own shimmering hair being so long and thick and golden. But the way Veronique rode her horse—for all that her back was knife-straight—was barely short of a swagger! And her gaze was far too aggressive. Veronique had a way of turning that imperious head of hers and staring directly into a man's eyes in exactly the same way—in Imogene's opinion—as the harlots of Cayona.

She dragged her thoughts from Veronique and bent over the clock.

"This is lovely," she murmured. "I would really like to buy it—but we already have so many things that must all be moved from Tortuga."

"Do you really think you'll be leaving?"

"Of course." Imogene straightened up in surprise. "*You* should certainly be aware of it. Your husband is negotiating to buy our house!"

"It will not happen." Esthonie shook her head decisively.

"And why not?" demanded Imogene.

"Because van Ryker will never change. Buccaneering is in his blood. Even if he leaves the sea, he'll come back to it."

"We will prove you wrong," said Imogene quietly.

Again Esthonie shook her head—this time with great finality. "You do not know men as well as I do. He'll never change now—he's in too deep."

Something cold seemed to filter down into Imogene's consciousness, for there was merit in Esthonie's remarks. Few buccaneers ever changed. Buccaneering was—truly—in their blood. The lure of the sea. Spanish treasure galleons sailing by temptingly. And women like Veronique to be rescued. . . . She tried to shake off this cold feeling that had gripped her.

"You are wrong about van Ryker, Esthonie."

"We will see." Esthonie's gaze had shifted. It was now fixed somewhere else. She had assumed what Imogene privately called her "hunting stance," for her dark head was cocked forward and her somewhat prominent nose pointed, quivering, straight ahead of her. "Do you see that woman?" she hissed.

"Where?" Imogene set down the clock.

"Over there, holding up that length of abominable green and orange striped taffeta. Oh, what awful stuff!"

"I still don't see—" Imogene stood on tiptoe to peer over the crowd.

"No, don't look now—*she's looking at us*!" cried Esthonie in distress. "Are you really interested in that clock, Imogene? You have three almost like it!"

"No, this one is different from those I have." At Esthonie's warning, Imogene had turned back to her consideration of the gilt table clock, but not before she observed that Esthonie had been speaking of the woman in purple, with whom Gauthier Touraille had been in such deep conversation a few moments before. "And yes, I am interested in it."

"You have too many clocks already," said Esthonie rudely. She lowered her voice. "I am told that woman wears red garters. *And* black lace on her chemise!"

"What woman?" asked Imogene carelessly—as if she didn't know!

"That woman in purple, of course, that Madam Josie. Who else?"

"Well, I really don't know who else, Esthonie." Imogene managed to keep a grave face.

Esthonie cast a look at the clock seller, who had stepped away to show a lantern clock to a swarthy Irishman busy loading his merchantman with goods purchased cheap in Tortuga. She lowered her voice. "I can tell you there's no one else. It's always *that* woman, that Madam Josie! Every time I turn around! I don't know what Gauthier sees in her. Her hips are as wide as—as—" She groped for a suitable word.

As yours, Esthonie! Imogene was dying to say, but prudence made her hold her tongue.

Esthonie snatched up a small lantern clock, studied it wrathfully. "Georgette needs one of these for her room," she muttered in a harassed voice. "She's so difficult to wake up. The only thing that wakes her is a piercing scream right in her ear! Oh, I'm too upset to decide on anything—and, anyway, this one looks to have been damaged in shipment." She set it back down regretfully and pursed her lips. She was pondering.

"Do you really think men count such things as important?" she asked presently.

"Which? Clocks or hips?" Imogene gave her friend a droll look.

"Red garters!"

"Oh—and black lace on the chemise. I see what you mean." Imogene gave the subject the consideration she felt it deserved and let Esthonie have the benefit of her wisdom. "I wouldn't think so. In my opinion, once they get *that* far they're really in transit to—" Now *she* sought for a word.

"Their objective," supplied Esthonie gloomily. "And you feel they'd be so hot to get on with it they'd hardly notice?"

"Exactly."

Esthonie heaved a deep sigh and the bronze plumes on her hat quivered. She clenched her black-gloved fingers together, rolled her eyes heavenward and shook her head. If it wasn't the red garters, she was plainly saying, what *did* Gauthier see in a frump like Madam Josie? Suddenly she gave a start and clutched Imogene. "I must get back to Georgette!" she cried indignantly. "Those men are studying the child's decolletage! Join me when you've finished looking at the clocks."

Imogene followed Esthonie's gaze to the little knot of men now surrounding vivacious Georgette. Among them she recognized kindly Dr. Argyll, who would see that nothing untoward happened to the girl. She thought Esthonie would be better advised to see to Virginie, who had drifted away from her father and was now in rapt conversation with the sandy-haired young buccaneer who had stood admiring her.

She sighed. Of a sudden her desire for a permanent home away from buccaneer Tortuga focused on the drum clock.

74

"How much is it?" she asked the clock seller. And when he told her, "I'll buy it," she said impulsively. "Have it sent to my home. Do you know where that is?"

"Everyone knows Captain van Ryker's house, my lady," said the heavyset buccaneer genially. " 'Tis the finest house on the island!"

Imogene flashed him a quick smile. "Arne, at the door, will pay for the clock," she told him—for she had no intention of interrupting van Ryker's conversation with Veronique even if they talked together in that conspicuous fashion all day. She would not let Esthonie Touraille have the satisfaction of knowing she was jealous!

Still, it was very irritating for the wildest lass in all of Cornwall to find herself eclipsed by a French-speaking hussy who seemed about to sweep her under the rug! That resentful feeling lingered with her as she strolled toward Esthonie and Georgette, stopping on her way to inspect some fresh green limes.

CHAPTER 4

"Madame van Ryker, could I have a word with you?"
came a hoarse voice from behind her and Imogene turned and
almost collided with the woman in purple satin, her wide hat
dripping an immense quantity of pink plumes. She realized
she was looking into the somewhat raddled but shrewd face
of the celebrated Madam Josie.

"Of—of course," she said, astounded.

"Over there behind those piles of barrels, where folks can't
see us."

Bewildered, Imogene followed those voluminous purple
satin skirts to a spot behind some barrels of sea salt, dried in
the salt pans of the islands. Although they had never met,
there was no point in pretending she didn't know who this
woman was. "What is it you wish of me, Madam Josie?"
she asked politely but with a slight frown.

"You're the right kind," approved Madam Josie, who had been born Josie Dawes in Liverpool and had made it to Tortuga by way of a London sporting house. "Van Ryker said you was a lady and he was right."

Imogene stiffened slightly and Josie caught that slight stiffening. She chuckled. "You needn't worry about the likes of me," she said with a wag of her hennaed head that set her pink plumes aflutter. "Your husband never had no dealings with me or any of my girls. Women was always mad about him—he had to fight 'em off every time he come to town. And when he built that big fine house and furnished it up so grand, everybody said it was to take a wife he was doing all that! And sure enough on his next voyage after it was finished, he brings *you* back with him." Madam Josie's broad smile said the town—and Josie Dawes—approved his choice. That smile also displayed a mouthful of teeth that were surprisingly white in view of the fact that Madam Josie was reputed to smoke a clay pipe with as much gusto as the male clients who frequented her establishment. She pushed back a straying lock of her abundant hennaed hair from her face, the complexion startlingly whitened with ceruse, or violet lead, cheeks and mouth made artfully pink by rubbing on Spanish paper. Her hazel eyes twinkled. "I know what you're thinkin'." She wagged her head again. "You're thinkin' decent women don't be conversin' on the quay with them as runs houses like mine, and that van Ryker wouldn't like it—that's why I'm talkin' to you behind these barrels."

"I'm very glad to converse with you, Madam Josie," said Imogene gravely, for she had by now regained her composure. "But I really can't imagine what it is you wish to see me about."

"It's about that woman you keep company with."

"Keep company—?" Imogene was bewildered. "Oh, you must mean Esthonie Touraille?"

"That's right, Gauthier's wife." Imogene was quick to note that Madam Josie used the governor's first name with a familiarity that spoke of long practice; his name slipped easily off her tongue.

"She's a bad-one, is Esthonie."

Imogene straightened up a little. She felt she must come to Esthonie's defense, even though she was sometimes inclined to agree with Madam Josie's assessment.

"No, don't be lookin' at me like that, Madame van Ryker. I know Esthonie Touraille is your friend and all that—leastways I know there ain't nobody else van Ryker will let you associate with around here."

"How do you know that?" asked Imogene sharply.

"Van Ryker told me so," said Josie simply. "We're old friends."

Imogene gasped. But then she got hold of herself. Everybody knew Madam Josie had an easy camaraderie with the buccaneers. She'd even been known to finance a venture or two herself. Van Ryker would naturally be thrown with her on occasions when he met with friends in the taverns and grog shops of Cayona. Imogene's face cleared.

"So you're thrown with Estie a lot and—"

"Estie?"

"That's Gauthier's pet name for his wife," explained

Josie. "He's fond of her, but she's awful hard to live with, Madame van Ryker. You wouldn't *believe* the things she—"

"Oh, yes, I *would* believe," interrupted Imogene hastily. This conversation was beginning to make her uncomfortable. She certainly hoped Madam Josie wasn't going to ask her to intercede for Gauthier in some way!

"I'm saying she tells *lies,*" said Josie earnestly. She was staring into Imogene's face as she spoke with an intensity that surprised the younger woman.

"And what lies is she supposed to be telling?"

"You know what lies I mean, Madama van Ryker." Josie bobbed her head so her feathers shook. "Lies about your husband. Gauthier tells me what Estie's been filling your head with! Tellin' you your husband's steppin' out on you. I know 'cause she tells Gauthier that too! Ain't no truth to it, Madame van Ryker. I never seen a man so stuck on a woman as van Ryker is on you! And that French—" Josie remembered abruptly that she was talking to a lady and that what she was about to call Esthonie wasn't ladylike. "That French—" She cast about.

"'Creature' is the word I think you're searching for," murmured Imogene in amusement. She thought the whole situation very funny.

"Creature," agreed Josie in relief. She told herself she must remember that word. In speaking to Gauthier, she had agreed Esthonie was a number of things that wouldn't do for the ears of van Ryker's bride. "So you just ignore everything she says about van Ryker," she told Imogene solemnly.

"Madam Josie—" began Imogene.

"You can call me Josie," said Madam Josie. "And don't

you worry, I won't call you Imogene. I know my place, Madame van Ryker.''

"Josie, why are you doing this?"

"Warning you?" Josie looked surprised. "Why, I thought you knew. 'Twas your husband chased down Captain Flogg's men the might they wrecked my place and made them pay to put things to rights! I don't know what we'd do without him around here!"

Imogene gasped. "You mean the governor didn't—"

Josie gave her a friendly smile. "Gauthier's a sweet old thing," she confided, "but he's scared to death of Flogg and his sort. It isn't as if Gauthier could call on constables or sheriffs or anything like that. He's just governor in name—'tis van Ryker has the power. But''—she grinned—"van Ryker's done me favors more than once and now I'm doin' him one—although I'd be beholden to you if you don't say I done it. I just wanted to warn you to pay Gauthier's wife no mind.''

"I do thank you." Imogene kept a straight face. Suddenly she could not resist asking. "Josie," she said hesitantly, "do you mind if I ask you a very impudent question?"

"Ask me anything at all," said Josie recklessly. "Ain't nothin' about men I don't know. Is van Ryker givin' you trouble in bed?" She leaned forward intently, ready to give instant advice on her favorite subject.

"Do you really wear red satin garters?"

Josie gave her an astonished look—and then she laughed. It was a throaty, rollicking, rumbling laugh rather like a cat's purr. "Sure, I do! You want to see them?" With a sudden gesture she hiked up her purple satin skirts and revealed a pair of plump legs wearing lavender and white striped stockings that were held up by the most majestic pair of garters Inogene had ever seen. Asparkle with brilliants, trimmed with black and silver rosettes, they were gaudy creations of crimson satin.

"I see you do!" she cried.

Josie let her skirts fall back down. There was a twinkle in her knowing hazel eyes. "It's Gauthier's wife wants to know, isn't it?" she guessed.

"Oh, I think she already knows," said Imogene demurely. "She's been making inquiries about you."

Josie slapped her large thigh and let out a hoot of laughter that made Imogene wince. "You can tell her I bought them off the old hunchback who sells trifles near the piles of bananas." She gave Imogene an impish look. "No wonder van Ryker likes you," she said. "You're not just a pretty face, you've got style!"

"Why, thank you, Josie." Imogene joined in Josie's raucous purring laughter. "So do you!"

Josie was still laughing as she billowed away.

Imogene went in the other direction to rejoin Esthonie and Georgette. It was clear the governor's wife hadn't seen her with the notorious Madam Josie because she was deep in selecting hair ribands for Georgette and her voice was quite calm. She held up a handful for Imogene's inspection. "Georgette wants this scarlet one but I think it's too—"

"Oh, Mamma, I can't wear white *all* the time!" Georgette's young voice was tragic.

Esthonie turned on her daughter. "You'll wear what I tell you to wear!" But at Georgette's petulant pout, she relented.

"Oh, I suppose we could take the red one as well," she sighed. "You can wear it to tie up your hair around the house but not in public or when we receive guests. Here, take these coins and pay the man."

As Georgette left their side to pay the trifling cost of the ribands, Imogene leaned toward Esthonie. "I can tell you where Madam Josie gets her red garters," she said airily. "She gets them from that old hunchback who sits by the bananas, selling odds and ends."

Esthonie gave her a suspicious look. "How do you know?"

Imogene's brows elevated innocently. She kept in check the laughter that threatened to well up, and took Esthonie's plump arm. "I have seen them! Come and look."

"Come along, Georgette." Esthonie moved forward to view the hunchback's selection of garters.

Imogene watched brightly as Esthonie picked out a red pair almost identical with Madam Josie's. She let Esthonie think she had found the display by accident. Esthonie would never know she had seen them on Madam Josie's legs!

They strolled about the market desultorily, idly inspecting shoe buckles and lemons and snuffboxes and candlesnuffers. When next Imogene looked, she saw that Veronique had disappeared and van Ryker had his back to her and was talking to a group of men. Apparently he had not seen her. She was content to leave it that way. What Madam Josie had said to her was strangely comforting. Esthonie did tend to blow things out of all proportion, she told herself cheerfully—and, besides, Esthonie loved drama. What would entertain her more than to have Imogene and van Ryker at each other's throats?

The white coral rock and shell of the street blazingly reflected the tropical sunlight as they rode home. Across from Imogene Georgette was studying her red hair riband, holding it up to admire it, while Virginie peered back expectantly toward the quay as if she expected her young buccaneer to be following the carriage.

"Mamma, can I have a pair of garters from the hunchback?" asked Georgette idly. "I'd like black ones trimmed in silver."

"Certainly not," sniffed Esthonie. "Most inappropriate for a young girl!"

"But they'd be under my petticoats," argued Georgette. "Who could see them?"

"*I'd* like a yellow pair." Virginie joined the conversation suddenly. "Trimmed in gold lace."

Imogene was wearing at the moment a pair of black silk garters trimmed with silver rosettes and she had at home, among a host of others, a pair of soft Chinese gold satin ones trimmed with gold lace, but since she had no intention of surrendering either pair, she chose not to mention it, for Esthonie would undoubtedly beg them away from her. She gave a tranquil look around her at the little white houses, half covered with fast-growing vines, lazing in the sun, breathed deep of the warm breeze that ruffled the silver plumes of her wide-brimmed hat and tried to tell herself that she would not miss Tortuga. She didn't quite succeed.

Eagle-eyed Esthonie leaned forward suddenly with a rustle of jet against bronze silk and interrupted her reverie. "There is that boy again!" she exclaimed. "I saw him lurking about on the quay. Wherever Georgette went, there he was! Who is he, Virginie?''

With a billow of pink organdy, Virginie turned and craned to see a slender taffy-haired lad who was just at that moment shyly disappearing behind one of the big live oaks under whose branches the horses were even now walking their carriage.

"I can't quite see him," she reported.

"It's Andy Layton," Georgette supplied in a bored tone. "He follows me everywhere." She suppressed a worldly yawn with a slightly grubby hand.

"Andy Layton?" Her mother looked blank. "And who might he be?"

Virginie wrinkled her brows. Then she laughed. "Oh, it's Cooper's little brother," she said derisively. "He can't be fourteen yet!"

"Cooper? Oh, you mean Captain Layton's younger son?" said Esthonie with mild interest. "You remember Captain Layton, Imogene? Tall, distinguished? When his merchantman was fully loaded and ready to sail back to Philadelphia, both his young sons came down with dysentery and Dr. Argyll counseled against their making the trip. He left them here with Dr. Argyll to recover and will pick them up on his next voyage. The older son, Cooper, was quite interested in Virginie for a time." She frowned. "We haven't seen him lately."

Georgette suppressed a giggle and Virginie gave her a warning look. Lanky, seventeen-year-old Cooper Layton had been one of those venturesome lads who had made the climb to Virginie's window—and descended like a shot when Virginie had hissed her father was coming. He had not been back since, fearing an enforced betrothal, for the Laytons were indeed a respectable Philadelphia family and his mother would have gone into shock if he had announced he was going to marry a girl—even a governor's daughter—from buccaneer Tortuga.

But of course Esthonie did not know that. The Captain, as was his custom with all women, had been very gallant with the governor's lady. She gave Georgette a tranquil glance. "Now *there* is a lad I would not mind having you speak to, Georgette. You might even invite him to have a glass of limeade in the courtyard if he comes calling. His people, I'm told, are well-to-do and his father well spoken. Not that I'd want you to *marry* one of these Colonials, mind you, but—" *But he would do to practice your wiles on,* was the plain inference. Inwardly shaken with mirth, Imogene wondered what Esthonie's daughters would grow up to be.

Georgette sniffed at her mother's suggestion. "Andy's a child," she said airily. "I take no notice of him! It's only puppy love anyway." Her shrug of enormous *ennui* would have done justice to a courtesan and nearly convulsed Imogene. "Besides," her eyes sparkled, "when I marry it will be someone dashing like Captain van Ryker and not a scaredy-cat like Cooper Layton or his little brother." This in scathing reference to seventeen-year-old Cooper's near record descent down the pepper tree.

Virginie knew when she was being attacked. She took up the cudgel with energy.

"Cooper Layton wouldn't deign to notice you," she said with a sniff.

"That's all you know about it!" cried Georgette. "He said I was a French *meringue* and tried to kiss me behind the camellia bush."

"He didn't, you're lying!" Her face flushed, Virginie gave her pink parasol an angry twirl.

"He did, I'm not!"

"Girls!" cried Esthonie in a quelling voice. They were just now passing Dr. Argyll's small white house and she shot a lowering look at his green-shuttered windows where this kissing fiend was undoubtedly lurking. "Virginie, if that boy calls on you again, make certain you keep him out in the open. You girls cannot be too careful of your reputations. Remember, not only was your grandfather a chevalier of France but you are both *governor's* daughters."

Once again Imogene fought back her laughter. She was rather of the opinion that the little Scots doctor had warned his genteel young houseguests of too close association with the wild daughters of Tortuga's French governor, and that that was the reason for Cooper's defection and Andy's skulking about.

But Georgette, having gained the center of the stage, was unwilling to surrender it. "That woman in purple that Papa was talking to," she told her mother importantly. "The one with all the feathers. I asked someone who she was and he said that was 'Old Rocking Chair' and laughed. What did he mean, Mamma? That doesn't sound like anybody's name to me."

"Of course it isn't!" Esthonie gave Imogene a wild look at this explicit appellation for Madam Josie. "Who told you that?" she demanded sharply.

"I don't know." Georgette's white dimity shoulders twitched in an indifferent shrug. "Just some man on the quay. Dr. Argyll came up and shushed him and sent Andy, who was with him, off to buy some tobacco and started talking right away about the weather, as if I—"

"How often have I told you not to talk to strange men?" shouted her mother, and Georgette fell back, frightened.

She watched her mother apprehensively as Esthonie began to talk very fast, to Imogene. Then Virginie began to squabble with her about the ownership of a pink hair riband.

Under cover of her daughters' bickering, Esthonie muttered behind her fan, "And what does *that* name suggest to you?"

That you'd better lock your husband in! Imogene wanted to reply irrepressibly. Aloud she said carelessly, "Don't concern yourself, Esthonie. People get called all kinds of names."

"Yes." Esthonie gave her a significant look. "And some of them are *deserved*! Did you see where Gauthier went? He had completely disappeared when I looked around after dragging Georgette away from those men. Virginie, stop tugging on that hair riband; let Georgette have it. I said, did you see where your father went?"

"No." Virginie let the hair riband go so suddenly that Georgette fell back against the carriage.

Imogene had seen the little governor rejoin Madam Josie and hurry away from the quay but she felt it best not to say so. "No doubt he'll be along," she said vaguely.

"No doubt! *And* smelling of wine that will never see our cellars! Well, I see we've arrived at your house, Imogene. No—don't ask us in, we must go straight home."

Imogene alighted and stood for a moment watching the

88

carriage drawn by its matched grays proceed down the street. Esthonie's strident voice carried to her.

"Georgette, Virginie, you must keep a sharp lookout for your father and call me the moment he arrives. *Mon Dieu*, I must get these stays loosed, they're killing me. Remember now, the very *moment* he arrives! Tell him I want a word with him!"

With a chuckle, Imogene moved through the iron grillwork doors that big impassive Arne, with his silver-studded wooden leg and his one dangling gold earring, held open for her. She moved through the second set of doors—these of heavy black oak and garnished with stout nailheads, for this house van Ryker had built in Tortuga was half fortress and built to withstand siege—and entered the coolness of the hall.

Outings with turbulent Esthonie, she thought wryly, were always interesting.

CHAPTER 5

"Van Ryker." Imogene flung her small purchases—a tiny steel mirror in a gilt frame for her reticule, a dozen pale green candles that burned with almost no smoke, a sachet scented with attar of roses—upon the bed. She turned her challenging gaze upon the tall dominating man who lounged in the doorway, watching her. Seeing him with Veronique had put her in a mood to quarrel with him. "I went to the market with Esthonie today. She says that you will never change."

Van Ryker had arrived just before her and gone to the storehouse next door to confer with the brace of buccaneers who guarded it. He had returned to hear Imogene's light step upon the stairway that led upward from the stone inner courtyard. Knowing he had something to tell her that would upset her, he had hesitated for a moment by the tinkling stone fountain. Then, because he was not a man to duck obstacles, he had set his booted feet firmly upon the stair and reached her bedroom door by way of the long open-air gallery that surrounded the courtyard, even as she was flinging her purchases upon the big square bed.

Now he leaned his broad shoulders against the doorjamb and cocked an eyebrow at his golden English bride. "And what would our governor's wife know about it?"

Imogene tossed her gloves after her purchases. "She says you will not be *allowed* to change, that your success in taking the Spanish treasure fleet is on everyone's lips and that you have become a target, not only for individual pirates or fleets of pirates but a target for *countries*—she swears a navy may be sent against you."

Van Ryker had pondered the same thought. He gave her a broad smile and his teeth flashed whitely in his dark face. " 'Tis true the king of Spain would love to chastise me—but until he has built or bought more ships he has not the floating bottoms to do so. As for the rest—" he shrugged.

"I think you discount this too much," frowned Imogene. "Esthonie says—"

"Come, let's not waste a beautiful afternoon talking about the wife of our French governor!"

Imogene stood her ground and watched him sardonically as he shed his clothes. The hot tropical sunlight pouring through the open shutters of their second-floor bedchamber revealed to her a long supple body, whipcord lean, with a deep chest, wide shoulders, and arms and neck bronzed to leather by the Caribbean sun. Her smiling gaze left those narrow hips and lightly furred chest and met his gray eyes squarely, intending that he should answer her.

"What are you going to do about it, van Ryker?"

"I am tired of counting gold. I am going to take you in ny arms," he said. "If you will ever get that damn dress off."

She gave a rippling laugh and with it her serious mood was broken. They had indeed spent long hours counting gold since that great coup when van Ryker's *Sea Rover* had surprised the broken treasure *flota* smashed in the wake of a great hurricane that had passed over the Antilles. Months they had been, making their arrangements to leave Tortuga. Always some new problem arose, such as the sale of the house, or what to do about the servants, or the ransoming of the Spanish prisoners, or the need to wait to get the best price for captured goods and fair distribution of the proceeds. A magnificent booty—ransom of a hundred kings. And it had all fallen to the hand of a single buccaneer captain.

And now that same buccaneer captain was waiting impatiently for her to undress.

She gave him a seductive smile, her eyes kindling. "If you will help me with these hooks? You know I can never manage them myself."

He complied with alacrity, moving toward her as a strong man does, with easy grace. His practiced fingers swiftly worked the invisible hooks of the thin gray taffeta and she thought ruefully that he had been good with hooks when first she'd met him—ah, the things other women had taught him! But the very feel of his long fingers along her spine had waked the wild girl within her and made her remember what it had been like the first time she had looked into his eyes, the first time he had held her, caressed her, made her his.

Her smooth buttocks brushed his loins as the gray taffeta dress whispered down her body and rustled to the floor, and for a moment fingers of fire seemed to set her alight. Then her embroidered satin petticoat slid gracefully down about her ankles and she stepped out of them both and turned in her sheer white lawn chemise to face him, cheeks flushed and blue eyes flinging him a challenge.

He gave a low exultant laugh and caught her to him, miraculously at the same moment loosing her chemise so that it feathered down between them like a lover's caress. She felt its lightsome touch drift past her hips and buttocks, felt it shimmer down around her stockings even as his arms went round her and her round breasts were crushed against his hard chest.

She managed to kick off her black satin slippers before he swooped her up and carried her to the big square bed. Together they sank into its soft surface in the sultry island heat, their hearts beating in a wild rhythm, their legs tangled, their heavy hair tangling too, making a frosted pattern of mahogany and gold upon the pillow.

"Let's rid you of these," he muttered, and she squirmed as his knowing impudent fingers found her garters and removed them.

"Van Ryker!" Her voice was breathless, for little currents of feeling were pulsing inside her, faster and faster, as they always did when he touched her.

But he was already removing her black silk stockings with an urgency that spoke fulsomely of his intentions.

"Be careful," she gasped. "They're finest silk!"

"Not so silky as your legs," he muttered, tossing one away and sliding his hands up her legs to secure the other. "And if I tear them, I'll replace them!"

But he had already replaced them a dozen times, for he loved to shower her with gifts, and her wardrobe—so much of it "lifted" from Spanish galleons carrying the best of stuffs to the wealthy ladies of Cartagena and Lima and Panama—rivaled the wardrobes of kings' mistresses.

But she did not really care if he ripped them. As the stockings left her legs and she lay naked in his arms in the tropical heat, she could think of nothing but the man whose strong arms held her, whose gentle hands caressed her, whose warm lips pressed demandingly down upon her own, and whose manliness was even now sinuously at work between her thighs, moving to some unheard but deeply felt lovers' rhythm.

Their joy in each other was a marvel. They drowned in it at night and waked to reimmerse themselves in it with each new day. For he had ever the power to move her, to shift her mind from all the pressing matters of the day and still it to forgetfulness and bring her heart throbbing to his bed.

I love him, she thought, forgetting Veronique as passion coursed through her veins like liquid fire. *I was born to lie in his arms like this, to let him take me, lead me into the wild byroads of passion. Ah, I was born to be his wife!*

And van Ryker, strong, intense man that he was, was lost again in the miracle of her beauty, her softness, her grace, her pliancy. He was beguiled anew by the depth and sweetness of her response to him, so that their lovemaking had all the magical grace of a lovers' dance in some secret hiding place known to them alone.

He had known she was the one woman for him from the first moment he had seen her that day in Amsterdam. All the heartache, all the wild venturing, all the scheming that had brought her at last to his arms had been worth it. Van Ryker knew in the depths of him that he would love this woman to his dying day—and that without her life would be shallow, worthless, not worth living.

They were—and they knew it—made for each other: mentally, physically, spiritually.

And there in the steamy heat of torrid Tortuga they moved as one being, exalted, star-reaching, dragged heavenward by great, far-reaching forces and a love that could never, never die.

To Imogene, van Ryker soared above other men as the eagle soars above the gulls. In him at last she had found her match.

They were—and all Tortuga knew it—the perfect couple.

Now in the afterglow of passion, he caressed her golden hair, let his sun-bronzed hand stray down tenderly to fondle her round white breasts.

"I have not been so idle as you have thought me," he murmured.

"I have not thought you idle!" she protested indignantly, her voice catching a little as tiny ripples of passion surged through her still quivering body.

"Not a trustworthy ship has left the port of Cayona without some small chest of gold or bullion on its way to a Dutch bank or an English solicitor—and all to be deposited well cloaked in other names."

"Can it not be traced to you?"

He shrugged. "Who would bother? The amounts are not that large. They trickle in, they are accepted as the rewards of some rich planter in the Caribbees. No, Imogene, they will not be traced to me.''

So that was what he had been doing all these long months when he had seemed entirely occupied with apportioning fairly the loot he had won, and with arranging for and receiving the ransoms of the wealthy and chagrined Spanish officers who had manned the treasure *flota*. Sometimes it had seemed to her that the very floors of their fortlike house in Cayona were paved with gold, for stacks of new-minted coins had been counted there, and great carved chests unloaded and refilled.

Her own reward had been the jewels. For van Ryker's generous crew—all now wealthy beyond their wildest dreams—had voted to a man that all the finest jewels taken should be showered upon the bride of the captain on whom they doted.

Such an avalanche of jewels had fairly taken Imogene's breath away. She had marveled over big white pearls from off the coast of South America, mounds of dazzling cut and uncut emeralds from the mines of Peru, caskets of carved jade and jadeite from Mexico and Central America, and an unending trove of intricately worked gold bracelets and crosses and chains.

Enough, she supposed, to make her the richest woman, jewelwise, in the world.

And yet from this fortress of a house, she dared not venture far. For she was now—like van Ryker, as Esthonie had maliciously reminded her—a target.

She was worth a queen's ransom and van Ryker would pay it for her willingly, all the world knew it.

There were many who would claim that ransom—if they

dared. All that stood between her and such men were van Ryker's buccaneers, still afloat on a sea of grog in Cayona, as they celebrated night after endless night their mighty victory. Them—and the reputation of the tall buccaneer who had married, of whom men whispered in awe that he was the best blade in the Caribbean and had spitted five men in a single sword fight on a slippery Spanish deck.

That she was a prize herself this golden woman discounted with a shrug. More blood would be shed for gold, she told herself cynically, than ever would be shed for love.

Still it was a troubled face she turned toward van Ryker on the pillow.

"I know the governor of Jamaica has put through a request for pardon for you," she began.

"It came today. A king's pardon. The governor of Jamaica sends you his greetings." Van Ryker's sardonic gray eyes were on her, and Imogene flushed, remembering how that same governor of Jamaica had sought to blackmail her to win her to his bed!

"So now the old charges are dropped and you may face the world under your real name at last," she murmured. "And I shall have to remember to call you 'Branch Ryder' and not 'van Ryker.'"

"Not yet awhile," he said lazily, bending to slide his warm mouth down over her breasts and deliciously along the smooth yielding flesh of her taut stomach. "Not till we've cleared Tortuga once and for all."

Once and for all! It had the ring of freedom to it.

"Oh, van Ryker," she whispered wistfully. "Will we really get away?"

"Certainly. I've been sounding out some of the men. There are those like myself who'd prefer to retire from the buccaneering life. Some of course will be away on pursuits of their own but there are some who'd like to go where we go, and make new lives for themselves."

"Enough to man the *Sea Rover*?"

He nodded. "And repainted and with a new name, who'll call her that?"

"Who indeed?" she murmured. "After all, she was once *El Cruzado*, the Crusader, when you took her from the Spanish!"

"So who's to know if a man named Ryder occupies his plantation upriver from Port Royal and comes and goes by way of a secret bay? And who's to know if a planter named Ryder, who's been a landgrave in Carolina all these years, even though an absentee owner, chooses to occupy his forty-eight thousand acres? We'll be safe, Imogene."

"We could even go to England," she murmured.

"Yes," he said. "I'll have my London solicitors enter into negotiations to buy Ryderwood back, now that my name is cleared."

Ryderwood . . . the home that had been sold out from under him long ago to ransom his father from a Spanish prison. Her eyes smarted at the thought, and a great encompassing happiness that van Ryker should live to see this day overwhelmed her.

"We'll see England again, then?"

"Certainly we'll see England," he promised her coolly. "And Paris and Amsterdam too. But my heart is in this New

World, Imogene, with the Colonies. I believe America has a great future. I'm for Carolina—with you beside me.''

Imogene thought of the wasteland the Indians had made of Longview, his secretly owned Carolina plantation, and sighed. It could happen again. But perhaps not with this determined forceful man at the helm.

"Perhaps we could see England first?" she suggested. "I'd forgot—'' her face clouded. "The old murder charge against you has been dropped but you'll still be wanted as a buccaneer and if anyone were to guess who you were—!''

"I'd chance that," he said calmly. "For the chance to show you London and to see Ryderwood again. I would ride those meadows of my boyhood again, Imogene, and leave them to the sons we will one day have.''

She was touched and turned away her head abruptly so that he could not see the tears that shone suddenly in her eyes. For she had borne—and lost—a daughter during her disastrous first marriage and the doctors had despaired of her ever having another child.

Even if it killed her, she promised herself, *she would accomplish it! She would give van Ryker the son he deserved!*

"Gauthier has finally agreed on a price for the house, so that's out of the way at last.''

"Yes, I know Esthonie has always coveted it—it is larger than the governor's mansion!''

He smiled. "And next week we will pack our things and be off!''

"Where are we off to?''

"To Amsterdam, I think—for we will be well weighted

down with jewels and gold, and Dutch banks are still the safest.''

"Then we will pass England on the way. . . ."

"England we will visit on the way back. I will take you to Ryderwood, Imogene, to visit the home of my boyhood."

Imogene forgot about Veronique and seductive amber eyes.

"It will be a lovely journey," she murmured. "Once again the two of us in the great cabin of the *Sea Rover*—only this time crowded in by chests of gold and jewels! It will be a second honeymoon!"

"No." He sat up restlessly. "Esthonie is right about one thing. Like hawks, there are sharp eyes about watching to see when I will go—and where. Ships will follow me, Imogene—even the Spanish fleet, or what's left of it now, may be alerted. For all I know there may be Spanish men-of-war lying off Tortuga right now, waiting." He rose decisively, ran a hand through his dark hair. "I would not have you with me on such a voyage."

"But surely you cannot leave me here!" she protested. "Remember, you will have sold the house over my head!"

"No, there is a merchant ship—the *Goodspeed*. She sails for Plymouth next week. You will be set aboard her under cover of darkness with but one trunk—the rest will be conspicuously hauled aboard the *Sea Rover* by daylight. And since none could expect that a woman of wealth and fashion would travel without her trunks, none will expect that you precede me aboard another ship."

Imogene sat up and gave him a rebellious look. "Let the trunks travel aboard the *Goodspeed*—I want to be with you aboard the *Sea Rover*!"

He shook his head. "No, it is too dangerous. There may be fighting—I would not have some cannon pick you out and blow you to bits before my very eyes!"

Imogene jumped up. "You mean I must travel all the way across the ocean without you?" she demanded.

"I will be close at hand," he promised, "pacing your ship to guard you from harm. None will notice—they will be too intent upon the *Sea Rover*, believing it to be gunwales deep in treasure."

"And won't it be?"

"To some extent," he admitted sheepishly. "But if the *Sea Rover* is attacked, the *Goodspeed* will sail fast away."

"And leave you?" she demanded bitterly.

"Certainly, leave me," he said, astonished. "What would you have the captain of a lone merchantman do? Take arms to defend a ship of forty guns like the *Sea Rover*?"

"Yes!" Her voice was argumentative. "In time of trouble, every cannon helps."

"I see you should have been my gunnery officer instead of my bride," he said lightly. "No, the four little cannons of the *Goodspeed* would serve more to incense an enemy than to smite him. If battle is joined, I will thank my foresight that you are not in range."

"And of nights, will you thank your foresight?" she asked pertly, standing with her hands on her naked hips.

"Of nights . . ." He sighed and, leaning over, traced with his fingers the hollow between her round breasts, pressed a kiss on one trembling pink nipple. "Of nights I will regret my decision, of course. But with every sail that heaves in sight, I will be glad again that I have made it."

"And, anyway, why the *Goodspeed*?" she demanded, thinking to postpone this parting. "There are many ships that touch here at Tortuga."

"The *Goodspeed* is an honest merchantman," he said slowly. "She put in here at Tortuga only to make needed repairs. I would trust you to her."

His meaning was clear: *Her captain is not the kind to make a deal with those who would seize you and hold you for ransom, Imogene.*

She tried a new tack, telling him she was not ready for the voyage. But there was no changing him, no swerving him from his purpose. She would be off to Plymouth on this merchantman, whether or no, there to be picked up by the *Sea Rover*, then on to Amsterdam.

Not even the protest that she had been involved in what had been accounted a murder in the Scillies could move him.

"You will not be going to the Scilly Isles, nor indeed to any part of Cornwall," he told her. "Indeed, 'tis my intention to take you off the *Goodspeed* at sea off Plymouth and journey with you thence to Amsterdam. I have already arranged this with her captain; he will wait for me off Plymouth."

"You said I have a memorable face," she reminded him. "Word of my near brush with England may reach Cornwall via the passengers arriving on the *Goodspeed*."

"No, for you will be traveling under an assumed name. You will be Mistress Tremayne for the voyage."

Apparently he had thought of everything.

"But will you sail the *Sea Rover* boldly through the English Channel?" she wondered. "Is that not tempting fate?"

"By then she will have another name painted on her hull," he said carelessly. "Should we call her the *Imogene*, do you think?"

He was teasing her!

"It might be an appropriate name for her," she told him in a quenching tone. "For, like me, she has seen many a battle!"

"I did not know you regarded yourself as so formidable," he grinned, reaching out to pull her to him and toy with a lock of her golden hair that fell fetchingly down about her ears.

"Van Ryker, be serious!" She pulled away from him.

"Very well, I intend to paint the name *Caribbee* on her hull and sail her to Amsterdam. There, those I take with me will all assume new identities, and we will all away to England and Ryderwood and thence to my plantation of Longview in Carolina."

Imogene knew these men changed identities as other men changed suits of clothes. Van Ryker's plans were always well laid. She sighed.

"What of my jewels?" she demanded.

"The bulk of them will travel with me for safekeeping. I suggest you take with you only the van Rappard diamonds, and in the bottom of your trunk—"

"My *one* trunk," she reminded him ironically.

But her buccaneer was not to be nudged into argument. He ran an exploring hand across her naked shoulder that made her flesh crawl deliciously and gave her back a bland smile. "In the bottom of your one trunk, I will place a money chain of gold. It should be enough to get you through any emergency that might arise."

It was more than enough. Even if the van Rappard diamonds had not been worth a king's ransom in themselves! Imogene knew that travelers often wore these golden chains around their necks, knowing that a link might be removed as payment for lodgings or for other purposes.

"I could *wear* a golden chain."

"You could but I would prefer you would not. And your dress should be simple, it should not cause comment."

"You mean I must make this voyage garbed as a serving maid?" Her annoyance showed in her voice.

To her surprise, he caught at that eagerly. "Yes, it would be a great protection. Wear something sober. Remember, Imogene, that spyglasses from other ships may be focusing on the *Goodspeed*. You are known for your extravagant gowns. No one will expect you to be wearing homespun."

Nor certainly had she ever expected it! She frowned at van Ryker, shrugging his hand away. "I see you have thought of everything," she said dryly. "Except one thing. How do you plan to get my consent to sail without you?"

He moved toward her, threw a lazy arm about her, pulling her close to him so that her breasts brushed lightly against his chest. "You will do it for love of me," he told her in a rich low voice that throbbed in her ears. "Because you know my only purpose is to keep you safe."

It was a hard argument to combat—especially with van Ryker holding her so breathlessly close. Against her will, her passion flared again, seeming to light the room with its fire. His warm mouth pressed down on hers, his lips moved over hers sensuously, his tongue probed deeply, ardently, past her lips—and her resolve, so strong a moment ago, weakened. His hair spilled over her shoulder to tangle with her own and his strong hands encircled and lifted her buttocks, moving her soft hips sinuously back and forth against his loins. A soft moan caught in her throat as her body waked anew to this magical lover who could always take her with him on voyages of delight—and discovery. The sultry air of the tropics seemed to press in upon them, laden with treasure. And the treasures of life they knew and plundered in the great square bed were accounted by them far dearer than gold, and their love was a molten river down which they plunged recklessly, to clasp and whisper and gasp at the very wonder of it.

Imogene's body melted against van Ryker's lean hard frame, his words of love were an unheard murmur above the roaring in her own ears. Uncaring now, she abandoned herself to the man and the moment, letting her hands and lips and body speak for her.

She loved him—dear God, how she loved him!

Van Ryker held her to him in triumph.

He had won the argument.

CHAPTER 6

" 'Tis a glorious day. Why so pensive?" van Ryker wondered as they sat at breakfast in the long dining room. They were seated at a makeshift table of boards laid atop carpenters' horses, for the handsome dining room suite with its carved high-backed chairs and trestle table were gone, already packed into the *Sea Rover*'s capacious hold. Gone too was the massive oaken table from the chart room and the precious charts over which van Ryker had so often pored. But the planking before which they sat had a white cover of finest linen and there were pink hibiscus blossoms in the silver bowl that served for a centerpiece.

Imogene laughed. "I was thinking of all I have to do today. All the linens must be sorted through, for I have no mind to take anything threadbare across the ocean!"

"Leave them," suggested van Ryker tersely. Now that

breakfast was on the table, he got up and closed the door. "Remember where you are going, Imogene," he said quietly— and that closing of the heavy door reminded her that even the servants were not to know their true destination; he was telling everyone they were sailing for Barbados, that they would head north first for a feint to confuse any who might lie in wait for their treasure-laden ship. "In Amsterdam the goods of the world come to market. You can buy the finest linens, Flemish lace, whatever your heart desires."

"I will not throw away good linens, van Ryker." Imogene helped herself to more of the delicious fricassee. Van Ryker had found for her the best cook on the island—Esthonie was always trying to win him away from her.

"Then sell them in the market on the quay," he suggested.

"Where they would bring buccaneer prices!" she scoffed. "For you know as well as I do that Cayona's prices are the cheapest anywhere—witness the ships from everywhere that flock in here to fill their holds and make their fortunes elsewhere! Besides, one must have linens and I would only be replacing them at a higher price in Amsterdam."

"I had thought you might want to order matched and monogrammed linens," he said quietly. "For you may find yourself entertaining frequently."

"In Carolina?" she laughed. "Where would I find the guests in that savage wilderness?"

"In Ryderwood, then. All the county will be mad to meet the bride I have brought home; you will need ball gowns by the score!"

He was smiling at her. He was looking very handsome this morning, she thought idly. And dressed somewhat more elegantly than was his custom for a morning spent provisioning the *Sea Rover*. His black trousers and wide rakish boots were in dramatic contrast to his short-sleeved scarlet doublet. And the white flowing sleeves of his shirt and the snowy froth of lace at his throat and ruffled cuffs—white as the strong white teeth that flashed at her in that smile—combined to give him a dashing look. As if he were out to impress a lady, she thought whimsically. A sinister look would be added when, before leaving the house, he stuck a big pistol into his wide leathern belt and buckled on the sword for which he was feared throughout the Caribbean.

"Or Gale Force," he said softly. He was speaking of his Jamaica plantation, where so much had happened to her during her short stay there. "Who knows, we may yet be entertaining the governor of Jamaica?" Ironically, for it was not lost on van Ryker that the governor of Jamaica was still in love with Imogene and had in the past proved a dangerous rival.

Imogene's color rose a little higher, for had things gone slightly differently she might have been in the arms of that same governor of Jamaica right now!

"I doubt we shall see much of Gale Force," she said vaguely. .

"Who knows, we may buy a house in London? You will have more than one home, Imogene."

"Yes, and if I wish to be worthy of it, I will not throw away everything we own and start anew. I will take the best of the linens with us, van Ryker, and have them monogrammed in Amsterdam." She was glad to divert him from the dangerous subject of Jamaica's rakish governor. Indeed, she told herself, van Ryker had no cause to be jealous of him. Her heart and her loyalty had never swerved from the lean buccaneer lounging before her. "As to buying new—yes, I will doubtless buy many new things in Holland, where so much is offered." She was silent for a moment, remembering the lighthearted shopping expeditions she had gone on there with Verhulst in that first blush of his love for her, there in Amsterdam where they had met. The young Dutchman had bought everything she admired—thick-piled Chinese rugs in blue and gold and lavender, subtle as paintings; delicate teakwood screens from the Orient; desk items of carved jade; brass paper knives with dragon handles; French wallpaper lavished with hunting scenes; lengths of rich brocades and velvets; silver salts—*silver salts*! She frowned, for that reminded her that she had not yet packed the silver and it must all be carefully crated for the voyage.

"Do you care which of the servants I take with me?" she wondered. "Of course I realize we will not need them all—nor would they all wish to go, but I thought perhaps to ask the cook and—"

"We are not taking any of the servants with us, Imogene," he told her evenly. "Arne has refused to go, for he is too used to the life here in Tortuga to change, he says."

"I shall miss him," laughed Imogene. "For surely he would add color to any place with that red rag tied around his hacked-off gray hair and that one gold earring—not to mention his wooden leg into which he has pounded all those pieces of eight he wins at cards. I marvel he can still lift it!"

"I too will miss Arne," sighed van Ryker. "For I have felt

that even in a place as wild as Cayona I could entrust you to his care. As for cook, Esthonie has asked cook to stay."

To gossip about *us*, no doubt! thought Imogene, knowing Esthonie. "But I am sure I could persuade cook to go," she said.

"You could, but you will not."

She gave him a puzzled look. "And the others?"

"Have all found good positions elsewhere, Imogene. I have already seen to it. We are starting a new life. We must begin it fresh and unfettered."

He was right, of course. She could see that. And these servants on Tortuga, while willing enough, were a slatternly lot. It was hard to imagine them in livery. No, they were not what the mistress of Ryderwood would need to serve her. Still, she was fond of them. She sighed. Esthonie would be taking over the servants, the house. The way of life to which she had become accustomed since van Ryker had brought her to this buccaneer stronghold was slipping fast away.

"You are thinking of covering up our past completely, then?"

"Burying it deep," he said. "To the world these last few years of our lives will never have been. We will fabricate a new past for ourselves."

It was tempting, this world he held out.

"And those men who have decided to join you, those who—like you—wish to become planters in Carolina? What of *their* pasts?"

"They have as much to gain by concealment as I," said van Ryker frankly. "For if we were to sue for pardon from the king for buccaneering, then we must render up one-tenth part of all treasure taken to the king and another tenth to his brother the duke.''

"Would it not be worth it?" she wondered wistfully. "We have so much gold now."

"I see you do not understand. The tenth part exacted from us would needs be a tenth part of all the ship took—and another tenth for his brother. We would have to make good for what others received—it would beggar us."

"I did not know that."

"I realize you didn't, else you would not have spoken."

She was silenced—and sobered too by what he had told her, for always it had lurked in the back of her mind that he would sue for—and receive—a king's pardon for buccaneering and his past would become as other men's, something that could be discussed around the hearth on rainy nights, or over tinkling glasses at some ball or other. Not forever cloaked and hidden, guarded watchfully. But now it seemed that it was not to be. They were to walk free only if they were careful. There was a difference.

"Will de Rochemont sail with you?"

"Yes, but he has longed to quit the sea. We will lose him to France, I fear, for he plans to pay off his old gaming debts and return in style to the home of his father. I expect this time next year will find him with a bride and an heir on the way!"

She was glad for the friendly ship's doctor, but she would miss him.

"And Barnaby?" she asked, wondering about their yellow-haired young ship's master.

"He may desert us too, but he has not yet decided. England calls to him, but Barnaby's heart will always be under sail. He has an eye for far places and has been muttering about Madagascar and the Spice Islands."

Barnaby, the poet . . . she would miss him too.

Suddenly it came to her, what she had not really realized before—that it was all breaking up, this easy camaraderie she had known with dangerous men. She was going back into a world of fashion and manners where prestige and deportment mattered. She wondered if she would be lost in it.

"Come, not so sad, Imogene. You will make new friends. You might take these plates along." Van Ryker indicated the fashionable blue and white ware on which their breakfast reposed.

"They are breakable, so I had thought to sell them—and replace them in Amsterdam."

Did she mistake it or did a shadow pass across his dark face? "As you like," he shrugged.

"Are they a symbol to you of some victory?"

He gave a wry laugh. "More a symbol of defeat, I should say. For I bought them on the day I met you in Amsterdam— as a tribute to your blue eyes. Even then I knew I meant to have you."

"You bought them then?" she marveled.

"Less than an hour after we met. I was strolling through the Kalverstraat and I went into a bookstore that dealt in maps. The owner had just received a shipment of delftware, which he intended for his wife. The box was open on the floor and I saw these plates. I remember thinking, *She would like these—they would match her eyes.*

"You never told me that," she said with a soft catch in her

voice. "And you kept them all this time? You carried them with you even when you thought I was lost to you?"

"In truth I forgot I had them," he said ruefully. "They were packed away, stored under my bunk. I kept your whisk, Imogene, the one that was fished from the sea. Kept it among my shirts."

"Did you really?" She was enchanted. "I had not guessed you to be so sentimental."

His lazy gaze took in the lovely woman before him, daisy-fresh in yellow sprigged calico. "I was sentimental about these small reminders because I had not the woman in the flesh before me. Now you may do with the plates as you will."

"I will keep them," she decided. Indeed they would become her most treasured possession—but she would not tell her tall buccaneer that. There was much of Eve in Imogene and Eve's voice whispered to her that part of the feminine mystery lay in carrying your heart not on your sleeve for all to see, but hidden away, a treasure that must be eternally sought for and won. Her blue gaze glowed at him.

"You seem to approve me today." Van Ryker finished his meal and leaned back and grinned at her. "Was it something I said this morning—or did last night?"

Her wicked gaze sparkled back at him, for last night had been a night of stars and sighs—the stuff that memories are made of.

"We've time for a bit of dalliance before I start my day," he suggested, his gray eyes kindling.

"Van Ryker!" Imogene jumped up laughing and flung down her napkin. "You are incorrigible! If we are not to

114

leave half our things here, I must be about it—I had not dreamt we had so many possessions!"

"*You* are my most cherished possession." He got up and moved toward her.

Warily, Imogene retreated around the table. She knew him in this mood! A few moments more and he'd be scooping her up and galloping upstairs with her in his arms and they would dally and lie abed till noon!

But it was not to be. Big Arne stuck his head in the door.

"That Irishman is here about buyin' the *Heron*," he said glumly.

"Tell him to wait, I'll be right out."

Imogene gave Arne a sympathetic look. Faithful as he was to van Ryker, he was not going with them. "I'm part o' the landscape here in Cayona," he'd told van Ryker bluntly. "I'd miss the town and the town'd miss me!" Imogene was sure that was true. She would hate parting with the blunt old buccaneer, who lately had been so lucky at cards that he had pounded enough coins into his wooden leg that it no longer looked silver studded—it seemed made of solid silver!

"I'll be taking the Irishman out to the *Heron*," van Ryker told her with a lingering look. "He'll want to inspect before he buys."

She nodded, her gaze following him fondly as he left.

Nina, one of the soft-footed half-Indian girls who helped cook in the kitchen, came in to clear the dishes and gave her a shy look. Imogene smiled at the girl, thinking that she would miss them all.

A sentimental feeling that was almost akin to homesickness drew her to the big kitchen. The servants were gathered there, drinking beer and eating at a long board that was almost as lavishly laden with food as that which the van Rykers had just departed. They were all absorbed in the fat mustachioed cook's boisterous retelling in broken English of his upbringing in a French brewery. One of the chambermaids, a redhaired slattern, countered with tales of her early life in the "whey houses" of London. And another, determined to top that, began amid a shower of giggles to brag of her "start" in a Liverpool brothel. Unnoticed, Imogene lingered by the kitchen door for a moment, then moved silently back into the open flagstone inner courtyard where the stone fountain tinkled.

Well, she must get started! And once she had fallen to sorting out the vast sea of linens she had stored in chests and boxes and stuffed into cupboards, she became absorbed by the sheer pleasure of it, for most of them were so beautiful and delicate that it was a delight to see and touch them. Esthonie would have wheedled them from her, had she thought about it, Imogene knew, telling her how they would mildew aboard ship or otherwise succumb to the voyage. Most of the linens were in excellent condition and Imogene shook them out and refolded them carefully into chests to be carried out by sweating buccaneers and stowed aboard the *Sea Rover*.

Sorting and packing the linens was a task that took up much of the day, and when she had finished she decided to pay a courtesy call on Dr. Argyll. The little doctor had been so kind to her that she did not wish to leave Cayona without calling on him again—even though he was not to know that it was the last call she would pay him.

She changed to a gown more suitable for calling. It was a

wide-skirted creation of shimmering peachbloom silk that swayed over a pale aqua silk petticoat, added a sweeping hat that matched the petticoat and supported a wealth of waving peach plumes caught by a gigantic aquamarine that flashed in the afternoon sun. She pulled on pale aqua silk gloves, picked up a ruffled peach parasol, and with Arne beside her she started out into the shimmering heat of Tortuga.

"Ye could take the carriage," he suggested, "for 'tis hot enough out here to melt nails."

"We've sold the carriage, Arne," she reminded him. "It was picked up yesterday."

"Aye, I'd forgotten," Arne sighed.

"Anyway, 'tis not far to walk." Imogene started out briskly with an airy wave of her parasol.

Arne nodded. She noted that he was heavily armed with a cutlass and a brace of pistols and—she had no doubt—a dagger concealed somewhere in that silver-studded wooden leg. He kept looking about him alertly as if expecting to whisk her away from an attack, but the streets were lazy and empty, and as Imogene had no intention of going down into the livelier part of town, Arne soon relaxed and stumped along beside her with the rolling gait that came of long years as a blue water sailor.

She gave a little screech as a land crab scuttled away from her feet and Arne kicked at it disinterestedly with his boot, without hitting it. The white coral rock and shell crunched under her slippers and reflected the sun blindingly. In the big branching live oaks birds were singing, and hanging vines and flowers were everywhere. There was a tang of salt in the air.

And somewhere off Tortuga buccaneer ships were sailing, searching for some passing galleon to plunder. . . .

It was in a mellow mood that Imogene reached Dr. Argyll's green-shuttered white house nestled among trees and vines.

She found him informally dressed in loose white cotton trousers and shirt, but he was delighted to receive her and ushered her into his pleasant courtyard at the back with great ceremony, urging on her wine or at least limeade.

"I'd prefer limeade," she told him with a smile. "It's so hot, I'm parched. And will you see that Arne has some, at the door? For he's weighed down with pistols and must be fairly steaming!"

"Of course I'll see to him. Indeed, we'll all have limeade," declared the little doctor gallantly. "Zazu," he called to the young black girl who kept house for him, "we'll take our limeade out here." He turned as two striplings appeared, coming out of the house. They were dressed somewhat less casually than the doctor but their shirts hung open in the heat. "You know my young houseguests, the Layton lads, I believe?"

"Of course," smiled Imogene. "Have you heard from your father yet, Cooper?"

"Not yet, Madame van Ryker," smiled the taller of the two. "But he won't forget where he left us!"

"I'm sure he will not. Are you enjoying your stay on Tortuga?"

"Oh, yes!" cried Andy, the younger brother. "I've never seen any place like it!"

Dr. Argyll and Imogene exchanged glances. "Well, there really isn't any place like it, I suppose," said Imogene thoughtfully. "You'll be able to keep your friends in Philadelphia enthralled for months with your stories about it."

"Indeed we will," agreed Cooper with a grin. "Like that green lizard that's just about to drop on your shoulder—we don't have *those* in Philadelphia."

Imogene gave a start, then relaxed as she saw that it was only a tiny green chameleon that was looking down at her. It opened its pink mouth as if it were laughing at her. "I'm sure you don't, Cooper," she said dryly. "You have other unusual things—like snow."

Before they could launch into tales of snow forts and snowball fights, of which he was growing rather tired during their continued stay with him, Dr. Argyll interrupted with a hearty "And what else will you tell them about Cayona, lads?"

"About the girls!" cried Andy irrepressibly.

Zazu in her brilliant blue and magenta flowered turban was just then serving the limeade and she rolled her eyes at him so that the whites showed.

Dr. Argyll frowned. That was not quite the answer he had hoped to elicit.

"But aren't there lots of girls in Philadelphia?" wondered Imogene.

"Not like Virginie and Georgette," crowed Andy—and winced as his big brother suddenly managed to dig a repressive elbow into his young ribs.

Imogene looked at Dr. Argyll in amusement. "I see you have your hands full," she said.

He sighed and gave her a rueful look from his honest blue eyes, and when she left he walked her to the door where Arne was waiting, smoking a long clay pipe. "I promised the boys' father I'd look after them," he told her in a worried voice. "But it's hard to keep up with them. Cooper was chasing after Virginie for a while, but now that's cooled off and little Andy is pursuing Georgette. I wouldn't want anything"— he coughed and grew a little red in the face "—anything *untoward* to happen. I wonder, do you think I should mention to Madame Touraille—?"

"I certainly wouldn't say anything to Esthonie, Dr. Argyll," counseled Imogene. "She is sure to blow it out of all proportion and become quite hysterical, wondering whether Andy and Georgette should not be married at once, despite their age!"

Dr. Argyll shivered. "I certainly wouldn't want *that*."

"No, of course you wouldn't."

"They're a worldly pair for girls so young."

"It's living with Esthonie has made them that way," laughed Imogene.

So glumly did the little doctor shake his head that she felt sorry for him.

"If you're worried about Andy seducing Georgette," she told him energetically, "it's more likely to be the other way around! But for your peace of mind, you'll be glad to know that Georgette considers Andy a mere child, unworthy of her steel!"

"I am much relieved to hear it," said Dr. Argyll sincerely.

"And, anyway, their house is locked at night and all the windows have bars on them!" laughed Imogene.

"Oh, I don't think Andy would be so rash as to *break in*,"

he assured her in such an earnest voice that she laughed again.

"Better you should worry lest he be *invited* in!"

"Oh, you surely don't think—"

"No, but only because she doesn't fancy him. If the older brother looks her way, beware!"

"I shall be grateful to get these two young bucks off my hands," vowed Dr. Argyll. "And I hope their father comes soon to pick them up."

CHAPTER 7

Imogene bade Dr. Argyll good-bye, but hardly had she cleared the corner of the building, airily twirling her peach parasol, before young Andy Layton darted out of the shrubbery. He looked flushed and excited.

"It's all right, Arne," said Imogene sharply, seizing Arne's arm.

Arne had had his big pistol half pulled out of his belt before he recognized Andy. He gave a disdainful grunt and stuffed it back in. "Oughten't to come up on a man sudden like that, lad," he counseled gruffly. "Get your head shot off someday, you will!"

But Andy was young and rash and spoiled. He ignored the old buccaneer's warning. "Madame van Ryker," he said in a low intense voice, "could you take a message to Georgette for me? Could you ask her to meet me down at the quay?"

"Of course I'll do no such thing," said Imogene. "Georgette's mother would be furious if she thought her daughter was running about unchaperoned! I'm surprised at you for suggesting it."

"But this isn't Philadelphia," protested Andy in disappointment. "Her father's only a buccaneers' governor and you're one of them and could—" He stopped, his eyes widening, for big Arne had taken a menacing step forward.

"Andy," advised Imogene quietly, "whatever you may think of me or of this island or of the buccaneers with whom your father does such a flourishing trade, you will find it no laughing matter if you seduce the daughter of a French governor. Esthonie will have you marry her—*and the marriage will stick*. So unless you choose to be dragged by your collar to the altar—young though you may be—I suggest you abandon the venture."

She swept away, leaving a hostile young Andy staring after her in chagrin.

But his attitude had ruffled her, his calm acceptance that because she was wife to a buccaneer she would also countenance—indeed assist in—behavior that would be frowned on in Philadelphia. It made her realize how far divorced she was from that other world she had lost—and that she must now reclaim again.

"Don't pay him no mind." Seeing how upset she was, Arne spat. "He ain't dry behind the ears yet."

"I know he isn't." She was silent for a while. Then, "Arne, have you seen Andy hanging around the governor's house?"

"Once or twice."

Imogene frowned. Perhaps she *should* warn Esthonie to have a care for her daughter.

She gave Arne a restless look.

"Let's take the long way home," she suggested. "The weather's so fine I feel like walking."

"Anywhere but the quay," said Arne. He touched his cutlass and pistols significantly. "I should have a couple more fellows to back me up if we're going to the quay."

"But I went there only yesterday with Esthonie!"

"That was then," said Arne with heavy emphasis. "There's been more talk come my way last night. Could be they'll try to seize you on the quay and bleed the Cap'n of his gold to get you back. He gave orders I wasn't to take you down into the town without two or three others to back me up."

She shivered. Up to now their stroll had seemed so peaceful. The sun was beating down, the palms were at their eternal rustling, overhead gulls and seabirds screamed at the land birds who sang back at them.

As they passed the church, she heard the soft thud of hooves and waited to see the rider.

Just as she had expected, it was Veronique. A disheveled Veronique with her hair quite tangled and her bodice not hooked properly. She gave Imogene a look of wild surprise and color rose up her elegant neck to tint the olive-toned skin of her face. With a curt nod, she struck her horse lightly with her hand and dashed by them, the horse's hooves setting shells and limestone flying from the make-shift road.

Imogene was thoughtful on the way home. Esthonie,

she was now convinced, was right. Veronique was meeting someone in the grove. Van Ryker? Ridiculous! It had to be someone Esthonie and the rest of them must not see her with. Could it be that Veronique had developed a tendre for Esthonie's husband? *That* would certainly explain all this slipping around and Veronique's flushed embarrassed face.

Back home, she consulted with cook, tasted the green turtle soup and agreed it was delicious. In the courtyard she stood for a moment to admire the tinkling fountain. She was going to miss this fortress of a house on this buccaneers' island, she thought ruefully.

At the sound of the iron grillwork doors opening, Imogene looked up to see van Ryker come swinging through the doorway. In one arm he carried a huge bunch of bell-shaped yellow flowers, each blossom about five inches across.

"You're early!" she cried. "And you've brought me those lovely Cups of Gold!" She used the familiar West Indian name for the blossoms.

"I had some unfinished business at home," he said with a grin.

Her breath caught as it always did when he looked at her that way. "Oh?" she said carelessly, finding a blue earthenware vase to put the flowers in. "And what business was that?"

"You know what business." He reached out and took hold of her wrist, drew her inexorably toward the stairs.

"We should dine first, shouldn't we?" she murmured.

"We should dine in Paradise—and then on earthly food," he said, dragging her with him as she playfully resisted.

"Who knows, the Spanish may attack tonight, there may be an earthquake, a hurricane may strike, fire may raze the town—it may be the last time we will ever hold each other in our arms!"

She was laughing as he whirled her into the big airy bedchamber that had known so much love and laughter. "You always make love as if it's the last time," she smiled as he kicked the door shut with an impatient boot.

"And should I not?" He drew her close to him, so close she could feel the strong beating of his heart through his white cambric shirt, so close she could hear her own heart beating like a muffled drum. "If death should claim me tonight, would I not die the happier for having held you in my arms once again?"

"Van Ryker, be serious!" she gasped. "Cook will wonder—"

"Where you are concerned, I am always serious—and let cook wonder all she likes!" Even as he spoke, he was carrying her to the big bed. He laid her down upon it, kept his gaze upon her as he unbuckled his sword and flung the big pistols he always carried, now that he had achieved such success and amassed so much treasure, upon a nearby table. She could still feel the pressure of that gaze as he bent down to tug off his boots, the ruffled cuffs of his wide flowing sleeves spilling over his lean bronzed hands as he did so.

She gazed fondly at those strong competent hands. Dangerous in battle, yet always gentle and caressing as they moved over her soft body. He was a myriad of paradoxes, this dangerous complex man she had married. He was a man's man, accounted the best blade in the Caribbean. He had carried on a quarrel with the might of Spain—and won. In Tortuga he was a national hero.

And yet in her arms . . . in her arms he was the lover she had dreamed of those nights in the Scilly Isles when she had looked up at the tall standing stones they called Adam and Eve and asked them to send her a lover. . . .

A great tenderness filled her eyes when she looked at him stripping off his clothes in their airy bedroom in the late afternoon, and her heart was full. She got up and toyed with the invisible hooks down the middle of the back of her bodice. Fumbling hands would add spice to her gown's removal.

"They are too difficult," she complained, watching him through shadowed lashes. "I fear I needs must have help or the dress will never come off!"

"It will come off," he promised her, stripping off his shirt and divesting himself of his trousers and standing before her with naked chest, clothed only in his thin white cambric breeches. As ever, the magnificence of his physique astonished her. On Tortuga one grew used to half-naked men toiling at the careening of ships, running like monkeys up the rigging— but none looked like van Ryker, whose mighty wingspread of shoulder and fencer-slim waist and hips gave him the look of an arrowhead poised to pierce the earth.

She had felt his magnetism that first day in Amsterdam, when he had appeared out of nowhere, sauntered up and demanded an introduction—she felt it now. Her heart was racing.

He stepped forward and put his arms around her. Skillfully,

without looking, he began unhooking—by feel—the recalcitrant hooks down the back of her bodice. She pressed against him, moving her breasts gently against his lightly furred chest and felt his muscles recoil suddenly, felt tension build within him. She gave a low exultant laugh that she should have this power to move him.

"Van Ryker," she murmured, "you have never brought me flowers before. Esthonie says Gauthier never brings her flowers except when he has been naughty. Have you been naughty?"

She was lightening a moment that was building explosively for both of them. Their bodies were so finely attuned to each other that they seemed to pulse as one. For them it had always been like this—since that first time when he had taken her in the great cabin of the *Sea Rover*—against her will, but from the purest of motives. She had been so despondent over the loss of her child that he had feared she was slipping away from him, slipping toward death. He had determined to give her a reason for living—hatred of him. And it had saved her life and her sanity, but it had almost destroyed that which was now so real and moving between them.

She knew he had maneuvered her shamelessly, yet she had forgiven him all, for his love for her was deep and wide and all-encompassing. Such a man deserved forgiveness. He had sometimes murmured against her golden hair that she was his passport to heaven and the only angel he would ever desire.

His answer to her was unintelligible, but it made no difference. He was unfastening the last hook now. In a moment the dress would come off, and then the chemise—

and her naked body would be locked with his in loving embrace. The tropical sounds of the day would become muted and blur into ecstasy as he swept her heavenward in a wild burst of feeling that would leave them both shattered and exhausted—and fulfilled.

"The flowers are lovely," she murmured breathlessly, unwilling to let him think she really suspected him, for she had been but teasing and she must be sure he knew it, for nothing must mar the perfection of this moment and those about to come.

He was sliding the dress gently over her shoulders now, easing it down around her hips. His gray eyes that could be so hard and unrelenting smiled down into hers as openly as a boy's.

"I remembered they were favorites of yours," he said simply, unfastening the tie of her petticoat.

"The Cups of Gold blooms are enormous," she said. "The biggest blossoms I've seen were no more than three inches across."

"When I saw them, I remembered how much you liked them." The aqua green petticoat slithered down to join the dress in a mounded circle around her feet. Only a sheer white cambric chemise and his thin cotton breeches separated their naked bodies. She could feel his manliness pressed against her.

Sirenlike, she would make him wait a moment more. "Wherever did you find them? And so many?" she asked airily, as if she was not already half suffocated with desire.

His answer nearly knocked her flat.

"In the pimento grove behind the church," he said carelessly, humoring this lady who wished to converse when there were other more desirable pursuits at hand. His hands roved over her body exploringly. "There's a great mass of Cups of Gold growing in there. Just walking through, you're apt to end up with yellow petals in your hair."

All of Imogene's thoughts came to a crashing halt. She stiffened in his arms. Veronique had come riding out of that pimento grove—and blushed at sight of her. Van Ryker must have come out somewhat later, for she could not imagine him wandering about the town or showing a ship for sale with a big bunch of flowers in his arms—no, he must have picked them shortly before he came in, which meant he had thoughtfully given Veronique time to clear the area and then sauntered out himself, having plucked an armload of flowers for his wife in the interim.

The answer to *who* Veronique had been trysting with screamed at her. Esthonie was right—it was van Ryker!

She twisted out of his light grasp suddenly, knocking away the hand that was about to tweak open the golden riband that held her chemise.

He gave her a swift questioning look as she turned away from him.

"I—have a headache," she said. She snatched up her aqua green petticoat and fastened it around her waist with trembling fingers. "Besides, dinner is ready."

"Faith, it seems to me this headache has come upon you suddenly," he murmured.

"Yes." Her voice was wooden. "Sometimes it is that way with headaches." She was slipping her dress back on as she spoke.

"And would this 'headache' be caused by something I've said? Or done?" His face was bland but the gray eyes were wary.

"Perhaps." She cast about for something, found it. "I have decided I must go with you. Aboard the *Sea Rover*. I will not be tucked away on the *Goodspeed* with a single trunk and a fare-you-well."

His answer was formal but the steel in his voice was unmistakable. "That will not be possible."

Her hands twisted together. "Van Ryker." She controlled her voice with an effort for her mind had taken fright at the thought of Veronique—Veronique the seductive, Veronique the fashionably flat, Veronique of the challenging amber eyes and the swift tense nervous gestures, Veronique whom men's eyes followed wherever she went. Perhaps it was true, what Esthonie had always insisted—that men craved variety and wives had to fight for their husbands! "Van Ryker." Her voice grew low and painful. "I entreat you—take me with you."

"No."

She gasped. It was unthinkable that he should refuse her. Her blood seemed to rush to her head. *"You will not?"*

"My concern is for your safety, Imogene." His warm compelling hands were on her shoulders now, the intensity of his voice forced her gaze to his. "Have you given thought to what the Spanish would do to the wife of a buccaneer? Especially to the wife of one who had seized the treasure fleet?"

"Oh, damn the treasure fleet!" she cried, trying to turn away from him.

But he held her fast. "There is another danger lurking: disgruntled individuals—like Flogg. If they band together, if they become a cohesive force—"

He left the words hanging meaningfully in the air, but Imogene seized upon them. Perversely she wanted to defy him.

"Go on," she said. "Don't stop there. Add that they may be ringed about Cayona harbor right now, just out of sight over the horizon. *Waiting for you to come out!*"

His answer caught her breath for he nodded soberly. "There have been reports. Hopefully they are untrue."

"I will refuse to leave the island without you!" she cried, stamping her foot. "Do you hear?"

His fingers tightened on her shoulders. "You realize, of course, that I am stronger than you?" he drawled. "And that I could simply pick you up—as now!" Suddenly he swept her up against his chest. "And carry you aboard?"

"Van Ryker, put me down!" She was in no mood to play and the strong throbbing of his heart against her left breast was disturbing. His touch had always affected her this way. In a moment little shudders of feeling would begin, and after a while the whole world would be blotted out—dominated by the pressure of this man's will—nothing else would matter.

But not today! Not with the shadow of Veronique between them! She began to struggle anew.

Van Ryker's eyes, with the softness of her in his arms pressed against his broad chest, had grown tender. She was very dear to him, this slip of a girl, more precious than all the gold in the world. He would not risk her but—he would not humiliate her, either, by carrying her bound and gagged, or

kicking and screaming, aboard the *Goodspeed*, thereby noti-
fying all Tortuga on what ship his lovely lady sailed. Imogene
must sail in secret—for her own protection. How he would
accomplish that must wait for later. For now, his cordlike
arms tightened about her and he drew a deep involuntary
sigh.

"Imogene, you'll be the death of me."

"Bah! How do I know you do not have a dozen women?"
She gave a furious jerk that almost tore her from his arms.

Van Ryker blinked. "I give you my word," he murmured.
"There is only one."

"Swear!" she cried perversely.

He laughed. "I swear on Spanish gold! May my sword arm
wither if I have lied—I have but one woman in my life!" He
looked at her keenly. "You have been listening to gossip.
Rumor would have me bedding half Tortuga! It is a recreation
here—inventing lies. And, anyway," his gaze on her was
incredibly soft, entirely honest, "your heart will tell you that
there is only one."

She heard that welcome note of awareness in his voice, that
softening, that timbred depth—and told herself she had been
wrong about Veronique. It was all a ghastly mistake, van
Ryker had had some other reason for going into the grove.

She relaxed, letting her slender body slump against him,
and turned to let her round breasts move seductively against
his chest. She could feel the sudden bunching of his muscles
in response and her body glowed with triumph that she could
so affect him.

His thick, shoulder-length dark hair fell over her expectant face as he leaned down to kiss her—a long, exploring kiss that left her breathless.

"Van Ryker . . ." she murmured luxuriously. "Forget about dinner, I don't want to quarrel with you."

Smiling, he carried her to the big bed.

"Aren't you going to throw back the coverlet?" she asked lazily.

Plainly, he was not. There was an urgency in him today, a violence that she could explain only by her having challenged his will by refusing to leave without him. But it was there—a felt force. Van Ryker could feel it rushing through him, this passion, this violence born of alarm for her safety, and frustration that she would not see that he meant only to protect her.

And Imogene, lying luxuriously beneath him, her hastily donned clothing tumbled, her bodice tugged down, her skirts sliding upward over her smooth hips to her waist beneath the urging of his impatient hands, succumbed to the warmth of his body, the fever of his lovemaking. She was drawn into his passion as a light skiff might be drawn into a maelstrom, borne irrevocably along, half swooning in his strong embrace.

And all the time a litany sang through her heart that he had not been unfaithful, that it was mere coincidence, that Veronique had gone to the grove to meet some other man, and van Ryker had merely passed by and remembered the Cups of Gold and paused to gather her some. *This* was the truth—what his body was saying to her now. Every sure measured touch, every gesture however tentative or delicate, sent aching bursts of pleasure shuddering through her slight frame and gave the lie to her foolish jealousy of so short a time before.

It was magical how van Ryker could draw her into splendor and send her hurtling over the brink of ecstasy. Not even Stephen, wild lover that he had been, could so seize control of her heart and mind and body so that they became one as surely as the heart and mind are one, locked in love forever. . . .

She drifted out of the magic slowly, as in a lovely lingering dream. Van Ryker was gently, playfully, stroking her breasts in the tender afterglow of passion.

She seized him with a sudden burst of affection and almost smothered him with her kisses.

"What's this?" he laughed. "Did I do something right?"

She was trying to tell him, wordlessly, that she had been a fool, and that all was right with her world.

The next day she plunged into supervising the cleaning and packing of the silver. It was an enormous job, for the house was laden with plate of all kinds—massive candlesticks captured from Spanish galleons, chargers heavy enough to support a forty-pound roast turkey or an enormous baked sea bass, giant salts and ornate bowls and salvers—all of them polished to a high sheen and packed away in hogsheads and barrels and whatever else could be found to carry them.

At the end of the day she was very proud of herself. She was glowing as she ran downstairs to greet the returning van Ryker. Despite a smudge on one cheek and several smudges on the bodice of her simple cream dimity gown edged in narrow bands of deep gold satin, she looked adorable.

Van Ryker stood at gaze, admiring the picture she made in her forward rush.

"The silver is all packed!" she cried merrily—and suddenly her smile froze on her face.

There were a couple of yellow Cup of Gold petals caught in the top of his scarlet baldric where it crossed over his shoulder and one long pointy spirally twisted yellow bud was tangled in his windblown dark hair.

The Cups of Gold had turned out to be cups of rue.

PART TWO
The Governor's Daughter

The governor's wife is sure she is right
To dress her youngest daughter in white
Like proper Parisian girls.
But the governor's daughter yearns for gold,
Indeed, indeed she would sell her soul
To wear black satin and pearls!

The Island of Tortuga, 1661

CHAPTER 8

Leaning silently on her windowsill in the tropical night, with the trade winds blowing through the heavy iron grillwork and open casements to ruffle her thick black hair, Georgette, youngest daughter of Tortuga's French governor, watched with interest the antics of the young buccaneer with whom her older sister, Virginie, had flirted day before yesterday on the quay.

For all she was but thirteen and her figure still flat and coltish, Georgette's dark eyes were cynical. This was a pantomime she had watched before—some young buck climbing up to Virginie's window in the moonlight, to be helped over the sill with a giggle while the householld slept like the dead below. Jaded Georgette felt she had seen it all: the eager ascent—and the quick retreat, for Virginie had told her wickedly how she always at just the right moment cried in a stage whisper, "I hear Papa coming!" and her swains scrambled out the window and away. "Except once or twice, of course," she had not been able to resist adding. "You must never be *easy*," she had counseled Georgette loftily. "Not so much as a kiss the first time they call."

Georgette's eager mind had skipped over the first call and rushed on to what happened after that. "You mean you actually *lost your virginity?*" she had gasped in delighted horror. And when Virginie had smiled mysteriously and giggled, she had demanded to know what it had been like. Virginie had made up a horribly exaggerated tale and Georgette had believed every word. Ever since, Virginie had been lording it over Georgette with her "ruin." Georgette's envy knew no bounds.

Georgette peered upward and breathed a deep blissful sigh. As soon as Virginie was married off—which would be soon, she had heard Mamma say—*she* could have that second-floor room they had added to the house last year.

Reaching that room from the courtyard had been easy when Virginie had had the balcony. But Dr. Argyll had quipped that balconies favored elopement and Esthonie had frowned and—over Virginie's tearful protests—had the balcony removed. Which was no real deterrent, because Esthonie had overlooked that big limb of the pepper tree that scraped the house and gave easy access to Virginie's room to any suitor agile enough to climb a tree.

Only this particular suitor had no convenient branch to aid him. This particular admirer, whose name was Thaddeus McCall, had managed to reach the roof tiles of the lower floor, and then clambered up to the roof above Virginie's room. He was now attempting a spectacular descent down through her open window and Virginie, still dressed as she had been at supper in pink and white striped cambric, was leaning anxiously out the window and directing his descent in sharp hisses.

Georgette's dark brows lifted in scorn as she saw the young buccaneer's hand slip, heard his soft muttered curse as he almost went plummeting down to the courtyard below. *She* would have more adroit lovers. Hers would never land awkwardly on marble benches and break their legs. They would never miss a step, or slur a name, or forget a face. Most especially they would never forget *her* face or anything else about her. They would carry her memory with them to their *graves*.

That, of course, was for the future, for Georgette was most closely guarded and chaperoned by her mother, who was well aware of her younger daughter's precocity. And, besides, there were the iron bars on the first-floor windows and the outer doors were always tightly locked before the servants went to bed. Even the door to Virginie's room was locked at night—lest she decide to wander. Georgette's was not but she could not get outside because the key ring reposed on her mother's night table and it would be a dangerous expedition to go in and get it. The keys might clink and wake her mother, who would then, to Georgette's vivid imagination, lock her in *for years and years*!

Her attention went back to the young buccaneer, his muscular body swinging from the roof tiles in the perfumed night. In the courtyard the palm trees rustled, blending in with Virginie's hiss as she leaned out the window clutching at her suitor's belt to pull him in. As Georgette watched, Thaddeus, now swinging by one hard-sinewed arm, caught hold of Virginie's casement, got both boots planted on the sill, and with a muscular ripple that tugged his flowing shirt near out of his trousers, disappeared inside.

Georgette sighed. She had been rather hoping for something more dramatic. A screech from Virginie perhaps as Thaddeus lost his hold, caught the windowsill as he fell— and hung there unable to climb up and afraid to drop to the potentially lethal stones below. Georgette could imagine the household awaking, lights appearing hastily, her father's nightcapped head thrust out, her mother crying, "What is it, Gauthier? Have the Spanish attacked?" And then her mother's near hysteria as she had realized the true situation.

That was the way it had been a week or so previously. Heartless young Georgette had thoroughly enjoyed everyone's discomfiture and especially Virginie's chagrin.

Now her thoughts drifted to what they were doing up there, Virginie and the blond young Scotsman she had attracted on the quay. For a good ten minutes Virginie had flirted with him from her window. He had stood in the courtyard with his long legs spread wide apart and grinned upward and beckoned her to come down.

Virginie had shaken her dark curls and smiled winningly. Thus encouraged, Thaddeus had leaped to the marble bench and held out his arms, indicating that he would catch her if she jumped.

Georgette had waited breathlessly for reckless Virginie to accept his challenge and throw herself from the window into his arms.

It had not happened.

Virginie, her face and figure dramatically lit by two candles set at strategic places near the window (Georgette helped her steal them from the kitchen; cook wondered what happened to them), pouted.

Realizing more bait was called for, Thaddeus reached inside his loose, coarse-textured maroon shirt and pulled out something that glittered. Georgette peered forward. It was a golden chain, delicately wrought, something he had picked up in his venturing.

Again he held wide his arms, lazily dangling the chain.

Georgette held her breath, firmly expecting Virginie to jump.

Instead, a low reckless laugh drifted down from the window above. With a languorous gesture of a slim young hand, Virginie beckoned to the man in the courtyard below. She whirled about once so that her black curls made a swirling cloud about her head in the candlelight. Mockingly, she blew out a candle and cocked her head at him and began taking off one of her big detachable sleeves (this had always sent the sons of merchant captains shinnying up the big pepper tree). She hesitated, toyed with the sleeve, seemed to change her mind and stood undecided, then slowly removed both sleeves with her wicked gaze fixed on the man dangling a golden chain in the courtyard below.

Then she blew him a kiss—and extinguished the last candle.

Thaddeus McCall was left in no doubt. The governor's daughter had flung him a challenge.

And he would meet it!

And now, surefooted as a cat burglar, he had made it through Virginie's window.

Georgette imagined the scene: Thaddeus, in his maroon shirt with its flowing sleeves, would be standing in the room facing a bridling Virginie. Virginie would have hastened to relight the candle and now the candlelight from behind would be haloing her dark hair (Georgette was sure of this, for Virginie had bragged to her about the "dramatic effect" of candlelight that "brought out the beast" in men. Georgette was not quite sure what the "beast" was, but she was eager to find out. So far, Virginie had not enlightened her). Virginie's pink and white striped bodice would be straining with the deep breaths she would be taking (Georgette had observed this from seeing Virginie in passionate conversation with gentlemen in the garden during parties Esthonie gave).

Thaddeus—what would Thaddeus be doing? Georgette reached for a mango in a bowl nearby. Thaddeus would—he would be on his knees to Virginie. No, that would come later after Virginie had led him on for a while and *before* she cried out that she heard Papa coming. Thaddeus would be bending over her, Georgette decided—like Captain Vartel had the night of the party when Mamma had come upon them in the dark courtyard; Virginie had been giggling and Mamma had said Virginie had drunk too much wine and had led her away.

Idly, Georgette rubbed the mango's smooth skin between her hands and her eyes grew bright. The night wind brought myriad scents through her barred window—lush tropical flowers, the salt sea, and something indefinable carried along on the trade winds . . . something wild . . . perhaps it was the scent of freedom.

Georgette's mind, however, was not on freedom but locked in that upper room with Virginie and her sturdy new suitor—that Thaddeus might not choose to marry Virginie if he could had never crossed the mind of either sister. Who would not leap at the chance to marry a daughter of the governor of Tortuga?

Georgette listened, hearing nothing. Her imagination raced.

Thaddeus's hot breath would be on Virginie's cheek now, on her pulsing throat, as his urgent lips drew closer, closer (Georgette saw it all in slow motion, as in a dream). Virginie would smell the scent of rum and tobacco. His arms would go round her and she would feel against her bodice the rough material of his maroon shirt. Georgette's short, rather stubby fingers were caressing the smooth peach-colored skin of the mango and her dark eyes had gone dreamy—*he would be kissing her now.*

And now his strong bronzed hands would be straying down her back, sliding down Virginie's pink and white striped bodice (Georgette had seen Captain Vartel do that) and he would be attempting to unfasten the invisible hooks that held that bodice together (as Virginie had later confided).

And what would he do next? Georgette's puzzled gaze sought the inscrutable darkness of the tropical courtyard where the palms scraped sensuously and the shrubs were hulking unrecognizable shapes. He would—well, he would give up on the hooks, Georgette decided. Virginie was always calling on her sister to help unfasten them and it was a near impossible job. Balked by the hooks, he would try a new tack. Georgette's eyes sparkled. He would crush a pulsating Virginie to him and his hot lips would drag away from

Virginie's eager mouth and trail impudently—she shivered—down the white column of Virginie's throat and bosom toward her taut round breasts straining against the cambric. Virginie of course would be covered with blushes and pushing him playfully away—for all that she was the heroine of several such encounters.

Entranced, Georgette bit into the luscious mango, unmindful that the juice had spurted on her night rail. Tomorrow Mamma would scold her, but tonight it did not matter, her very soul was seething in that upstairs room with Virginie and her buccaneer.

And now . . . now Thaddeus would have reached a questing hand down inside Virginie's bodice, just at the cleavage, she supposed. And Virginie would slap his hand away—but not too discouragingly hard a slap. She would mince about, tossing her head in mock fright—in Georgette's opinion, Virginie always minced—and mutter how he must *not* make advances—oh, la! her parents would hear! And *then* there would be the devil to pay!

Georgette tried hard to imagine Thaddeus blanching at the threat of Papa charging up the stairs and gave up. No, she decided regretfully, he would not blanch. Nobody blanched at Papa here on Tortuga for all that he was the governor—and most especially not the buccaneers, who were a fierce lot and considered van Ryker their leader if indeed they had one. Virginie had already enjoyed several lightsome affairs almost under the parental noses. Georgette shrewdly decided that Mamma had decided Virginie's uncertain virtue was already lost and that was the reason for her sudden urgency in corresponding with her French cousins about a mate for

Virginie. Otherwise she would probably have let her go her way until she chanced upon some really good catch like—like Captain van Ryker if he were free.

Georgette sat dreaming. Imagine . . . all that gold and the glamorous captain too! How lucky Imogene was! She wished *she* were grown-up and could try to win him away like their houseguest Veronique Fondage was doing. Georgette was certain she herself would win. For although it was true that Imogene had a heavenly beauty—she, Georgette, would have an overwhelming appeal that would bowl men over like tenpins! She had long ago decided that. When she was as old as Virginie she would be a *femme fatale*—just like ruined Cousin Nanette in France! Of course, she had yet to prove her universal allure, but there would come a day—and she hoped dismally that there would be *some* Spanish treasure left, so that she could reap herself the golden rewards of buccaneering—not as Virginie upstairs was doing with the gift of a simple golden chain, but as Imogene had done, with the glamorous Captain van Ryker pouring out the wealth of the Spanish plate fleet at her feet.

Georgette missed entirely the love Imogene bore the tall buccaneer or the way he worshiped her. In her youth and inexperience, she was sure sex was everything and that by her very youth and vivacity she could *at this moment* transport van Ryker—if she but had the chance!

She was not likely to get the chance either, she knew. Not only Imogene, but now Veronique, stood squarely between them. And although she had made eyes at him, it was obvious that he considered her too young. Georgette heaved a deep sigh. She wondered if Virginie would really go to bed with Thaddeus—she had always claimed the next morning that she had not.

"He nearly had my clothes off!" she had whispered to an ecstatic Georgette on more than one occasion. "But I was too quick for him. I told him I heard Papa coming and he slithered back down the tree in fright!" Her low wicked laugh had thrilled Georgette.

But now there was no tree branch, and the admirer in question was not one of the sons of merchant captains, for the most part fairly genteelly brought up, who might take fright at the thought of being pursued by the furious governor of a buccaneer island—entirely misunderstanding the governor's position here as a puppet for the buccaneers. Virginie's new admirer—like the last one, who had fallen and broken his leg before he could bed Virginie—was a wild buccaneer and unlikely to run away at a mere whispered threat.

Had Georgette but known it, Virginie, who had tempted fate so many times and won, was at the moment hard pressed and on the run. Thaddeus, spurred on by Virginie's exhibition from the window, had arrived in a mood to begin at once. If Virginie had expected some conversation from him, she was not to have it. He scooped her up impetuously in his arms and was about to bear her to the big square bed when he was stopped in his tracks by a hiss from the squirming creature in his arms, followed by a stinging slap.

Surprised at such hostility, Thaddeus stopped in his tracks and peered down.

"I want to light a candle," muttered Virginie. "Put me down, Thaddeus!"

Thaddeus gave an uncertain chuckle. He wanted to please

the wench, God knew. And if she wanted to make love in light instead of darkness, he felt he should accommodate her. He'd known a wench back in Scotland who'd make love only in the heather right after a rain—there was no accounting for tastes!

He put Virginie down and leaned against her, reaching round to fondle her breasts as she tried with trembling fingers to light the candle. His breathing was heavy and indeed his breath came so hot and vigorous on her ears that it blew her curls about.

"Here," she said petulantly, trying to strike his body away with a shrugging shoulder. "You do it. I'm all thumbs."

Excited, was she? Well, his friend Jim Notley had told him she was a hot wench! Thaddeus took the flint and promptly lit the candle. It flared up to reveal Virginie's slightly scared face. She was even more alarmed to see Thaddeus's triumphant, almost gloating expression.

Virginie was of no mind to have her virginity plucked as carelessly as one might pluck an orange from a tree. She stepped cautiously away from Thaddeus, wishing she still had the meager protection of her big detachable sleeves—they had the virtue at least of always getting in the way.

"Sit down," she said, regally indicating a high-backed chair with a leather seat.

Again Thaddeus looked surprised. But he remembered Jim Notley telling him that for all her passion, Virginie was a "real lady." And with "real ladies" (he had never known one), he had always heard it was slow work.

He set the candle down carefully on a table—aboard ship

one learned to be very careful with fire. "And where will you be?" he wondered.

"I will sit on the bed," Virginie said, somewhat regaining her composure. At least, she told herself, looking at the brawny young buccaneer before her, she had been able to stop him! For a moment there, she had had her doubts.

Thaddeus nodded thoughtfully. That was a very good place for the lass to compose herself, on the bed. If this was how she wanted to do it, he had no objection. He was about to settle onto the chair when he realized it was already occupied—with feminine apparel.

"Oh, those sleeves—" for Virginie had flung her detachable sleeves on the chair. "Just toss them to me." She caught them as Thaddeus tossed them and laid them carefully on the coverlet. She was watching Thaddeus out of the corner of her eye as she might some dangerous animal about to spring.

Thaddeus picked up the chair, meaning to bring it closer to the bed.

Virginie jumped. "Oh, don't move it," she entreated in an anguished whisper. "The floor squeaks over here by the bed—my parents are sure to hear!"

Well, he certainly didn't want that. Carefully, Thaddeus put the chair down. He sat upon it. It occurred to him that this was not a winning situation for him. Certainly it was not the way he had imagined it would be from Jim Notley's bawdy (and entirely imaginary) recounting. Jim had told him Virginie had melted like butter in his arms and given him a night of dazzling thrills. By now Thaddeus had fully expected to be tickling a half-undressed Virginie, dangling the gold chain above her naked nipples and making her reach up to snatch for it. Now for some reason he was afraid to bring up the subject of the gold chain, much less display it.

"D'ye have something to drink?" he muttered restlessly.

"No, I thought we would sit and talk for a while." Virginie plucked aimlessly at her skirt. In their concentration neither of them noticed Malcolm, who had been sleeping under the bed's heavy fringe and who now got up and stretched.

"*Talk?*" Thaddeus gaped at her. Did the wench think he had climbed her roof at peril of his limbs to *talk*? Then, to Virginie's terror, he threw back his blond head in a roar of silent laughter. The wench was putting him on, and he'd been too dumb to know it! When his head came down, he got up and swaggered confidently toward her. "Lass, Jim Notley told me all about ye. A hot wench, he swears ye to be, and I've a gold chain to be had by a lass with looks like yours—and more too where that comes from."

Virginie gasped. She had not bargained for this.

"James Notley knows nothing about me," she protested. "He fell before he reached my room!"

He was towering above her shrinking figure on the bed. "But there were times before that," he pointed out tolerantly. "Jim told me so!"

"There were *no times before that*," whispered Virginie in fright. She leaped up, intending to elude him.

Thaddeus was more aware of her flashing cambric skirts than of her protests. Reckless of the sound his heavy boots might make upon a squeaking wooden floor, he plunged toward her, intending to take control of the situation.

His timing could not have been worse.

Malcolm had just poked an orange and white head through the bed fringe as Virginie leaped up. Finding too many legs and feet about for his liking, he elected to dart between them—this just as Thaddeus made his move.

Thaddeus's toe caught Malcolm's tail—and Malcolm retaliated in the time-honored fashion of cats.

To an electrified Georgette, the sounds from above came as a sudden thump, as Thaddeus instantly found a new place for his boot, simultaneous with a cat's loud angry screech and a sudden masculine howl as Malcolm took vengeance by slashing the flesh above Thaddeus's wide, turned-down boot. And all accompanied by a clearly heard thin wail from Virginie pleading, "*Do* be quiet! They'll *hear*!"

There were noises of awakening all over the house. Georgette, her teeth clamped for a last luscious bite, tore the mango free and dropped it on the windowsill as she unwound her long body for a rush to the door. She flung it open and catapulted toward her father's room, from which the stairs led up to Virginie's second-floor bedchamber.

Her mother, who occupied the bedroom next door, was already there when she arrived. Esthonie slept heavily, but when she woke, she woke like a buccaneer, ready to fight or fly. Tonight, realizing the racket came from overhead, she had flown unerringly toward her husband's door—and collided with Georgette in her night rail in the entrance.

"Get out of my way!" She gave her younger daughter a push. "Gauthier, Gauthier, put on your trousers—no, don't wait for that, come along in your nightshirt. And bring your pistol."

That last remark electrified the plump governor, who tumbled out of bed in his long nightshirt, pushed back the tasseled nightcap that had fallen over his eyes, and, barefoot, rushed to open a chest by his bed and pull out a long dueling pistol.

"What is the matter?" came Veronique's voice.

"Nothing!" snapped Esthonie. "Go back to bed. Oh, Gauthier, hurry!" Esthonie was already halfway up the stairs. "Someone is attacking Virginie!"

How this could be when the only access to that upstairs bedroom with its locked door was past *him*, Gauthier never questioned. He surged to the defense of his women, a plump charging figure brandishing a big pistol, only to meet Esthonie's anguished wail at the closed door. "I forgot the keys—Georgette, go get them from my night table. At once, Georgette! *Mon Dieu*, what was that?" at a sudden scuffling sound from inside the room. "Virginie, are you all right?"

"Yes, Mamma," came a shaky voice from inside.

"Who is in there with you?"

"No one, Mamma." A firmer tone.

Racing upstairs with the heavy key ring, which contained the keys to the entire house, Georgette heard that and marveled at Virginie's aplomb. After all, in a minute or two her clandestine visitor would be found and only heaven knew what would happen then—maybe Mamma would have Virginie put in irons and transported far away to France!

This exciting thought caused Georgette to trip on the top step and plummet into her father, who said "Oooof!" as he dropped his pistol. It went off with a deafening report that brought forth a united scream from all his womenfolk as well as two female servants downstairs who had crept out of their quarters, round-eyed, to ask each other what was going on upstairs.

"Don't shoot, Papa!" implored Virginie as the door burst open. She was at her dressing table, desperately trying to rearrange her hair and she was holding the torn front of her bodice together with her other hand.

"Virginie, what has happened to your dress?" cried Esthonie.

"Nothing, Mamma." Virginie turned a shade paler. "I was fiddling with the lace at the neck and tore it in fright when I heard Papa's gun go off."

The explanation seemed reasonable enough to the governor, who was beginning to feel foolish. But Esthonie was not satisfied. "What happened?" she demanded loudly, her ears still ringing from the report of Gauthier's pistol.

"I stepped on the cat," sighed Virginie.

"Then where *is* Malcolm?" Esthonie cast a suspicious look around.

"Maybe he's gone under the bed, Mamma," offered Georgette helpfully. She fell to her knees, peering through the fringe under the bed—fully expecting to meet the scared blue eyes of the young buccaneer and see him put a finger to his lips to command her silence. Instead she saw Malcolm, his orange and white fur fluffed out, his assaulted tail swelled out like a porcupine, his golden eyes baleful. When she reached out a tentative hand, he drew back and spat at her. "Malcolm's under the bed," reported Georgette. "He's frightened and he won't come out. He hissed at me."

"Oh, do let the cat alone." Esthonie was pulling open Virginie's big press and pummeling the clothes hanging there as she spoke. She gave the big full skirts a couple of kicks with her carpet slipper for good measure, half expecting a yelp. She seized the top of Virginie's big trunk and yanked it open, and brought both fists down smartly upon the contents.

"Mamma." Virginie's eyes were round. "What are you doing?"

Her mother did not deign to answer. Instead she swept toward the window that looked out on the courtyard. "These casements should be shut," she rasped.

Virginie slid in front of her to bar her way. "I'll close them after you've gone, Mamma," she quavered. "But right now I need some air!"

So that was where the intruder was! Clinging to the sill, dangling above the courtyard! Esthonie's eyes gleamed.

"I will close them right now!" she cried. "Yes, and have your father nail them shut!"

"But, Mamma, I'll suffocate in here!" Panicky, Virginie still barred the way. She jumped as Georgette, having seized Malcolm by the paw, tried to drag him forward. Indignation rose in Malcolm—first trod upon and now this! Growl rose to yowl. He bit Georgette's finger and she shrieked—her wild yelp nicely covering the sound of a thump as Thaddeus's fingers gave way and he fell to the courtyard. He landed on the side of one boot, toppled, and before he could save himself, struck his head against the corner of the same marble bench that had broken his friend James Notley's leg. He crumpled and his falling body shot between the bench and a large enveloping shrub, which met above his fallen form in a way that hid him from onlookers from above.

In effect, Thaddeus had disappeared. And when Esthonie at last managed to brush by her protesting daughter and looked out before she slammed the casements, she saw nothing. With a frown, she turned to Virginie. "Nevertheless, these casements will be nailed shut!"

"Tomorrow, Esthonie," sighed Gauthier, who felt that the whole thing was a tempest in a teapot. "Tomorrow I will have them nailed shut. Now let us get some sleep—if that is possible in this house."

Grumbling, Esthonie had to be content with that. Together they all trooped away, with Georgette sucking the finger Malcolm, still skulking angrily under the bed, had bitten.

Back in her own room, Georgette peered out with interest— and saw from this angle the fallen figure of the young buccaneer. She studied him with relish. What if the fall had killed him and his body was discovered there tomorrow morning? Everyone would remember the incident of the night before and realize that he had been visiting Virginie. There would be a rare scandal and Virginie would be ruined. Callously, Georgette wondered what it would be like to be ruined—not secretly ruined as Virginie insisted she was, but publicly ruined like Cousin Nanette. Of course those overdressed bawds with their loud voices and raucous laughter who hung about the buccaneers at the quayside market were also ruined. Georgette would not care to be like *them; they* lived in tawdry squalor. But Cousin Nanette, who had deserted her family for a fabulous life in the theater in Paris, was also ruined, according to Mamma. And now Cousin Nanette, who had never had two petticoats to her name when she lived with her family in Lorraine, had clothes and jewels to rival a duchess and was the talk of Paris.

Plainly, there were different levels of "ruin." Georgette

up. He's responsive, whatever that means, but he's got a ways to go to be all right. Still great news. Anyway, I wanted you to be the first to know. Love you, babe. Call me."

"Not home?" asked Beau.

"Probably out in the yard," said Nick, hitting a speed-dial number. Tig Sutter answered on the second ring.

"Nick—you heard?"

"I heard. We're on our way to Lady Grace now. Do we still have the jurisdiction here?"

"Oh yeah. Case is still open. I've already called the doctors down there. They're saying the kid's not coherent, but he's definitely conscious. They're going to do a bunch of tests on him, but I told them to keep him alert until you got there."

"Incredible, Tig," said Nick, his heart lightening in a way it hadn't ever since the case kicked off. "You know I've never even talked to the kid?"

"Yeah, well, remember, he doesn't know his parents are dead. That's going to be a tricky call."

"He's not going to hear it from me. Not today, anyway—"

"He'll be asking."

"Yeah. I can't reach Kate. She's his legal guardian. She ought to be there, see to what he needs, sign whatever has to be signed."

"Nick, this is going to sound crazy, but the docs are saying the kid calmed down when he heard Lemon Featherlight's voice. If Kate's not available, maybe you could go in that direction?"

"We should think about that, Tig. Guy's a CI, a drug dealer—"

"Lemon connected with the kid last year. Even Tony Branko at Vice thought Lemon's heart was in the right place. I think it's worth a shot."

Nick thought it over.

"Okay. I'll give him a try. Did you hear from the lab yet?"

Nick and Beau Get Word

Beau and Nick were only a block north of where Byron Deitz and Zachary Dak were concluding their discussions. Nick was still brooding on Bock.

"You get a look at that guy at the table by the railing? All in black?"

Beau stopped to think.

"I saw him," he said. "He drove up in that lime green shit-box Camry. Why?"

"I know the guy. His name is Tony Bock. He's the guy in the Dellums custody case. Kate handed him his ass on Friday afternoon."

"Weird-looking guy."

"Yeah. Did you see what he had shoved down the crack of his ass? He had one of those collapsible steel batons. What do they call them? An ASP? Must have been damn uncomfortable."

Beau nodded. "Or maybe he had his dick on backwards."

"Yeah," said Nick, pulling out his cell phone. "Happens to me all the time."

Nick's cell phone rang as soon as he turned it on. He got

into the car on the passenger side—a couple of Advils had eased the pain in Beau's butt cheek enough for him to drive.

Nick hit ANSWER.

"Lacy?"

"Nick, I've been trying to reach you."

Her voice was tight and urgent, but not the tone she had when she was calling with a problem.

"I can see that. Four times in the last hour. Is everything okay?"

"Yes. No. Well, maybe."

"That pretty much covers the ground."

"Nick, Rainey Teague woke up."

The words ran around in his skull like those tigers chasing the black kid in that book nobody was allowed to read anymore. For some crazy reason he remembered it from his childhood. *Little Black Sambo*. His mother had waved it around as an example of what she called endemic racism. On some level Nick knew he was thinking of that stupid book right now because what Lacy had just said completely rocked his world.

"How awake?" he asked when he could speak.

"They're saying he's responsive. He's talking. He's been immobile for a year, so he can't sit up or control very much. But he's definitely not in a coma or a caledonia or whatever it was."

Nick turned to Beau.

"Lady Grace, Beau. Right now."

"What's up?"

Nick told him.

Beau took it in, made a U-turn to a chorus of outraged honks, accelerated into the street with the siren on. Cars on both sides swerved to the curb to give them room. Nick, busy getting the story from Lacy, only half registered Byron Deitz in his big fat yellow Hummer driving slowly north, staring at them as they flew south down Long Reach Boulevard.

Lacy had gotten to the part about Lemon seeing a man in the elevator.

"What does he mean? Like, a ghost?"

"No," said Lacy, who wasn't sure what the hell Lemon had been trying to say. "Just a guy with a really wicked vibe. Lemon said he sort of radiated crazy. Crazy and spooky. I don't know. Whoever he was, he scared the hell out of Lemon, which is pretty hard to do."

"He get a description?"

"Yeah. He'll tell you when you get there. He's in the lobby, waiting for you."

"You got his cell?"

Lacy gave it to him.

"What was Lemon doing there in the first place?"

"After he talked to you, he wanted to go see the kid. He says he went to smoke the room."

"What? You mean like that bug-killing stuff?"

"No, you mutt. It's a tribal thing he does. All the Indians have it. He takes some sweetgrass and burns it in a bowl and calls the kid's name."

"Looks like this other guy had a better method for calling the kid. What's this name Rainey was saying again?"

"He was asking for somebody named Abel Teague."

"*Abel Teague?* You sure?"

"Yeah. He was also talking about a woman named Glynis Roo . . . something. Glynis Ruelle. I don't know what this all means," said Lacy, "but you better go find out."

"I will," said Nick. "Thanks, Lacy."

"Keep me in the loop, will you?"

"When I know, you'll know. Bye."

He switched off, hit AUTO-DIAL. The phone rang six times, and then went to voice mail.

"Kate, when you get this, call me on my cell. You sitting down? Great news. Rainey Teague just woke up. Yes. Woke

"You mean that goddam cat? What'd you do to her, anyway? Yaztremski says the thing's crazy."

"He get anything off her coat?"

"Not much, so far. Blood, and it was definitely human, but it had broken down a lot. Yaz thinks it might have come from a body been dead quite a while. Not the same blood type as either Delia Cotton or Gray Haggard. We've got a forensic team going over the house now—"

"Yeah? How they liking the house?"

"What? Liking the house? Like how?"

"They talk to the Armed Response guy? Dale Jonquil? He said he saw some weird shit in the mirrors there. So did Mavis Crossfire."

So did I.

Skulls.

Coffins.

Slaves.

"CSI didn't say anything useful, Nick, but those people *never* say anything useful. You follow that thing down at Saint Innocent?"

"From a distance. I hear Mavis did good."

"Yeah. I talked to her a few minutes ago. They're going to give her a commendation. Giving Coker one too, for spotting that stovepipe round. Saved that man's life, between the two of them. They've got Dennison in Psychiatric for now, but all in all, he may not even do much time."

"You getting anywhere with the snitch?"

"I asked Byron Deitz to put one of his IT guys on it, but so far no word back. I'm hoping, though. Deitz says the guy's the best there is."

"I saw Deitz a minute ago, going northbound on Long Reach in that gigantic Hummer. He was gunning me like he wanted to talk, but I had the lights on. He and Phil Holliman still stomping all over Boonie's investigation?"

"I told him to jerk Holliman's chain. He said he would. You wanted to know about that metal shit you found in the dining room at Temple Hill?"

"I thought it was shrapnel. Was it?"

"First take from Metallurgy was that it was shell fragments from . . . get this . . . a German .88."

"How'd they figure that?"

"One of the guys at Metallurgy is a fragments freak. Has cans and boxes full of various bits of shell casings, debris from car bombs, whatever—he's compiling a sort of reference library about it. He takes one look at the bits, scrapes some shavings, puts them under a scope, looks up and says German .88. Here's the thing. Haggard was at Omaha, and he got a chest full of shrapnel when he got to the top of the cliffs. From a German .88, according to the After-Action Reports."

Nick thought about that. "Okay, well, if that shrapnel came out of Haggard's chest, I'd say we've gone from a disappearance to a homicide."

"That's what I think too. We're declaring Temple Hill a crime scene. And we've got everybody we can spare out looking for any sign of either of them. Are you going to go back to Delia's house after you see Rainey?"

I'd rather stick hot needles in my eyes.

"I don't think so. We'd just get in the way. But keep me in the mix, will you?"

"I will. I talked to Mavis, a while ago. She called in to ask exactly the same thing you asked. 'How did Nick like the house?' What the hell went on up there, anyway?"

Nick was quiet for a moment, watching Lady Grace fill up the windscreen. He realized, abruptly, that he had not heard back from Kate, and for some reason that bothered him more than it should have.

"I don't know, Tig. Beau and I saw some crazy stuff, hard to explain. Got to run, Tig. We're at Lady Grace."

"Okay. Check back."

"I will."

Beau pulled the cruiser to a stop at the main entrance to Lady Grace. Lemon Featherlight was waiting outside, under the arch, smoking a cigarette and watching them, looking jumpy and spooked. He came up to the passenger window as they cracked their doors.

"Nick, they won't let me back in to see Rainey! Talk to them. I really think I can help."

"So do I," said Nick. "Let's go."

Saturday Night

Danziger Checks In

After a very hectic but productive afternoon during which he worked out and executed a seriously entertaining way to manage the Cosmic Frisbee Exchange with Byron Deitz, Charlie Danziger was back at his home, a mid-sized horse farm he ran a few miles up into the rolling countryside just north of Niceville, a large log-framed rancher furnished mainly in bare wood, Mexican rugs, gun racks, and saddle-leather chairs with steer-horn arms—Danziger, like Ralph Lauren, was a man of simple cowpoke tastes—and some brand-new pine-board stables, beside a fenced-in paddock for breaking and training, a few acres of rolling grassland, enough to keep eight quarter horses happy.

He showered, shaved, showered again to be on the safe side, replaced his bandages—he had to admit for a Sicilian pervert dentist, Donny Falcone knew how to sew up a chest wound—changed into clean clothes, burned his old ones, with the exception of his navy blue boots. A prudent cowboy never threw away his lucky boots.

He cooked himself a huge bloody steak and poured himself a massive jug of cold Pinot Grigio, consumed both with real enjoyment, lit himself up a borrowed Camel—he owed

Coker three packs by now—and then, rested and reasonably calm, he sat down at his computer to see how well the flash drive that he had given to Boonie Hackendorff had actually worked.

Because, aside from the names of all his Wells Fargo associates, the flash drive he had given to Boonie had also carried a program, available on CopNet, which, when the flash drive was plugged into the mainframe, did some cyber-voodoo thing that gave Danziger a backdoor look at everything that was going on in Boonie Hackendorff's desktop computer.

His PC got all warmed up and he typed in a few keystrokes, listening to the cross talk between the Niceville PD and the State Patrol on a police scanner set on a sideboard in his dimly lit office, the walls of which were covered with very nice oils showing various scenes of the Snake River country and the Grand Tetons where he had grown up and the Powder River country where he hoped to be buried if the circumstances of his demise left enough of him to justify the trouble and expense.

The screen flowered into cool blue light, and he was looking at the crest of the Federal Bureau of Investigation, over a red-lettered warning bar letting it be known that all ye who enter here had better have their shit together or else.

A few minutes later, he was looking at Boonie Hackendorff's notes on the Gracie Bank robbery, Incident Number CC 9234K 28RB 8766.

Boonie's notes on the Gracie robbery were clear, concise, well organized, very professional, in Charlie's view a credit to the service. By the time he had gotten to the end of them, he had concluded that he did not have nearly enough Pinot Grigio in the house to drown this ugly-ass bad news, or enough cigarettes to smoke it away.

He and Coker needed to talk.

He called Coker and told him so.

Coker replied that he was very glad to have heard from Charlie because he, Coker, had a pretty young Indian woman

named Twyla Littlebasket lying on the leather sofa in his living room and sobbing great racking tear-loaded sobs into the
cushions in a way that would very likely be the ruin of them—
meaning the cushions.

"My place or yours?" asked Danziger, when Coker had
brought his narrative to a natural pause.

"My place," said Coker. "You may recall I still got the proceeds here."

"Shit. Holy shit. Twyla see it?"

"Yep."

"How the fuck how?"

"She has a key. She was here when I got home."

"It was still on the fucking *counter*?"

"You left after I did, Charlie."

"Shit. I never thought."

"You're slipping, son."

"Is that why Twyla's crying?"

"Nope. She's got more important shit to deal with than
what's sitting on my kitchen counter."

"Like what?"

"That you got to see to believe. You hear from Deitz yet?"

"Didn't I say I was spending the rest of the afternoon fucking with Deitz's head?"

Charlie, already up and looking for his gun and his jacket
and his boots, pulled the pay-as-you-go cell out of his hip
pocket. There was a text message, badly spelled, as if the guy
doing the texting had really large thumbs.

> OK HOW M UCH WEAR WHEN
> GOT 2 B 2 NITE GOT 2 B
> NO TRI X M OTH RFCKERS

"I guess it slipped my mind, Charlie. You may recall I was
kinda busy not shooting a Barricaded EDP. This what you did
after you left us at the church?"

"My labors never cease my wonders to perform."

"Yeah yeah. Is it really from Deitz?"

Danziger looked at the text message again.

"Well, the guy can't spell *motherfuckers*."

"That's Deitz."

Merle Walks the Town

On the way back down Gwinnett, Merle passed the same appliance store where the crowd had been watching some sort of police standoff at a church on Peachtree. The television sets were all showing the same loop, a small chubby man in a green work shirt and matching pants, cuffed and bleeding, being duck-walked along the sidewalk by an impressive-looking redheaded female cop who was grinning hugely and talking to a tall silver-haired man in a charcoal suit, who was leaning back on the patrol car with his arms folded across his chest.

The man in the suit was Coker, Merle realized with a jolt, and, some distance away, looking on with a big grin, was Charlie Danziger, with a group of uniform cops, smoking a cigarette and looking right at home.

Merle stood and took that in for a time and was surprised to find that, in some strange way, and by no means all at once, he had gradually ceased to give a rat's ass about what those two were doing there. It was as if they were part of another life, an old life that he used to have, and they had ceased to have any meaning in his new one.

Maybe for now, he decided, he would side with Glynis, because he needed a place to stay, and she was a damn good-looking woman, and there was still the matter of Coker and Danziger to be handled.

He took a long last look at Coker and Danziger on the television screens, both of them smiling and talking with the cops, looking pleased as punch with themselves, and he locked them away in his heart under *unfinished business*.

Down the street he plucked some peaches off a rack outside a grocery store, tossed a five-dollar bill onto the pile without stopping, and strolled around Niceville with as easy a heart as he had managed to have since before he got sent to Angola.

Later that evening, as the dark was coming on, he rested his bones on a park bench in the shadows of the town square, lit up a cigarette, and sat there watching the people of Niceville come and go.

Around ten the man from the Blue Bird, the sad guy in the seat beside him, came and sat down beside him again. Merle offered him a cigarette, which, after some thought, the man accepted without a word, and they both went back to watching the strolling citizens in an odd but companionable silence. By ten thirty the park was full of silent figures gathered under the trees. Merle counted at least fifty people, some of them women, no kids, but far more people than the two dozen or so silent men who had arrived on the bus that afternoon.

Some of the men and women smoked cigarettes and some of them had small silver flasks that they shared in silence.

Fireflies sparked and glimmered in the summer night and the city lights grew brighter. Stars glittered high above and the evening magnolias gave off their scent.

Spanish moss shivered in the scented breeze and the live oak branches creaked and groaned in the blue velvet darkness over Merle's head.

At fifteen minutes to eleven, the Blue Bird bus wheezed

around the corner, lurched to a halt in a squeal of brakes. The driver came down and stood on the steps, smiling as all the riders lined up politely. The man greeted each person with a kind word. When they had all taken their seats, he got back behind the wheel, put the bus in gear, and drove away into the darkness beyond the edge of town.

Danziger and Coker
Consider the Lilies of the Field

Coker maintained a kind of informal pharmacy in his house, as a defense against an accidental overdose of reality, which was sure as hell the case with Twyla Littlebasket. She had cried herself into a puddle on his leather couch and was now lying there curled up into a ball of inconsolable grief, staring up at Coker and Danziger with a wounded look in her wide brown eyes.

She was wearing her version of a dental hygienist's outfit, a tight powder blue smock that buttoned down the front, and it had ridden up her thighs as she lay there.

Looking at a pretty young girl in that state of semi-erotic-undress made it sort of hard for either man to pull out a pistol right there and shoot her, which they had both agreed was the only sensible thing to do, considering what she had seen piled up on the kitchen counter. But there was a limit to what even a hard man could do, at least without a couple of hits of Jim Beam under his belt.

So instead of shooting her, Coker had drawn on his pharmacy for a few Valiums, sharing them equally with Twyla and Danziger. He watched as Danziger covered her up with a soft blanket and smoothed her cheek with a gentle hand until she drifted off to a fitful sleep.

When she was asleep, Coker and Danziger looked at each other, shook their heads, and walked out into the golden afternoon light, going all the way down to the bottom of Coker's driveway for a smoke and a consultation.

They lit up and stood there together, looking out at all the civilians up and down the tree-shaded block, with their gardens and their lawns and their uncomplicated lives.

"Bet none of these folks have to kill a dental hygienist this evening," said Coker, watching a slightly wavy dad teaching his toddler how to pull-start a gas-powered weed whacker.

"Guess they don't," said Danziger.

A pause, while they inhaled and exhaled and generally felt the nicotine and the Valiums and the Jim Beam doing their holy work.

The sun was warm on their cheeks and the air was hazy with glowing mist. The Glades smelled like flowers and cut grass and barbecue smoke.

"How would *you* do it?" asked Coker.

Danziger sipped his Jim Beam, looked down at his blood-stained navy blue boots, which reminded him that he had yet to fill Coker in on just how much plug-ugly trouble they were looking at.

"You mean Twyla?"

Coker nodded.

"Right now, I'm thinking she overdoses after finding those nudie shots on her e-mail."

"I sure would," said Coker, thinking about those shots. "What a twisted old motherfucker. Good old Morgan Little-basket, pillar of the Cherokee community."

"Wonder who sent them?" Danziger asked.

"And how did *that* puke get them?"

"These are good questions. We will address them later. I

was thinking maybe we ought to kill old Morgan Littlebasket first? Maybe let her watch?"

"Maybe let her do him herself?" said Coker. "Give her the satisfaction? Then pop her afterwards, while she's still on a high?"

He thought that over, and then shook his head. "Nope. I don't think she has it in her to shoot her daddy, not even for taking nudie shots of her."

"She had it in her to blackmail Donnie Falcone for fifty large," observed Danziger after a moment.

"So she did," said Coker.

"This is all getting a bit . . ."

"Complex?" suggested Danziger.

"I mean, we already got Donnie involved, now we got her—"

"Plus wherever the fuck Merle Zane is."

"You heard back from him yet?"

"Not a peep," said Coker. "Phone just rings three times and goes to his voice mail."

"Any sign of him?"

"Nope."

"You try getting a fix on where his phone is?"

"Haven't had the time. You?"

"Me neither. You figure he's still laying in the tall grass, waiting to make a move?"

"Or he's laying in the tall grass stone dead and the crows are pecking out his eyes. Could go either way."

"A guy wrote a movie once about these mutts who find a bunch of money and then they have to start killing each other over it. With that weird-looking actor in it, used to be married to Angelina Jolie?"

"Billy Bob Thornton. *A Simple Plan.*"

"Yeah. That was it. They started by just trying to keep the money, and then they had to start popping guys, ended up popping each other—"

"First one was Billy Bob. And he was the nicest guy in the film. What's your point?"

"I'm just saying . . ."

A silence.

The weed-whacker dad was helping his kid whack weeds. Dad was blitzed to the eyebrows on beer, and the kid was waving the weed whacker around like he was Luke Skywalker. It wasn't going to end well.

"All I was saying, Coker, was the way we're going right now we're going to end up having to shoot each other."

"We're not there yet."

"Okay. Good to know."

"Where are we on Deitz and the Frisbee?"

Danziger grinned. "I had him bouncing around Tin Town going from Piggly Wiggly to Winn-Dixie to the Helpy Selfy and back to the Piggly Wiggly. Coker, I tell you, it was a thing of beauty."

"Where we going to make the exchange?"

"No exchange needed."

"We gotta get the thing to him, don't we?"

"He's already got it."

"He does?"

"He just doesn't know it yet. I had a Slim Jim, popped the rear hatch on his Hummer while he was inside the Piggly Wiggly reading my note. Shoved it into the jack storage slot under his spare tire. Lest he has a flat, which Hummers don't get, he'll never find it on his own."

Coker stared at him.

"What if Deitz doesn't wire us the money?"

"Then we snitch him out to the Feebs. Make a call, we say Byron Deitz is diddy-bopping around Niceville with a top-secret Frisbee in the back of his Hummer. Either way, we're not stuck holding something will get us in deep shit with the CIA."

"Risky," said Coker.

"No. It was *audacious*," said Danziger, savoring the word. "Another thing. I also tucked a packet of bills from the First Third inside a cable hatch down behind the gas pump shutoff switch."

"Jeez. How much?"

"One hundred thousand—"

"Holy fuck, Charlie. That's a lot of cash."

"Yeah, well, you're not going to like this either, but I also threw in some of the shit we scooped out of the lockboxes."

"Like what?"

"Like that antique gold Rolex and those emerald cuff links in the Cartier case and a string of—"

"*Fuck*, Charlie. I had my eye on that fucking Rolex—"

"Rolexes are out, Coker. Everybody's wearing Movados now."

"Says who?"

"Says *GQ*."

"Fuck *GQ*. What did you do that for?"

"For verisimilitude," said Danziger, savoring that word too.

"*Verisimilitude?*"

"Convincing supportive evidence. Just in case we need to dump this whole thing onto Deitz."

"I know what *verisimilitude* means, Charlie. Getting that twitchy, is it?"

"It is. It always does, at least in this town."

Danziger looked out at the sky, saw a slice of the old forest on top of Tallulah's Wall.

"You ever wonder, Coker, about that?"

Coker's smile gradually went away, and he cut a sideways glance at Danziger.

"What? Wonder about Niceville?"

Danziger folded his arms across his chest, kicked at a tuft of saw grass.

"Neither of us was born here. I'm from Bozeman and

you're from Billings. Before we got here, neither of us ever did anything like we just did yesterday, did we?"

"Regrets are for losers, Charlie."

"I'm not talking regret. I *like* money, Coker, and I intend to enjoy every fucking dime. It's just that, this job, killing those cops, you get right down to it, it was sorta out of character for us. Both of us."

Coker gave it some thought.

"You, maybe. You're basically a nicer guy than I am. Hell, I was twelve when I kicked my old man to death in the back-yard."

"Your old man deserved it, what he was doing to your mom. Hell, even the Bighorn county deputies said he had it coming."

"What the fuck are you saying, Charlie? Like, Niceville put some sorta *spell* on us? Jesus, Charlie. We saw a business opportunity, we took it. End of story. Don't go all mystical on me now."

Danziger was staring up at Tallulah's Wall.

"Them old Cherokee, Coker, they thought this place was cursed, before ever a white man got here. Said there was something evil . . . living up there."

Coker followed his look.

"You mean Crater Sink?"

"I guess."

"Something evil lives up there, that it?"

"You don't like the place yourself, Coker. I heard you talking to Merle about it."

A silence.

"Well, maybe I don't."

He threw his cigarette onto the road, lit another, sucked the smoke in deep.

"Hell, maybe I *am* getting meaner since I got here. Maybe something came outta Crater Sink one cold winter night and slithered into my ear and it's eating through my brain right now. You think?"

Another pause while Danziger thought it over.

"If all it had to eat was your brain, Coker, then the fucker died of starvation a while back."

"Fuck you, Charlie."

"Thank you, Coker. And fuck you too."

"Well, one thing," said Danziger, after a another long pause and in a thoughtful tone, "I don't wanna shoot poor young Twyla in there without we have a good reason. I mean, why add to my sins?"

Across the street the weed-whacker episode was ending, as it had to, in tears. Somebody called their names.

"Charlie. Coker."

They turned around and saw Twyla Littlebasket framed in the open door, her powder blue semi-porno hygienist's outfit askew, half the buttons all undone, her hair in a tangle, and her pretty nose as red as a rosebud.

"You guys got a minute?" she said, her voice hoarse from crying and her big brown eyes rimmed with runny mascara. She looked like that sexy Betty Boop doll, only with two black eyes.

"We sure do, sweetie," said Coker.

"We need to talk," said Twyla.

Danziger and Coker looked at each other.

"Oh shit," said Danziger.

Lemon and Rainey Meet Again

Beau and Nick stood back from the bed, letting Lemon take the lead. Nick was wishing that Kate were there. She still hadn't called back.

Two young doctors, one a black woman in a Muslim head scarf and the other a Somali man with horn-rimmed glasses and a disapproving frown, stood far enough apart from everyone else to signal their professional objection to this intrusion.

The boy was on his back, skeletal, his lips cracked, his pale cheeks raw from the sheets, but his large brown eyes were wide open and he was looking at Lemon Featherlight with a sweet, slightly drugged expression that was touching in its vulnerable affection for Lemon Featherlight.

Lemon was leaning over the bed, holding Rainey's hand in his.

"There are some men here with questions, Rainey. Can you think about answering some questions?"

"I . . . was awake . . . some of the time. I could hear people in the room. I remember you would come and talk to me. I smelled smoke. It smelled nice. I tried to answer you but I couldn't make my voice work. I couldn't move. But you were there. Then you were gone. Then everything would go away again."

So much for catatonia, Nick was thinking, glancing over at the docs, who had their heads well down and were busily whispering to each other in magical medical mystery words.

The boy was still speaking.

"I want to see my mom," he said.

"I know. You love your mom."

"Is she here?"

"Not here, no," said Lemon, refusing to lie to the boy.

"Soon?"

"She loves you very much," said Lemon. "Can I ask you an important question, Rainey?"

The kid blinked up at Lemon.

"Yes, Lemon," the boy said, yawning.

"When you woke up, was someone in this room?"

A silence, and then a whisper.

"You mean, just now?"

"Yes."

"A man was here."

"Did you know him?"

"His name is Merle."

"Merle?"

"Yes."

"Was he a nice man?"

Rainey hesitated, as if he didn't know how to form an answer to that.

"He wasn't mean."

"Did he frighten you?"

"No. He woke me up."

"He woke you up?"

"Yes. He called me."

"That's all? He just called you?"

Rainey tried to nod, didn't have the muscle tone for it yet. He was looking at weeks of therapy just to sit up straight, Nick figured. Kate would see that he got it. Kate would see that Rainey got everything he needed. Under Kate's care, Rainey's estate was in better shape than the year before. Rainey Teague was a very wealthy young boy.

"He just called my name a couple of times. I heard him and I . . . came back."

"Came back? Do you remember where you were?"

"I was at a farm."

Lemon glanced over his shoulder at Nick, and then back to Rainey again.

"You mean like a park?"

Rainey tried to shake his head.

"No. A farm."

"A farm?"

"Yes. There was a lady. And a really big horse, brown, with a long yellow mane and big white hooves. His name was Jupiter."

Nick heard that, tried to take it in, thinking about the heavy horse he had seen last Friday night, running wild on Patton's Hard.

A really big horse, brown, with a long yellow mane and big white hooves.

The thought took him places where he disliked going, so he set it aside. Maybe he'd deal with it later, but not if he could avoid it.

Lemon went on.

"Do you remember the lady's name?"

"Yes. Her name was . . . Glyn . . . Glynis."

"Glynis. Was she nice?"

"She wasn't mean. She was in charge. I don't want to talk about her. She wouldn't like it."

"Okay. We won't. When Merle woke you, did he say anything else to you?"

A pause.

The boy's dry lips worked and Lemon held a glass of water

with a bent straw up to him. The boy drank, softened into a sleepy state, his eyes closing. The doctors started to step forward but Lemon simply held up a hand and they stopped in mid-stride.

"Merle told me to ask for a man."

"Did he say the man's name?"

"Yes. His name was Abel. Like in the Bible."

"Like Cain and Abel?"

"Yes. Abel was the good one."

"Rainey, when you woke up, I heard you say some more of the man's name. Do you remember what more you said?"

Rainey closed his eyes again. Nick wanted to step in but he wouldn't have done half as well as Lemon was doing. And Lemon was being careful about his questions. He wasn't leading the kid at all.

"It was my name. My last name. Teague."

"Abel Teague?"

A shadow slipped across him and the boy flinched as if struck. Lemon straightened up and looked at the doctors, as if releasing them from his spell.

They stepped in, shoving them out of the way, the Somali doctor hitting the red CALL button. Lemon moved away from the bed, his eyes on Rainey as the doctors started to poke and prick and stab. Nick touched Lemon on the shoulder, nodded at the door, and they all walked softly out of the room.

As the door hissed shut they could hear Rainey asking for his mother.

The three men stood together in the darkened hallway. Nurses were jogging towards them from down the hall, making squeaky sounds with their rubber soles, hissing at the men like geese.

They gave way and headed for the elevator. There was a Starbucks down in the lobby.

They got themselves three tall ones and sat down at a jiggly tin table while the towering temple-like lobby grew slowly less crowded and the light from the window wall over in the waiting area changed from bright gold to amber, slender needles of light shifting in the haze, giving the whole echoing space an underwater feel.

"Well, what did you make of that?" said Nick, leaning back, checking his cell phone to see if Kate had called yet. She hadn't.

Lemon studied the surface of his coffee, and Beau waited in silence, feeling deeply blue and sad for the kid up there who was asking for his dead mother.

"A caller. This Merle guy was a caller."

"And what's a caller?" asked Nick.

"Just a superstition. My mother believed in them. They were people who could live in some place between the worlds, not dead and not really alive, but sort of in both places at once. If a caller came to you in a dream, when you woke up you knew you had something important to do."

"What'd he look like?"

"Tall, tall as me, shaved head, a hard-looking guy, like he had maybe been in prison. He had that yard boss look, or like a drill instructor, no looking away. Straight at me, eye to eye—"

"What was he wearing?" asked Beau, writing this down under block letters MERLE — PRISON?

"Farm clothes. Rough jeans, heavy boots—looked old— the boots—marked up and dirty—jeans with the cuffs rolled up. His belt was old and worn and cinched in tight, way past the last hole, as if he had lost a lot of weight, or it was borrowed from a bigger guy. Wide across the shoulders, looked real strong, thick neck with what looked like a burn scar on one side, had on an old plaid work shirt, looked paper thin, like it had been washed too much. He was carrying some sort of canvas bag, on a strap over his shoulder. It looked heavy. It had markings on the side. Black Army stencil. First Infantry Division, and the letters *AEF*."

"American Expeditionary Force," said Nick. "First World War."

"Yeah. That's what I thought. It looked old enough. He moved . . . funny . . . as if he had a stiff back. He smelled of diesel fumes."

Beau wrote down BUS STATION?

"This Glynis woman? Her name mean anything to you?"

Lemon shook his head.

"No. I've never heard of her. But the guy in the grave, his last name was Ruelle, wasn't it?"

"Yes. Ethan Ruelle."

"Do you know a Glynis Ruelle, Nick?"

"I know a woman signed her name GLYNIS R. on the back of the mirror that Rainey was looking at in Uncle Moochie's window."

"Wasn't that a real old mirror?"

"Yes. From Ireland, Moochie figured. Real old."

Lemon shook his head.

"I don't get any of this."

"I don't think we're supposed to. I think someone is having a lovely time playing around with our heads. There are a lot of Teagues in this part of the state," said Nick, flicking a look at Beau, who was scribbling fast. "We'll run the names and see if anything comes up."

Lemon had a question.

"Did the name Abel Teague ever come up back when you were looking for Rainey?"

"No. Look, Lemon, this morning you were saying that Sylvia Teague was looking into her ancestors a few days before she died. Maybe this Abel Teague is on her computer somewhere."

Nick sipped his coffee, checked his cell again.

Kate. Where are you?

Nick looked back at Lemon.

"So what do you think?"

"I told you this morning, Nick. I thought this stuff was from . . ."

"Outside. Yeah. I remember."

Lemon sat back, looked at them, said, "Whatever is going on here, I want in."

"This is a *police* investigation," Beau said.

"I'm a CI."

"For the *drug* squad," said Beau.

Nick held up a hand.

"I can't let you all the way in," he said. "But I think we can use you."

"How?" asked Beau, looking at Nick.

"Can you handle a computer?"

"I did quartermaster inventory and supply for the Corps. But how can I get access?"

"I'll ask Tony Branko to let you come over to us for this case only. I'll give him some reason. But this will get you off the hook with the DEA."

Nick's cell phone rang.

It was Kate.

"Kate? Where have you been?"

She was crying.

"Nick. Come home. Please."

Nick sat up straight.

"Honey. What is it?"

"It's Dad."

Byron Deitz Really Dislikes the Chinese

Deitz was sitting in the parking lot of the Helpy Selfy Market on Bauxite Row in Tin Town, across from the needle exchange, watching a skinny Goth chick with spiky blue hair undress in the window of her flat over top of the needle exchange.

In the normal course of events Deitz's sexual fantasies did not involve skinny Goth chicks with spiky blue hair. He ran more to the Large-Breasted Nordic Twins with Zero Gag Reflexes.

But seeing as how she was showing every sign of getting all the way down to naked and he had nothing else to do right now but wait for Zachary Dak to arrive so they could be cordially dishonest with each other, this was as good a way to pass the time as any other.

A swarm of addicts and gangbangers and dead-enders was circling the Hummer, some of them clearly trying to get up the nerve to hijack it, or at least to spray-paint a gang tag on it, or just to ask for a handout, but the fact that Deitz was sitting there with the windows wide open and a very large Colt Python sitting on the dashboard was creating a certain delicacy of feeling in this regard.

The Goth chick getting naked above the needle exchange,

who Deitz did not know was Brandy Gule or that if he had gotten anywhere near her with a workable hard-on she would have taken it off with a pair of nail scissors, was talking on the cell phone—to Lemon Featherlight, as it happened—and seemed to have halted her strip-down at a studded black leather push-up bra. Deitz was dealing with his disappointment by rearranging his courting tackle. It seemed that he was living in this fucking truck these days.

He was still doing that when the long black turtle-limo pulled up alongside the Hummer and Zachary Dak rolled down his window.

The arrival of the second luxury vehicle in this sorry-ass part of Tin Town was creating a major sensation—so much money so close—but thus far none of the locals felt like making a sortie.

"Mr. Deitz," said Dak, showing his tiny baby teeth. "I gather we have made progress?"

"We have, sir," said Deitz. "I have established contact. I have an address to wire the funds."

"And it is?"

"If I tell you, could you trace it?"

Dak nodded.

"Of course. But this will not be done. I ask merely to determine how reliable the network of transfer would be. If the destination is in Zurich or the Isle of Man, we may be content. If it is in Dubai or Macao, less so. May I know the numbers?"

Deitz had them on a slip of paper.

He handed it down to Mr. Dak.

Andy Chu, fifty feet away in a heroically dull beige Toyota, had been following Deitz's bright yellow Hummer around for the better part of an hour now, and he happily snapped a very fine telephoto shot of this exchange, which, from a graphic point of view, literally oozed furtive and sneaky and coconspiratorial.

Dak read the note, handed it back to Deitz.

"This is a Mondex cash card account."

"Yeah? What's that?"

"The deposit will go into, basically, a private ATM card. It's a cyber-transaction that can't be traced. It hides inside all the other ATM transactions that occur around the world, millions every second. It's not traceable in any way. I congratulate you. You're in business with a professional. How much do you have to send them?"

"Well, that's the thing. They're asking three-quarter mill. I only have two-fifty available."

Dak got colder, and seemed to recede.

"When we acquire the object, you will receive the payment we agreed upon, and in the manner we have agreed upon. This will not be altered."

"Yeah, I get that. It's just that I can't come up with the other five large. I can go two point five large, maybe even three. I was hoping you could come up with the difference, because I just can't make the vig on this. I mean, I can't get my hands on the thing without you kicking in, sir, and that's a fact."

"So you are asking us to 'kick in' five large, as you put it, on top of what we are already paying you, so that you can then pay these people seven point five large, which you contend is the only way to acquire the object for us. Is this correct?"

"Yeah, see, plus, since this is an unforeseen eventuality, maybe you could cover some of my additional expenses that would need to be, like, addressed, you know, for the extra services I'm performing? It's just that I—"

Dak lifted a languid hand, showing a length of his pale gray shirt under the charcoal suit. He had cuff links made of some small lavender stone that perfectly matched his lavender tie and his lavender socks. The stones were set into solid gold. His nails were buffed, glossy and perfect.

Deitz hated the man's guts, for reasons he could not have adequately explained, even to himself. Basically, Deitz was just

a really good hater, the way other people are good at basket-
ball or dancing the tango.

"Mr. Deitz, have you seen the movie *The Godfather*?"

Deitz knew where this was going.

It wasn't good.

He didn't really need any help with the five large the pukes
were *actually* asking for—he had it ready to go—but he *hated*
getting fucked all by himself. He wanted to share the experience.

The pukes were asking five, not seven point five, so if Dak
kicks in with the five and Deitz pretends to cover the other
two point five that nobody was asking for, then he actually
fucks Dak for the five large the pukes were asking and he still
picks up the one mill Dak has to pay him on delivery, so Dak
gets fucked and it's a wash for him, he'd skim off the cream,
and his life would just be that much . . . creamier.

None of which it looked like Dak was going to go along
with.

"Yeah. I did."

"You'll remember the line 'Either your signature or your
brains will be on that contract'?"

"Yeah. Great fucking scene. Doesn't change—"

Dak did more of that hands-up palm-out stuff.

Talk to the hand.

"Mr. Deitz, I believe we understand each other. We regret
that we cannot accommodate your request. It is not a busi-
nesslike proposal. You bear the burden of executing your end
of the bargain. Unforeseen eventualities should have been
foreseen by you, not by us, who are merely your grateful customers. As I say, deepest regrets, but when can we expect
receipt of the object?"

Deitz looked up at the Goth girl's window.

The blinds were shut.

Then he looked at the Colt Python on his dashboard, had
a brief and bloodred urge to just fucking shoot the living shit

out of everybody in range, gave that up as counterproductive, had a second fantasy about having been old enough for the Vietnam War so that he could have gone over there and shot the shit out of a whole boatload of wily Asiatic slimeballs just like Mr. Dak here, but that war was over, so Deitz had to go back to looking at Dak's irritatingly serene expression.

"They say I'll get the item as soon as the wire transfer hits that number."

"Who will effectuate the exchange?"

"What?"

"What agency will do the actual wire transfer?"

"My guy at the First Third."

"Ah. The unfortunate Mr. Thad Llewellyn?"

Dak smiled, therefore Deitz was able to infer that some sort of joke had just been made.

"Yes. That guy."

"And this will be done very soon?"

"Yes."

"That is to say, this evening?"

"Yes. That is to say."

All the same. Andy Chu, this snake-head, Joel fucking Cairo, Mousy Dung, Charlie Chan, the Dragon Lady, Kim Jong Il, King Ming of Mong, all the wily fucking Asiatics all over the world. Hate 'em all.

"How will the exchange be effected?"

"They say it's in a readily accessible location. As soon as the payment is made, they'll tell me where the item is."

"And you have obtained, how to put it, proof of actual possession?"

"They knew the number of the deposit box it was taken from. And they described the box. And what was inside it. They've got the fucking thing."

"So you feel confident that the object will be successfully retrieved?"

"It's no good to them. The money is."

Dak saw the wisdom in this.

"Mutual and balanced expectations create happy and harmonious outcomes. Good. I approve of this. We will leave this in your capable hands, trusting that you will do nothing to create uncertainty or discord between the parties. We will be at the Marriott. We will expect you in two hours. Yes?"

There has to be some way to fuck these guys.

"Yes."

Has to be some way.

Dak withdrew his head like a turtle.

The window rolled up, the turtle car glided away soundlessly, Andy Chu snapped a few more shots, grinning ferociously, having one of the very best Saturdays of his entire life.

Deitz looked up at the Goth girl's shuttered world, and from somewhere inside his skull he heard that goddam mysterious walnut-cracking sound again.

Has to be.

And then, like Saul on the road to Damascus, it came to him in a flash of brilliant light.

There was no fucking way to fuck these guys.

Morgan Littlebasket Comes to Regret

Morgan Littlebasket, pillar of the Cherokee community and highly respected comptroller of the Cherokee Nation Trust head offices in Sallytown, alas now a widower, lived all alone in a big old rambling rancher-style wood-and-brick home on a full acre of rolling grass and live oaks just a half block away from Mauldar Field, the regional airport for Niceville and Sallytown, where he kept a very fine Cessna Stationair 206.

Being a pillar of the Cherokee community had its perquisites, and one of them was this nimble little plane that he liked to fly on sunny Saturdays such as this one, soaring high above Niceville like an eagle, sometimes following the meandering course of the Tulip River as it flowed south and east out of Niceville, winding its way eventually to the sea, or perhaps he would glide at treetop level above the ancient trees along the crest of Tallulah's Wall, terrifying the legions of crows that nested there, catching a fragmented glimpse, if the light was right, of the glittering coal black eye of Crater Sink in a rocky clearing below the canopy, the circular sink looking exactly like a black hole in the middle of the world.

Around six on this particular Saturday, as the light was changing and the sun was sliding down towards the far west-

ern grasslands, Morgan Littlebasket was driving home from
the airfield after just such a flight, calm, relaxed, feeling that
warm meditative glow, that holy transcendence, that he always
got from flying.

He was at the wheel of his classic old Cadillac Sedan de
Ville, wearing his genuine reproduction Flying Tigers flight
jacket and a pair of original Ray-Ban Aviators and listening to
Buckwheat Zydeco on the stereo, tapping his left foot in time
to the rollicking beat, and wondering, in an idle way, just how
much money a man would have to assemble to leverage himself into a plane like that exquisite scarlet and gold Learjet 60
XR that was parked on the tarmac back at Mauldar Field.

That beautiful jet, according to the field boss, was owned
by some Chinese syndicate called Daopian Canton, apparently an outfit with money to burn.

But, the man had pointed out, sensing a buyer, given the
late recession, there were still an awful lot of cheap second-
hand Lear and Gulfstream models lying around.

And, so ran Morgan Littlebasket's thinking, the Cherokee
Nation Trust was getting to be a pretty sizable financial entity,
with a lot of travel required to attend to its variegated interests.

Maybe it was time for the Cherokee Nation Trust to think
about acquiring a secondhand Lear—strictly for business, of
course.

The idea, although far-fetched, was pleasing to entertain,
so, in short, on this soft summer afternoon, Morgan Littlebasket was a contented old man truly at one with his universe.

When he turned into the driveway he was surprised but
not unhappy to see Twyla waiting for him, leaning on the
trunk of her red BMW with her arms folded across her chest
and her eyes hidden behind a very large pair of sunglasses.

There was something in the set of her mouth that sent a
bit of a tingle down his spine, but he was in far too dreamy a
space to let it ruffle his feathers.

He rolled to a stop next to her "Bimmer" as she liked to call it, rolled down the window and smiled at her, a well-fed well-dressed craggy-faced deeply tanned leathery old man with a full head of silvery hair that he liked to wear long. Catching a peripheral view of himself in the driver's-side mirror, a habitual conceit, he thought he looked like a cross between Iron Eyes Cody and Old Lodge Skins, in other words a classic example of the Noble Red Man at his most iconic.

"Twyla, honey, how nice. Can you stay for dinner?"

Twyla had come forward to the car door, her look still cool and wary.

Clearly something was on her mind.

Well, that's what fathers were for, wasn't it?

"Hi, Dad," she said, not offering a kiss this time. "Can we go in and talk for a bit? I really need your advice."

Littlebasket unspooled his lanky frame from the car, placed a large veiny hand on her shoulder, felt her slip away from under it as she turned to walk ahead of him to the front door.

Definitely something wrong, he decided, watching her make her way up the flagstone pathway, trying not to notice that she was wearing a wrinkled blue smock that was much too short for a girl with such a lovely body and that under the smock, from what he could make out, she might have been wearing thong panties.

He shoved that image out of his mind—an ancient weakness from long ago—gathered his gear from the backseat, and made his creaky way up to stand beside her as she keyed the lock.

He had always made sure the girls had their own keys to the house, even after dear Lucy Bluebell had passed. It gave them all a sense of family, and it was all about clan and family, wasn't it?

Twyla went in first, going a few feet down the long wood-paneled hallway and stopping in the entrance to the great room—low rough-cut beams and a stone fireplace, leather sofas and chairs and wall-to-wall Native American memorabilia—before she turned to face him, taking off her sunglasses as she did.

Morgan Littlebasket stopped in his tracks, his heart missing a beat and a cold black feeling rising up from his lower belly.

The look she had was unmistakable, a look he had been afraid he would see there ever since his little . . . weakness . . . had led him astray.

Her eyes were red and swollen from crying, but she was chilly and composed.

The certainty hit him like a boot in the solar plexus, literally stopping his breath cold.

She knew.

He came towards her, his mind working fast, rehearsing again, to himself, the several complicated lies he had ready in case this terrible moment should ever arise, but when he reached the door into the great room he saw they weren't alone.

There were two large men by the fireplace, both of them hard-faced weathered older men in shirts and jeans and cowboy boots, lean and competent-looking, range-hand types, one a long-haired blond guy with a shaggy white handlebar mustache, cold blue eyes, the other clean-shaven, white-haired, with an eagle beak, prominent cheekbones, and gunfighter eyes.

Morgan Littlebasket glared at Twyla.

"Who are these men? Why are they in my house?"

"My name is Coker," said Coker, "and this here is Charlie. Twyla's a good friend of ours, and she asked us to come along and help her ask you a few simple questions."

The man's tone was calm, casual, and packed with latent menace. Littlebasket felt his left knee begin to quiver. To cover it, he went over to a bar and cracked open a bottle of vintage Cuervo, making a ceremony of pouring four fingers into a crystal glass with the logo of the Cherokee Nation Trust on the side.

Everyone let him fumble around for a while, but once he got settled into a big leather chair and opened his mouth to start in on one of his prepared speeches, the man called Coker lifted up a remote and aimed it at the big flat-screen Samsung above the fireplace.

It bloomed into light and everybody was looking at a picture of Twyla and her sister, Bluebell, both girls obviously in their very early teens, together at the entrance to a large tiled shower area, arms folded across their breasts, naked, engaged in what looked like some serious girl chat. No one said anything.

Morgan Littlebasket swallowed hard a few times, worked out what he was going to say, opened his mouth to say it, but Twyla cut him short.

"Don't, Dad. Just . . . don't."

Littlebasket looked over at her, composed his features into a semblance of outrage.

"Twyla, why are you showing me these nasty—"

Twyla held up a hand, nodded to Coker, who pressed the FORWARD button, rapidly flicking through a series of images taken over a period of years, shots obviously copied from a larger digital file, but clear enough, color shots of the girls— alone, together, occasionally with their dead mother, Lucy— in their bathroom, doing all manner of things that all people do in their bathrooms, and in each shot the girls were growing older, filling out, blooming, as if the shots were taken from a time-lapse film of two naked young girls turning into grown-up women.

No one spoke.

Coker never looked away from the screen, Charlie never looked at it, instead fixing his hard flat stare on Morgan.

Twyla had never taken her eyes off her father, and her father, after a few frames, was staring into his tequila glass, his shoulders slumping, his hands shaking, his breathing labored and heavy.

After a while Twyla held up a hand and Coker shut the flat screen down.

Twyla walked over and looked down at the top of her father's head.

"Look at me, Dad."

Littlebasket slowly raised his old bull buffalo head, his glazy eyes wet, his large mouth sagging.

"Say that you did this."

He shook his head, mouth working, but only a small squeaky whisper came out.

"I didn't hear that," said Twyla, in a low whisper, her head cocked to one side, her expression as white and hard as quartz, her eyes burning.

Littlebasket tried again.

"Your mother . . . Lucy . . . she asked me to. It was only for . . . your safety . . . in case you fell down—"

Crack.

No one saw the move. Just a blur, but the sound of the slap filled the room like a whip crack. She followed through, Morgan reeling, and brought it back fast and mean at the end of the arc, raking him across the left cheek with the back of her hand, a well-aimed strike from a very strong, very angry young woman. Blood came out of her father's open mouth, his teeth showing red with it as he stared up at her.

"Don't even *try* to blame Mom for this, you shit-heel fucking coward. *Say* that you did this."

A silence, while the old man moved his lips, his eyes darting around the room, as if rescue was at hand.

No one moved a muscle.

Outside, the shafts of sparkling bright sunlight faded into pale golden beams, filling the earthy, comfortable room with a gentle amber glow.

"I . . . did this," he said, after a long time.

He lifted his hands to his face, started to sob. Twyla stepped in and ripped his hands away, leaning down to speak directly into his center.

"You're dead to me. You understand me?"

"But . . . Twyla . . ."

"No tears, no tears from *you*. You're only crying because you got caught. All those years, you made Bluebell and me feel like whores, just because we were growing up into women. You treated us like lepers, never hugged us, never said we were pretty, never made us feel . . ."

Her voice choked into silence.

She pulled herself together, stood up straight again.

"And all the time, you were doing . . . that," she said, her hand sweeping out towards the television, the sudden motion making Littlebasket flinch as if she was about to hit him again.

"Listen to me now, Dad. Listen and remember. You will never know what this has done to me. You will never know what you took away from me—"

Littlebasket whispered something barely audible. Twyla cocked her head, her mouth tightening.

"*Bluebell?* Have I told Bluebell? No, I have not told Bluebell. I am not going to tell Bluebell, now or ever. She's the reason why I'm not going to tell *anyone* about this. I don't want her to know. You'll have to find some way to explain why you're dead to me. I don't care what it is."

She stopped, seemed to center herself.

"But one thing *will* happen. Bluebell must never have to know what I know. That's one thing you can do. One good thing."

Littlebasket's mouth was working, trying to form some kind of an apology.

Twyla brushed it aside.

"You will find a way for her not to *ever* know. If you decide to shoot yourself, don't leave a note explaining it all. If you decide to crash your plane, just go do it and let everybody go on thinking what a great guy you are. I don't care about any of that. You're dead to me from the moment I leave this house. Tell Bluebell anything you want. Just make sure that Bluebell never knows about those pictures. Say that you understand me . . . say it . . . Daddy."

The word rocked him and his tears suddenly became much more convincing.

He nodded and covered his eyes again.

She stepped back, looked over at Coker and Danziger, both of whom were really wishing they had had a lot more to drink than a couple of glasses of Jim Beam and a bucket of Valiums.

Coker and Danziger exchanged looks, and Danziger came over to the old man, stood in front of him. "Listen up, old-timer. Listen up. Shit. Coker, he's turning into a puddle of warm piss here. Pour the old man some more tequila."

Coker poured them all some tequila, handed a glass of it to Morgan Littlebasket, for whom he had no feelings of any kind at all. This *thing* here, this deer tick—squashing him wasn't worth the stain on the sole of his boot.

He walked away, stood beside Twyla, and she eased herself under his arm, spent and shaking now that it was done.

Danziger took his glass, sipped at it, took a knee in front of the old man.

"These shots are small-file jpegs taken from a digital hard drive, or a mainframe, right?"

No word, just the head moving up and down.

Yes.

"But when you started doing this, years back, there were no digital recorders, so at some point you took the earlier images and had them scanned into digital shots, right?"

Yes.

"And then you switched to a digital recorder so you didn't have to use film, right?"

Yes.

"How did you get the pictures scanned? Nobody at a camera shop would have done that. They'd have called the cops. So you did it all yourself?"

Yes.

"Okay. Big question here. Lie and we find out, Twyla's not the only one you're going to have to worry about. Did you ever take any of the shots and sell them? Put them on the Internet to trade with other kiddy-porn freaks or sell them to a porn mag?"

The man looked up, a spark there, and then gone again. "No. Never."

"Twyla got an e-mail today, with about fifty shots taken from that camera you got rigged in her bathroom. Looks like it's been there for years. How many years?"

Lips dry and working, eyes down.

"Since Bluebell was fifteen."

Danziger glanced at Twyla.

"Ten years ago," she said, a harsh whisper.

"Ten years? That right?"

"Yes."

"Is the camera still there?"

"No. I took it all out when Twyla moved away."

"When was that?"

"Two . . . two and a half years ago."

"Did you throw the recorder away?"

"No. I wanted to, but then . . . I didn't."

"Is the camera still in the house?"

"Yes. In a trunk. In the attic."

Danziger looked at Coker, who looked at Twyla, and they both left the room.

"These shots here, they look like they stopped a while back. Like when the girls were younger. The shot where Twyla is helping Bluebell shampoo her hair, in the shower together—did you see that?"

"Yes. I . . . I remember it."

"It looks like the last shot in the series that Twyla got. I want you to place it in time."

"Why?"

"Because if you never let those shots out, then somebody else did. If we can figure out who that was, then Coker and Twyla and I are going to go see him and make sure he stops doing shit like this. So can you place that shot in time?"

Silence, but he was thinking.

"I think . . . it was Bluebell's birthday. She was going to have her hair done special. Twyla was helping her in the bathroom."

"Which birthday?"

"Her twentieth. She was going to be a full-grown woman. In our clan, twenty is the age—"

"Her twentieth. What date?"

"Bluebell's birthday is the seventeenth of July."

"So after that date, you were still taking shots of the girls, but none of those shots are in the e-mail Twyla got. So maybe that's just because he never sent them, or maybe that was all he got when he got into your camera. It's all we got to go on right now. Bluebell is twenty-five, right?"

"Yes."

Coker and Twyla came back into the room, Coker carrying a large digital recorder. Twyla was carrying a box of mini-disks and looking sickly.

"So can you remember anybody coming into the house around that time five years ago? Was there a party, where maybe somebody could have gotten upstairs and found the camera?"

"No. The party was at the Pavilion."

"How about cleaning staff? Do you have a cleaning lady?"

"No. Lucy did it all."

"Did you have any kind of repairs done to the place around then? Any construction workers in?"

"I can't . . . I don't think so."

"Coker, any dates on those disks?"

Coker took the box, opened it, flicked through the plastic cases. "Yeah. Most of them have labels."

"Jesus," said Twyla in a whisper, and then she walked away down the hall and went into a bathroom, closing the door behind her.

"See if there's anything for August five years back."

Silence from Littlebasket while Coker flicked through the cases. He pulled out one.

"Here's one labeled for August and September, same year."

"The recorder still work?"

Coker checked it.

"Battery's flat."

"Does it have an AC converter?"

More digging.

"Yep. Hold on, I'll see what we got."

He plugged in the converter, inserted the disk, stared down at the flip-out LED screen. Twyla came back into the great room, wiping her lips with a towel, her forehead damp, her hair brushed back.

Littlebasket stared at her until he realized that she was never going to look at him again in this life or the next and then he lowered his head.

"Here's something," said Coker, handing the box to Danziger. In the screen a man was bending over the shower drain, on his hands and knees, only his back visible, a dark-haired white male with a thick neck and a puffy waistline, the usual plumber's hairy-assed butt crack, wearing some sort of uniform jacket with a logo.

The logo was blurred, the man moving energetically, prying up a shower drain for some unknown reason.

"Go to the next frame," said Danziger.

Coker hit the tab, and the images jumped a bit, and now the logo was more visible, a white oval with black lettering.

NUC

"That's Niceville Utility Commission," said Danziger, turning to the old man. "Looks like you had a service call that August from the NUC. You remember that?"

"No. I don't."

"It might be on his computer," said Twyla. "He keeps a record of all his financial transactions on a Quicken program. Archives it every year. Let me go see."

Twyla left, went down the hall, apparently to some sort of home office at the rear of the house. She was back in less than a minute.

"He paid $367.83 for an energy audit from the NUC on Friday, August 9."

"Energy audit? So the guy's no plumber. Why was the guy in the shower stall?" asked Coker.

"Any name on the bill?"

Twyla shook her head.

"Just the bank transaction. The actual receipt might be in the box of tax receipts for that year. He always took care to save everything, if the IRS ever wanted to jack him up."

"Those boxes in the house?" Danziger asked.

"Yes," said the old man. "In the basement."

Coker sighed, looked at Twyla, and they left the room again, this time going downstairs.

Danziger went back at it.

"You remember anything at all about this energy deal, Morgan?"

The old man went away for a time, his red eyes glazed and unfocused.

"He was young, a middle-sized guy, black-haired, white guy, pale white skin. Homely, but not mean-looking. Ordinary. He was all over the house. Went everywhere. Took several hours to do it all—main floor and basement, the attic. I never thought . . . all those guys are bonded, you know? You never think. He had a funny name. Short. It reminded me of some kind of beer."

"What, like Coors? Schlitz, Beck's?"

"Short, like that, maybe Beck's . . . but . . . I can't remember. I can't think. Are you a policeman?"

"Yeah. But you're not getting charged."

"It's not that. Do you think . . . in your experience, do you think she'll *ever* forgive me?"

Danziger looked at the pitiful old man, seeing his desperate need for comfort, for sympathy, the hope of redemption, for anything at all—no matter how small—to ease the sting, the burning shame.

"Not a chance," said Danziger. "I were you, you sorry son of a bitch, I'd eat my gun."

The rest was silence, and the old man wheezing, until Twyla and Coker came back into the room, Coker holding a rumpled receipt with the NUC logo over a row of figures and a handwritten signature along the bottom line.

C. A. Bock, NUC Energy Auditor

"Bock," said the old man, hearing Coker read it out. "That was the name. He called himself Tony. He was a nice young man. You don't think he's the one who . . ."

"I don't know," said Danziger, taking out his cell phone. "But we're sure as hell going to ask him."

Nick Drills Down

Nick was at the house, in the backyard, facing away from the conservatory, staring out into the lindens where Kate said she had seen the woman in the bloody dress, but he wasn't thinking about her right now.

He was listening.

He was listening to a detective sergeant with the Lexington, Virginia PD, older, a calm baritone voice, some gravel in it. Nick was trying to visualize him. His name was Linus Calder, and he was standing in the doorway of Dillon Walker's office in the Preston Library at VMI, the cop talking to Nick on his cell, describing what he was looking at.

Kate and Beau and Lemon Featherlight were in the conservatory, in a row all facing out, all watching Nick in the twilight of Kate's garden with his cell phone at his ear, every line of his body as tight as piano wire, intensity in every angle of it, but in a still place, his mind far away in Virginia, seeing through another man's eyes.

"No sign of a struggle, Detective Kavanaugh. Office in order, nothing broken. Papers on his desk, held down by a model cannon, window open, but onto the parade square, and he's four floors up. He always worked alone here, according to the cleaners—place is closed on Saturday afternoons when the cadets are out on an exercise."

"And his quarters?"

"Been all over them. Nothing out of line, according to the staff. I mean, there's no sign that anything is wrong in any of this—"

"Except that he's disappeared and nobody knows where to?"

"What can I tell you, Detective Kav—"

"Nick. Call me Nick."

"Nick. Call me Linus. What can I tell you? Guy's seventy-four, a prof, lives alone, he goes for a walk, he doesn't have to check in . . . only reason we're having this talk, to be honest, is you're a cop and I'm a cop and your wife is a very persuasive lady too, and now we've got her brother, who's also a cop—what's his name—"

"Reed Walker. He drives an interceptor for the State Patrol."

"Now I hear we got him racing up here in his pursuit cruiser, and he's already called me four times to let me know how far away he is."

"Reed's a good kid. He just can't sit still."

"Well, State guy or no, he'll be sitting on his ass in his car with a box of donuts and staying out of my way. I'm not having some wild-ass highway cop cowboy my investigation. I mean, Professor Walker's only been off the grid for a few hours—"

"Which he's never done before—"

"And he always answers his cell when your wife calls him, even if he's in a lecture, and they always talk on Saturdays—"

"Have for years, every Saturday at five—"

"Except for today, when they just talked a while ago, and he said he'd be coming down there in about four hours. I get that, but—look, you're a detective, you know how this thing works—unless he's a kid, or diagnosed as having Alzheimer's or dementia, which he isn't, then all we can do is ask the uniform guys to keep an eye out and we wait for him to show up—"

"Or not—"

"*Especially* not. As soon as we get to *not* then the machine kicks in. You'd do the same thing."

"I'm on a Missing right now. Two old people went missing last night or this morning, here in Niceville. Both of them knew Kate's dad very well. The guy was in the Big Red One, like within a mile of him at Omaha Beach, and the lady was a family friend. You see where I'm going with this?"

"Pattern."

"Yeah. Look, Linus, I know this is crazy, but look around the office—"

"Nick, with respect, what the hell you *think* I'm doing? Playing with my dick? I'm looking—"

Silence, while Nick listened to the guy breathing, rapid and wheezy, like he had asthma or a cold.

"What is it?"

"I'm just . . . okay, the floor here . . ."

Nick's chest froze solid, but he said nothing.

"There's like . . ."

The man was moving around, stepping back. Nick could hear his shoes on the floor.

"Okay, there's like a stain here, like something got spilled on the floor and took the varnish off—"

Nick couldn't help himself.

"Is the floor warm?"

"Warm? You mean, like, to the touch?"

"Yeah."

"Hold on a minute"—creaking leather, the man's wheezy breath coming shorter—"Yeah, it is. I mean, you can feel it pretty—"

"Try outside the stain. See if the stain is warmer than the rest of the floor."

More rustling.

"Yeah. Yeah, it is—okay, hold on. There's something under the desk here . . . rolled under . . ."

More creaking, the man breathing hard as he reached under the desk, Nick wondering why people always held their breath when they were reaching down to pick something up off the floor. It was why their faces got all—

"Little metal rods. Sorta corroded."

Nick's mind went on a short trip to Tahiti because it was a long way from here and Tahiti was supposed to be a real nice place to get away from all the bad things in life, but then Nick had to go get it and drag it all the way back to here and now.

"Little rods. Okay. How many?"

"Let's see. Five . . . no, six."

"Steel rods? About two inches long?"

"Yeah. That's right. Stainless steel."

He had to convince the guy, not just say it right out loud.

"Kate's dad had a medical every year. At the VMI clinic. I'm going to tell you something, going to sound weird as shit, so you're going to need to know I'm not crazy. I want you, after I tell you what I'm thinking, I want you to go over to the clinic and ask to see Dillon Walker's X-rays—"

"Nick, I'm like off duty in a half hour—"

"Dillon Walker served in the Hundred and First Airborne. He dropped into France on D-Day. He landed on a stone fence and shattered his right femur. They had to put pins in it to hold it together. They've been there ever since."

A silence, but it was that special kind of cop silence that you hear while the cop is thinking *oh please God not another fucking fruitcake.*

"That's why I want you to go over to the clinic, Linus. Take the pins and go over to the clinic and if they're not the same damn pins Dillon Walker had in his femur then you're right and I'm just another fucking fruitcake."

"Hey. I wasn't thinking that."

"Yes you were. Will you do it?"

More silence.

"Okay. What the hell. I'll do it. Will you be at this number?"

"Yes. Anytime. Day or night."

"You're serious, right? I mean, if what you're saying is true—"

"You're screwing around in a crime scene."

"Oh jeez," said Linus, and clicked off.

Nick put the cell in his pocket, drew a long breath, and turned around to walk back to the house and tell Kate something other than what he firmly believed to be true, which was that her father was as dead and gone as Gray Haggard and how it was done was a complete mystery to him.

She opened the door and stepped out to meet him halfway and as soon as she looked at him she knew what was in his heart. She dropped to her knees and began to cry, and Nick stepped in and held her.

"That," said Beau, watching from the conservatory, "doesn't look good."

"It isn't," said Lemon Featherlight.

"What the hell's going on in this town?" asked Beau. A rhetorical question, but Lemon tried to answer it anyway.

"Whatever it is," he said, watching Kate Kavanaugh trying to pull herself together, "it's been going on for a long time. Too long."

Kate came in, gave both of them a harried, puzzled look, as if wondering what to do with two strangers in her house.

Both men saw it.

"Nick, I think maybe I should turn the cruiser in. I can drop Lemon off somewhere?"

Nick thought about it, about the day. He was done, and Beau looked the same. Lemon was quivering with a drive to do . . . something. Kate was about to collapse. The old line from the Bible came back:

Sufficient unto the day is the evil thereof.

"Lemon, you said you wanted to take a look at Sylvia Teague's computer. At what she was doing with the Ancestry program. You still feel like doing that?"

"Yes," said Lemon, "I do. Is it all still there, at their house?"

"Yes. Kate's Rainey's legal guardian. She's kept the house up. Everything's just the way it was when it all started. Wait a second."

Nick took out his notebook, wrote down a string of numbers, ripped the sheet out and handed it to Lemon.

"That's the entry code to Sylvia's house."

Lemon looked at it.

"It's different."

"Yeah. Had it changed. Beau, will you drop him off there? Pick up some beer and a pizza on the way, okay, Lemon? You have some money?"

"I'm fine," said Lemon. "But I hate pizza and I hate beer. They've got a wine cellar and I'll call out for some KFC."

"Okay. Beau, let the NPD patrol guys for Garrison Hills know that we've got someone at the Teague house. I don't want them kicking in the door because some nosy neighbor sees a light on."

"I will. What about the rest of it?"

"You mean Delia and Gray Haggard? Tig's had the house locked down. Crime Scene is already out of there. Dale Jonquil and the Armed Response guys are sitting in the driveway. NPD is out looking for any sign of Delia. It's getting dark, and we're all dead tired. Tig went home an hour ago. Nothing else is going to happen on that file until tomorrow. You go home, see to May. Lemon, you want somebody to go see if Brandy is okay?"

"I spoke to her this afternoon. She's at her place over the needle exchange. She'll stay there."

"Hope her teeth are all okay," said Beau, with an edge. "Hope she didn't break one off in my ass or something."

Nick took a long look at Lemon Featherlight.

"You really up to going over to Sylvia's?"

"I'm not going to get any sleep until I do."

Bock Works Late

Vangelis Kinkedes was the night shift supervisor at the NUC field office on North Kennesaw. He was an avocado-shaped second-generation Greek with droopy bloodhound eyes and bad skin. He was up to his ears in grease from a souvlaki pita when Bock appeared at the glass doors of the office and slipped his ID card through the reader. Bock was wearing all black and looked bone weary.

"Tony, hey, Tony, what the fuck you doing here at this hour? And what's with the ninja suit?"

Bock slumped into the padded chair in front of his computer station, reached down into his pack, and pulled out a six-pack of Rolling Rock, peeled one off and tossed it across to Vangelis.

"The AC is out at my flat. Too damn hot to sleep. I have a bunch of reports to key in. I figured I'd get them done here, where it's cool. Is it just you and me, or is everybody out on a call?"

"We got two trucks out, on account of the heat. Everybody has their AC on—"

"Except me."

Vangelis grinned at him over the top of his Rolling Rock.

"Except you. We got rolling brownouts and people calling in all over the place. You want to post on as R2R? I'll put you down for double OT. We could really use you."

"Works for me," said Bock, typing in his password and looking at the system entry screen. He was concerned about having to log in with his own ID, but he had no choice.

Chu had him by the throat.

I chose you when I saw what you did for a living. You can go into any house in the city and no one will pay any attention to you. That is why I chose you. I have studied the Niceville Utility computer. I know that you can disable his home climate-control system from the head office. Then you will arrange to take the service call—

How?

That's your problem. You will go to Deitz's house and you will search his home office and you will find a way to copy the hard drive on his home computer—

Why can't you do that from—

Because he never goes online with that computer. I need what's on his hard drive—

Why?

To complete my dossier. Deitz was in trouble with the federal government. What he did was bad enough to force him to resign from the FBI. I also believe that he betrayed four men who were conspiring with him, and these four men went to jail in his place. It would be useful to know the names of these men, in order to persuade Mr. Deitz that his interests may best be served by cooperating with me.

What did he do?

I believe the details will be on his computer or on files in his home office. I want to complete my dossier on him. I wish to possess the whole story of all his crimes. I want the names of those four men.

Why?

As I have said. To complete my files. Deitz plans to leave the country and go to live in Dubai. He's rich but he needs to be much richer if he is to live safely in Dubai. So he is stealing all he can—

Did he rob that bank in Gracie?

No.

Do you know who did?

I could find out, if I cared. I have cloned his BlackBerry. I infer from what I hear and see that Deitz is dealing with someone over an item taken from the bank during the robbery, an item belonging to Slipstream Dynamics, an item he has promised to deliver to a man named Mr. Dak. But I am concentrating only on Byron Deitz. If I have all the details of his betrayals, including the full story of his dismissal from the FBI, the names of those four men, it will help me control him. With a complete dossier, I can compel him to give me a large share of BD Securicom. Then as the co-owner of a security corporation I will qualify for a green card.

What if he just has you killed instead?

The game is worth the risk. He will know I have taken steps to protect myself.

You're nuts.

No. I am angry. He is a very bad man. I wish to own him. I wish him to know that I own him. So. You will go there on a service call as I have planned and you will find some way to gain access to his records and his personal computer—

It's not necessary—you said so yourself—you said you had enough to break him already.

I wish to complete my dossier. You will assist.

I can't—

Yes. You can, and you will.

Chu had him, and that was that.

But, if he did this thing right, no one would ever connect him to the stunt, and he'd be free of Andy Chu. And after eight years he knew the NUC system as well as anyone in the commission.

Besides, playing at Jason Bourne again was going some distance to restoring his shredded ego.

"Good," said Vangelis, turning to his screen and typing Bock's name in on the R2R list—short for Ready to Roll. Over his shoulder he asked Bock about how things had gone at family court on Friday.

"I got screwed blue by the judge," said Bock, feeling the burn again in his lower belly. "Lost custody, lost access, got a no-go order, plus in front of everybody he as good as calls me a cockroach and says he's going to be keeping his eye on me. My head almost exploded."

"That's the way it always goes," said Vangelis, whose domestic situation was no better than Bock's. "The broads always win. Ask my bitch wife. Whole game is rigged. Bitches. All of them, all ages. The young ones are only BITs."

"BITs?"

"Bitches in Training," he said, which always got him a laugh. "What did that rocker dude say—Mick Jagger, I think, about giving away a house?"

"Keith Richards. He said, 'Forget marriage. Next time I'm just going to find a woman I hate and give her a house.' "

"That's it. Who was the judge?"

"Monroe. Teddy Monroe."

"Jeez. He's a hard guy. You lip off at him? I mean, after he calls you a cockroach?"

"I gave him some edge. You know, in a cold kind of way. Told him that with all due respect I felt he had crossed a line and the way he was talking to me was bringing justice into disrepudiation. I said I was an honest citizen and as such I deserved a basic level of respect."

Vangelis swiveled around in his chair.

"No shit. You said that?"

"Couldn't just lay there like a punk, all those people watching. You gotta stand up. It's like Glenn Beck says. Respectful resistance. Question with boldness. That's what America's all about."

Vangelis was duly impressed, and they tossed around a few more dumb-ass clichés about dozer-dyke broads and cold-assed effin cees.

After a while they gradually settled down to the plodding pace of the graveyard shift in America's heartland, the only light in the electric glow of computer screens and the beep of phones ringing in empty offices.

Back in familiar surroundings, Bock felt his nerves begin to settle. He logged on to a website for streaming audio and found some classical music—Ofra Harnoy doing Vivaldi cello sonatas—and his panic and his shame and his dread of Andy Chu and his fear of the immediate future ebbed slowly away.

Back at his flat over Mrs. Kinnear's garage his phone was registering a fifth call from an unknown number. Every time his phone rang Mrs. Kinnear's little dog would throw a hysterical rang and run around the backyard yapping like a castrated hyena and Mrs. Kinnear would shuffle to the screen door in her house smock and her rabbit-ear slippers and scream at it to shut the hell up, and then shuffle back to her movie—*Gigi*—and her bucket of Zinfandel and when she did she'd always let the screen door slam, which drove her neighbors nuts.

After eight rings, the line would switch over to voice mail and the machine delivered Tony Bock's recorded voice, pretty wise-ass, saying, *"This is a machine, you know what to do"* and then the beep. No message was left.

Charlie Danziger Calls It a Day

Charlie was a patient man.

It was Saturday night. Maybe Bock was out having a few beers with the boys.

Maybe Bock was just a regular guy.

Maybe Bock had nothing to do with screwing Twyla Littlebasket and her entire family in the ear.

Maybe Bock was a Cub Scout who helped old ladies across the street whether they wanted to cross or not.

Maybe Charlie Danziger was just an ugly-ass old coot with a suspicious mind.

Fuck that, Danziger was thinking.

He's the one.

Danziger set the cell phone down, yawned, stretched, looked at the clock on Coker's wall, looked across at Coker and Twyla, both sound asleep on the couch, Twyla all curled up in Coker's lap like a big tawny kitten, Coker's silver-haired head flopped back and his mouth wide open.

No formal decision had been made, but neither Coker nor Danziger had any stomach, right now anyway, for punching Twyla's ticket, so it looked like they had acquired another partner.

She'd probably be okay.

The way she'd handled the Donny Falcone thing had called for a streak of cold-ass larceny as tough as boot leather.

And she knew she was in business with people it was risky to fuck with, at least in the metaphorical sense.

God, look at Coker.

How the fuck old was he?

Coker was fifty-two, the same age as Danziger, but he looked about eighty, lying that way. He wasn't snoring yet, but Danziger knew he was going to start any minute. You didn't want to be around for something like that.

Danziger pulled the blanket up over both of them, shut off the cable news—apparently the Rainey Teague kid had come out of his yearlong coma and started yapping about some guy named Abel—some biblical shit, sounded like—anyway, how nice for the kid—welcome back to reality, you poor little bastard—and they were *still* running a loop of the sniper take-down at Saint Innocent Orthodox, including that long shot of Coker and Mavis Crossfire and Jimmy Candles and Danziger having a good laugh by the cruiser.

So far nothing more about the cop killings from Friday—*the investigation continues* was the phrase—Boonie Hackendorff and Marty Coors, the State guy, had given a press conference—Boonie looking like a club bouncer in a nice blue suit and the tie around his neck all askew—saying that they were *following breaking leads* and *expected to make multiple arrests very soon.* Coker snuffled, swallowed, and then began to snore.

Oh Christ, there he goes—sounds like somebody pulling a rubber boot out of a bucket of mud.

Adenoids probably.

Well, as Dandy Don Meredith used to say on *Monday Night Football, Turn out the lights, the party's over.*

Danziger got his jacket and his boots and the last bottle of white wine and tiptoed out Coker's front door, locking it softly behind him. The night was dark and smelled of cut grass and flowers and leftover barbecue smoke.

Stars were out.

The long day was done.

And tomorrow promised to be interesting as hell. Way it looked right now, he'd either end it a rich man or a dead man. Maybe Boonie Hackendorff and his boys would come calling. Maybe Coker would wake up early and decide that he needed to do some preventive maintenance on his life, this time including Charlie Danziger.

Either way, he intended to be up before dawn and ready for whatever came down the road. One thing he knew, anybody wanted a slice of him, they'd have to pay for it in a couple quarts of their own blood.

This was the sort of life-or-death drama that gave a lonely man some spring in his step, put some jalapeños in his chili. Maybe it was even the reason he'd planned the First Third robbery in the first place. One thing for sure, he wasn't bored.

So, all in all, he figured, a good two days of work. He particularly enjoyed imagining the look on Byron Deitz's face when he read the text message telling him where the cosmic Frisbee actually was.

Deitz had one of those faces where it was easy to picture it going all veiny and bulgy and knotting up purple while he was reading that the fucking thing had been in the back of his Hummer all afternoon.

He tippy-toed halfway down the drive, sat down on Coker's garden wall to slip his boots on—his super-lucky blue boots—got slowly to his feet—damn, he was tired—getting too old for sucking chest wounds and all that shit—walked stiffly the rest of the way down to his truck, favoring his ribs, the bullet wound really throbbing now.

He started up the truck, slipped in a Caro Emerald CD, rolled down the window and lit up a cigarette, unscrewed the cap on the bottle of white wine and washed down two Oxy-

Contins and one of Donny's bootleg Heparins. He swallowed hard, sucked in some smoke, dialed the AC up, put her in gear, and rumbled off into the dark.

When Danziger's truck reached the corner and braked at the Stop sign, the red glow of the truck's brake lights was reflected in Coker's pale brown eyes, two tiny red points of light flickering in his irises, as he stood there at the picture window, smoking a Camel, watching Danziger make the left turn and disappear.

Merle Zane Finishes It

Glynis woke Merle up at midnight. He came up out of a nightmare with a snap that almost broke his neck. He was in his attic room, lying on top of the sheets, sweating with the heat. Outside his window the moon was gliding through a field of stars. Cicadas were humming in the pines and the generator was muttering away beyond the barn. Glynis was naked, poised at the foot of his bed.

"It's time," she said.

Merle reached for her, and she came softly into his arms. Afterwards, in the peace and stillness of that moment, she turned to him and asked him if he would do what he was going to do at dawn under another name. He looked at her, stroked her cheek.

"Yes. If you want it. What name?"

"When you reach him, if you reach him, will you say your name is John?"

"John? Your husband?"

"Yes. His name was John. Can you do that?"

"Of course," he said, drawing her in again.

In the early morning they dressed in silence, and shared cigarettes and a cup of her cowboy coffee in the kitchen, and she walked him to the Belfair Pike gate, where they watched Jupiter for a while, out in the field of dewy grass, cantering, his hoofbeats shaking the earth under their feet.

The Blue Bird bus was already there, idling by the gate, the old black man leaning on the door and smoking a hand-rolled cigarette.

Glynis handed Merle the canvas bag, heavy with the Colt and the spare magazines, kissed him, this time with heat, broke away and buried her face in his neck. And then she turned and walked back down the lane to the farmhouse.

Jupiter trumpeted from the far end of the fields, tossing his huge head. Halfway along the path Glynis turned to wave, but he was already climbing up the Blue Bird steps and he didn't see her. By the time he was seated, she was gone into the shadow of the live oaks.

"Niceville?" said the old man, putting the bus in gear.

"No. Not that way. You go by Sallytown?"

The old man nodded towards the house.

"Mrs. Ruelle hired us for the whole day, me and the Blue Bird. Take you all the way down to New Orleans, you want. How about that? Have us a real Houlihan and we can come back in a Black Maria."

Merle smiled.

"Wish I could. Maybe next week. Right now I'm going to Sallytown."

"Any particular place in Sallytown?"

"Gates of Gilead Palliative Care Center. You know it?"

"Oh yes. I know it," said the old man, more to himself than to Merle, and he didn't speak again for several miles. After a while the Belfair Pike broke out of the old forest and uncurled into the rolling grasslands that spread out to the north of the Belfair Range.

The rising sun was a sliver of bright red fire above the eastern hills when the old man spoke again.

"I don't believe I know your name, sir?"

"My name is John Ruelle."

"The lady's husband?"

"Yes."

"It's good you came back, Mr. Ruelle. Mrs. Ruelle, back there, she is a very fine lady. That plantation is cruel hard work, and her running it all alone since Mr. Ethan got shot by the Haggard man . . . well, folks have all admired her for her courage. She's like that Penelope lady whose husband had to go off and lay siege to Troy. Been alone for a long time. Since the war. I'm glad to see you safely home."

"Thank you."

The driver shook his head.

"My son got killed over there."

"Did he? I'm very sorry."

"Damn fool war. No offense, sir."

"None taken."

"My son was conscripted."

Since he was reasonably sure the draft had been ended by Congress in 1973, Merle decided to change the subject.

"I didn't catch *your* name, sir?"

"My name is Albert Lee, like in the general, not like in the Minnesota," he said, with a grin, obviously repeating an old line.

"Mr. Lee. Good to meet you," said Merle.

"Please. Call me Albert."

"If you'll call me John."

A polite pause.

"Would you be a drinking man, sir?'

"Well, I do enjoy a bourbon from time to time."

Albert Lee's cheek pulled back and his teeth glinted in a shaft of the rising sun.

"I just happen to have a flask of Napoleon with me. I'd be honored if you would join me?"

He took a hand off the wheel, reached up into an overhead compartment and brought down a fat silver flask. Merle got up from his seat, took one next to the driver's side. Albert Lee took a sip, handed the flask back to Merle, who took one too. The cognac went down like a ribbon of blue silk soaked in liquid fire.

It warmed him to his boot heels.

He handed the flask back.

"That, Albert, is a very fine cognac."

"I do admire my liquor, although I would never drink such on a normal driving day. But today does have sort of a different feel to it, doesn't it?"

"It does," said Merle.

They shared the flask back and forth for a while in friendly silence. Merle offered the man a cigarette, which he accepted, twirling it in his arthritic hands, his palms shining in the golden light, his eyes bright with humor and intelligence.

"A filter tip. We don't see much of those here in the Belfair Range. Down in Niceville, maybe, but not up here. Used to buy them at the Belfair Pike General Store and Saddlery, put them on the ticket, but they stopped giving out credit last year, on account of the economy."

Merle was privately thinking that they probably stopped giving credit at the Belfair Pike General Store and Saddlery because Charlie Danziger had burned the place to the ground late Friday afternoon. However, in keeping with his *don't rock the boat* policy and his growing suspicion that Albert Lee, although amiable, was another one of those slightly crazed Belfair Range locals, he declined to point this out.

Instead he lit up Albert's cigarette, and then one of his own, and they both watched the countryside roll towards them, a morning mist rising up out of the fields and all the trees a hazy blue, the dim black shapes of cattle in the golden fields of canola moving in slow motion through a soft, shimmering light.

They both saw the silvery spire of a church as the sun glinted off it, a needle-sharp nick in the far horizon, and

Albert, pointing with the stub of his cigarette, told Merle that was the steeple of Saint Margaret's Church in Sallytown.

At the name, Merle's belly tightened and he sat back, watching the church spire as if it were the tip of a knife.

Albert sensed the change.

"Don't want to push myself in on a private affair, but could you use some help, when we get to Sallytown?"

"What sort of help?"

"Well, pretty much everybody knows you going up there to call out Mr. Abel Teague."

"They do?" said Merle, surprised but not shocked. It would be damn unnatural if the word hadn't gotten around.

"Yes, they do," said Albert Lee, looking over his shoulder at him. "And many think it's been a time coming, too. Mrs. Ruelle knows, I suspect."

"Yes. She does."

"I thought she looked long at you, like she was afraid she might not see you again. Were you going to follow the Irish rules?"

"He had his chance."

A silence.

"The lady said there might be two others coming along, relatives of hers who owed the Ruelles a debt, a Mr. Haggard and a Mr. Walker, but you are here alone, so I guess there won't be what we used to call seconds, and anyway, Mr. Teague, he has been asked to stand before, and refused."

"So I hear."

They were rolling in past the edge of town, a tiny cluster of Victorian houses, still in the shadows, neat redbrick homes with narrow windows, white-painted porches, sheltering under tree-shaded avenues. They bumped and chugged along the single main street, all the stores shuttered and closed at this early hour. Merle's heart was racing and he was making an effort to slow it down.

"The hospital is set apart from town, over on Eufaula Lane, inside an old park there, about two block up and we take a right. You never said if you wanted some help, John? I always keep something in the bus against bad men who might get on."

He leaned to his left, reached down beside his seat, and pulled out a medium-framed revolver, stainless-steel, angular, brute-ugly but so clean it shimmered in the light.

"It's a Forehand and Wadsworth I had from my daddy who went to the South African War. It fires a .38-caliber bullet. Not good for long-range work, but it will do pretty good for in close. I would take it as a personal favor if you were to allow me to walk along with you."

He wheeled the bus around the corner and pulled it to a stop about a hundred feet down from the gates of a single-story flat-roofed structure made of pale yellow brick, looking very much like a blockhouse instead of a palliative care center.

The neighborhood around it was shady and old-fashioned, a few warm yellow lights showing in the windows here and there, porch lamps glimmering in the early-morning light. A dog started to bark in the distance, and from somewhere else came the sound of music. Swifts and swallows and mourning doves were calling in the leafy canopy over the street.

The palliative care center was fenced off by wrought-iron spikes eight feet tall, with a single open gate in front of the entrance. The clinic sat in the middle of a large green park studded with willows and live oaks draped in shaggy tendrils of moss, still shrouded in a heavy morning mist. The clinic had few windows, some of which were showing a cool institutional light. They could see only one set of doors, two broad wooden slabs under a wide stone archway, in front of a circular drive.

There was a small metal sign, blue, with gilt letters, mounted on the fence near the open gate.

GATES OF GILEAD
PALLIATIVE CARE CENTER
PRIVATE NO VISITORS

Two white men in blue shirts and black trousers were sitting under the shelter of the archway, tilting back in wooden chairs, smoking cigarettes, and by the set of their heads, watching the Blue Bird as it sat there, idling, its engine wheezing and chuffing.

"I think we are expected," said Albert, looking at the men under the arch. "What would you like to do, John?"

Merle stood up, reached for the flask on the dashboard, sipped at it, handed it to Albert Lee.

"I accept your offer of walking along with me, if you still feel like it?"

This brought a huge smile.

"Thank you. I could use some excitement."

He took a sip, twisted the cap on tight, put it away in the compartment, and shut off the bus. He took the keys out and put them in the compartment beside the flask.

"Best to leave the keys here, in case one of us is coming back alone."

He pushed himself up with a groan, looked at the revolver in his hand, checked to see that he had all six chambers loaded, and then looked at Merle, his eyes calm and clear, watching Merle's hands as he slid out the magazine, checked the chamber and the magazine, loaded the magazine back in, and racked the slide, a satisfying metallic clank. They shook hands and Merle stepped down out of the bus. The two men in shirtsleeves were on their feet now, and staring hard at them.

And then something *happened*, almost as soon as his boots hit the sidewalk. Merle was standing there, fighting his adrenaline, taking in the street, the low brick building, the sleepy residential neighborhood, when, in some indefinable but powerful way, the entire street *changed*.

The comfortable old houses were engulfed in a thickening mist, their porch lights dwindling into yellow sparks and then winking out, the warm yellow windows going black. They were alone in a dense fog with only the Gates of Gilead showing dimly through the haze, a low barrow-like bulk.

The milky light of the early morning turned yellowish and sickly. The scent of spring earth and cut grass and cool morning air changed into a brackish reek, sulfur and ammonia and the stink of dead things half-buried.

The low brick building seemed to dig itself deeper into the green lawn surrounding it, and grow darker, more sealed, more remote from the normal world, like an animal pulling back into a cave. The live oaks sheltering it grew blacker, larger, and their branches creaked like old bones, their leaves rustling as if they were suddenly alive.

A palpable miasma of resentment, of menace, seemed to breathe in the air above them and slip snakelike around their bodies as they stood there in silence. The cool fluorescent light at the windows was now gone, the window slits black and closed.

The calling of birds in the trees stopped abruptly, the dog was no longer barking, there was no distant music on the wind. The morning breeze withered away into a low whispering murmur that seemed to come up from the earth under their boots.

Wherever they'd been a moment ago, they weren't in that place anymore. Merle walked a way along the lane and turned as Albert came up and stood beside him.

"Did we just see that?"

"We saw it," said Merle, in a tight voice, swallowing his fear. "Everything changed."

"I know. But how?"

Merle swallowed again.

"I don't know."

Two man-shaped figures with shotguns were walking towards them out of the mist, tall black shadows in the fog.

"More of them," said Albert Lee. "Maybe we should get back on the bus. This is all wrong."

"It is," said Merle. "But we have to finish it anyway. I won't blame you if you want to get back inside. Just don't pull away until it's settled."

Albert Lee shook his head.

"If you're staying, I'm staying. Do we have a plan?"

"Not get shot."

Albert straightened his back, adjusted his jacket, blew out a breath, flashed a wry smile.

"Good plan."

They walked slowly up the street, lowering their heads as they passed under a hanging willow, keeping a good distance apart, Merle with the Colt in his right hand, down at his side, Albert with his revolver in his left hand, held at an angle. They were looking at four men at least, the two in the street in front of them, and the two waiting by the wooden doors of the hospital.

One of the shirtsleeved men turned around, opened the wooden doors and went inside, leaving the doors open. The other man, older, with a salt-and-pepper mustache and the look of a small-town sheriff, stepped out through the gate when they were twenty feet away, walked out into the middle of the road, blocking the lane, stepping a few feet in front of the other two men. They could see he had a double-barreled 12-gauge hanging down by his right side, held in one rough hand.

"State your business."

"We're here to see Abel Teague," said Merle, still moving forward. He could feel Albert stepping out to his left. Depending on the choke and the shell, a 12-gauge at twenty feet had a cone of fire three feet wide.

The man frowned at them.

"He's not seeing your kind. He never sees your kind. You read the sign?"

"Our kind?" said Merle. "What's *our kind*?"

The man's eyes flicked from Merle to Albert and back to Merle.

"You know what you are."

"What are we?"

His face grew less human.

"Bounty men. You're from her."

"And who are you from?"

Now he looked confused by the question.

"We're with him."

"Abel Teague?"

"Yes. We're with Mr. Teague."

"And what are *you*?"

The man's eyes grew remote, and a cold light grew there.

"We are here. We live in this place. We don't go anywhere else. There isn't anywhere else. We live in this place and we take care of Mr. Teague. We do his work."

Albert spoke, in a shaky voice.

"John, I think we need to stop talking to this man."

The man turned to watch as Albert spoke, his features seeming to shift and shimmer as he did so.

There was a long silence.

"Albert, you still with me?"

"Yes. I am."

Merle took another step forward, set himself.

"We're here to see Abel Teague," he said, his anger welling up. "Step out of the way and let us go by."

The man stared at Merle for another second, his eyes still

changing, and then he lifted the shotgun, the muzzle swinging around, and Merle shot him in the middle of the forehead.

The slug took most of the top of the man's head off. The sound slammed around in the misty parkland and a huge flock of birds—crows—rose up in a faint cloud in the mist and flew in circles, shrieking and calling.

The man went down onto his knees, the shotgun clattering away, and then he pitched forward, landing on his face with a meaty crunch.

He stayed there.

Albert had his pistol up and the sharp crack of its muzzle blast rang in Merle's right ear.

One of the men behind the fallen man had a large black hole appear in his face, and he tumbled back and fell. The other man had his weapon raised—there was a deafening crack and a billow of blue fire exploded from the muzzle.

Merle felt hot lead pellets plucking at his neck and his left ear as the shot cloud flew past him. He stood straight up as the figure racked another shell into the chamber and shot the man four times in the head. The skull exploded outwards, black blood and bone chips flying away in a ragged cloud, but the man stayed on his feet for another half second, still fumbling at the shotgun.

Albert stepped in and fired two rounds into the man's chest and he finally went down. Albert leaned in, tugged the shotgun free, tossed it into the fogbank, where it struck with a muffled clatter.

He looked down at the bodies, then at Merle.

"Well, ghost or man, looks like we can kill them."

They reloaded, kept walking, stepped past the three dead men, reached the open gate and turned into the walkway. A jet of blue flame erupted from the dark inside the open doors.

Merle felt a stinging lash of fire across the right side of his face. He heard Albert's .38 snapping at his right shoulder.

Someone inside the doorway fell forward into the light,

collapsed onto the walk, still moving, his thick arms trapped under his chest. Merle put a round into the back of the man's skull, the explosion ringing up and down the darkened hallway.

Albert stepped past him and walked farther into the hall. At the far end, there was a sparkle of blue fire and then several popping cracks. A slug snapped past Merle's cheek. Albert grunted, slumped sideways and went down on a knee, raising his revolver. Merle and Albert both fired at the same time, the solid boom of the Colt and the lighter crack of the .38 blending together, the muzzle flares lighting up a crouching figure at the far end of the hall, a figure in dark blue.

Albert's rounds struck the terrazzo floor and went wild and then he was out of ammunition and had to stop to reload. The figure down at the end of the hall was still firing at them, visible only by the tiny blue flash of his gun muzzle.

Merle reloaded the .45, racked the slide, stepped past Albert, and walked farther down the hall with slugs plucking at his shirt and hair.

He steadied his hand and put three heavy rounds into the man, aiming by his own muzzle flash. He saw the rounds hit, saw the guard falling back.

The hallway was full of gun smoke and the reek of cordite. His right ear was ringing like a bell.

"See if there's a light," said Albert, still on his knee, holding his belly with his left hand, the revolver in his right. Merle felt around the entrance, flicked a switch: nothing happened.

Albert sighed, pulled his hand away, looked at his bloody palm. Merle realized he was still standing in the pale light from outside, a perfect target. He knelt down, got a grip on Albert's coat, and pulled him along a few yards, getting their backs up against the brick wall.

Nothing moved.

There was no sound at all.

The place was black and silent.

Albert was having trouble breathing.

Merle could smell blood on him.

"I have to go on down," he said to Albert. "Will you be all right?"

"You go on down," said Albert. "I'll be fine."

Merle checked his magazine, changed it out for his third—and last—magazine, racked the slide again. He patted Albert on the shoulder, stood up, keeping his back off the wall, remembering from somewhere that slugs fired in a hallway tended to ride the surface of the wall, if they hit, so if you stood out a few inches, the slug would zip by you. Merle hoped this was true.

He made his way down the long narrow hallway, past a series of doors that reminded him of the doors he had passed on his way to Rainey Teague's room at Lady Grace. He got all the way down the hall and felt his boot stepping on something soft.

He knelt down and felt a hand, a man's hand, cold and limp, and wet. He lifted his hand and smelled cold copper on his fingers.

The man on the floor moved and now he could hear his breathing, short and ragged. He touched the floor around him, found a small semi-auto pistol. He knelt there for a few minutes, listening to the man die, trying to see into the darkness.

"Albert?"

His reply came back, faint, hoarse, echoing.

"I'm here, John."

"How are you doing?"

"I'll do. How are you?"

"I think there's nobody left. I'm going to go look around. Stay there. Reload."

"I already reloaded. You take care."

"I will."

Merle stood up, moved forward to the end of the hall, reached a flat brick wall. The place had no windows. No glass inside either. No mirrors. It really was a kind of block-house. From outside, you could see the building was in the shape of a T.

He reached the end of the main hall.

The T went right and left, although he couldn't see a thing and might as well have been blind. Whoever lived here didn't like bright lights, didn't like windows, didn't like glass. He looked into the dark on his left, saw nothing, looked around to his right and saw a thin sliver of flickering light at the far end of the passage.

A doorway, closed, with something beyond it, flickering. A familiar flickering blue light.

A television.

They may have cut the power out here, but it was still on in that room. He reached up and felt his left temple, touched raw flesh and warm wet liquid. He flexed his cheek and regret-ted it.

He touched his left ear, or tried to.

He didn't have one anymore.

But he was still on his feet and still moving.

Sliding his hand along the wall, stepping carefully, he counted off a hundred paces down to the closed door at the other end of the hall.

There was more light down here, coming from under the door, and as his eyes adjusted he saw that he was coming up on a gurney, parked outside a room. Something was lying on the gurney, covered by a sheet. He reached it, keeping the Colt on the shape, put out a hand, and lifted the cover.

A dough-faced old man, cheeks blown out, eyes wide open, glazed in death. He reached down, felt for the wrist, and lifted it into the light coming from under the door, read the wrist-band:

Zabriskie, Gunther (Plug) DEMENTIA—DNR

Not Abel Teague, anyway.

They had emptied out the whole place, except for the dead. He let the wrist fall, which it did slowly, rigor setting in, covered the old man again, and came to stand in front of the last door. He could hear voices, tinny and brittle, clearly coming from the television.

He reached out, tried the handle.

The door wasn't locked.

He steadied the Colt and used his left foot to ease the door open. A dark cell-like room, completely windowless, four tiled walls, the room about fifteen by twenty, almost completely empty, tile floors, a flat painted ceiling.

There were only a few pieces of furniture in the room, a small flat-screen television set sitting on a card table, its glow lighting up the room, tuned to a cable news station, a large green leather armchair placed in front of the television, its back to the door.

Over the top of the chair back Merle could see a dome of age-spotted skin surrounded by a halo of light from the television. On the television, two very blond females were having a heated argument over something to do with Israel.

Merle came forward into the room, looking around carefully, stepped around the chair, and looked down at the man in the chair. A very old man, but not a ruin, still erect, completely bald, his skin spotted and withered, his cheeks sagging down in folds, his eyes nearly shut, glinting in the light from the television. The man was wearing an ornate silk bathrobe over blue silk pajamas. He had leather slippers on his feet, lined with lamb's wool. His large bony hands were resting on his lap, one hand holding a television remote, the other a heavy glass with something pale in it, the liquid also luminous with the light from the television.

A crystal decanter full of a clear liquid was sitting on the card table beside the television, next to a silver bucket full of ice.

The man lifted the remote, turned off the sound, looked up at Merle, his wide-set gray eyes empty and cold. His thin blue lips moved.

"I heard shooting," he said. "I guess you've shot all my people, or we wouldn't be talking."

"I guess I did."

Abel Teague studied him.

"You could *see* them?"

"I shot them, didn't I?"

He blinked at Merle.

"If you could see *them*, son, and they could see *you*, then you're in more trouble than I am. You're more than halfway gone already."

"What were they?"

The man shrugged, waved a bony hand in dismissal, took a sip of his drink, smiled up at Merle. His teeth were strong and white.

"My people. I found out how to call them. Like she figured out how to call you, I guess."

"And now here I am. Get up."

"You know about her?" he asked.

He had a soft Virginia accent and his voice, although weak, was clear.

"I know about *you*."

"Do you? I don't think so. You'd be better off knowing what she really is. Knew I'd be seeing you as soon as that boy down in Niceville woke up and started asking for me. Saw it on my television here. I knew it was her work. She ask you to call yourself John, when you saw me? Just to remind me of my sins against her family?"

"Yes. I'm here in the name of John Ruelle, and in the name of his brother, Ethan, to settle an old score. Now get up."

The old man smiled up at Merle.

"Why? You can shoot me right here."

"She wants you to be on your feet."

Teague stared at Merle, looked around the room, and then back at him.

"She uses windows, you know? She uses glass. She uses the mirrors. I figured her out, after a while. Everybody else in the families, they're just *gone*, one after the other. *The windows*, I said. I told them all, *the windows and the mirrors.*"

He sighed.

"But nobody listened."

He seemed to drift on the memory, and then he came back to Merle.

"So I live in this room, son, no windows, no glass, no mirrors. My window is the television. Takes me everywhere I want to go. You see, with her, young man, the trick is not to open the way."

He started to wheeze, and then Merle realized the old man was laughing.

"You don't even know the thing that sent you. You think its name is Glynis Ruelle. You think she's been wronged by me. Clara Mercer was a real fine piece. But I already had her in my bed and there are lots of fine girls in the world. Besides, I didn't like to be told what to do. And look where it's got me. A prisoner in this cell. I haven't left this room in fifty years. Think about that, young man, if you get a minute to ponder."

He stopped wheezing, gave Merle a sidelong look.

"But the thing that sent *you*, my friend, that's not Glynis Ruelle. Glynis died in '39. What lives in her now, what keeps her going, what keeps all of this going, that power goes back as far as you can go. I spent a lot of my fifty years here wondering what it really was. All I figured out was, it lives in Crater Sink. It hates Niceville like it hated the Creek and the Cherokee before ever we came here. It *hated* before there ever was anything to hate, before the world was made, as far as I can tell. And it has to *feed*. It was riding on Clara Mercer's angry spirit to help itself feed. Oh yes. I saw those markings on the floors, or in the dirt, or in their beds, where people had been *taken*. Over the years, almost two hundred souls got eaten alive that way. I knew what I was looking at. But it has *rules*. It will do some things, and not some others. I found out if you're real careful, you can get it to do things for you. How I got my helpers, the ones you shot up just now. Maybe how Glynis got you."

"Stand up."

He looked at Merle more carefully.

"You're not *listening* to me, son. You should. You know how old I am? I am one hundred and twenty-one years old. Look at me. I can still stand up, I can still hold a drink, I can still eat good food, and I piss when I damn well feel like it and not when I don't. Cost me a fortune to stay alive this long, and stay this healthy, but then I had a damn good reason, didn't I? I knew *she* was waiting for me. I know about that field she has down at her plantation and what gets buried in it, what gets dug up, and what poor souls do the digging. They dig each other up, son, the dead do, and then they trade places in the moldy old caskets, and those who were waiting help the dead get out and then they lie down and take their places, and the ones who got dug up do the burying. Over and over again. Year after year. Until the sun falls and all the stars go out. Glynis, she calls it *the harvest*. She does it because the thing that lives in Crater Sink wills it, although she doesn't know that. I've stayed away from that awful harvest for a long time. And if you're a reasonable young man, with a taste for unusual pleasures, I can put it off a few more years. What do you say?"

"I say no. Get up and come with me."

Teague considered Merle's face for a while, saw nothing there that he could appeal to. He sighed heavily, leaned forward, set the glass down on the card table, put both bony hands on the arms of the chair, and straightened slowly up.

Merle stepped back as the man got to his feet and turned to look at Merle.

"Here?"

"Outside," said Merle.

"Why not here?"

"Outside. In the park. Under the trees."

He stared hard at Merle.

"You're proposing we fight?"

"I'm here to kill you. Glynis said that if you were willing to stand to the scratch line, I should let you. Are you ready to stand?"

"I have no one to second me."

Merle studied his face.

"I can find you a second. Will you stand?"

A flicker of cunning rippled across his face.

"I will. But I have no weapon."

"I brought two."

"Swords? Or pistols?"

"Pistols."

The man stood looking at Merle for a full minute, and then he tightened his robe and began to shuffle towards the door.

Merle followed him out.

Albert Lee got to his feet when he saw them coming back down the long dark hallway, the tall old man in his bathrobe and slippers.

Albert stood aside as they got to the door, the old man's glittering eye studying Albert as he went slowly past. Albert had gone to the Pensacola shore one year, as a boy, and they had a bull shark in a big glass tank, the shark gliding around in there and looking out at the people, his gills working, his eyes like shiny black pebbles in his dead white hide. That was the look in the old man's eye.

Albert followed them through the waist-high mist, his feet leaving a dark trail behind him in the dewy grass. There was wondered which level Virginie would find—if Thaddeus were indeed dead. She watched him as a cat might a mouse as the minutes ticked by on the lantern clock in the hall. Finally she heard a hiss from above and looked up at Virginie's open casement.

"Can you see him?"

Georgette nodded vigorously.

"Is he *dead*?"

"I don't think so," whispered Georgette. "I just heard him groan."

"Oh, dear," came a sibilant whisper from Virginie. "I do hope they don't find him *here*. If he *must* die," she added petulantly, "let us hope that he staggers away somewhere to do it!"

Georgette nodded in complete understanding.

It was near dawn before Thaddeus came to and shook his head to clear it. His vision seemed to have doubled. He muttered a curse and wondered what had happened to him. Then he looked up at Virginie's window and remembered. The house had gone into an uproar and he had fallen from the window. Still giddy, he crawled under the bush and retrieved the cutlass he had left there. With a manful effort he made it to his feet. The golden chain slipped from his sleeve unnoticed as he staggered away. No one remarked his going. By then both Georgette and Virginie were sound asleep.

They had come by their hard hearts naturally. They were, after all, Esthonie's daughters.

CHAPTER 9

In the morning the sisters fought over the gold chain, which Georgette found glittering by the marble bench.

"Give it to me!" grated Virginie, in a temper. "I near lost my virginity for it!"

"You haven't *got* your virginity," mocked Georgette. "And besides, *I* found it—finders keepers."

Virginie made a snatch for the delicate gold chain, missed and boxed her younger sister soundly on the ears. Georgette shrieked and dropped the chain as Virginie pursued her, skirts flying, around the courtyard.

Lured by the sounds of warfare, Esthonie came out into the courtyard. Her eyelids were heavy, she had a headache brought on by lack of sleep, and she was in no mood to cope with her angry daughters.

"Virginie! Georgette! Stop this nonsense at once and come here!"

Sulkily, Virginie approached. "Georgette took my gold chain," she said, bending down to pick it up.

"It's not hers—*I* found it!" cried Georgette in a passion.

"Where did *you* get it, Virginie?" asked Esthonie tonelessly.

"I—why, it was—!" Virginie colored, for once at a loss for an explanation.

"I see." Still tonelessly. Esthonie reached out and took the offending chain from her reluctant daughter's hand. "*I* will settle this argument by keeping the chain myself."

Regally she turned to go back inside while two pairs of dark eyes watched her with furious indignation.

"It was a gift *to me*!" Virginie grasped Georgette's arm as she moved to follow her mother.

Georgette shook free. "He never gave it to you, he fell out the window."

"He *didn't* fall out, he was dangling from the sill and his fingers must have given out."

"Or he let go because he knew Mamma was going to slam the casements and break his fingers and he would fall anyway," said Georgette loftily. "And *then* Papa would have had to go out and finish him off with his pistol—to save your reputation."

"*Mon Dieu*, you're bloodthirsty!" Virginie shivered.

"What was it like?" wondered Georgette, big-eyed. "Upstairs? *With him*?"

Virginie gave her younger sister an irritable look. "He was very rough," she said. "He pounced on me and tore my bodice. And *now*," she groaned, "Mamma will have my window nailed shut and I will not be able to stand the heat."

"No, they'll put up iron bars. Like mine."

Georgette was right. The iron bars she had predicted went up that same day. When Virginie saw them, she stalked around like the heroine of a tragedy. Esthonie took her daughters driving—to quell any rumors before they started. And when the carriage passed Thaddeus with his head bandaged and James Notley with his splinted leg stretched out, both of them lolling in a doorway, Virginie turned away with a sniff, elevated her pointy chin and refused to look at either of them.

The two friends gave each other a startled look. Their guilty eyes met. And for the rest of the day, they vied with each other as to who could invent the most erotic story about his encounter with the governor's eldest daughter.

Fortunately, something happened to divert the governor's daughters from their shared resentment over the iron bars that had gone up over Virginie's courtyard window—resentment from Virginie because it stopped her diverting "social" life, and from Georgette, aggrieved that her role as voyeur had been abruptly cut off. They were already scheming to steal the house keys and "go out on the town" some evening, but Esthonie must have guessed their temper, for she began hiding the keys whenever she was not wearing them. Still, both girls were ready for diversion and that diversion came in the person of Imogene, who that very afternoon paid a surprise visit to the "governor's palace," bearing gifts.

"Imogene, you'll set a bad example for my daughters!" chided Esthonie as her guest floated into the cool hall from the brilliant sunlight outside. "I can see right through you—like one of those cutout silhouettes they sell down by the quay!"

Imogene, who had spent a sleepless night and whose eyes felt heavy, answered in a curiously clipped tone that she couldn't care less. The tissue-sheer cream linen she was wearing was simply one of the few dresses left in the big fortresslike house—all the rest were packed away in lavender in big trunks aboard the *Sea Rover*. Esthonie would have chided her for not wearing gloves but she held her tongue as Imogene motioned to Arne to bring in the big linen-wrapped bundle he was carrying. Grasping Esthonie's eyes brightened. She loved a gift.

"Why, what is this?" she cried in a pleased voice.

"A little something for you to remember me by," said Imogene dryly. "At least, for a season." The brittleness of that remark entirely escaped Esthonie as Virginie and Georgette came running at her call. They all gasped at the beauty of the gowns Imogene was unveiling from their linen wrappings.

"Georgette, you said you yearned for a gown as bright as a mango. Now you have your heart's desire." Imogene held up a remarkable dress of peach silk with slashed sleeves lined in rose satin, and with a petticoat of rose and gold squares stitched lightly with gold threads.

Georgette was ecstatic. "It's beautiful!" she gasped. "Not like those hateful white cotton dresses that make me look like a schoolgirl!" Impulsively she threw her arms around Imogene. "I shall never wear anything else!"

"Then you will soon wear through such thin material!"

warned her mother jovially. "But we do thank you, Imogene. And look, Virginie, what she has for you!"

They all gasped at the sight of the regal white taffeta heavily overlaid with creamy lace and accompanied by a lustrous embroidered white satin petticoat edged with heavy point lace.

"It can serve as a bridal gown," suggested Imogene, "since I had it from you, Esthonie, that there might be a marriage in the offing?"

"You must stay and see me married in it!" cried Virginie, her eyes shining.

"I am afraid I cannot do that." Imogene smiled, but her eyes were not smiling. They were very bright and anger smoldered in them—anger directed at van Ryker. "And this, Esthonie, is for you." She held up a black taffeta dress overlaid with gold tissue heavily ornamented with gold silk embroidery. And with it a petticoat of rich gold satin heavily embroidered with black silk peacocks. Esthonie, Imogene knew, loved glitter.

"How elegant," purred Esthonie, cradling the showy dress in her arms. "And with my diamonds and jet!"

Imogene winced inwardly. The dress by itself was overpowering enough, but Esthonie would try to outshine it with all the jewelry she owned, no doubt.

"I have also told van Ryker that I am leaving the marquetry long-case clock he gave me in the house for you."

She had told van Ryker several other things, but she forbore to tell Esthonie about those. Yesterday at dinner, after the initial shock of seeing the Cup of Gold petals on van Ryker's shoulder and realizing the plain implication of what that meant, she had been pale and distant and remote. When her announcement that she would take the jewel case containing the van Rappard diamonds on board the *Sea Rover* at the last moment did not move him, her eyes had narrowed. Knowing how proud he was of the handsome marquetry long-case clock, which was a miracle of English clockmaking, she had added coldly, "I intend to leave the marquetry standing clock for Esthonie. She has admired it."

He cocked an inquisitive eyebrow at her but made no comment. He was very thoughtful all through dinner and when she jumped up immediately after they had finished their dessert and announced that she had a splitting headache and intended to bathe her forehead in rosewater and retire at once, he said only, "Is there anything I can do?"

Was there irony in that simple question? she had wondered as her angry feet carried her upstairs. Fury made her slam the bedroom door hard enough to shake the house—and certainly in a way that no woman with a violent headache would do.

Downstairs van Ryker poured himself another glass of wine and frowned as he heard the door slam. He sat drumming his strong bronzed fingers on the table. Something was very wrong and he had a pretty good idea what it was. He jammed his hat on his head, left Arne to see to guarding the house, and wandered down to the taverns to see if he could learn anything of what men might be planning to his detriment. When he returned, he tried to open Imogene's door and found it locked.

Walking softly not to disturb her, he went to his own room, pulled off his boots and went to bed. In the morning, on his way down to breakfast, he knocked on her door and heard only a jumbled mutter that sounded like, "Go away, I'm sleeping." With a wry look at the barrier of the sturdy door that lay between him and his tempestuous lady, he went down, ate a hasty breakfast and spent the day out as usual, seeing to the seaworthiness and provisioning of the *Sea Rover*, concluding the deal on the *Heron*, and bargaining over the other vessels with hard-eyed Dutch and English traders who inspected them, stomping about with their big boots, poking into the holds, examining the rigging. With luck the ships would all be sold before he left and soon be sailed away by men who had paid cash for them and filled their holds full of trade goods purchased in Tortuga.

It was hard parting with some of these vessels but he realized wryly that although there were some among his crew who bewailed the breaking up of van Ryker's fleet, his young wife was not among them. That fleet, Imogene felt, had kept him anchored to Tortuga and the buccaneering life. Without those ships, he would be free to find his destiny someplace else.

So be it. He sighed and signed papers and bade good-bye to sturdy vessels that had served him well. He would cut free from the old life.

He would begin again.

Van Ryker had hardly cleared the house before Imogene, who had not slept at all, was up. She watched from the window as he strode away down the sunlit street, a handsome and dominating figure who had mastered his world—and her. For a moment she hated him because even now her body called to him, urging her to forgive him, to reconsider, to forget.

In violent answer to her own inner pleadings, she swept the embroidered coverlet entirely off the bed with an angry arm and sat down trembling before the mirror at her dressing table. Tangled golden hair and heavy-lidded eyes greeted her inspection. And a soft mouth with a new tinge of bitterness.

Too upset to eat, she drank a cup of the new "China drink," as tea was called, and set to work furiously sorting the kitchen things. She rattled pots and pans blindly and astonished the kitchen help—she who was usually so calm—by throwing one three-cornered brass pot at the wall just because it fell over when she touched it. When she had finished she wasn't sure what she had done. Had she really picked out the pots and pans that would be of excellent use in Carolina? Or had she consigned them to be sold on the quay?

Unable to swallow solid food at lunch, she drank instead two cups of the new "West India drink" that had become so popular and which would come to be known as chocolate. She told herself she must not forget to pack the special covered cups in which it was served, but she was unwilling to disturb the help at their meal of hog's harslet and pease and fritters, so she went upstairs to pick idly at her wardrobe, unwilling to come to grips with packing anything.

The gowns she had chosen for Esthonie and her daughters caught her eye and she dressed quickly in a light linen dress. It was not split up the front so she omitted her petticoat, careless less questing eyes catch a shadowy glimpse of her figure against the glaring sunlight. She had loaded her arm with gold bracelets and put a gold chain dangling an enormous topaz around her neck. Her hair was casually dressed but topaz eardrops sparkled from beneath her huge wide-brimmed cream straw hat.

It was not her purpose at the moment to be demure. Rather, she wanted to be startling. Tossing aside both whisk and gloves, she told Arne she was off to see the governor's wife.

Arne elected to carry her bundle himself, saying complacently the Cap'n had found no new mischief afoot in the town last night, although who knew what tomorrow might bring?

Imogene gave an impatient sniff. Who cared what tomorrow brought? If Veronique already had her claws into van Ryker, her own world was lost already.

In near unbearable heat, they had walked the short distance to the governor's green-shuttered house, baking in the sun. And now in the courtyard, beneath the shade of the big pepper tree, with Malcolm purring at the hem of her skirts and leaving little tufts of his shedding orange and white fur on the creamy linen, she dragged herself back from bitter thoughts of van Ryker and the scene they would undoubtedly have tonight in that thick-walled fortress of a house.

"What were you saying, Esthonie?"

"That the clock is a regal gift, *ma chère*!"

It was on the tip of Imogene's tongue to say, *You have earned it, Esthonie—for warning me of what I was too blind to see for myself.* Instead she looked about her with some distaste. "Where is Veronique?"

If Esthonie caught the implication, she showed no sign of it. "Out riding. She will wear that poor horse out!"

"I doubt she rides him for long at a time," said Imogene ironically. "I imagine he finds long periods to rest and graze." She could not quite keep the bitterness from her tone.

"Veronique is very happy these days—she sings a lot," put in Georgette. She studied the peach dress raptly. "Will it need to be altered?" she asked her mother.

"Of course. It will have to be let down, for you are taller than Imogene—at your age! I cannot understand it. And it will have to be taken in at the bust, for you have not her figure."

"I am fashionably flat," said Georgette complacently.

Ordinarily, Imogene would have smiled at that, but it was a reminder that Veronique too was fashionably flat—and *her* charms were undoubted and compelling.

"I would like to grow up and look like Veronique," said Georgette perversely, knowing this would irritate her mother.

"You are too like her in manner already," sniffed Esthonie. "The manner of a worldly woman does not become a child."

A child! Georgette held up the "mango" dress. "In *this*, all the men will say I am stunning!"

Beside her, Virginie, who had bent to pet the cat, burst into wild laughter. She picked up the purring animal, who flexed his wide paws delightedly. "Listen to her, Malcolm," she cried. "Georgette yearns to be a *femme fatale*! Perhaps she may yet go on the stage like Cousin Nanette!" Malcolm convulsed her by yawning. Georgette gave her sister an intimidating look but Virginie was not to be intimidated. "Perhaps she will give us some advice about men?" she asked the cat.

"*I* will give you advice about men," said Esthonie tartly. "They are all untrue. Do not expect anything else."

Imogene was temporarily diverted from her own problems.

170

"Gauthier bought that liquor shipment on the quay!" she guessed.

"Go put your dresses away, girls." Esthonie waved her fan at her daughters. "And take mine with you." She waited until they had departed before leaning toward Imogene and saying in a dramatic stage whisper, "He said he did not but I am sure that he did!"

Imogene waited, brows elevated, for more revelations.

"And I am certain—although I cannot prove it—where it reposes today," Esthonie added heavily.

Imogene could guess. It was well known that the little French governor frequently found solace from his nagging wife with Madam Josie, one of Cayona's more elegant "madams."

"So you think the wine is in *her* cellar?" murmured Imogene.

"Exactly." Esthonie began to fan herself violently. She leaned forward. "Men are not to be trusted. I will not have my girls brought up believing they are saints, but I cannot blacken their papa to them either. It is a terrible situation."

"It must be," agreed Imogene.

"I should not burden you with my troubles. You are but a bride although—did someone not say you had been married before?"

"At sixteen," said Imogene in a soft sad voice.

"So then you know about men!"

What I know has been hard learnt, thought the fragile beauty whose broad-brimmed straw hat shaded her pale set face. *I gave my heart to a copper-haired lover who deserted me and who has since married someone else. And my hand to*

171

a mad Dutchman who nearly killed me—and then I told myself I had at last found the only man for me. And now he too has proved unfaithful . . .

Her cup of bitterness was full. But she would not burden Esthonie with that.

"Men crave variety," grumbled Esthonie. "No matter how beautiful the wife, other fields are greener!"

Imogene rose. "I must take my leave of you. I only came by to deliver the dresses and tell you about the clock. Good-bye, Esthonie." This was to be a real good-bye, although Esthonie was not to know it, for Imogene doubted she would ever see the governor or his family again.

Esthonie took her outstretched hand. "I can see by your eyes that you have found out about van Ryker. Veronique has told me nothing, but I have eyes to see. All men are false."

Imogene wished she could deny it.

"Do you know yet where you will be going?"

"Barbados, according to van Ryker."

Esthonie gave her a bright-eyed, commiserating look that said, *You will not be gone long. You will sail away and van Ryker will chance upon some Spanish galleon, a prize too tempting not to be taken, and he will sail back to dispose of his goods. Your life will never change. And now he is enamored of a new woman.*

Imogene could not bear that look. A dull pain pounded in her head. At that moment she cared not where they went.

From the hall came the chiming of Esthonie's much despised lantern clock. It reminded her that at about this time thrice before she had seen Veronique leaving the pimento grove.

"But I had hoped you would stay longer." Clucking, Esthonie followed her to the door. And as Imogene peremptorily beckoned to a lounging Arne, her curiosity surfaced. "Where are you off to in such a hurry?"

Imogene gave her a mocking look. "I am off to pick some flowers. For my hat."

She left Esthonie staring at her open-mouthed from the doorway.

To Imogene's chagrin, Veronique had already cleared the grove and the church. They met her smiling dreamily, walking her horse, already halfway back to the "governor's palace." She gave Imogene a scrupulously courteous bow as she passed and got a frosty bow in return.

"Where we be goin'?" demanded Arne, bewildered.

"To pick some flowers," Imogene repeated grimly and walked fast toward the grove. It was possible, she told herself, that van Ryker was still there. If so, she would confront him!

Neither of them noticed a head that poked around the corner of a low shed, nor the silent wave with which that head's owner beckoned to others behind him.

Arne gave her a wild look as she headed into the grove. "Here now," he began unhappily. "I don't know as how the Cap'n would like this."

"Perhaps we'll run across him and we can ask him," Imogene flung sweetly over her shoulder. "Who knows, he may be picking me another bunch of flowers?"

Arne had his hands full warding off palm fronds that snapped back at him from Imogene's impetuous forward rush through this green jungle. Muttering in alarm, he surged after her, blundering into tangles of vines that snatched cruelly at his wooden leg, for Imogene's slender form could swish sinuously through narrow openings in the brush that big Arne had to smash through.

In her anxiety to find van Ryker, and Arne's concentration on following her without having a snapping branch blind him or a twisted root hurl him headlong, both were oblivious momentarily to what was going on around them. The grove could have been full of people and they would have been unaware.

So suddenly did Imogene come to a halt that Arne nearly plummeted into her.

Here before her at last lay the secluded clearing she had been afraid she would find. It was small and private and seemed surrounded by a breathless hush. Pimento trees and climbing vines rose around it and arched over it like a green roof, and it was here the Cups of Gold bloomed. Their vines ran riotously over the pimento trees, hanging from their branches, festooning them with brilliant yellow flowers, five inches across. This tiny clearing was at once spectacular, perfumed, and intimate—a perfect trysting place for lovers.

Imogene drew a quick hurtful breath. For there beneath the trees was a place where the soft waving grasses had been pressed down as if two bodies had lain on them, straining together in this place of enchantment. Van Ryker had gone but—the imprint of his body was still here.

A sudden blur of tears misted her eyes. She had so hoped to be proved wrong.

Imogene never knew why she turned. Perhaps it was a

sound, perhaps some grunt of warning from Arne, but turn she did.

She was just in time to see a heavy cudgel swung. While she and Arne had been crashing about, four men had stolen up behind them—and now the lead fellow had felled Arne like an ox.

A scream tore from Imogene's throat and she whirled to run. She was half across the little clearing before a big hand clamped down on her shoulder. She managed to jerk away but not before she heard a ripping sound and felt the wrench as her big detachable sleeve was torn from her arm. In a wild plunge she was away from her attacker and heading for the wall of yellow flowers at the opposite side of the clearing.

But she never made the trees.

Her head and arms were actually halfway through the hanging vines before she was brought down, grasped roughly and swung around so hard she stumbled and went down on her hands and knees. She would have been up again but that a hamlike hand clamped down on her naked shoulder and she was jerked unceremoniously to her feet.

She found herself staring into the hard blue eyes of a smiling giant with a mustard-colored mustache and unkempt oily hair. He was naked to the waist, wearing only coarse cotton breeches, a belt that supported a cutlass, and scuffed leather boots. The sun had bronzed his massive chest muscles almost to mahogany and his large white teeth gleamed as he grinned at her.

"Got 'er!" he called triumphantly over his shoulder, and Imogene's dazed gaze swung to the others now crashing through the underbrush. They were dressed like the first fellow, in coarse drawers, boots and cutlasses—and they looked as murderous as he. One of them sported a mouthful of broken yellow teeth, another a fresh new scar that zigzagged down through his tan, and the third a single silver earring that looked as if a woman of quality might have worn it once.

Her gaze fled to Arne, stretched out unconscious on the grass. He was so still he looked dead.

The bright courage that had always marked her came to aid her now. Her delicate chin went up.

"It is plain you do not know who I am," she said coldly. "But before you die of your mistake, I will tell you. I am Imogene van Ryker. All the Caribbean knows the temper of my husband's steel. He is not likely to forget an injury done to me or to Arne. You had best clear out before he finds you."

"Talks good, don't she?" The giant, whose grasp had in no way relaxed, gave her a look of grudging admiration.

"And not afeard of us," marveled Yellow Tooth.

"That's 'cause she don't know us yet," chuckled Silver Earring.

Scarface spat.

"I give you this warning only to save your lives," she told them steadily, her courage dimming a bit as she saw her words were having no effect on them. "Which are surely forfeit if you harm me."

"Harm you?" The giant who held her laughed delightedly. "Who said we'd *harm* you?" He reached out and casually tweaked her breast with impudent fingers. She struck his hand away. He gave her a light cuff, but heavy enough to

176

make her ears ring. "Easy, mistress," he said lightly. "You be good to Ferdie, an' Ferdie'll be good to you." His voice had a kind of insinuating crooning note in it that frightened her more than the blow. The softness of her woman's flesh, the silkiness of her bright hair, the clean sweet scent of her had mesmerized him.

"Bring the wench and come along, Ferdie," called Scarface. "We got a ways to go to reach the ship."

"Can't take her through town till after dark," Ferdie flung over his shoulder. He was staring raptly down at her. Imogene felt pinned by that gaze like a butterfly. "Plenty o' time," he said lazily and flung her to the ground.

Imogene landed twisting and would have been up and away but that a heavy boot suddenly pinned her thigh to the grass. She gave a painful cry, only half aware of Yellow Tooth's muttered, "Are you goin' to let that Portugee have 'er first, Toss?"

What Toss answered she was never to know, for an arm with a pistol in it was stuck suddenly through the flowering vines and fired at point-blank range into Ferdie's bronzed chest. The bullet entered just at the breastbone and Ferdie's blank face mirrored his surprise. Imogene screamed as he went down, felled like a tall tree. She barely had time to roll out of the way before van Ryker dropped his smoking pistol—which contained, after all, only one shot—snatched up Ferdie's cutlass and met the murderous charge of Yellow Tooth, who was closest.

Looking up, she thought she had never seen such a satanic expression on van Ryker's face. He was white beneath his

177

tan, which gave his face a strange gray cast, his lips were drawn back and his white teeth gleamed savagely.

To the accompaniment of Silver Earring's explosive "My God, it's van Ryker!" her lean buccaneer met Yellow Tooth's charge with a ferocity unmatched in her experience. When Yellow Tooth's cutlass took a vicious swipe at him, he was not there to receive it. But even as it bit into the bole of one of the old pimento trees, his own wide-swinging cutlass, which he had borrowed from the man he had just shot, described a wide savage arc and caught Yellow Tooth across his naked midsection. It went in far enough to sever the spine and send Yellow Tooth screaming to eternity. Simultaneously came a roar from Arne, who had been only stunned and now lurched to his feet.

The pair of remaining cutthroats hesitated, glanced at each other, and as one man took to their heels. Van Ryker wrested the cutlass free and flung it after them with deadly accuracy. There was a howl as it bit into Scarface's muscular shoulder, but he stumbled on with Arne now in clumsy pursuit. They heard two shots.

Van Ryker made no effort to pursue. He bent in concern over Imogene, who had risen and whose knees had suddenly refused to support her. She was now sitting on the ground, trembling in every limb.

"Did they hurt you?" he asked tersely and there was fear in that face men said knew no fear.

She shook her head, shuddering. "A bruise only. 'Twill soon be mended."

"I give thanks for that," he muttered. "Rest a bit," he

counseled, watching her keenly. "You look as if you're about to be sick."

Imogene *felt* about to be sick. She kept her eyes averted from the pair of dead men on the ground. She cast a stricken look at van Ryker. A fearsome picture he presented: cold gray eyes still flashing, jaw still grim, face alert and watchful. His doublet was slashed halfway across where Yellow Tooth's cutlass had grazed him before it sank into the pimento tree, and the flowing sleeves of his white shirt hung in torn streamers where briars had caught and ripped the fine cambric. He picked up his pistol and stuck it back in his belt.

Imogene bent her head down on her knees, trying to control her nausea. When her world stopped reeling, van Ryker helped her gently to her feet and she leaned against him. By now Arne had come back. He held a smoking pistol in each hand.

"I couldn't catch up with 'em, Cap'n," he cried, aggrieved. "They wouldn't stand and fight! I shot twice at the one you got in the shoulder—missed him both times!" He looked frustrated.

"That's all right, Arne. They'll not escape Tortuga—we'll get them later." And then the harder question. "What the devil were you thinking of, letting my wife wander into this thicket?"

Arne looked sheepish. "I couldn't stop her, Cap'n," he mumbled. "She took off ahead o' me and I was hard put to keep up."

"I don't doubt it," muttered van Ryker with a frown at Imogene. "Well, we'll away from here before that pair

179

collect their wits and bring back a few more of their fellows to work their devilment.''

"How did you find me?" asked Imogene soberly. She was still shaken as he led her out of the grove, holding back the thrashing palm fronds so that she might pass through.

"A rumor reached me that something might happen to you, so I came home to check up. When I learned you were at the governor's, I went to collect you and escort you home. Esthonie told me you had gone to pick some flowers—I could guess where. On the way here I passed Veronique who said she had seen you entering the grove. I was in time to see four husky fellows slipping into the grove and followed them.''

" 'Tis a lucky thing you come along, Cap'n,'' interposed Arne morosely. "For they slipped up on me unawares.''

"How's your head, Arne?"

"Aches somethin' awful," admitted Arne with a grimace.

Imogene threw him a remorseful look. She felt steadier now.

"I'll send for Raoul to have that head looked at. That was a solid blow that felled you. I came up in time to hear it.''

Arne grunted his gratitude and disappeared toward his own quarters when they reached the house. By mutual consent van Ryker and Imogene continued on through the stone courtyard and up the stairs. The wide-eyed servant who scurried away to find the doctor thought the Captain looked exceedingly grim and his lady's lovely face bore a threatening expression that boded him no good.

For all he had rescued her—and the danger had driven everything else temporarily from both their minds—they were now back on the track.

Imogene was furious with van Ryker, who had, she was now certain, betrayed her with Veronique, and van Ryker guessed what she was thinking.

He kept his hold on her, almost dragging her into his bedchamber. Then he closed the door firmly behind him and turned to face her. She jerked away from him pettishly.

If she had expected him to hold on to her, she was surprised. He let her go with a suddenness that shocked her. The gray gaze that raked her was as cold as winter ice. "Take off your clothes." It was not a suggestion, it was an order. As he spoke he was tossing his pistol aside, unbuckling his belt.

"In *your* room?" she asked contemptuously.

"Or yours. Whichever you like." His indifferent voice told her he couldn't care less in which room she disrobed.

CHAPTER 10

Imogene sniffed, noting warily that van Ryker was stripping off his torn doublet. She had no intention of taking off so much as a shoe while he was in the room!

"Off with them," he said peremptorily. "Strip!"

Did he think he was going to make love to her? *Now?* After nearly being caught with Veronique? Certainly he had made haste to drag her to his bedchamber! The astounding thought that van Ryker might be considering imminent contact with her flesh filtered through Imogene's brain, making her feel dizzy. And with it—ancient as Eve and as crafty—came another thought. She would approach this thing obliquely, she would surprise him into an admission of guilt.

As he flung away the shreds and streamers of his torn shirt, she turned away from him so that she did not quite meet his eyes. "Georgette is growing up," she said carelessly, just as

183

if none of the events of the past hour had happened. "She is experimenting with new hairdos. Veronique"—she could not resist a spiteful emphasis on the name—"is teaching her that overdone hairstyle she affects. Esthonie does not favor it." She watched him catlike out of the corner of her eye.

Van Ryker made no comment.

"In the carriage the other day, I mistook her for Veronique. Was it not strange?"

"I would rather hear less of Veronique." Van Ryker's eyes narrowed. He was already pulling on another shirt.

"Would you? *Would you?*" She turned on him in fury. "Do you ask me also to be blind, that I do not see you meeting her, spending time with her?"

"Ah," he said, "so that is it. You are jealous of Veronique. Ask yourself, have I given you cause?"

"*Yes!*" she shouted. "*Yes, you have given me cause!*"

He studied her for a minute; she could not read his gaze. He advanced upon her. So formidable did he look that she almost gave ground.

"Come, if you will not strip, at least let us see that bruise. That bastard tramped down on you pretty hard with his boot." He reached down and would have pulled up her skirts but that she slapped his hand away.

"Don't touch me, van Ryker!" she almost spat at him. She was thinking how that strong bronzed hand that he now extended toward *her* must have fondled Veronique, touched her intimately.

His hand dropped away instantly. "If you will not suffer my inspection, then I will send Raoul round to examine you."

"There is no need," she flashed. "I'm not hurt."

He accepted that. "Were there any others besides the two who fled?" He was buckling on his rapier as he spoke, checking out two large pistols. "I saw only four."

Her anger was winding down. "I saw but four. You're—going after them?" she asked raggedly.

"Yes." Curtly. "I am. And find them too."

She had no doubt he would.

"Stay in the house until I return," he said dispassionately, and shouldered past her. She could hear his boots clattering down the stairs, striking the stone floor as he strode across it.

And Imogene, caught up again in jealous impotent fury, swept her arm across a low cabinet and sent van Ryker's comb and brush and two silver tobacco jars flying across the room.

She was a long time picking them up and her hands trembled as she did it. Van Ryker was off to avenge her but—had he only this afternoon broken faith with her?

Her thoughts gnawed at her, allowing her no rest. She paced the floor and finally went back to her own room. Time passed. She refused dinner.

A long scented bath refreshed her and she drank a tall glass of cooling limeade and slipped into her night rail. A big orange moon crept over the skies. The palm fronds rustled restlessly. Although she would not admit it, she had begun to be afraid for van Ryker. He would thrust himself unhesitatingly into any danger, she knew. Perhaps they had set a trap for him. Perhaps . . .

But all her anxiety translated itself into anger again when at last she heard van Ryker's quick step in the hall below, heard him speaking to someone—the guard drowsing at the door, no doubt. She debated pretending sleep, but jumped up instead. She wanted to confront him!

She thought he looked tired as he swung into the room and closed the door behind him. There was a long rip in his doublet but—her heart gave a lurch—it was not bloody. One of his shirt sleeves had been torn entirely away—but the sinewy arm beneath was unscathed. And that bruise on his cheek (where a tankard had been thrown at him by a dockside whore in the brothel where he had at last run down Imogene's attackers) was light enough, considering the mayhem he had wrought.

"You found them?" she asked. And at his curt nod, "What—did you do?" But she knew already.

"I rid the world of them," he said conversationally, tossing his sword into a corner. "What would you have had me do? Leave them about to attack some other poor woman who had no strong blade to protect her?"

"No." She shivered. "I'm glad you killed them." A frown crept over her face as she saw that he was undressing. "You're not planning to sleep here tonight, are you?" she asked sharply. *"In my bed?"*

He looked up in some surprise. "That was my intention."

His calm assumption that he could assert his marital rights with her made her fury wash over her again.

"I don't see how you can face me!" she cried. "After what you've done?"

"And what have I done," he asked coolly, pulling off his boots. "Except to save your pretty hide and chastise your attackers as a warning to others?"

She had been lying on her elbow on the bed and now she bounced up. "You'll not sleep in *my* bed!"

He drew back, eyebrows elevating sardonically. "So? I had noticed a change in the weather. You have been blowing hot and cold lately. Let us have it out between us, whatever is bothering you."

"You *know* what is bothering me!" she shouted, feeling he was making a fool of her.

Again he quirked an eyebrow at her. "Do I now?" he wondered. "Let me see. You visit the governor's house frequently and come back looking preoccupied and worried. Suddenly you decide to gift Esthonie with one of your favorite possessions—the marquetry standing clock. I would suggest it is in the nature of payment for something. And what would Esthonie have to sell? Information, perhaps. Am I right so far?"

Choked with rage, Imogene stared at him. How dared he stand there playing at word games with her? Her hands balled into fists. "And what could she tell me, van Ryker?" she asked at last in a tone of suppressed fury. "What would Esthonie know that I don't?"

"I have no idea," he said blandly. "I suggest *you* tell *me*."

"I do not need to have Esthonie tell me anything! With my own eyes I saw Veronique coming out of the grove behind the church—where she goes day after day! With my own eyes I saw you brush the Cup of Gold petals from your shoulder!"

"And you assumed I was meeting Veronique in the grove?"

"Of course!" she shouted.

"Well, you are wrong. I only escorted her there. She was meeting someone else."

"Liar!" she accused bitterly.

"Imogene." He frowned. "Have I ever lied to you?"

"Yes!" she cried.

A ghost of a smile played over his sardonic face. "You are right," he agreed, then countered with, "but have I ever lied to you for other than a good purpose?"

"You are now!" she flung at him. "Esthonie is right. You are like Gauthier and have wandering ways. You have found a new woman!"

His face seemed to harden. "Esthonie's opinion is of little interest to me."

"Tell me it is not so!" she flashed.

Van Ryker studied the flushed face before him in the bright moonlight. Imogene's golden hair was disheveled but shining. Her breast, beneath the thin lawn of her lacy night rail, heaved mightily and he could see the pink tips of her nipples surging against the delicate fabric. A tiny scratch marred the white column of her pulsing throat where a twig had scraped her this afternoon. Somehow his gaze seemed to focus on that scratch and a great overpowering tenderness stole over him. He loved this girl so much, and the accusations she had made—she had made because she was jealous. Of him.

It was a thing to be forgiven.

He gave a deep sigh. "Imogene," he said. "I had not intended to tell you this, but now I will. Come and sit down."

"I can take it standing," she said promptly. "If you have taken a mistress, be good enough to say so." Her voice was filled with stinging contempt. "Do not beat about the bush!"

Van Ryker gave a rueful laugh. He left her side and walked over to the window, stood before it looking out into the midnight blue sky drifting serenely over Tortuga. His broad muscular back was to her so she could not see his face but something distant in his voice told her he was seeing other skies, other shores.

"What I tell you now is told in confidence," he said sternly. "A woman's life depends on it—yes, and a man's too."

Imogene gave a contemptuous sniff.

He ignored that and went on. "The woman you know as Veronique Fondage is not French but Spanish."

Imogene's racing thoughts skimmed back to that gliding walk of Veronique's. The ladies of the Spanish court walked that way, she had been told. It took endless practice but they gradually achieved a gait that sent their long skirts floating over the floor as if they had no legs at all. And that unusual coiffure—it was made to support a high-backed tortoiseshell comb, as indeed it must have done in Spain. She should have recognized a Spanish aristocrat, she told herself in surprise. A woman who had been born to command, to walk over people; had Veronique been a man, she would doubtless have faced van Ryker from behind the guns of some majestic galleon, challenging his right to use the seas.

"But she was a captive aboard the galleon *Delgado*," she burst out. "Esthonie said so!"

"She was not a captive in any ordinary sense," he explained. "Although she was indeed a captive. She is the runaway wife of Don Luis Alvarez, the duke of Sedalia-Catalonia—of whom you may have heard."

Imogene gave that broad back a startled look. Who had not heard of Don Luis? He was a grandee of Spain whose many ships ranged the seas, mortal enemy of all buccaneers. She sank down upon the bed and listened raptly as his level voice continued.

"It was one of Don Luis's ships that attacked my father's merchantman, sank the vessel, and carried him away to Spain. It was in one of Don Luis's dungeons that my father languished in chains, starving in darkness, gnawed by rats. It was to Don Luis that my mother sent the ransom—raised by selling our family home of Ryderwood and all we possessed. And it was that same Don Luis who accepted that ransom and sent my father back to us—starved, maltreated, and dying."

"And Veronique is his *wife*?" gasped Imogene. "But she is young and I had heard that he is an old man!"

That dark head, turned away from her, nodded soberly. "In Spain marriages are arranged. Veronique's maiden name is Maria Theresa del Rio de Guarda. Hers is one of the loftiest families of Spain. She was thrust at sixteen into the arms of a man old enough to be her grandfather."

And you are rescuing her, thought Imogene, feeling hot jealousy pour over her.

"Not only old, but a cold man, a proud man, a cruel man. Maria Theresa—"

"Call her Veronique."

"Very well. Veronique was young and reckless. Appearing at court, she one day wore a dress cut too low—and the queen remarked it. Don Luis set out to punish her for this slur on his honor. He had all her clothes gathered together and burned while she watched. Then he ordered for her a new wardrobe of heavy fabrics in solid black with long sleeves and neck-lines that reached to her chin. She was young and spirited and she cast her gaze elsewhere; it was a harmless enough affair, to hear her tell it.''

Imogene doubted anything Veronique had ever done was entirely harmless and she knew Spanish ladies of rank favored black, but her heart—the heart of a girl who was forever tossing away her whisk—went out to anyone obliged to wear stiff garments that reached to the chin.

"Don Luis heard of her straying ways. He could prove nothing, but he determined to exact vengeance on his young wife. He sent her from court in disgrace under armed guard, exiled her to one of his country estates and told her that she would never leave it, that she would receive no visitors, buy no new gowns, be forbidden even to ride, that she should spend her days on her knees seeking forgiveness and her nights in prayer that such forgiveness be granted.''

"But surely he couldn't have meant *forever!*" protested Imogene, shocked.

Again that large head nodded. "Veronique believes Don Luis would never have relented, that she would have grown old there—alone. For Don Luis had said that he intended never to lay eyes on her again. She managed to bribe one of the servants, sold some of her jewels—jewels that were part of her dowry—and secretly secured passage to Cartagena. She intended to go on to Lima, Peru, and live out her life under a new name. What that name was cannot matter now—she never reached Lima. Don Luis tortured the servants until they revealed what she had done. He then sent one of his ship's officers—a most intrepid fellow—to the New World to collect her. She was to be returned to Spain for execution as a heretic.''

Imogene shivered. She knew that in Spain the Inquisition had been twisted in strange ways: a disobedient child—or a disobedient wife—could be declared a heretic and disposed of under church law.

''The man he sent to accomplish this was Don Diego Navarro, who had little heart for his task. He found his quarry easily enough—a woman with a face so striking is hard to conceal.'' Again that little quiver of jealousy went through Imogene. ''He loaded Veronique on to one of the galleons of the treasure *flota*, intending to deliver her back to Spain.'' *Like other treasure wrested from the New World*, she thought suddenly. *A woman with amber eyes and hair of flashing jet....* ''There was one trouble with his plan.'' Van Ryker's voice grew ironic. ''Diego Navarro, gentleman of Spain, had fallen in love with the lady.''

''And he is the man whose leg you injured in the fighting on the beach the day you took the treasure *flota*?''

If he was surprised that she knew that, his voice did not show it. It continued even and calm. ''The same. Diego Navarro had toyed with the idea that he and Veronique would make their escape in Spain when the ship landed, make their way to some out-of-the-way place and live as peasants in the hills.''

Hard to imagine elegant Veronique doing that!

''But then the storm came up and *you* captured the treasure *flota* and all that changed,'' she murmured.

''Right. At that point, Diego decided to sell his life dearly.'' There was admiration in van Ryker's voice. ''We must have seemed an overwhelming force, sweeping in across the beach, but Diego, almost alone, leaped forward to meet us. I was the first man to reach the shore and he waded out in the surf to meet me. We clashed swords and he came off the worst of it. I pray that his wounded leg will not leave him crippled—Raoul says it will not although it still pains him and he will limp for some time to come.''

Imogene's gaze was misty. She could understand van Ryker's feelings about Diego—gallantry calls to gallantry. "So you are telling me they are lovers," she said at last.

"I am telling you more than that. I am telling you they are *lost lovers* if something is not done to help them, for although Diego's ship's company died to a man and the surviving Spanish prisoners have apparently accepted his story that she was a French captive being returned to Spain to be ransomed, they have no future. They cannot return to Spain."

"What will become of them?"

"They meet secretly in the grove each day. I have let the world believe it is I she trysts with—but that is only to aid Diego, whom I have come to admire and like. She is teaching him French, which she speaks so fluently she has even been able to fool the governor's family into believing she is French. When *La Belle France* leaves our harbor for Marseilles she will carry with her Monsieur and Madame de Jonquil, an unfortunate French couple who were shipwrecked and lost their papers. In Marseilles they will buy new papers—her jewels, which I restored to her, will keep them going—to prove beyond doubt that they are Monsieur and Madame de Jonquil. Veronique will leave without saying good-bye. Her horse will be found riderless beside the sea. She will be presumed to have drowned. Diego will be presumed to have escaped—I will say so.''

"So you arrange this happy fate for Veronique because you admire Diego's gallantry," Imogene murmured. "And not because she is a poor helpless female of striking attributes?"

He swung about and the anger in his dark face struck her like a physical blow. He looked satanic as he spoke.

"I do it for both those reasons," he agreed in an icy voice. *"But I would do it in any event to discomfit Don Luis*. Not a day have I sailed these waters that I have not yearned to find one of his ships looming over the next horizon—and Don Luis himself aboard her. I have longed to face him across the length of a sword.''

"Feeling as you do, I am surprised you have not sought him out in Spain!" she exclaimed.

His gaze narrowed. "Be assured that I have thought about it on many a long night," he said tersely. "But reaching Don Luis is like reaching the king of Spain himself—he is almost as heavily guarded." His sudden laugh chilled her. "But some reward has come my way at last. Don Luis must have valued his young wife to wreak such vengeance upon her. I will see that word is circulated throughout Spain that she lives, that she has sought the very arms of the buccaneer who took his flagship, *El Cruzado*, from him and turned her into the *Sea Rover* that seized the treasure *flota*. And that he is further dishonored because the buccaneer holds her in light esteem, keeping her about as a sometime mistress and plaything.''

Imogene flinched before the cold fury of his merciless tone. "'Does Veronique know that you plan this?" she gasped.

He cocked a cynical eyebrow at her. "She joined me in planning it. She hates Don Luis with a bitterness that almost surpasses my own. She says that he will crawl inwardly and worms of doubt will gnaw at him, that he had sought to entomb her while living and now—neither dead nor alive as he sees it, but flitting by like some wraith, ever striking at his pride—now he will be made to suffer eternally, for he will not know what to believe."

And together they would bring about that eternal suffering— van Ryker and Veronique. Imogene realized with sudden loneliness that their very hatred was a bond between them. A bond that, much as she loved van Ryker, she could not really share.

"I owe Don Luis a debt," van Ryker told her softly, speaking almost to himself. "A debt for the murder of my parents, for my mother died of grief, a debt for the impoverishment of my family. It is a debt that will have something on account before ever I leave Tortuga." He roused himself from his angry reverie. "So now you understand, Imogene. Now you know all."

"Yes," she sighed. "Now I understand."

But any woman would dislike having her husband seek another woman's company, flaunt it to the world—even in a charade. And Esthonie had been so certain there was something between them.

Could there be? Could love be founded on hatred?

At that point something half remembered came back to torment her. She had hated van Ryker before she had loved him. Veronique and van Ryker were drawn together by strong

195

passions and who could say what random spark might ignite a flame between them?

She pushed the thought from her mind and melted seductively into his strong arms, fitting her slender body to his, telling herself fiercely that she would bind him to her with a thousand intimate caresses, a sweetness beyond anything he had known, a night of unforgettable passion that would erase from his mind all other women and make him remember only her. Only her.

Sensing the tinder of her mood, he took her fierily, elegantly, teasing her, caressing her, sweeping her along with him, driving her to heights of ecstasy. His touch was liquid fire in her veins, each thrust an agony of delight, each retreat a madness. Her senses wavered, dazzled, righted themselves— careered and careered again. So overcome was she, she was near fainting in his arms. Her breath gasped in her throat, tears of joy stung her lashes, and feelings so deep she felt that before tonight she had only splashed about in the shallows of them, immersed her, enveloped her, overwhelmed her, left her drowning in desire and pleasure.

The night noises of Cayona reached them muted, ethereally transformed. Drunken laughter from buccaneers staggering home assumed an angelic sound as it drifted past them on the perfumed trade winds. A night bird's sleepy call to his mate, the rustle of the palms—all of it added to the night's magic for these star-crossed lovers.

As Imogene strained against her buccaneer's sinewy frame, moaning, sighing, whispering, loving, in the turbulence of her tumbled thoughts she became truly one with him, flying to the stars. And the full moon over Tortuga bathed them in its golden light and looked down tolerantly on the storm that shook them, consumed them, ennobled them—and flung them to the farthest shores of passion and fulfillment.

Still, the woman who lay sleepless, staring at the ceiling after van Ryker had been long asleep that night was very thoughtful. His masculine body could not lie to her, could it? The marvelous delicacy, the tenderness of his touch . . . it could not be a sham?

Oh, no, she told herself with a shudder, *it could not.*

Morning dawned at last and she turned over in bed to face him, letting her long fingers trail over his splendid naked chest to wake him.

"Van Ryker," she said softly.

His gray eyes opened and she realized that he had been awake, for he was looking at her keenly, half humorously. "You were a wild lover last night," he grinned.

Imogene thought of the storms of passion that had tossed them. "I had—thought I was losing you," she admitted shyly.

He drew her to him, stroking her back. "I never knew you to be jealous before," he said tenderly. He was caressing her hair as he spoke, separating out big soft curls and winding them around his fingers and blowing them away to watch them bounce and gleam.

"I never realized I *could* be jealous before," sighed Imogene. "I wanted to scratch your face and tear her eyes out!" She laughed ruefully. "Now I know the feeling I must have caused in so many women."

" 'Tis a gnawing pain," he agreed, "that will not be

assuaged. The thought of the Dutchman bedding you was more than I could bear.''

''He never did,'' she said carelessly. ''He wasn't capable.''

''His ill fortune was my good luck,'' he grinned.

''No, it was nobody's luck,'' she said soberly, leaning against him. ''His love for me cost him his life. Let us not talk about Verhulst, van Ryker. It makes me sad. It makes me remember. . . .''

She did not have to tell him what it made her remember. It made her remember Georgiana, the child who had been born to her only to be snatched away.

But there was comfort to be found in van Ryker's arms—comfort and forgetfulness. ''I have sworn in my heart to make you happy, Imogene,'' he said softly against her ear. ''Let me do it.''

''You speak of happiness but your heart is set on vengeance.'' Her voice was muffled as her lips brushed his chest. ''Against Don Luis. Your hatred is absorbing your life.''

''I will have done with it before ever you set eyes on Amsterdam,'' he promised, rubbing his cheek gently against her hair. ''And in England your mind will be occupied with other things—like redecorating Ryderwood. I have heard it is in sad shape, that the new owners let it run down badly.''

''I will be all right when at last we are at sea and watching the stars through the big stern windows of the great cabin.''

She felt a slight stiffening of the strong male figure that held her. ''I have said I will not risk you,'' he reminded her. ''You sail aboard the *Goodspeed*.''

''No.'' She twisted herself into a position so that she lay sprawled along his naked body, her soft breasts resting on his lightly furred chest. "Nothing good has ever come of our separations. If you had snatched me from the Governor's Ball in New Amsterdam as you threatened, Georgiana would be alive, Elise would be alive, Verhulst would be alive. . . . If you had not left me in Jamaica, so many terrible things would not have happened. No, it is settled." She rolled over and rose from the bed, stared down at him regally, a golden woman at the height of her beauty.

For a moment his steely gaze bit into hers.

"I am going with you!" she cried stormily. "If we die, at least it will be together!"

To her surprise, he did not argue about it. Instead he reached out and drew her back to the bed, flinging a long arm about her pliant naked waist, dragging her slender form lingeringly along his long body, caressing her, making love to her. All quarrels were forgotten in the glory of those long pulsating moments as their passions flared as hotly as the golden ball of a sun that stormed down upon Tortuga and plundered its dark secret places.

Later—much later when it was too late—she was to remember with bitterness that he had said neither yes or no.

CHAPTER 11

The day that was to remain for a long time like a scar on Imogene's memory dawned brightly.

They were leaving Tortuga at last. Everything was packed, crated. Most of it was already aboard ship—the remainder would go tonight under cover of darkness.

Last night there had been an urgency in van Ryker's lovemaking and his fervor had communicated itself to Imogene, who had clung to him desperately. She had flung herself into his arms with reckless abandon, letting her body tell him more vividly than words that she forgave him for letting all Tortuga think he had taken a mistress even if it was not so. She had moaned in his arms, nuzzling, caressing, thrilling to his every touch. Caught up in a web of passion, their storm of love had shaken them, sent them reeling past the wild reaches of desire and—at last, for van Ryker had chosen to drag out this heartfelt ecstasy, holding them ever back from the brink—swept them breathlessly into shuddering fulfillment.

Remembering the wild passion of that joining, Imogene was puzzled. She stood in the late morning sunlight of this, her last day on Tortuga, a slight lovely figure in a wide-skirted calico dress of soft yellow with a figure-hugging bodice, and asked herself what sense of panic had seized them the night before? There had been none of the tantalizing, languorous, half-playful lovemaking they had known of late. All spirit of playfulness had departed, leaving instead a sense of desperation—as if they played for great stakes and well might lose. It was the feeling of the night before the battle that had stalked them, driving them violently into each other's arms. *A last kiss feeling*— as if, whatever happened, they both knew they were going to be separated for a long time. That was the feeling van Ryker had summoned up in her, communicated to her.

Which was ridiculous, for she had announced that she was going with him on the *Sea Rover* and van Ryker, for all he had looked thoughtful, had not demurred.

She frowned as she saw Esthonie's carriage drawing up. Esthonie must not see that the house had by now been completely dismantled—it would tell her that their departure was imminent. She ran to the door to intercept her before she could alight.

"I was just leaving for the market," she told the governor's wife. "We are in need of fresh fruit. I certainly never expected to see you here today, Esthonie—not when you sent word yesterday that Virginie's fiancé has arrived from France!"

"Jean Claude has indeed arrived," sighed Esthonie. "I

will admit he is not quite what I expected. He is years older than I was led to believe and has a dissolute air. He took an immediate fancy to Veronique and I have asked her"—Esthonie's face took on a kind of fury—"*I have asked her*—quite pleasantly, you understand, since she is after all my guest—*to stay away from him.*" She looked about to gnash her teeth.

Imogene hid her amusement. "And what did Veronique say?"

"She was quite vague in her answer. She said of course she never *intended* anything untoward, that it is not her fault if men fall in love with her at first sight. 'Love'!" cried Esthonie derisively. "He is interested only in women of easy virtue and I am afraid he is not good enough for Virginie!" She peered at Imogene from beneath her bronze silk hat and her bronze plumes quivered. "Can't your servants attend to the marketing? Never mind, I'll take you there—my next stop is to be the quay, anyway. I am looking for Gauthier. I will tell him that both Veronique and Jean Claude have disappeared and that he is to *find* Jean Claude and bring him back. Immediately. Well, do get into the carriage, Imogene—no, of course you must go back and get your hat and gloves. I will wait for you. Hurry!"

Imogene dashed back inside and struggled into a pair of fashionably tight yellow silk gloves. She could not help chuckling at Esthonie's determination, even in the face of such formidable vexations as Veronique and Jean Claude, to keep up appearances here in lawless Cayona.

She, of course, knew where Veronique had gone—although where Jean Claude was, she could not imagine. Probably searching out the grog shops and taverns for suitable company. But Veronique and her Diego were at this very moment on board *La Belle France*, sailing out of Cayona Bay on their way to whatever lay in store.

Van Ryker had told her the plan. Veronique had donned her riding habit this morning as usual and ridden through the town on the black stallion van Ryker had lent her. This time she had kept on riding until she reached a secluded beach where Diego waited for her with a coarse brown kirtle and a tattered shawl and a big basket of fruit. He too would look threadbare—in a battered, wide-brimmed straw hat to hide his face, hunched over and stumbling—which would be easy enough since his limp still plagued him. Her lovely riding habit would be consigned to the sea, tossed far out, and together the pair of them, weaving as if they had had too much to drink, would meander through the uncaring crowd on Cayona's quay and board *La Belle France* as if they were hawking fruit to the departing passengers. Once there, *La Belle France*'s captain, who had been alerted to this charade, would quietly spirit them below where they would doff their beggarly clothes and dine soberly tonight as Monsieur and Madame de Jonquil, on their way back to their native France.

It was a lovely plan and it had some chance of success, for Veronique's jewel case was already waiting for her in that cabin reserved for the de Jonquils—van Ryker had seen to that.

The horse might not be missed, for the governor's grooms were a careless lot, but Veronique's absence at supper would surely be noticed. Esthonie, already at outs with her guest, would probably assume Veronique was keeping some romantic rendezvous, so it would be tomorrow before any real search would be instituted combing the island for the governor's houseguest, who might have come to harm.

The searchers would find the black horse, wandering saddled along the beach (Arne would find him, for van Ryker had already told him where to look and given Arne the stallion for his own). A woman's footprints would lead down to the sea and disappear (the tide would have washed clean the footprints of a man and a woman as Diego and Veronique hurried away through the lacy surf to their destiny). And all would conclude that Veronique had decided to wade out into the sea and come to grief—perhaps from a shark or barracuda.

Imogene grinned as she settled a wide-brimmed lemon silk hat, afloat with golden plumes, onto her thick shining blond hair. Tortuga's gossip being what it was, the governor's wife might well be rumored to have murdered her splendorous guest—if word got out that Esthonie feared Veronique might take Jean Claude from Virginie!

Arranging her features into a suitable gravity, she went out to join Esthonie, who was tapping her slipper and fanning herself in the heat.

"I am surprised you stopped by when you were in such a hurry to find Gauthier," she observed as she climbed into the carriage. "When you are so worried," she added innocently.

"I am surprised Captain van Ryker allows *you* out without a guard!" countered Esthonie in a tart voice. She let her fan drop upon her bronze silk lap. "Oh, I heard how those men attacked you!" She gave a brief theatrical shudder.

"Look behind you, Esthonie," directed Imogene casually as she settled her light yellow calico skirts on the seat opposite the governor's wife.

Esthonie turned her head, her bronze-plumed hat dipping as she did so—and blinked.

Arne, who had fully recovered from the blow he had taken in the pimento grove although his head was still bandaged, had fallen in behind them. And behind him lounged half a dozen other rough-looking fellows, all armed to the teeth.

"Oh." Esthonie gave Imogene a rather blank look. "So we do have an escort. I must say, I think that is wise. Is that a new dress?" And at Imogene's nod of demurral, "Well, *I* have not seen it before. How clever to trim it in yellow silk ribands! Van Ryker spoils you shamefully, Imogene." She reached up and tapped the driver on the back with her fan. "We'll walk the horses, Ramon. There's no need to make Madame van Ryker's guard run to keep up with us." She nodded graciously to the men who slouched along behind her carriage, delighted to move thus conspicuously through the town with an armed buccaneer escort. For, to strangers—and Cayona was always full of strangers—it would appear that the governor's valuable wife always roamed about under heavy guard.

"I stopped by to see you, Imogene"—Esthonie's heavy bustline strained against the black-braided bodice of her bronze silk gown with the import of her words—"to invite you and van Ryker to my party tonight."

"A party?" But this was awkward. How could they attend a party when they were sailing around midnight? There would be so many last-minute things to see to! "Isn't this rather sudden?" she asked, playing for time. "You always plan your parties days in advance." And why had Esthonie come herself, instead of sending around a note?

Esthonie looked uncomfortable. "Jean Claude arrived so unexpectedly—we had not expected him till next month, as you know. Of course, it seemed very fortuitous at the time—" She stopped. She did not intend to tell Imogene that after all the excitement over buccaneers climbing to Virginie's window, she had questioned the girl closely and learned that Virginie had skipped her period the month before. That alarming news had led her to welcome Jean Claude with open-armed relief and when Veronique had set her velvet claws into him, she had reacted with surging anger. "The party is to announce that the wedding will be held next week—here on Tortuga. We shall not wait to send her to France to meet his family and hold the wedding there as originally planned."

The fierceness of her tone caused Imogene to study her keenly, and Esthonie, before that level blue gaze, realized suddenly that Imogene must have guessed the whole situation. Her reserve melted. "It is terrible having daughters," she groaned. "Isn't it?"

Imogene, who would have given anything to have had her own daughter beside her at this moment, said stonily, "I am sure it is," for it was evident that Esthonie was very upset. "But—is Jean Claude *ready* for this?" she could not help asking. "I mean, he had not expected anything so soon, surely?"

"He had *better* be ready," declared Esthonie wrathfully. "After the way he was pursuing Virginie in the garden last night! Why, he had worked one of her sleeves down before I—" She cast a sudden look at the driver's back and lowered her voice to a conspiratorial whisper. "I do not know *what* might have happened if I had not chanced by at that moment. Virginie was giggling and leaning back in his arms—you know how innocent she is," she added quickly. "She did not realize what might have happened. Why, he had her half stretched out on one of those stone benches!"

"And her skirts might have ridden up," pointed out Imogene with dancing eyes.

"Indeed they might!"

"I doubt he would have been shocked, if he is the chaser you claim him to be," laughed Imogene. "Indeed, it might have helped Virginie's chances for a quick betrothal if they had!"

"Her *chances*? Ah, you need not worry about her *chances*! Jean Claude's father and I have already agreed by letter that he is to marry Virginie if they get along well, but I will *not* have him deflowering her ahead of time. Indeed"— the fan waved furiously—"I have changed my mind. He shall marry her tonight! Gauthier has the power to issue a special license and the minister will make no remonstrance, for we just had the leaks in the church roof repaired. Yes! That is what we will do!" She smote her bronze silk lap with her fan and lapsed into muttering over the details.

Esthonie would work it out, Imogene decided fatalistically. She always did. There was a certain wistfulness in her gaze as she rode for the last time through these hot narrow streets, winding down to the quay. About her sprawled a hodgepodge town of scattered houses lazing under the tropical sun. Stark white lime-washed walls and wooden shutters with peeling green paint shimmered past them in the heat as the carriage wheels turned lazily behind the walking horses. Through the satiny dark green leaves of citrus trees the tropical sun blazed down on faded terra-cotta roof tiles and sturdy iron grillwork, Spanish made and installed by captive artisans. And everywhere the enormous cascading vines of the tropics. The air was heavy and sweet with the scent of flowers. It was strange to ride through these crooked streets and realize that this was the last day she would ever spend in this buccaneer stronghold. Behind came the clank of cutlasses from the walking men, reminding her proudly that they were *her* guards—as wife to the unofficial mayor of Cayona!

She started as Esthonie leaned forward and tapped her with her fan. "We will of course expect you and van Ryker at the wedding tonight."

"Of course we will come," smiled Imogene, wondering distractedly if she could keep that promise!

"I don't see Gauthier anywhere, do you?" cried Esthonie as they reached the quay.

"No," said Imogene, but her gaze was fixed not on the crowded market but on the departing sails of *La Belle France*, just now clearing the harbor.

Van Ryker was having his revenge on his old enemy Don Luis, she thought. With cold precision he had engineered it and now before her eyes it was taking place.

Veronique and her lover were aboard that ship, sailing away to an uncertain future. Esthonie had no reason to fear Veronique any more—but of course she did not know that. Imogene, watching the great sails billow, wished them well. Instinctively she felt that Veronique had been right in her decision—lovers should not be separated. Veronique *should* go with her Diego wherever that led her. Just as she herself would follow van Ryker wherever the winds of fate blew them, to the very ends of the earth.

They alighted, and Esthonie was delighted at the stir caused by the contingent of watchful buccaneer guards who kept pace with Imogene as they strolled through a winding maze of piles of oranges and fresh coconuts and guavas and mangoes and big stalks of yellow bananas and breadfruit.

"I thought you said you needed fresh fruit for your table?" she remarked mildly.

"Yes, I do think I will have some of those bananas sent to the house," she decided hastily. "And some of those oranges as well. Attend to it, Arne." Making good her comment about needing fruit, she bought coconuts and lemons as well—at least Arne would enjoy them even if they themselves were far out to sea when he ate them.

She was distracted from her thoughts by a sudden gouge from Esthonie's fan. "Is that not Georgette?" she cried in horror. "Alone? And without her hat or gloves?"

Through an opening in the crowd Imogene did indeed see Georgette's dark shining curls bent over a collection of pearls being displayed on a keg top by a sun-blackened buccaneer, before the crowd closed between them, shutting off her view.

"Why—there's Virginie too!" gasped Esthonie. She was fairly dragging Imogene toward them as she spoke, puffing along in the heat in her rustling bronze silks through mountains of lemons and limes.

They came up behind the girls. Georgette, in white dimity, was rapt in her inspection of two short strands of pearls that she was comparing by holding them up to the light, dangling them from her short fingers. Virginie, in pink voile, was gazing with delight at a single baroque pearl that she held between thumb and forefinger. She made a little pirouette that brought her face to face with her mother.

"Mamma," she cried blithely. "Look what Jean Claude has just bought me!" She displayed the handsome pearl.

The look on Esthonie's face was ludicrous. It veered somewhere between anger and shock. Imogene choked back her laughter as Esthonie looked wildly about her.

"Where *is* Jean Claude?" she gasped.

"Over there." Virginie nodded toward a pile of wine kegs over which Jean Claude was bent in inspection. Now he rose and strolled in their direction. "Papa took him on a walk to view the town this morning and they rushed back right after you left, Mamma, to tell me they'd seen this beautiful pearl and Jean Claude wanted to buy it for me as a bride's gift if I liked it."

"And they told Virginie to hurry down before it was sold," Georgette finished for her. "*I* came along to select a necklace." She held up her choice meaningfully for her mother to view.

Her mother ignored that obvious invitation to purchase. "But where is Veronique?" she gasped, bewildered at this new turn of events.

"Oh, she rode out early before any of us were up," said Georgette. "It was barely light out and I called to her and she said hush, I would wake everyone up. She said she might stop by the market before coming home. I guess she changed her mind." The girl gave Imogene a slanted look of enormous malice—Georgette envied Imogene inordinately.

"What an odd expression you have on your face, Georgette," said Esthonie suddenly. "Have you some great revelation for us?"

Georgette cast a half-triumphant, half-taunting look at Imogene. "No," she said airily.

Imogene caught the menace of that sudden bold glance. She wondered uneasily if Georgette knew that Veronique had sailed. She knew that alone among the governor's family, Veronique was fond of Georgette and might have confided in her. No, surely even Veronique would see that it would have been folly to entrust such knowledge to a child. Georgette would never keep her secret, she would brag about what she knew that others were unaware of, and slowly, surely, word would reach Don Luis in Spain of what had happened and his long arm would reach out and pull his errant young wife back to him.

Imogene shivered. These were cold thoughts that raked her in the hot Tortuga sun.

Jean Claude had reached them now. He was a gangling fellow of medium height with narrow shoulders, a rather caved-in chest and a sallow complexion. Veronique, Imogene thought in amusement, could not possibly have been interested in him. Indeed, if she had she would have been the death of him—he looked too fragile to satisfy such a lusty woman. Still he did have a languorous air and wore his unnaturally orange hair unconscionably long and wavy. A drooping orange mustache hung from his noticeably long upper lip and his small bright brown eyes looked out over a beaklike nose. His age was uncertain but Imogene agreed with Esthonie— the closer one looked the older he became. It was as if he kept up the facade of youth, the trappings of the young, but behind it one sensed an enormous *ennui*, a boredom, a lack of purpose.

Imogene judged him to be a failed fortune hunter whose family had despaired of finding him an heiress in France and had sent him here to this disreputable island. She did not care for him, but she knew how anxious Esthonie was to get Virginie wed.

"Why, Jean Claude," Esthonie simpered with more truth than she would have liked to admit, "I thought we had lost you!"

"Never, madame." Jean Claude swept them all a bow so low that his long orange hair grazed the dust.

Esthonie tittered. "Then I am sure what I have to say will come as good news to you. Madame van Ryker here—" she paused to introduce Jean Claude to Imogene and at her beauty Jean Claude came instantly to attention. Esthonie frowned. "As you know, we are buying Madame van Ryker's house."

"Yes," murmured Jean Claude raptly, his eyes never leaving Imogene.

Esthonie's voice sharpened. "As a friend of the family, Madame van Ryker desires to attend the ceremony. Since she is leaving so soon, I could not but oblige her." She beamed at Jean Claude as if she were bestowing on him a gift. "So I have promised her the wedding will be held tonight!"

"Tonight?" Jean Claude was staggered. The face he turned to her had a jaw gone slack with shock; his future mother-in-law had at last his full attention. "But Madame Touraille," he protested in confusion, "my family expects me to return with Virginie and marry her there. In France!"

Roguishly Esthonie waved her fan beneath his beaklike

nose. "Ah, but they could not but approve when you tell them that if you are married tonight Captain van Ryker plans to give our Virginie a little *gift*!"

Imogene winced at being used in this manner, but Jean Claude straightened suddenly and blinked. The mixture of expressions on his face was a wonder. He knew there was no way to escape this marriage—he had come to that dismal conclusion back in France. But he had planned to postpone it as long as possible—even though he was in desperate need of her dowry to pay off his gambling debts, which had piled up so monstrously. He had been lured here only because Virginie's father, Gauthier Touraille, was amassing a fortune selling letters of marque to the buccaneers of Tortuga. And now if he wed the girl tonight, the buccaneer who had taken an entire Spanish plate fleet would bestow on him a large gift!

"Madame Touraille, you are right," he agreed gracefully. "There is no sense waiting. We should accommodate the van Rykers. Tonight would be excellent!" He gave Virginie a sunny smile and she managed a virginal blush. Imogene envied her aplomb.

Esthonie's attention was diverted. "Do I see your father over there behind those wine kegs?" she demanded of Virginie. "Yes, I am sure it is he. Jean Claude, do go over and collect him. See that he does not buy any more wine—tell him I said he is not to do it. And bring him back with you. He must inform the minister and make all the arrangements. Now, this afternoon, if we are to have the ceremony tonight."

Jean Claude bowed and left them, and the buccaneer sitting on his haunches behind the keg that served as a table for the pearls reached out a gnarled hand to retrieve the short pearl necklace Georgette seemed about to make off with.

"Fine pearls, my ladies," his big voice boomed at them. "Fit for queens like yourselves!"

"*That's* the necklace I want," Georgette told him airily as she surrendered it.

Imogene peered at the two necklaces. "The other necklace is better matched," she said wickedly, as a prod to Esthonie. "Why did you choose the one with smaller pearls, Georgette?"

"Because there are ten more pearls in that one," Georgette pointed out impatiently.

"I would still prefer the other one," laughed Imogene. "It's much better looking." She was amused that Georgette did not yet understand the value of larger, better matched pearls—that was something grasping Esthonie obviously had forgotten to teach her!

"Well, *I* wouldn't," insisted Georgette. "A string of pearls just can't *be* long enough—queens wear great ropes of them wound around their necks and around their waists and some-day I'll have ropes of pearls too—like you do! I wouldn't bother with a lumpy pearl like that." Her lofty shrug dismissed Jean Claude's gift to Virginie.

Nettled that her handsome baroque pearl should be thus cavalierly dismissed—and on her wedding day too!—her sister gave a heartless laugh. "You'll never get them," she told Georgette. "Papa is going to be short of funds what with having to raise my dowry in such a hurry!" She gave her sister a winsome smile. "Jean Claude says he will buy me a string for Christmas. In Paris."

Georgette was not one to be bested. "I don't need Papa to

buy my pearls," she stated recklessly. "I'll have my pearl necklace, you'll see—in fact I may even have *that* one!" She indicated the strand those gnarled hands had just taken from her.

"Ha!" said Virginie. "Braggart!"

"And I won't have to wait till Christmas, either!" Georgette's voice rose shrilly.

"Two pieces of eight say you don't!"

"Five say I will!" flashed Georgette.

"Girls, girls," chided their mother. "You are making a scene here on the quay. *Mon Dieu*, what will Imogene think of us?"

Both girls subsided, pouting, and immediately—pearls and wagers and weddings forgotten—began studying with appraising glances the buccaneers who swaggered past. Once again Imogene was reminded that the governor's daughters had the air of very young, very determined prostitutes prowling about looking for their first customers. For a wild moment she wondered if Georgette intended to acquire her string of pearls *that* way. Esthonie had better hang onto the house keys or she might find Georgette swaggering down into the town some night!

Jean Claude came back with Gauthier, who looked floored when his wife airily told him the marriage would be held that night. With her usual domination, she overrode his weak protests and he trotted off dutifully with Jean Claude to find the minister.

"Imogene, I have no time to buy Virginie a proper pair of bride's garters," twittered Esthonie. "And you have such lovely things. Could we stop by your house and borrow a pair?''

''No, I''—Esthonie must not see that empty house and jump to the right conclusions—''I am still in a flurry of packing and will have to look for them. You and the girls had best drop me off and I will find a pair and have them sent over.'' And *that,* she thought with irritation, meant that she would have to send one of the servants down to the quay to buy a pair, for all of her own, save those she was wearing, were already on board the *Sea Rover.*

''Is that woman Papa and Jean Claude are talking to a whore?'' wondered Georgette as they climbed into the carriage.

Esthonie's bronze bodice lurched as if pierced with a pin. She whirled to view in the distance the stylish madam with whom Gauthier kept company—and for whom he bought vast quantities of wine.

''Virginie said she was,'' insisted Georgette.

''I said she was a madam,'' corrected Virginie.

''What's the difference?''

Esthonie looked about to choke. ''Have you no sense?'' she cried. ''Nice young girls do not speak of whores. *Or* madams! Ramon, drive on!''

Imogene saw the driver's shoulders shake, convulsed at Georgette's question. In spite of himself, Ramon was beginning to feel a real fondness for the French governor's unconventional family.

''I hear Captain van Ryker prowled the town in search of the two men who attacked you,'' said Virginie, who had not seen Imogene since the incident. ''And killed them.''

''Yes,'' said Imogene shortly.

"What did they plan to *do* with you?" breathed Georgette, her eyes growing enormous.

"I think they planned to hold me for ransom."

"And rape you too?" said Georgette in admiring horror.

"That too," said Imogene.

"Georgette!" cried her mother. "Ladies do not use the word 'rape'—it is indelicate."

"What *do* they call it?" Georgette was fascinated.

"They say"—Esthonie cast a rather hunted look about her and found no help from Imogene—"that a man forced his attentions upon them."

"Or that they were evilly *used*," supplied Virginie smugly.

Georgette shivered happily. "Jean Claude is all very well but I want a man like Captain van Ryker," she stated loftily. "Someone who will litter the Caribbean with bodies in my behalf!"

Her mother, vexed as the carriage gave a sudden jolt when it hit a piece of coral rock, turned on her menacingly. "I will paddle your bottom with my hairbrush if you say another word on the subject, Georgette! Be silent—and sit straight!"

Georgette's back stiffened even as her lower lip stuck out in a pout.

But Imogene was not looking at the governor's younger daughter at that moment. She was looking at Virginie, leaning back against the carriage seat and holding the baroque pearl up for inspection. They were just leaving the quay and a handsome young buccaneer leaning on a crutch had stopped to study them.

As she watched, Virginie gave him a brilliant smile, then

airily considered the pearl and turned kittenishly to cast a
slanted, inviting look at his face.

The young buccaneer got the message. The governor's
daughter was not priceless—but her price was high. Swearing
an inward oath that he would garner the pearls of the Indies
for her favors, he beamed and stood on one boot to wave his
crutch enthusiastically as the carriage swept by full of bright
billowing skirts and wide-brimmed hats and waving plumes.
With a self-satisfied expression, Virginie leaned back sensuously,
continuing to regard her baroque pearl with absorbed interest.

Imogene's delicate brows elevated. It occurred to her that if
Virginie stayed on Tortuga, she might not have to wait till
Christmas for her pearls. Indeed, she thought that fortune-
hunting Jean Claude might have met his match in Virginie.

And down the coast a longboat was just arriving that would
have grave consequences for them all.

CHAPTER 12

Virginie's wedding swept by Imogene in a haze. It was an evening wedding, held in the drawing room of the "governor's palace," a room reeking of fresh paint for Esthonie had not been able to resist having the room hurriedly painted lavender to complement the red and pink hibiscus and bougainvillaea blossoms in which the room had been draped for the occasion. The painters, all Spanish captives working out their two- or three-year terms in lieu of ransom, were still working while the flower decorations were being hung and propped up, and many of the waxy green leaves had been turned to lavender by coming into contact with a too hasty paintbrush. The painters were giving their last strokes as the first guests arrived. So the unfortunate wedding guests had now not only to brush off an occasional caterpillar or spider that fell upon satin shoulders from the flower garlands festooned from the ceiling—they had to be careful not to get too close to the walls else a smear of lavender paint would adorn whatever they were wearing. As a result, the guests tended to huddle in the middle of the big room for safety as a surprisingly dewy-eyed Virginie took her vows beside an erect—and for once entirely sober—Jean Claude.

Van Ryker and Imogene were almost late for the ceremony, for van Ryker was full of last-minute preparations and instructions. They would leave the wedding reception early, he told her. Imogene, with a concealing scarf thrown over her head, would proceed at once to the quay with Arne and be rowed out to the ship. Van Ryker meantime would saunter about the taverns, making himself very much in evidence, and at the last minute would slip out to the *Sea Rover*, which was anchored far out in the bay. Not till morning, it was hoped, would it be noticed that the great ship had sailed.

Imogene, looking glorious in tangerine silk over a rustling changeable taffeta petticoat that changed from gold to tangerine to flaming Chinese red as she walked, moved like a flame among the guests. Her peach-gloved hand held a heavy silver goblet with which to toast the bride. It was one of a dozen such goblets the van Rykers had sent over to the governor's house this afternoon, along with the bride's garters that Imogene had promised Esthonie she would send. An excited Virginie called her into her bedchamber to view how the new garters looked on her handsome legs. Imogene thought they were in execrable taste, more turquoise than blue, garnished with pink rosettes, and aglitter with gold and copper lace and brilliants as they were, but then what could one expect of Arne, who consorted with tavern wenches and trollops? And there had been no time to send him back to buy another pair. She made Virginie ecstatic by telling her she could keep them.

On any other night Imogene would have noticed that Virginie's smile was too bright, her ecstatic thanks for the gift of the garters bordering on the hysterical. But absorbed as she was with her own plans to leave Tortuga that night, Imogene did not notice that the governor's eldest daughter was fast reaching a state of panic about her impending wedding night.

Virginie stayed in her bedchamber after Imogene swished out in her tangerine silks, and studied her face in the mirror. Rather pale. Her mother had suggested rubbing on a bit of Spanish paper to brighten her cheeks and that was why she had retired here, calling to Imogene to accompany her and view the garters, but right now rouging seemed unimportant.

What her sister Georgette had said to her after they reached home this afternoon and fled to Virginie's room to escape the painters kept running through her mind.

"Are you going to undress yourself? Or let Jean Claude undress you?" Georgette had wondered, sinking down upon the bed.

Virginie had shrugged but Georgette was not to be put off. "I mean tonight. Your wedding night," she elaborated.

"I knew when you meant." Virginie looked away. "I haven't decided yet."

"Well, when you *do* decide, let me know. Or I shall worry about you all night, thinking about you up there alone with him."

"Oh, you will be the *first* to know!" said Virginie in a scathing tone.

Georgette ignored her sister's tone. "I shall expect to hear everything, you know. Tomorrow afternoon by the latest. For I expect," she added thoughtfully, "you will decide to sleep late—after so much exertion."

"*Everything?*" Virginie's dark brows shot up. "Really, Georgette!"

"Well, how *else* am I to know how it's done?" wailed Georgette.

It was on the tip of Virginie's tongue to say, *You can watch the cats, as I did!* But that would be to let Georgette realize that she was still a virgin, and she would never hear the last of *that*! She personally did not consider the cats' rendezvous, which she had watched pensively from her window one moonlit night, very exciting, but everyone made so much of that sort of thing that it *must* be worthwhile.

Big orange and white Malcolm had certainly enjoyed it. He had crouched on the paving stones of the courtyard with all his fur aquiver, and howled mournfully. Across from him Tiffin, a very independent female tabby, had crouched, watching him warily. After a few undecided moments she had answered Malcolm's howl with a demonic shriek.

Malcolm had roared back and run three paces nearer. Tiffin had opened her mouth and let forth a banshee wail—and retreated coyly two steps.

Virginie had watched fascinated as Malcolm gradually eased to within three feet of Tiffin, whose fur was fluffed out and who was watching him balefully from her big green eyes that flashed phosphorescent gold against the darkness.

There was a sudden furry melee as Malcolm rushed forward and pounced upon his lady, seizing her by the scruff of the neck with his big white teeth and holding her firmly as he worked his will. Virginie had nearly fallen out of the window trying to see better. All she could really see was Malcolm, with Tiffin hidden beneath. Both of them seemed to be howling wildly, but whether from rage or pain or joy, it was impossible to tell.

Suddenly her father had called up the stairs, "Virginie, are you up? Throw something at those cats!" He had not, she realized, been able to find the proper door key on the ring by Esthonie's bed, and was prevented from throwing anything sizable out the window himself by the decorative iron grill-work that prevented prowlers from entering.

"I will, Papa—as soon as I can find my shoes," called Virginie, never stirring from her place as she hung out the window watching that jumble of fur below.

The caterwauling continued—indeed it seemed to reach a peak of fury. And at that point, regretfully, for she had wanted to see the *dénouement* and learn whether they would part friends or foes, Virginie threw down one of her old slippers—being careful to miss the combatants, of course.

But the shoe landed close enough to disturb them and they were off into the night, yowling. Virginie never knew if they continued the encounter or not, for the sound dwindled away in the darkness.

The next time Tiffin came in for food—which was seldom for Tiffin was a good hunter and spent most of her time in the bush elsewhere—Virginie looked at the high-stepping tabby with a sigh; she wished she could ask Tiffin if she had enjoyed it or whether she regretted the whole thing. Virginie thought Tiffin lived in the pimento grove behind the church.

At least, she had once seen her carrying home a kitten from there. Tiffin had all her kittens away from home, obviously not trusting the energetic Tourailles to leave them alone until their eyes were opened. Once they were grown strong and playful, she would bring them back one by one in her mouth and deposit them carefully under the bush by the marble bench.

The French governor passed out kittens along with his letters of marque, and they were well received by the buccaneers, who had little on which to lavish affection on their voyages. They grew very fond of their ships' cats and gave them exotic names like Jolly Roger and Marooner and Pieces of Eight. Virginie sometimes thought that between them Malcolm and Tiffin had sired half the cats that kept the buccaneers' fleet free from rats.

She came back to what Georgette was saying.

"I said, aren't you going to *practice* undressing for your wedding night? You haven't much time, you know!"

"Why should I practice?" demanded Virginie. "I've been undressing all my life!"

Georgette sighed. "*I* practice all the time," she volunteered. "First I twirl about undoing my hooks and *then* I ease my bodice down over—"

"I do hope you remember to untie your sleeves first," put in her sister cuttingly.

"Oh, of course," said Georgette. She gave Virginie a tranquil look. "If you'd like to practice before *me*," she offered, "I could tell you how you look doing it. And what's awkward and what's not."

Virginie was half tempted to take her little sister up on that offer but it wouldn't do to let Georgette get the upper hand. "I shall probably let Jean Claude undress me," she said airily. "So much more romantic!"

"He'll ruin your hooks," predicted Georgette. "Don't say I didn't warn you!"

Virginie turned on her. "Maybe I won't go through with it, maybe I'll stalk out and refuse to marry him!"

"Of course you won't," said Georgette, picking up a mango and holding it up to the light to admire its color. "You'll marry him whether you want to or not—Mamma will see that you do!"

"Nonsense." Virginie sniffed.

But before supper, standing in front of the mirror, she had practiced what Georgette had mentioned, twirling around undoing her hooks. It had taken an unconscionably long time, she had decided—and one of the hooks had quite eluded her, leaving her in a half-dressed condition. Which must have looked ridiculous to Georgette when she had called down to her, asking her to come up and undo it.

And it would never do to look ridiculous tonight!

Virginie's reflection told her that her color had become indeed very high. Even Mamma would admit she did not need Spanish paper now!

Lifting her head higher to help allay her fears, Virginie ran downstairs to rejoin the company, who were happy to see her and lifted their glasses in bridal toasts. Virginie's gaze fled to Imogene—perhaps she should have asked *her* what to expect. She sighed, knowing that she had lost her chance to ask the buccaneer captain's lady.

Unaware of Virginie's predicament, Imogene clasped people's hands and smiled—and avoided going too near the freshly painted lavender walls. Her mind was so full of the details of leaving tonight that she found herself making polite conversation with no thought at all of what she was saying. It amused her that Esthonie, strikingly overdressed in stiff black brocade overlaid with gold tissue and black lace heavily adorned with gold brilliants, muttered darkly that Veronique must have been put out that the ceremony was being held so soon "before she could get her hooks into Jean Claude" and had not shown up for supper—in fact she had *ignored* the wedding! Well, she knew how to deal with *that*. She had instructed the servants not to go near Veronique's room until she came out and made a formal apology!

Imogene smiled and thought that some people were lucky in their timing. For Veronique it had all worked out. She imagined Veronique in the wine red velvet gown she herself had picked out for her and given to van Ryker to stow aboard *La Belle France*—too hot for the climate of the Caribbean, but Veronique was on her way to a colder climate where she would find velvet useful. And its deep decolletage would be a delight to a woman who had been forced for so long to wear gowns that almost hugged her chin! She had chosen too the foppish clothes to turn Diego into a French dandy, and added an enameled French snuffbox for good measure. She imagined Veronique and her Diego standing romantically by the taffrail in the moonlight watching the phosphorescent water glide by like shining silver—as she and van Ryker would be doing before the night was out. All of them gone while Esthonie and her household slept. . . .

She hoped Veronique would like the delicate black chemise

and the sheer black silk stockings and black satin garters she had packed beside the wine red gown—and the dainty black satin slippers. And the flowing night rail of black silk trimmed in black lace. She had been so jealous of Veronique, and her generous spirit had been moved to make up for it by giving Veronique a trousseau such as the Spanish girl might have chosen for herself; A deep vivid green dress ornamented with yards and yards of black braid for dusty travel in France from Marseilles to Paris. And dainty toilet articles, and perfume and ceruse and Spanish paper for rouging her cheeks—ah, she had forgotten nothing! And because Veronique was Spanish and would miss her homeland, she had included a lovely black silk shawl, thickly fringed and brilliantly embroidered with red and yellow flowers, and a flowing black lace mantilla and a high-backed Spanish comb. Veronique might not dare to wear that mantilla and comb where she was going—but she could wear them for private dinners at home with Diego and dream of the life they had lost.

For Imogene was deeply aware of the dangers Veronique and Diego faced. A man such as Don Luis would have agents everywhere, and Veronique's face, as van Ryker had once said, was memorable. She could only hope that Veronique's luck would hold.

Near her van Ryker was listening patiently to an English trader who was in Tortuga to fill his ship's hold with captured Spanish goods.

"I tell ye, sir," the man was saying, "Tortuga is a bastion against these Spanish marauders! A bastion, sir! Without Tortuga, we'd all have had our throats slit some fine night, not an English settler in the West Indies would be safe—aye, nor a French or a Dutch settler, either! We're beholden to ye, sir, for ye've made our lives safer." He blew-out his cheeks and looked at van Ryker admiringly. "They tell me ye're leaving us, and I've come to tell ye I hope 'tis not true. Egad, sir, what would the Indies be without ye?"

"Better perhaps," said van Ryker with the ghost of a smile. "But I'm leaving none so soon." He clapped the admiring fellow briskly on the shoulder. "Perhaps we'll have the chance to sup together later in the week."

Imogene heard and thought in wonderment how bold van Ryker was—and yet how cautious. He did not want even this enthusiastic gentleman to know that he sailed tonight. Not that he thought this English trader, who hailed from Barbados, would betray him to the Spanish—nor yet to such buccaneers as might wish to band together and make an attempt on his treasure. It was just his native caution, she told herself with an inward smile.

Little Dr. Argyll, looking a bit woozy with drink, came up and asked her to dance. He led her—stumbling only once—out upon the floor.

"I thought I saw Andy Layton lurking about the entrance as we arrived," Imogene told the doctor. "But I don't see either Andy or Cooper Layton here. Don't tell me Esthonie didn't invite them?"

"She invited them both," hiccuped Dr. Argyll. "But I didn't convey the invitation. I intend to hand them back to their father the way I got them—unmarried and unbetrothed. And if that young devil is sniffing around outside the house, I'll go out and send him home!"

He might have interrupted the dance to do just that, but that

Imogene laughingly dissuaded him. "I was probably mistaken," she said indulgently. "And, anyway, even if he is skulking about, what harm could he do Georgette out there?"

Dr. Argyll gave that owllike consideration and finally nodded his head with drunken dignity. "What harm? I do agree with you. What harm, indeed?" He gave her another whirl about the floor, sweeping her tangerine skirts perilously close to the fresh lavender paint on the walls.

Van Ryker was very gallant tonight, Imogene thought. Even for him, a man to whom gallantry was second nature. Over Dr. Argyll's shoulder she smiled at van Ryker, who was now dancing with the bride. He smiled back, handsome in dove gray silks laced with silver and with a diamond flashing in the frosty white Mechlin at his throat. An arresting figure . . . as always, she was proud of him. He looked carefree and young tonight, now that he was leaving Tortuga at last. He looked, she thought in amusement, as if he should be the bridegroom, for he far outshone Jean Claude. In his arms an excited Virginie spun out her big, flowing, lace-overlaid taffeta skirts and displayed the handsome white satin petticoat edged with point lace that Imogene had bestowed upon her as a going-away present.

The dance ended—a good thing, for Dr. Argyll was puffing with the heat and the exertion. He bowed with tipsy dignity and tottered away.

Esthonie's voice shrilled in her ear. "He's drunker than I've ever seen him."

"Who?" asked Imogene.

"Dr. Argyll, of course. And you know why, don't you? That trollop he's so enamored of, and who has kept him chained to Tortuga for she refuses to leave it, has run off with someone else at last. I suppose he's drowning his sorrows.''

Imogene gave the little doctor a sympathetic look. She saw that Gauthier was urging on him yet another glass. Perhaps he would find oblivion in wine, and tomorrow, when his world settled down, he would realize that Tortuga offered him nothing and seek passage back to Scotland where he belonged. She hoped so for she liked the little doctor and had never thought he belonged on rough buccaneer Tortuga.

''Do you know, those two Layton boys who are staying with him never even put in an appearance? And after being invited especially too! I shall not be so hospitable to their father after a slight like that!''

Imogene could have told Esthonie why the Laytons had not put in an appearance, but loyalty to the little Scots doctor forbade that. ''They are young,'' she said tolerantly, as if that excused everything.

Esthonie sniffed. ''Not too young to lurk about in the bushes! I saw that Andy Layton hanging about the house this afternoon, but he disappeared when I beckoned him to come closer.''

''You probably frightened him, Esthonie,'' laughed Imogene. ''He may have heard how quickly you arrange marriages!''

Esthonie gave her an uncertain look, but her expression softened as Virginie danced by with Jean Claude. ''They make a handsome couple, don't they?'' She was staring proudly at the bridal pair.

''Yes, they do.'' Imogene accepted a glass from a tray brought by one of the brightly turbaned servants.

''I shall hate to see them go. Do you know, Jean Claude

232

actually suggested they sail on the *Goodspeed* tonight? *Tonight!*'' Esthonie rolled her eyes.

Rushing home to spend the dowry! thought Imogene cynically, but she did not tell Esthonie that.

''I told him poor little Virginie should not lose her virginity on board a bouncing vessel!'' Esthonie sounded indignant, remembering the soft, giggle-smothering feather bed in which she had lost her own virginity—a full two years before she had met Gauthier!

''I don't imagine it will mean much to her *where* that event takes place,'' said Imogene ironically. And then to soften that she added quickly, ''I mean, it isn't *where* but who, Esthonie, that counts.''

Esthonie, poised to give her a withering look, was mollified. A slight frown crossed her face. ''How much do you think a girl needs to be told on the day she is wed?'' she asked bluntly.

''As much as she needs.'' Imogene gave Esthonie a wry look, for gossip had it that Virginie might well instruct her mother in such matters.

''Perhaps I had best have a talk with Virginie,'' said Esthonie uneasily. ''Before they retire.'' She heaved a sigh. ''Poor little Georgette. All this excitement has been too much for her. Do you think I was too hard on her about the pearls? She threw up—not half an hour ago! I would hate to think—''

''It was probably all the heavy food she ate at supper,'' laughed Imogene, who had observed that teenage Georgette consumed enormous amounts for one so thin.

''Yes, I suppose that was it. I told her to go to her room

and not to stir until she is quite recovered. Ah, here is Captain van Ryker to claim a dance with you.''

Van Ryker offered her a gray silk arm and swept her away. ''What was Esthonie looking so perturbed about?'' he wondered.

''She is contemplating instructing Virginie in the art of sex,'' laughed Imogene. ''Do you think she is too late?''

''I would doubt it.'' Van Ryker looked across the room at the flushed-faced bride who was fast acquiring a hunted look in her eyes. ''I rather think Virginie's vaunted wantonness is a fake.'' He gave her a knowing smile.

''You could be right,'' said Imogene thoughtfully. ''Anyway, Esthonie is obviously having second thoughts about pushing her daughter unadvised into the arms of a *roué*.''

''She should fare very well in the arms of a *roué*.'' Van Ryker's brows rose. ''Better than in the arms of some untried youth!''

Their eyes met in perfect agreement—and amusement.

Meanwhile, Esthonie had sought out her daughter and was having—perilously close to some paint-spattered green leaves—a belated talk with her.

''Virginie,'' said her mother, her voice necessarily low, for people were dancing by. ''I know I have been late in counseling you, but I cannot caution you too strongly: Do *not* let Jean Claude get the upper hand!''

Virginie, who had been dwelling in her mind more on the physical aspects of losing her virginity, looked harassed. ''How am I to avoid it?'' she asked plaintively, for it seemed to her that men—except for Papa, of course, and he was the exception—always seemed to take *and hold* the upper hand.

''By taking firm measures,'' said her mother impressively.

She was thinking bitterly of that Josie Dawes she was always seeing Gauthier with down on the quay. How a woman of *that* sort could appeal to a man of Gauthier's fine sensibilities she could not imagine. Ah, she should have taken a firm hand with Gauthier early on!

"What *sort* of measures, Mamma?" Virginie was growing impatient. Her bridal bed was growing nearer by the minute and she could use all the advice she could get.

Dragged back to Virginie's immediate problem, Esthonie asked sharply, "Did Veronique tell you *nothing*? About the—ways of men?"

Virginie sighed. "Veronique is Georgette's special friend. They are always together, laughing, talking—I am never sure about what."

Too bad! thought her mother. Veronique could have had her uses at a moment like this. Instead, she had chosen to ignore the wedding altogether! Across the room she noted that two of her guests—one a dissolute aristocrat who made his living arranging ransoms, the other a cardsharp who had been banished from a good county family back in England—were beginning to shout at each other. Red-faced and angry, their voices rose clearly over the sound of the harpsichord and the viola and the stamping feet of the dancers. In another moment swords might be drawn and Virginie's wedding might be remembered for the amount of blood shed rather than the number of toasts drunk to the bride's health!

"I am sure you will manage," Esthonie told Virginie vaguely, keeping her eye on what was going on across the room. "There is really nothing to it. Just—" Her voice rose to a shriek as the ransom arranger gave the cardsharp a dusting across the teeth with his fist, and the cardsharp slid back with a snarl and snaked out his rapier. "Gauthier!" shrieked Esthonie. "Do something!"

But it was van Ryker who did something. He was suddenly there with his blade out, encouraging the pair of them to settle their differences tomorrow in gentlemanly fashion beneath the oaks instead of here tonight on the ballroom floor. After a few wild moments during which Esthonie rushed forward and clung to Gauthier's arm with a numbing grip, wondering if van Ryker's suave words would work, both gentlemen put away their swords and settled down to serious drinking in different parts of the room.

Esthonie forgot Virginie, allowing herself to be claimed for a dance, and Gauthier bore down on Imogene, expressing his relief to her that van Ryker had acted so quickly.

Imogene could hardly refuse to dance with her host. The plump, panting governor whirled her away. And then another partner claimed her. And another. The music of the harpsichord and the viola tinkled on. She made polite conversation, she danced—and she kept an eye on the clock. She wished van Ryker would rescue her. But van Ryker—and now her gaze swept the room searching for him—was nowhere in sight. He had been missing now for some twenty minutes and the party, full of Tortuga hangers-on, was beginning to wear on her nerves. She knew she must endure it, must wait until nearly midnight to make her escape, but this rather tawdry wedding was not the way she had meant to leave Tortuga. She would have liked to slip away in the dusk through the flower-scented air and skim with her memories across the silvery phosphorescence of Cayona Bay and let that tall ship, the *Sea Rover*, take her where it would. But, obviously, it was not to be.

She took another goblet of wine and turned to see Esthonie approaching.

Esthonie's gaze traveled up and down the flamelike gown Imogene was wearing. Why was it, she asked herself, that Imogene always looked marvelous? *Surely* she must have off days like the rest of us! But Esthonie had never caught her looking otherwise than wonderful; it was most upsetting. As she reached Imogene's side, her dissatisfied gaze traveled to the blaze of topaz and diamonds at Imogene's neck, which were only matched by the large topaz and diamond pendants hanging from her ears and the brilliant emerald that flashed from her peach-gloved finger.

"Your jewels are *stunning*," she said enviously.

Imogene had at first intended to wear the van Rappard diamonds but now she was glad she had not. They were so overpowering it was best to let them repose in their little jewel case. If ever she were presented at court—which was unlikely—she would wear them. In the meantime, the topaz and diamond jewelry flashed brilliantly and complemented her striking gown.

"Is that a new ring?" Esthonie seized her hand and studied it.

"Yes, it is. Van Ryker gave it to me yesterday." She smiled down at the square-cut emerald set in gold—an exact duplicate of the one he wore himself. *If ever we become separated and you should need me,* he had said earnestly, *send me this ring and I will know the message comes from you. I will do the same.* She had tried to laugh it off as

237

melodramatic but she had been touched all the same. Now she touched the ring gently to her cheek. "I intend to wear it always," she said softly.

"But then you have so many jewels! Lord knows when you will find time to wear them all!"

Imogene was spared a retort, for van Ryker showed up at just that moment. She knew it must be near midnight.

"Esthonie," she said apologetically, "you must forgive me, I have a splitting headache. I have asked van Ryker to take me home!"

Van Ryker had been right. Getting away from the governor's house proved easy. Perhaps Esthonie was even a little glad not to have Virginie's wedding reception overshadowed by the beauteous Imogene!

Van Ryker took her outside where the music and the laughter from the "governor's palace" drifted out to them. The wind sighed through the palm fronds and the night was full of stars. Black velvet studded with diamonds. Imogene breathed deep of the heady air.

"On a night like this," she murmured ruefully, "it seems a shame to leave Tortuga."

"We cannot put it off," he said. "Arne will take you to the ship."

From somewhere Arne materialized, carrying a yellow silk shawl.

"Aren't you coming with me, van Ryker?"

"No, I want to close up the house. A few details. Go with Arne. I'll be along."

He swung away from her, a tall broad-shouldered figure disappearing into the night. Imogene stood and watched him go. Then she drew the light yellow silk shawl over her head to conceal her bright hair and the blaze of her jewels and accompanied Arne down toward the quay.

They were halfway there when Arne stopped. "That little jewel case of yours," he said suddenly. "I saw it in the hall when I left—I'll wager the Captain will pass it by and leave it."

And that little jewel case contained the van Rappard diamonds!

"Oh, he mustn't leave it, Arne," exclaimed Imogene. She would never be able to wrest those jewels away from Esthonie once she occupied the house. Esthonie would be vague, she would say she had not found them, someone else must have taken them. "Go back and get them, Arne."

Arne hesitated. "The Cap'n said I wasn't to leave you. Not even for a minute."

"I'll go back with you, then. We can catch van Ryker there if we hurry. Perhaps we'll meet him coming this way—with the jewel case."

Arne grunted and the two of them set off through the darkness toward the house.

It loomed up before them, that massive pile of lime-washed stone that she was seeing for the last time. A pattern of waving shadows played across it as palm trees bent in the moonlight, driven by the trade winds. Imogene paused wistfully for a moment. Since she had married van Ryker she had really known no other home than this and now all was to change.

Silent and pensive now, she let big Arne push the well-oiled iron grillwork door open; in silence she moved into the

239

dark familiar hall vaguely illuminated by moonlight filtering down into the inner court where the fountain tinkled. No, not entirely illuminated by that. There was a light burning in the chart room. Van Ryker was still here, then!

Moving quickly and soundlessly on her satin slippers, Imogene moved toward that light and stood in the door of the chart room.

Like the rest of the house, the chart room had been evacuated. Left in it was only a rude table, adjudged too insignificant to move, and a long red velvet divan that Esthonie had fancied and which Gauthier had asked to be included in the sale of the house. Tonight a single candle burned on that small table, stuck into a bottle, tavern fashion. The red divan's back was to her and the rest of the room was bare.

But on that divan was such a tableau as caused Imogene to stop short, her breath catching in her throat.

A man and a woman reclined on that red divan. Their backs were turned toward her but it was easy to see who they were.

The man was unmistakably van Ryker. That dark head she knew so well, the long sinewy arm in gray silk with a ruffle of white lace at the wrist, the fine bronzed hand with its square-cut emerald ring that matched her own.

But that familiar sinewy arm was loosely thrown about a woman who was equally unmistakable. A spill of shining black curls in a distinctive coiffure that seemed to cry out for a high-backed Spanish comb cascaded down the woman's long neck, over her black satin back, and spilled over the carved back of the long divan. Imogene saw that one of her slender languorous arms was extended and lay caressingly along van Ryker's broad silk-clad shoulder. The long fingers that toyed lightly with a lock of his dark hair were encased in black gloves. But between the glove top and the beginning of a spill of black lace from the woman's elbow-length sleeve was a small expanse of creamy skin—and the mark of a strawberry heart was plain upon it.

Veronique.

Veronique and van Ryker trysting before the *Sea Rover* sailed.

A kind of thunder roared through Imogene's head. It had all been a lie, then. . . . Veronique had not gone anywhere with Diego. She had come *here* to meet her lover—as she must have been doing in the pimento grove every day. Esthonie had said men craved variety and here before her was the solid proof of those words!

As she watched, frozen into immobility, beyond speech, that dark head she had often stroked so lovingly bent toward the gleaming mass of black curls. He was going to kiss her!

A strangled protest rose in Imogene's throat—and was instantly stilled by the hand that fled to her mouth. Everything in her revolted. Warring forces roiled within her—dismay and disbelief. Veronique was not—*could not be*—van Ryker's mistress. Van Ryker loved *her*, she was sure of it. His eyes, his face, his body told her that every day, every night. No, this was something else. . . .

What, then? In sudden shock, she understood.

A feeling cold as death stole over her.

This was revenge.

Van Ryker, the master planner, the man who thought

241

everything out, was taking his final revenge on Don Luis of Spain. With cold-blooded premeditation he was seducing the fiery young wife Don Luis had sought to isolate from the world. When he had taken Don Luis's woman and made her his own, then left her and sailed away, that revenge would be complete.

And tonight in the great cabin of the *Sea Rover* he would embrace his wife as if nothing had happened. Fresh from his triumph over Don Luis, he would take his wife in his arms. . . . The lips that had pressed Veronique's full sensuous ones would press *her* lips, the exploring fingers that had brought forth moans of rapture from Veronique would then rove over her own body—*oh, no, they would not!*

Quivering, she backed away from the sight of them. She would have crashed into Arne, who stood waiting outside, save that he reached out and caught her. As he let her go he opened his mouth to speak but she motioned him to silence. The big man inclined his head in deference to her wishes and followed her, stumping along on his coin-blazoned wooden leg, as she moved unsteadily down the street.

Around them was the warmth of the Tortuga night, wrapping them breathlessly as a blanket. A breath of air from the sea ruffled Imogene's fair hair and found tendrils stuck to a forehead gone damp with the turbulence of her emotions. A large land crab, disturbed by her footsteps, scuttled away from her slippers with a rattle. Normally Imogene would have shied away from the awkward creature, but tonight her tangerine skirts swept by it as if it did not exist. Her heart was too full, her feelings too tumbled, to care.

They had walked halfway to the quay before she could make her voice obey her.

"Arne," she asked shakily, "has the *Goodspeed* sailed?"

"Not yet." Arne peered ahead. "I can see her lights up ahead. But she sails with the tide."

Like the *Sea Rover*. . . . sailing with the tide.

Imogene came to such a sudden stop that Arne almost ran into her. In the moonlight she had drawn herself up and her blue eyes flashed dangerously. He would tell his captain later how fiery she had looked, standing there.

"Then you'll take me aboard her, Arne. No"—she held up her hand to ward off his protestations—"I'll brook no interference in this matter. Van Ryker has already paid for my passage aboard her and he told me the *Goodspeed*'s captain refused to refund the money. I will take up that passage now!"

Before Arne could reason with her, she was again moving toward the quay. Her feet began to pick up speed, putting distance between her and that house with its scarring memory.

"But what'll I tell the Cap'n?" cried Arne in real distress.

"Tell him—" Feelings too overwhelming for words drowned her voice. *Betrayer, betrayer*—the words hammered a litany in her heart. "Tell him I've gone," she choked. "And that I'll not be back. Tell him I'm leaving him. Tell him that, Arne."

"But your baggage, my lady!" gasped practical Arne.

"I care not if I wear this same dress all the way to Plymouth!" she cried.

And suddenly it was all too much. It crashed in on her in a single mighty wave, sweeping away all her reserves. She gave a great gasping sob and flung away the light yellow silk shawl that was meant to obscure her glitter and her worth.

Picking up her light skirts, she began to run, sobbing. Tears streaked her face and the wind felt cold where they fell. She was running away from all that she had loved, down toward the quay, and those who saw her pass stopped to stare, jaws dropping. For she passed them like the perfumed wind, like a wraith in the night, a woman with flying golden hair and flying flame-colored skirts, ablaze with topazes and diamonds.

Her present destination was the *Goodspeed*, about to take sail. But her real destination was much farther than that.

She would go anywhere—anywhere that led her away from van Ryker!

BOOK II
The Runaway Lovers

Jealousy drove deep the knife—
'Twas hurt that sent her forth.
Fast away from her southern love
The tall ship carries her north!

PART ONE
The Masquerade

Noble oak and swaying pine
In the dark may seem similar trees,
And a wench may be mistook for a queen
'Neath the moon in a sheer chemise!

The High Seas
1661
CHAPTER 13

Dawn—that swift hot dawn of the tropics—burst over the wild blue wastes of the Caribbean. It gilded a flight of gulls streaming out over the ocean to feed. And it picked out the lone figure of a woman leaning on the rail of the *Goodspeed* as that stout merchantman careened over the waters on the long journey back to England. The freshening breeze that came with the dawn was a relief to the early-rising passengers, who had tossed and turned on their bunks in the sultriness of the night. But although it blew the light silk skirts of her tangerine ball gown and ruffled her golden hair into a wild halo, making her a remarkable and striking figure aboard that staid ship, Imogene never felt it. She was wrapped up in her own somber thoughts, lost in a world that did not include the *Goodspeed* or its sober crew.

The other passengers nudged and whispered. They gave her

area of the deck a wide berth—but Imogene was not aware of that either. There was some reason for their wariness, for had she not burst aboard weeping last night, making a great scene and demanding a cabin just as the ship cast off?

"I am Imogene van Ryker," she had cried dramatically. "My passage has been fully paid and I *demand* to be taken aboard and transported to England!"

With an alacrity that had surprised the passengers, Captain Bagtry had agreed. One might almost have thought he had been waiting for this late arrival, so swiftly did he cast anchor after she came aboard.

Why had van Ryker done it? Over and over Imogene had asked herself that through that long night. Was revenge then so sweet? Or . . . were Veronique's slender arms even more tempting?

Whatever had driven him, everything was over between them now. She had left him, the dark buccaneer who had swept into her life with the force of a gale and swept her along with him into what had seemed at the time such a glittering world. She no longer needed Esthonie's warnings or van Ryker's protestations—she had seen the truth with her own eyes. And been shattered by it.

A false dawn had appeared and then the sun had come up and she was hazily aware through her grief that there were people walking about, muttering when they looked at her. They must think her actions exceedingly strange. She looked down at her fluttering tangerine skirts and realized that she was still wearing her ball gown, still glittering with jewels. They would assume her to be a runaway from Tortuga, as indeed she was.

But they would not guess the reason.

Moving stiffly, she left the rail and walked slowly to her cabin. She leaned against the door, loath to go in, and told herself she must try to sleep—and after that, to think. There was nothing for her now, nothing left, and it seemed to her in her despair that no man had ever been true to her. Not Stephen, the copper-haired lover who had deserted her in the Scilly Isles, not Verhulst who had loved her madly and nearly killed her with his jealousy, not van Ryker who had seemed so steady and so true.

All of them, faithless in the end. . . .

A dry laugh crackled. She realized vaguely it had come from her own parched throat. Annoyed that she should make such a sound, she flung open the door.

She had expected an empty cabin with naught but a blanket on the bunk and perhaps a rude chair and table. What greeted her made her grasp at the cabin door in shock.

It was obviously the best cabin on the ship—after the captain's—that met her gaze. Upon the wooden table in the center of the room reposed a large silver bowl filled with fresh fruit—mangoes and grapefruit and oranges and limes. A tall stalk of bananas graced one corner and there were open kegs of golden lemons, bright oranges, deep green limes. Upon the bunk was spread no ordinary ship's mattress but a fluffy feather bed, spread with a handsome blue coverlet that she recognized, and three pillows. Two blankets of fine white wool reposed at the foot against the colder nights that would come on the North Atlantic. And—there was a leathern trunk. *Her* trunk.

With an exclamation of surprise, she ran to it and threw open the heavy curved lid with its shining brass fittings.

Inside she saw a mirror, a silver comb and brush. But there were fresh undergarments as well, a dressing gown of soft rose-colored wool against any chill, a light blue silk shawl and another of fine white wool to wear on deck. There were perfume vials and several bottles of fine wine. And—thoughtfully—a beautiful dress she had never worn. The fabric had been of van Ryker's own choosing, a gift to her from the buccaneer goods on the quay. It was of sky blue velvet, simple and tailored and figure-fitting, with a wide skirt, a deep-cut neckline held together artfully with an amethyst clasp, and a blue silk petticoat embroidered in shimmering silver roses. The big sleeves too were heavily embroidered in silver.

She recoiled from that dress. It reminded her both of Stephen, who had loved her in blue, and of van Ryker, who felt the same way. Angrily she pushed the dress back in the trunk. She would remain dressed in her tangerine ball gown rather than wear it!

As she did so, the glitter of gold caught her eye. Slowly, almost in fear, she pushed aside the finery and peered into the bottom of the trunk. There, underneath the perfumes and toilet articles and several bottles of fine wine, was a heavy gold money chain, enough to keep her for years.

White-faced now, she sank to her knees beside the leather trunk and felt like ice in her hands the smooth cold metal of the money chain. Its presence had for her a bitter significance.

Van Ryker had cast her out. Here indeed was the evidence of it.

He had found another woman to share his life but—his was a handsome nature. He had spared Imogene a confrontation, spared himself recriminations and explanations—he had let her see with her own eyes what he intended, knowing full well what she would do about it.

He must have asked the *Goodspeed*'s captain to wait sailing on her sure arrival, knowing she would fly like an arrow toward the fastest escape route once she had seen him with Veronique.

Now, stunned, she realized he had *contrived* for her to see him with the Spanish woman, *he had staged it*! To give her a way out. So she could leave him of her own will, proudly, defiantly—instead of being cast aside as other less thoughtful buccaneers cast aside their women.

Doubtless at this moment Veronique's dark curls reposed on van Ryker's pillow!

A sob caught in her throat.

She flung herself down on the bunk but sleep refused to come. Instead, memories chased each other around her mind, making her feel strangely disoriented. Memories of perfumed nights in the arms of her dark buccaneer, memories of long sultry wonderful days spent lying naked beside him on some strip of isolated white beach in Tortuga, or walking proudly beside him through admiring crowds on Cayona's quay, memories of the way it had been . . . before Veronique with her long legs and her restless gestures and her challenging amber eyes had come over the horizon like a lean pirate ship and taken van Ryker by storm.

Galled by the thought, Imogene jumped up and paced frenziedly about the cabin.

Abruptly her footsteps slowed. It had occurred to her suddenly that something was missing.

The van Rappard diamonds! She had forgotten all about them. They reposed either in the hall of their house on Tortuga—where avid-eyed Esthonie would stumble upon them. Or they had been stowed aboard the *Sea Rover*, where Veronique would find them a foil for her own dark blazing beauty. A bitter laugh welled up in Imogene's throat. Either way, some other woman would wear them.

The cabin was too oppressively small to contain such large emotions. Again she sought the deck.

And bumped into Captain Bagtry. "Ah, I was just seeking you. Mistress—Tremayne, is it?" And when she frowned, he jogged her memory with "That is the name Captain van Ryker said I should call you, but when you came aboard last night crying out that you were Madame van Ryker!" He gave an expressive shrug. "I am afraid your secret is out."

"No matter," she said wearily. "I *am* Madame van Ryker. Let the world know it!"

Captain Bagtry pulled at his pointy brown beard. He cleared his throat. "The man who brought you aboard handed me a note before he left. He said it was from Captain van Ryker and that I was to give it to you the minute the ship cleared Cayona Bay. He left and I was just sticking the note into my doublet when"—he looked sheepish—"I saw that little Miller lad had climbed the railing and was about to fall into the sea. I leaped forward to seize him and when I looked for the note later I could not find it. I fear the note must have fallen into the sea, instead of the lad."

So van Ryker had thought to pen her a good-bye. . . .

"It's all right," she told the captain dully. "I know what was in the message."

Captain Bagtry nodded and left her and Imogene, painfully, in her mind, worded the message van Ryker might have written her: *You will be better off without me*—yes, that was what he would have said. *You do not believe it now, but you will come to realize it later.*

And he had sent her off exactly as he had meant to—with one trunk and a blue dress and a money chain. And kept the van Rappard diamonds, like the buccaneer he was.

All her lovely clothes would be worn by another woman— just as another woman would admire her beautiful marquetry long-case clock. Another woman would wear the jewels that had in a way been her dowry—the van Rappard diamonds, gift of her tragic first husband.

But it was not the loss of those things that dulled her eyes and made her stare straight ahead of her, past the whispering passengers. It was the loss of the dangerous man who had filled her life and her heart.

From the taffrail of the *Sea Rover*, the object of all this travail considered through a glass—for the distance was too great to see her with a naked eye—the dipping white sails of the merchantman up ahead. He noted with approval that the *Goodspeed*'s captain held his course well.

He lowered the glass and turned a grim face toward his own ship.

Van Ryker had reason to be grim. He was not proud of himself this day. Last night he had tossed restlessly, unable to sleep, his mind and his heart filled with thoughts of the woman who would have been clasped in his arms, save for his own conniving.

He had tricked Imogene.

Aware of Georgette's obsession with pearls, he had sought the girl out and made a bargain with her. If she would pose as Veronique, complete to unique hairdo and heart-shaped birthmark duplicated by the use of the Spanish paper women used for rouge, if she would don the black satin gown Veronique so favored, and slip away from the wedding party shortly before midnight and accompany him to his house for just a few minutes—

At this point Georgette had interrupted. Having leaped to the natural conclusion that van Ryker was setting up a rendezvous with her and wanted her disguised as Veronique so she could safely come and go from the governor's house, she gave him a melting look. For already she could see herself replacing Imogene, set up in splendor in the house her mother so coveted. "Would not some tavern be better?" she suggested. "Or some house in the town where we are less likely to be interrupted?"

Van Ryker had given this presumptuous miss an impatient look.

"I do not set out to seduce you, Georgette," he said bluntly. "You will but *pretend* that I am courting you and afterward I will personally escort you back to your father's house. Safe and unmolested."

A petulant frown had creased Georgette's creamy forehead at this brusque rejection of her young charms. "I have other things to do," she said loftily, "than play games with you, Captain van Ryker. But," she added in a spiteful voice, "I think your wife might be interested to know that you had asked me."

The coldness that stole over van Ryker's dark features

chilled Georgette. "I would not do that if I were you," he said silkily. "For if I hear that you have spoken to Imogene about it—governor's daughter or no—I will lift up your skirts and spank that white bottom of yours until it is cherry red!"

Georgette paled. She had no doubt van Ryker would do exactly what he said. She sidled away from him in panic.

"I but seek to play a trick on my wife, who is jealous of Veronique," van Ryker explained. "And since you have the same height and coloring, and are a talented actress"—he flung this in ironically—"I thought of you."

Georgette gave him an uncertain frown. He had called her a talented actress! She thought of Cousin Nanette, dancing through life across the Paris stage.

"Of course there is a string of pearls in it for you," he added casually.

Pearls! Avarice flared in Georgette's dark eyes. "Let me see them!" she cried. "Of course I will do it!" And then, to save face, "I did not realize it was but a trick on your wife, Captain van Ryker," she added hastily. "Or of course I would have said yes immediately."

"Of course," agreed van Ryker gravely. "The pearls you may select for yourself from among the strands Stoddard has down at the quay. You know who I mean?"

Georgette nodded raptly, and entered with enthusiasm into the planning of the venture.

Now, from the taffrail, van Ryker thought wryly that Georgette had indeed flung herself into the part, stretching herself seductively upon the long divan, extending a tantalizing gloved arm across the back. He had personally pulled that glove down far enough to display the heart-shaped birthmark rubbed onto that arm with Spanish paper. He had wished they could dispense with the gloves, which threatened to creep up, but Georgette's young and slightly grubby hands were easily differentiated from Veronique's long slender ones. They had stuffed the fingertips of Veronique's gloves with cotton at the last minute and made the picture complete. Georgette had meticulously copied Veronique's hairstyle. The black satin dress was a shade too tight and perhaps an inch too long but lying on the divan with the back of the divan concealing most of her thin young figure, who could see that?

It had gone well. Perhaps too well. At moments she had seemed almost real to him as Veronique—probably, he told himself wryly, because she yearned so much to be like Veronique.

He wondered idly if he would overtake *La Belle France* and see in the distance the ship that carried Veronique and Diego to Marseilles. For it had been with a sense of triumph that he had watched her clear Cayona Bay.

CHAPTER 14

As the merchantman *La Belle France* cleared Cayona Bay on her long voyage to Marseilles that morning of what was to be Virginie's wedding day, the woman who had called herself Veronique Fondage when she was a houseguest of Tortuga's French governor—but was in reality Maria Theresa del Rio de Guarda, duquesa of Sedalia-Catalonia and runaway wife of Don Luis Alvarez—was standing by the taffrail, leaning against the strong figure of Diego Navarro, who had an arm clasped about her shoulders. His dark head was inclined toward hers in a most loving way.

Veronique was dressed in a strikingly low-cut, wine red velvet gown of van Ryker's providing, and her hair was arranged differently, swept back so that only one "heartbreaker" curl hung over each ear, and she had cut a fashionable fringe of bangs across her forehead. For van Ryker had warned her that she must look as different as possible, so that Don Luis's agents would not be able to thrust a miniature painting of her into the hands of those people she met from now on and have them instantly identify her by her distinctive hairstyle and manner of dress. Unjeweled in Tortuga, she had dipped into her jewel case, which van Ryker had sent aboard, and was now wearing a blaze of rubies—and they were vastly becoming against her pale olive skin.

Diego too looked strikingly different. He had lost the rakish—indeed, somewhat sinister—look of a Spanish officer, emissary of that mighty grandee, Don Luis Alvarez, duque of Sedalia-Catalonia, and was got up as an elegant French cavalier, in doublet and trousers of rich viridian green satin. The lime gold silk of the lining showed fashionably through his slashed sleeves, there were lime silk rosettes at his garters, a spill of frosty Mechlin at his throat and cuffs—for van Ryker had spared no expense in outfitting his gallant former adversary. And if the clothes were a bit too flamboyant for Diego's taste, he told himself that too was a part of his disguise, for he must learn henceforth to think of himself as a French aristocrat, with a Frenchman's elegant taste in clothes.

Such a pair could hardly escape attention. Anyone could see they were lovers and the other passengers gave them indulgent glances, for had not Captain Ducroire told them that Monsieur and Madame de Jonquil were still honey-mooners—indeed, their wedding trip to Martinique had been unpleasantly interrupted when their ship had been taken by the Spanish and they had found themselves briefly captives of the Spaniards. Was it any wonder after such an experience that upon being rescued they should elect to proceed not to their original destination of Martinique but back to their native France by the first available vessel, which had turned out to be his own *La Belle France*?

The passengers had agreed heartily with the wisdom of such a move and the honeymooning de Jonquils' name was on everybody's lips, for the distinctive pair had attracted much notice. Many speculative looks were given them. And one of those passengers, a fragile lady in elegant plum silks and spiderweb lace, named Mademoiselle Pernaud, who was traveling with her maidservant, gazed at them longest of all, and her gaze was sad.

"L'amour," she murmured. *"Mon Dieu,* how marvelous it is. . . ." There was desolation in her voice—and with reason. For Mademoiselle Pernaud was frail-looking for a reason: she was wasting away. The handsome gown that now hung on her thin body had fitted her well but two short months ago. Mademoiselle Pernaud was sister to the French governor of Martinique and she was returning home to France to die, for the doctors had given her but a few months to live. Now her wistful gaze caressed the lovers. "If only I . . ." She let the thought trail off and turned her head away from the sight of those two striking and romantic figures that seemed to blend in the morning light, and gazed instead out across the vivid turquoise wastes of the Caribbean.

Seeing her lips move, her watchful maid hurried up. "Did you speak, Mademoiselle?" she asked anxiously. "Do you wish me to bring you something?"

"No, Colette." What Mademoiselle Pernaud wished for, anxious little Colette could not bring her—the gift of life. Poor Maurice, her brother. He had accused her of not wanting to live! It was an expression of his burning disappointment in her, for over the years Mademoiselle Pernaud, who in her youth had been blessed with a rare and fragile beauty, had managed to reject the advances of half the noblemen of France—indeed, she had rejected them all, he said, to moon over the memory of a tiresome Huguenot who had managed to get himself killed in Brittany! He had hoped that this sea voyage to so exotic a place as Martinique would at last make her forget Andre and take a "normal" interest in life. If she would have none of the Frenchmen at home, perhaps she would become interested in one of the French planters who were even now carving out island empires on the beautiful volcanic island of Martinique.

But Maurice's plans for his sister had not worked out. Her lovely sad face had not brightened at the dazzling sight of Mont Pelèe towering against the sky. And although she was fond of her brother and had greeted both him and his pregnant wife affectionately, she had hardly bothered to sniff the flowers that overran his beautiful gardens in Fort-de-France. Indeed, she had taken little interest in anything, passing her days as if exhausted, lying recumbent upon a chaise lounge in his sunny loggia, being fanned by an impassive black servant. Nor had she evinced any joy at the succession of hopeful— and single—planters who had journeyed to the governor's residence to make a leg to her and gallantly offer to show her their handsome plantations. Not a single such invitation had she accepted. Indeed, the governor told his pregnant wife in disgust, his sister would be an old maid to the end of her days.

When a few weeks before her sudden weight loss had

become alarming, the doctors had been called, but they gave conflicting diagnoses. Her alarmed brother had been for sending for a doctor from France, but Mademoiselle Pernaud, who had never been a burden to anyone in her life and was determined not to become one now, had vetoed that suggestion. It was easier for her to go back to France to see a doctor, she had told him gently, than to have one sent out. But when she had kissed her brother good-bye as she boarded *La Belle France,* she had known it was for the last time.

Mademoiselle Pernaud did not understand her condition any better than did the puzzled doctors of Martinique, but she was shrewd enough to project the outcome. No one knew better than herself that she was going home to France to die. She hoped only that she would have time—and strength—to make the journey to Brittany to place a last wreath of flowers on Andre's grave, where he had lain these dozen years past.

Colette's timid voice interrupted her reverie. "The de Jonquils," she suggested hopefully, "appear to be very aristocratic." For Colette, who was devoted to Mademoiselle, was well aware that Mademoiselle had resisted Esthonie Touraille's effusive invitations in Tortuga to attend dinners and balls, claiming quietly that her health was so poor she dare not leave the ship. *I will not spend my last days in such company,* she had told Colette contemptuously. *Mon Dieu, what a common woman she is! And did you see how horribly overdressed she was? Going on and on about her husband being the governor, as if to equate him with my brother! Why, this is nothing but a buccaneer island and her husband hardly better than they!* Dutifully, Colette had nodded. Indeed it was impossible to overlook what Esthonie Touraille had been wearing the day she had called—all dancing gold and jet and inappropriately placed rosettes and braid and ribands. Plump Esthonie was not *chic* and elegant like Mademoiselle!

"You are right, Colette, the de Jonquils do look very pleasant," Mademoiselle Pernaud sighed. "Perhaps in a day or two, when they can take their eyes off each other for a few moments, I will invite them to share a glass of port with me."

Colette looked pleased, for the governor's last instructions to her had been, *Try to help my sister to find friends, bring her out of this despondency for it may well be the end of her.* And then he had muttered something under his breath about that damned Huguenot being the root cause of all this! Colette had nodded wisely. She had been jilted by a butcher's helper back in France—indeed, it was for that reason she had been willing to accept this journey to the islands, which she had always thought of as the outer rim of civilization. Colette knew what it was to love and lose—and her heart had gone out to fragile Mademoiselle Pernaud, so lovely and so lost. She had curtsied to the frowning governor, agreed earnestly to do her best by his sister, and now, aboard *La Belle France*, was doing her best to interest Mademoiselle in something—at this moment it was the de Jonquils.

Standing by the rail, that lady of many names who now called herself Veronique de Jonquil, snuggled closer to her lover's broad chest. "It has happened," she exulted. "We are on our way! Oh, Diego, we are going to have our chance at happiness at last."

"You must remember to call me Jacques," he reminded her gently.

"And *you* must remember to speak to me in French," she countered, giving him a smile of great tenderness.

Diego's strong arm around her tightened. "I will make you happy, Veronique. That much I promise you," he said hoarsely.

She gave him a lightsome answer. "Of course we will be happy. We will live on love and play all day in the orange groves—" Her voice came to an abrupt halt. The de Jonquils' eventual destination was Paris, which she had heard was cold and rainy. It came to her with force that she would not see the orange groves of Valencia again.

Diego felt her sudden inward quiver—just as he always seemed to catch her thoughts, so in tune with this tense blazing beauty was he.

"Perhaps we will yet win through to the orange groves, Veronique," he promised recklessly.

"No." Sadness stole over Veronique's beautiful aquiline features for a moment. "We will never see them again, Diego, or walk in Spanish sunlight, or see our homes again. Our sons will never take their rightful places in the land of their heritage. We will forever be wanderers, cast out."

"Only while Don Luis lives," said Diego grimly. "Then we will marry, and return with some wild story." *Which may or may not be believed.*

"He will live forever!" she burst out. "Oh, how can fate be so cruel? Why was I forced into marriage with a tyrant?"

"A moment ago," he reminded her dryly, but there was a twist to his own lips as he spoke, "you were congratulating yourself that we had got this far."

"That is true, Diego." With a mercurial change of mood that was part of her charm, Veronique turned to him with a sunny smile. "The sun is warm, the sky is blue, and I am full of hope! At this moment I know in my heart that we will win through to the orange groves of Valencia, that God will strike down Don Luis and let us marry—that we will have strong sons, every one exactly like his father." She surged against him so strongly that Diego said hoarsely, "I think we'd best repair to our cabin, Veronique."

And those staid married passengers on the deck exchanged glances and watched the de Jonquils go—with knowing smiles, remembering when it had been the same with them on honeymoons long ago.

The walls of the de Jonquils' cabin could have been blackened with smoke or hung with tinsel that day—it is doubtful they would have noticed. To Veronique and Diego it was a cabin of sighs and dreams, for this make-believe "wedding trip" under assumed names was all the wedding trip that either believed they would ever have. And what they could not claim before the world they would have in secret here: the wine of passion, the sharing of dreams.

Hardly had Diego closed the door behind him before Veronique kicked off her black satin slippers and melted against her tall lover. Diego held her to him, his lips sought the curve of her white throat, found the little pulsing hollow at its base, and trailed down lingeringly to the top of her low-cut gown to nuzzle at the pale smooth hollow between her breasts.

Veronique felt her breath come in short fast bursts as his lips and fingers worked their magic. Beneath the ardent urging of those fingers her hooks were soon released, her sleeves and bodice loosened. A little involuntary moan escaped her lips as she felt the wine red velvet of her gown drift down her tingling body to lie in a soft velvet mound around her black-stockinged ankles. Next her black lace-trimmed chemise—and his fingers were more hurried now, more urgent as they touched the fragile undergarment that was so dramatic against the pale olive of her skin—floated down past her hips and trembling legs to join it. Then Diego lifted her to the bunk and himself removed the black silk stockings and black satin garters that were all the barrier that remained between him and the last of her nakedness.

Although they had made love many times and passionately in the pimento grove behind the stone church in Tortuga, this was the first time either one of them had ever dared to disrobe. In their flower-hung bower in the pimento grove there had ever been the need to be furtive and quick lest someone come along—and there had been the need for French lessons as well, as Veronique earnestly taught Diego enough French to survive as a staid and remarkably silent Frenchman.

But now at last they had all the time in the world for dalliance, and the very smallness of their cabin, the very confinement of the voyage, which most passengers deplored, would be for them one long embrace interrupted only by dreamy walks along the deck, hand in hand, and the occasional need for food.

Silent, intent, they lost themselves to love, the only sound in the cabin Diego's hard breathing and Veronique's occasional moans and small impassioned sighs as his hard body strained against her lithe yielding form.

Diego clasped her to him gently, reverently, and with a new

and terrible tenderness. He had made a rash, desperate, and eternal commitment to this woman, and in his heart with each impassioned thrust he was vowing silently to love her always, to stand beside her, care for her, shelter her, protect her, and shield her against all the world. His strongly beating heart sang with the depths of his commitment to this spirited woman, a woman of silk and fire and dreams, that he had loved with a boy's exuberance—and now as a man clutched fiercely and tenderly in his arms.

And with every shudder of feeling that coursed through her slight body, each burst more overwhelming than the last— flowering, surging, pulsating—Veronique was passionately promising herself that she would somehow make it up to Diego for all that he had lost in snatching her from Don Luis's vengeance. Diego had sacrificed all that a man held dear *but she would make it up to him somehow*—her breath caught sobbingly as those rhythmic shudders of feeling mounted and soared and spilled over into ecstasy—*somehow, somehow.* . . .

Eventually—as all things must—their sudden wave of passion ended and they drifted back to earth like ordinary mortals and lay companionably together on the bunk, damp naked bodies touching, and began, as lovers will, to talk about the wonder of it all, and to review the events that had brought them thrilling to each other's arms.

"Ah, Diego, Don Luis would never have sent you to find me if he had known we had loved each other since childhood," sighed Veronique contentedly, running caressing fingers along his thigh.

"Lovers only in dreams then." Tenderly Diego ruffled her dark shining curls. "Lovers in fact now."

Veronique slid backward away from him and sat up in the bunk. She leaned forward and her dark curls fell over on his lightly furred chest as she stared down into his face.

"Did you know that I fasted for a fortnight when they told me I must marry Don Luis? I swore that I would stay locked in my bedchamber and never eat again!"

"What made you break your vow?" he asked curiously, for he knew how resolute she was.

Veronique made a gamin face at him. "The smell of chicken frying under my window! I determined that I would find another way to your side than starving—I ran away."

He looked startled. "I did not know that!"

"No, of course you did not." Her naked breasts were lowered now and brushed his chest tantalizingly. He felt ripples of desire flame through him. "My family kept it a close-guarded secret lest my virtue be deemed impaired! But I climbed down from my balcony and traded clothes with a gypsy girl and tried to reach your house."

He reached up and tried to pull her down to him. "Poor little Veronique," he said, much moved. "Had I but known!"

But she was in a mood to talk and resisted him. "The gypsy girl ended up in a dungeon—for helping me!" She grimaced at the memory.

"Did they let her out?"

"Yes, but not till after I was safely married to Don Luis, so she could not talk about my wild ride." Her dark eyes pondered the past, irrevocable now. "I stole my father's fastest horse that night. But he went lame halfway there and they caught up with me, dragged me back. And later I learnt that you were not even at home, Diego, you were in Madrid. So it would have been futile, anyway.''

"How did they ever coerce you into marrying Don Luis?'' he wondered, knowing well her valiant spirit.

"They almost despaired of me. My father was beside himself—he even dragged me down to the dungeons and threatened me with the Iron Maiden.'' She shivered, remembering that silent armorlike suit with spikes turned inward into which a person could be locked, and must stand frozen and rigid forever or be instantly impaled. "He told me that if I did not submit he would lock me inside it and I dared him to do it! It was then he said he knew how to break me, that I would come screaming to him on my knees and beg him to allow me to marry Don Luis.''

Diego felt a chill of horror go through him. He waited silently for her revelation.

"All in my family know my weakness, Diego—that I have a terrible unreasoning fear of small enclosed spaces. My world darkens and I feel suffocated by them—it is as if I cannot breathe. It has been so ever since we went to see the great caverns near your home and a bit of the cavern flooring gave way beneath my feet and I was trapped in darkness for hours before they could get me out.''

Diego nodded soberly. He remembered those caverns—he had nearly lost his way in them himself once or twice.

"So he locked me in the oubliette.''

It was Diego's turn to shiver. For the oubliette was the darkest deepest hole of any dungeon—and the most feared. It was a tiny space enclosed in stone with an opening only from the top. The very word *oublier* meant "to forget" and into those dark grim holes the "forgotten ones" were lowered, without hope, and left to die. *And they had done this to her. . . .* His muscles tensed and at that moment he would have lunged with glee at her father's throat and brought him instantly to his reward. He controlled himself with an effort, for although her eyes were closed, she was speaking again.

"I fought back my screams and they left me there. I nearly went mad." Her pale fists clenched and her whole body trembled with the memory. "Not till just before the wedding did they take me out and at that moment I would have done anything, *anything* not to be put back into that lost darkness. I had had only bread and water and I nearly fainted during the ceremony. People remarked afterward how pale I was—they never guessed the reason." *It had gone by in a dream, a nightmare, that enforced wedding ceremony—but a lesser nightmare, for it took place in the lofty airy dimness of a great cathedral and not in the tight, stifling, airless darkness of a black hole with only the sliminess of cold stone walls to the touch and the only sound the scratching and squeaking of rats running overhead.*

Diego was sitting up now and for a moment he bent his head to shield his face from her view. He did not want her to see the raw emotions that coursed across his strong features. But he need not have done so; Veronique was staring stonily ahead, seeing other places, other times.

"I remember when Don Luis's emissaries came. Ah, they were royally decked out, I can tell you. There was enough gold gilt on that carriage to become the altar of a church! They strolled about our courtyard arrogantly in their satins and plumes with their talk of great doings at court—and my father, who was a simple man at heart, and who had spent almost all of his days at our family estate in Valencia, never stirring forth, was impressed. I watched them from a distance and my heart sank, for I could see that he was flattered that a great man like Don Luis should ask for me. *Flattered!"* The bitterness of her tone cut Diego to the heart. In it was all the rejection she had suffered when, young and tender—and frightened although her pride would never let her show it—Don Luis had taken her to his bed. She had not produced a son—although he had striven manfully with her—and he had become impatient and packed her off to court where her dark beauty would at least be a credit to him. There, in his view, she had disgraced him—and she had been made to pay for it.

Now, groping for the words, she tried to make Diego understand how it had been.

"That night my father called me into his *estudio*. He bade me sit upon the high-backed balustered chair that had belonged to his great grandfather. I remember staring at the inlaid ivory of his tall trestled writing desk as he spoke. Even now that design is etched in my memory. At first he strode about extolling the virtues of life at court, a life he was quick to mention that I had been denied. When I proved intractable, he seated himself on the big carved chest that contained his papers. He was very silent for a while, studying me, for I had proved obdurate. Outside the nightingales were singing."

Listening, Diego suffered with her, castigating himself for not having been there to snatch her away, to save her.

"He told me, appealing to my pride, that if I married Don

272

Luis, I would become a duquesa, and was that not worth having? I told him that I did not wish to become a duquesa if that entailed marriage to Don Luis! His lips tightened, but he was determined to reason with me. He told me that Don Luis had only one son from his first marriage, Carlos, and if that son died—and indeed Carlos was reputed to be on his deathbed at that very moment, Don Luis's emissaries had told him so—that I would sire the heir to Don Luis's noble line. I told him that mattered not at all to me, that I wished to marry for love or not at all.

"My father assured me that I would learn to love Don Luis, that he had been long a widower and I would bring joy into his life again, that I would be happy with him. Happy! Don Luis wanted to marry me for one reason and one reason only: when the doctors had told him that Carlos, his only son, could not live much longer, Don Luis had cast about for a suitable bride to assure the continuance of his noble line! He had chosen me because the women of my family were considered to be prolific. He did not even bother to come courting himself, in fact he never called at all. It was all arranged through his emissaries. Don Luis had seen me once, they told my father, at a fiesta, and I was passable-enough looking. Passable!" Her indignation flared. "His only questions were about my health: would I conceive quickly? For the rest, my lineage he knew was of the best; my clothes, my jewels he would choose himself—I would be molded to his will!" She gave Diego a tormented look. "Can you imagine a man like that, who would take a bride in cold blood for no other reason than quickly to replace a son who lay dying?"

Diego shook his head in wonder. "It is hard to believe,"

he agreed, viewing the splendid creature before him. How could any man, he asked himself—even Don Luis, on his urgent search for a bride—overlook the fire, the passion that lay just beneath the surface of her amber eyes?

"It is true, I swear it," she declared passionately. "Don Luis told me on my wedding night what my mission in life was to be: I was to produce a son to bear his noble name."

A memorable night that had been, the sudden dark emptiness of her eyes told him. But her lips would not form the words to describe it. Veronique knew she would never tell Diego the horrors of that night, the callousness with which Don Luis had pierced her maidenhead, his heartless cruelty in the methods he had used on his exhausted bride to ensure that she would become pregnant during that first week of marriage. In another woman such harsh treatment would have created frigidity, a trembling terror of all men, but in proud, strong-willed Veronique it had created only a sense of outrage, and a hatred of Don Luis that ran deeper than any river on earth.

"And then," she said, her mouth dry from the very memory of it, "when I did *not* become pregnant—and for that I thank God, for it would have been a curse to bear his son—and when his son Carlos made a miraculous recovery, in spite of leeches and doctors and endless bleedings, Don Luis had no further use for me. He brought me to court as an ornament. I was to reflect further glory upon him!"

"I would I had been there," sighed Diego. "I would have taken you from him though I died of it."

"I know you would, Diego." Her mood shifted suddenly to tenderness and she gave him a soft look. "The change to the world of the court was to me a welcome one. There was much to interest me there. And since Don Luis came no more to my bed, for a time I even thought it might work out, that we would reach some compatible arrangement, Don Luis and I. But then I shocked the queen by wearing my bodice cut too low.''

Diego cocked an eye at the mound of wine red velvet lying tangled with her black lace-trimmed chemise upon the floor. That gown had a stunningly low decolletage. ''You have made up for it since,'' he observed.

''I have tried,'' she admitted demurely. ''I asked van Ryker to find me the most shockingly low-cut dress he could find, and he laughed and said his wife had many such and would choose for me herself. I feel, Diego, as if I had been denied my girlhood,'' she added, almost shyly. How to tell him what it had been like to be laced up in iron stays to keep one's budding breasts from developing so one would be ''fashionably flat,'' to be continuously chaperoned by a stern duenna who kept ordering one to one's knees to pray for sins only imagined? How to tell him how the wild-hearted young girl in her had yearned to leave her long enforced hours of embroidery and ride out and swim and make love in sylvan glades? And most of all, how to tell him what it had been like to meet and fall in love with the brave young stripling from a neighboring estate—young Diego Navarro, and to dream in her room of nights when the pale moon gilded her olive skin to ivory, how Diego would one day sweep her up on a white Arabian steed and carry her away through the orange groves and olive groves to make her mistress of his estate! She touched his hand shyly. "I used to dream about you, Diego. Long ago."

"And I"—his voice had a stirring quality—"took one look at the lovely young lady who came riding so correctly by the *Lonja de la Seda*, the silk exchange, looking neither to right nor left—"

"I looked," she laughed. "Every time I came to the Plaza del Mercado I looked for you. You just didn't see me!"

"And lost my heart," he finished gallantly.

But had he? she wondered wistfully. She had heard wild tales of Diego's adventures with women, his frolics, his gaming. For a while it had been rumored that he would be excommunicated and she had prayed to the Virgin to spare him. Had Diego really been thinking about her, dreaming about her then—as she had dreamed about him?

She would never know. But now she looked deep into Diego's dark eyes and saw there an expression that told her she would never *need* to know. He was hers now. Hers alone.

"I thought," she told him with a catch in her voice, "that we would marry and live among the orange groves of Valencia, with the air filled with the scent of blossoms. And instead I was dragged off to a mountain stronghold in Castile with freezing winters and hellish summers. And a man who hated me." She turned to him and her voice was the impassioned cry of a hurt child's. "Oh, Diego, why did you not come for me then? When first you learned I was to marry him?"

"I heard too late," he sighed. He had often told her so but she stubbornly refused to believe that his soul would not have heard the urgent cry of her rebellious heart. "I rode for Valencia but—the thing was already done. You were just coming out of the cathedral when I arrived. The bells of El Miguelete were tolling—and you were already his wife." He had no need to tell her what it had been like for him, a fiery young man, to see her thus; the face he glimpsed beneath her white bridal veil pale and set, her slim back arrogant and straight even as now, walking with measured steps beside the old grandee. "It was because of you that I went into Don Luis's service," he said simply. "I was not really offering *him* my sword—it was to *you* I offered my sword, *querida*."

"But I never saw you again after my marriage," she complained. For her dazed eyes on her wedding day, seeing the world through her bridal veil, had completely missed a dusty young man who had ridden up to the edge of the crowd, viewed for himself the bride and groom departing the cathedral, and dashed away with a haggard face to drown himself in wine.

"At first I hated you," he admitted. "I felt you had betrayed me by marrying him. And then I came to realize that my father had had wind of your betrothal and he had quickly sent me away before I learnt of it lest I do something rash and end up a scandal—or dead. I could not understand why you had not sent me word."

"*I tried, Diego*," she whispered. "But I was closely guarded, watched. And no one sends word from the oubliette."

He winced, blaming himself for not trusting her—for not being there when she needed him. "You were always with me," he said quietly. "I saw your face in every hearth-fire, in every glass of wine." Veronique's face flamed in triumph at this admission and her gaze on Diego was very soft. "Not a day passed that your memory did not strum across my heartstrings. It was torment, knowing you were in his arms. And then the day came that I knew I had to see you again. And what better way than to go into Don Luis's service? I was so certain we would meet, that I could at least view you from a distance, perhaps even exchange a few words with you. But always Don Luis kept me busy elsewhere—far away where I did not even hear the rumors about his treatment of you that must have been circulating. Perhaps he had heard of my early fondness for you and that is why he chose to keep us apart.''

"No. He would have mentioned it. He was quick to mention any man at whom I dared to smile, telling me in his cold harsh way that I would not see *that* face again!''

So they had kept their secret well. . . .

"He would never have sent you to the New World to find me, Diego, if he had thought you cared for me—or I for you. You do not understand him if you think that.''

"Perhaps he thought that I would find you *because* I loved you, but that my honor would make me restore you to him.'' Diego gave a bitter laugh. "He did not know how utterly lacking in honor I am where you are concerned.''

"Oh, do not say that!'' cried Veronique. "You have saved me from a monster!''

"I have taken another man's wife,'' he said soberly. "A man to whom I swore fealty. I have broken my oath, I am dishonored before God and man.''

"Never!'' She threw her arms about him as if to shield him from his own self-recriminations. "Oh, Diego, without you I am lost!''

He sighed. She had a hypnotic power over him, this

woman. Her nearness swayed his senses like some dark perfume wafting his way—heady, overpowering, unreal. It seemed to him that he had loved her from the first time he saw her—a child and dramatic-looking even then as she walked sedately to church beside her duenna, with a white lace mantilla draped over her heavy black curls—and with her bright eyes darting merrily sideways to see the world passing by. She had seemed to him so vivid, so full of joy.

And Don Luis had sought to wall her away from light and laughter. His heart hardened again against this man to whom he had sworn an oath of loyalty.

"Have no fear, *querida*," he said more gently, ruffling her dark hair. "If we are lost, we are at least lost together. Perhaps we will find ourselves again—in France."

She clung to him silently, dry-eyed but crying inwardly, for she knew what this love of his had cost him: his honor, his country, his fortune, his family, even his name—all these he had sacrificed for her. Passionately she promised herself that Diego would never regret—no, not for an hour—that he had made this sacrifice. She would fill his bed, his heart, his world.

"I will take a turn around the deck," he said restlessly, detaching her arms from him. She lay on her elbow and watched as he rose and began to dress. She knew that it tore at him, the fact that he could never again return to Spain. But when he was fully dressed and starting for the door, she could not let him go.

She slid back down in the bunk and held out her bare arms to him.

"Diego," she called softly. "Come back to bed."

He turned on her a bittersweet smile. "But it is not yet dusk," he said. "And we have already had our *siesta*."

"I know." Her voice was throaty. "But life is short and the world is sweet. Take me in your arms again, Diego, for who knows what hour may be our last?"

It was a cry of sweetness from the heart and it touched him. Swiftly Diego shed his doublet and trousers and fell with her to a wondrous oblivion there in that small cabin aboard the merchantman *La Belle France*.

Their lovemaking refreshed them, for they were used to these pleasant afternoon *siestas*—had they not enjoyed them every day, though with more brevity than they would have liked, in their private bower in the pimento grove on Tortuga? Alone among the Cups of Gold . . .

Hearts still communing, they dressed and went back to the deck, found a place apart and stood there watching the long light lengthen.

"Why did you not tell van Ryker that we knew each other back in Spain?" he asked her curiously, for it was something he had long wondered about.

She twitched a velvet shoulder. "I thought he might look with less favor upon restoring a runaway wife to a former lover—and, besides, we were not lovers in any real sense back in Spain. It seemed better to tell him that we had just met and I had won you to my cause. And having said it—" She shrugged.

And he had propagated the lie. He supposed it did not matter, but he would have preferred to be entirely open with the buccaneer who had made their future possible.

Beautiful Veronique was more complex than he.

"How did you bring yourself to ask van Ryker for his help?" he puzzled. "It would not have occurred to me to ask him."

"When I saw that his ship, the *Sea Rover*, was the former *El Cruzado*—it gave me hope. I spoke to him about it, and discovered that he nursed an old grudge against my husband. It was then that I revealed to him my true circumstances and he agreed to help me. I think it was not just for myself," she added frankly, "but because he respected your gallantry in defying him and his buccaneers as they stormed ashore in the Antilles."

" 'Gallantry'?" Diego made a gesture of dismissal that shrugged that off. "I attacked him in the surf and he overwhelmed me. *Nombre de Dios*, what a swordsman!"

"He told me you near bested him," she insisted.

"Never! He could have had me through the heart but he chose instead to let me live."

"And crippled you," she said dryly.

"But only temporarily," he protested. "The French doctor, de Rochemont, says I will soon be as good as new. The ligaments are slow to heal, that is all."

For Diego's sake, Veronique hoped so. For her own, she knew she would love him even if he could not stir from his chair. She would love him if he was hurt or sick, she would love him when he was old. She would love him always.

And now they were together again. For a moment it was as if the old terrible days had never been, as if they had always known they would win through to this.

Smiling, they looked deep into each other's eyes. Indeed, they might have gone back to their cabin there and then but that there was a shout from above and Diego drew back from her and peered intently into the gathering dusk. Beside him, Veronique leaned upon the rail and stared too, for around them suddenly there was pandemonium.

Out of the dusk a handsome galleon was bearing down upon them—and she flew the flag of Spain.

"I know that ship," said Diego in an expressionless voice. "She is the *Maravilloso*."

"Then she is one of Don Luis's ships!" cried Veronique. "And she will have many guns, she is sure to take us!"

"Yes, that much is certain," agreed Diego quietly.

"She will take us—*to Spain*," whispered Veronique.

Before Diego could form an answer the guns of the *Maravilloso* thundered and a warning shot ripped through the water across *La Belle France*'s bow. They had been signaled to stop—or be blown out of the water.

The Island of Tortuga, 1661

CHAPTER 15

No one in the governor's family would ever forget Virginie's wedding night.

Georgette, having told her mother she had thrown up and was very dizzy—and proved it by wavering on her feet—had been briskly packed off to her room, where she had shut the door and immediately started transforming herself into a reasonable facsimile of Veronique. Her hair was swiftly done, for she had been practicing arranging her hair like Veronique's for days. She slipped into the black satin gown that was Veronique's favorite for evening wear, and which she had earlier filched from Veronique's room. She was just applying with great care the strawberry birthmark with Spanish paper when Virginie, attired in bridal white, burst into the room.

"Why—what are you doing got up like that?" gasped Virginie.

"Shut the door and I'll tell you." Georgette never looked up. She continued to concentrate on making the "birthmark" into the identical heart-shaped mark that graced Veronique's slender forearm.

Virginie shut the door and leaned against it. Beneath her elaborately lace-overlaid taffeta bodice she was breathing rather hard. Jean Claude, who was by now drinking heavily, had suggested with a leer that they go upstairs, and Virginie had said "later" and escaped the dance floor, meaning to hide in Georgette's room until she could get herself together. "Veronique will kill you when she finds you've worn her gown, Georgette." She stated that in a flat voice for her heart was not in it—she was caught up in her own problems and Veronique could fend for herself.

"Maybe," agreed Georgette complacently. "But she won't know about it till after I've worn it tonight."

"Where is Veronique?" wondered Virginie. "Mamma says she's miffed about something and sulking in her room."

"No, she isn't there. At least she wasn't when I borrowed this dress." Georgette nodded downward at her sleek low-cut gown. "Now that you're here, Virginie, will you help me with these hooks?"

Virginie moved forward like someone in a dream. Her world seemed to be coming apart at the seams. A tipsy bridegroom would soon be bringing her to bed and here was her younger sister getting herself up as a duplicate of their sophisticated houseguest.

"You won't dare come out among the guests in this," she warned Georgette as she fastened the last of the hooks. "Mamma would skin you alive!"

"Oh, I know that." Georgette twirled before the mirror. "You know, I *do* look like her!" she exclaimed in delight.

"You certainly do, but you'd better take it all off. Right now before anybody sees you."

"If anyone sees me, they'll believe I'm Veronique!"

"Not if they see you close up!"

"Nobody's going to see me close up except—" Georgette let that trail off tantalizingly, smiled a secret smile and twirled again before the mirror. The gleaming black satin skirts behaved as expected; they swung out in a lazy arc, then fell back into gleaming folds against her long legs. "I know you'll find this hard to believe, Virginie, but I have a rendezvous tonight. With a man." She watched her big sister out of the corner of her eye.

"You're right, I don't believe it," said Virginie bluntly.

Virginie's disbelief irritated Georgette. "Well, I do," she said airily, reaching for the pair of black silk gloves she had taken from Veronique's room. "And you'll never guess who it is!"

"It's Andy Layton, I don't doubt—I saw him come to the house yesterday when you thought I was taking a nap. I saw you talking to him in the courtyard and serving him limeade!"

Georgette made a face at her and laughed.

"Be careful of Andy," Virginie warned. "Unless you really do want to marry him. For Mamma will make you marry him, you know, if she thinks he has had his way with you."

"I don't see why!" Georgette tugged at the black gloves. "After all, Jean Claude won't be the first to have his way with *you*—and Mamma didn't make you marry any of the others.

Of course," she added in fairness, "maybe she would if she'd known about them."

"Don't say that!" Her nerves rubbed raw, Virginie's voice had gone waspish. She had been distracted for a minute by Georgette's masquerade, but now she was back facing her main problem and she couldn't bear to be twitted about her worldliness by Georgette.

"Well, *you* said—" began Georgette argumentatively.

"I don't care what I said! *None* of them ever had his way with me and you'd best take care with Andy, Georgette! I mean that!"

"Then you really *are* a virgin?" Georgette stopped struggling with the gloves. She looked awed.

"Of course!" snapped Virginie.

Georgette gave the recalcitrant glove a mighty tug. She was thinking indignantly how Virginie had lorded it over her with that loss of virginity. *She* would strike back!

"I shouldn't want to lose my virginity to my husband," she declared with a lift of her chin. "It sounds very dull. *I* intend to lose *mine* to some exciting married man."

Virginie gave a scornful laugh. "Who?"

"Captain van Ryker," said Georgette airily. "I have a rendezvous with him tonight. At his house."

"At his *house*?" Virginie stared. "I don't believe it! And, anyway, he's downstairs."

"We'll slip away. I'm to meet him outside." And to Virginie's disbelieving look, "Why do you think I am got up like this? He wants me to look just like Veronique so that I can come and go without being suspected."

"You do know that everybody says she's his mistress?"

286

"Yes, but I don't believe it," scoffed Georgette. "Else why would he—"

Virginie didn't let her finish. "Georgette, he's married to *Imogene.* She'll never let him go!"

"She doesn't have to," said Georgette with a heartless smile. "He can cast her out and we can have a buccaneer's marriage."

"Oh, you wouldn't! Mamma would *die*! And Papa would—" Her older sister peered into Georgette's face. "It's none of it true!" she accused.

"Wait and see," said Georgette blithely. "Captain van Ryker has promised me a string of pearls in the bargain—just for this *first* time." She emphasized that strongly. "Who knows what gifts he will shower on me later?"

Virginie sniffed.

"I don't intend to be a fake like you," Georgette told her, striking back for that sniff. "I intend to come back from this rendezvous—" She lifted her arms and pirouetted as gaily as a child "—a woman of the world. And *rich*!"

"A string of pearls won't make you rich," said Virginie tartly. She was half inclined to believe Georgette now and she found the thought alarming.

"No, but it's a start," Georgette told her. "And one must start sometime."

"I've half a mind to tell Mamma!" said Virginie.

Georgette's dark eyes narrowed and her gamin face assumed an ugly expression. "If you do," she warned her sister menacingly, "I'll tell Mamma *and* Jean Claude that I saw Jim Notley climb into your window *and stay all night*!"

Virginie hesitated. She knew Georgette would do it! "All right," she said in a resigned voice. "I won't tell."

"Better than that," suggested Georgette, seizing her advantage. "Tell Mamma you looked in on me and I was asleep. She'll believe it."

Virginie was quite sure Mamma would believe it. She was too busy keeping track of her party guests to keep track of her daughters. For a moment she felt bitter about that. "Georgette," she began halfheartedly. But it was no use. Having tugged the gloves on, Georgette gave her sister a wave with one black-gloved hand. "Georgette!"

But Georgette was already slipping from the room. She'd make it unobserved into the courtyard and then outside where Captain van Ryker would be waiting for her. Not only would she win a string of pearls tonight by acting out a lie, but she would triumph over Virginie by telling one! And Virginie, she told herself, would be gone to France, shipped out with Jean Claude, before she could ever learn the straight of it.

Idly she wondered where Veronique was—and dismissed the thought. Veronique was keeping her own rendezvous, no doubt—perhaps she had quarreled with Captain van Ryker and was teaching him a lesson. Or perhaps she'd met someone else and that was why Captain van Ryker needed *her* to play this trick on Imogene. Or perhaps . . . her mind was full of vivid imaginings as she reached the courtyard.

Meanwhile, shaken, Virginie sat down and stared white-faced into the mirror. She had already forgotten all about Georgette and was imagining in lurid detail what might happen tonight upstairs in her bedchamber. She was not only tired—she was scared to death.

Just as he had promised, van Ryker was waiting for Georgette outside and he escorted her swiftly—and unnoticed save by one sharp pair of eyes—to his house. That particular pair of eyes belonged to Andy Layton, who had been skulking about the shrubbery out front trying to get up the nerve to crash the party. Every time anyone wandered by, Andy had hastily shrunk back into the concealing cover of the shrubbery and he did the same when van Ryker appeared with a tall black-satin-clad creature who appeared to his eyes in this indifferent light to be Veronique. He held his breath as they passed, and indeed he never got a good look at the slender lady the buccaneer captain was escorting away from the governor's house.

Andy had heard the gossip, of course, that linked Veronique's name with van Ryker, but it was the first time he had actually seen them together and alone. He thought about that for a long time and regretted not having followed them, for it would have been interesting to see where they went. Van Ryker, Andy felt, could hardly take Veronique home with him. Suppose Imogene came back and discovered them together?

The laughter and music from the house drifted out to him, making him feel disconsolate. In spite of his show of brava- do, Andy was a timid soul. He could not quite summon up the courage to present himself uninvited at the governor's door—for Esthonie Touraille had a sharp unforgiving face and suppose she ordered him cast out? He would die of embar- rassment and, besides, he would cut a ludicrous figure before Georgette!

He had almost decided to give up his fruitless vigil and return home to Dr. Argyll's house, where his brother was spending the evening absorbed in one of the books from the little doctor's excellent library, when his attention was suddenly attracted by the sight of a dozen men who were moving purposefully and with remarkable silence toward the house.

Some internal mechanism warned Andy that he had best stay out of sight until they passed. To his surprise, they did not pass at all, but melted like shadows into the shrubbery and disappeared, he thought, into the courtyard. Andy blinked his surprise at this, for they had all been cutlassed and carried big pistols. They had looked to be buccaneers, and this was the governor's house of a buccaneers' island, so why were they hiding?

Meanwhile van Ryker had settled Georgette on the sofa, given her some cotton to stuff the fingers of her gloves so that her short-fingered grubby hands would look long-fingered like Veronique's. He had shown her graphically what he expected of her. And hurried back with Arne to collect Imogene.

Bewildered now—and afraid to leave lest he attract the attention of the cutlassed crew who were even now, he was certain, hiding in the bushes, Andy saw van Ryker stride up to the governor's house with Arne. He saw Arne and Imogene come out, saw her throw a scarf over her head and walk off in the direction of the quay while van Ryker strode off in the direction of his house. Afraid to leave and curious too, Andy waited there, puzzled, certain that things would eventually be made clear to him. Unknown to him as he waited, Georgette performed her little charade on the long sofa of van Ryker's house like the accomplished actress van Ryker had assured her she was. She never saw Imogene come into the house—or leave it. All Georgette heard was a sudden gasp behind her, and van Ryker kept a tight grip on her to discourage her from looking around.

He was frowning as he brought her back to the "governor's palace" and Georgette, who was finding it hard to keep up with his long stride, was afraid she'd jeopardize her pearls if she asked him why.

"Hurry in before you're missed," van Ryker told her in a taciturn voice and turned on his heel. Georgette scuttled away from him, snapping back a branch in Andy's face as she passed the place where he was hiding. Andy, who had leaned forward meaning to get a good look at "Veronique" and see whether she looked happy or sad, was hard put not to cry out for that whiplash blow nearly blinded him. When he could see again, he saw that "Veronique," as he believed Georgette to be, was strolling through the shadows of the courtyard—for indeed Georgette was enjoying her masquerade and was loath to have it end. She only hoped one of the guests—some dashing buccaneer preferably—would leave the house and come out into the courtyard for some air and she could stand in the shadows and make believe that she was Veronique and lure him on. . . .

The door to the courtyard opened and with that in mind, Georgette stepped back deeper into the shadows. But it was only Dr. Argyll tottering out to knock the fire out of the bowl of his long clay pipe. She watched as he made his unsteady way back inside.

Georgette gave a sniff. She supposed the rest of the guests were in no better condition, for the drinking had become heavy even before she had left the party. She decided she'd best go back to her room and get out of these clothes before Veronique came back and found her in them and perhaps set up an outcry. With that in mind, she moved to step onto the moonlit stones that would take her back inside.

For a moment as she brushed aside a palm frond, her arm was gilded by moonlight. Her sleeve had fallen back and the red heart was suddenly shown in vivid relief.

There was an abortive movement nearby. Georgette's head swung around sharply. She would have cried out but that a hand suddenly crunched down over her mouth. Georgette struggled. She tried to scream. In the darkness she could see still darker shapes converging around her. She thought her heart would stop, so wildly was it beating.

And then a gag was thrust into her mouth—but not before she bit the fingers that thrust it in and was rewarded by a grunt of pain. Then something large and dark and smothering—she thought it was a blanket—was thrust over her head and she was heaved up onto a sturdy shoulder and carried away. Terrified, half fainting from being stifled, she heard the sounds of the party recede in the distance.

In sudden blinding terror it came to Georgette that none of the Tourailles would notice her disappearance. She had instructed Virginie to tell her mother she was sleeping—and Esthonie would undoubtedly let her ''sleep'' till next day, never dreaming that she was on her way to God knew where, being carried away by a party of grim and silent men who had not spoken since they had taken her.

Georgette had never much believed in God, but now in panic she prayed to Him, making all manner of heartfelt promises if only He would get her out of this.

But the watcher in the bushes had seen it all.

Appalled, Andy Layton crouched in the sheltering shrubbery, afraid to move a muscle, and saw "Veronique" taken by this group of "buccaneers" who had come out of nowhere and snatched her up and were carrying her fast away.

Piled on top of the other events of the night, it was too much for Andy. He gave no alarm—indeed his throat was too dry to speak. With saucerlike eyes he watched the men depart, moving silently on a path that would avoid the quay and lead them out of town and down the coast. And then Andy—who would have fled all the way to Philadelphia at that point if he could only have walked on water—took to his heels and made it back to Dr. Argyll's green-shuttered house in record time.

"That you, Andy?" His brother looked up sleepily from his book. "I wondered where you'd got to."

Andy made a strangled sound in his throat. He was too scared even to tell his brother where he'd "got to." His teeth were chattering for he'd seen, he knew, an abduction. And he wasn't about to get involved in it, no, sir! That was a group of buccaneers who had fallen upon "Veronique"—and just after van Ryker had brought her back to the house! Could van Ryker have been in on it? If so, it behooved a young man from Philadelphia to forget all he'd seen. At least until tomorrow.

Even though it was a hot night, Andy hastily pulled a sheet over his head and pretended sleep when toward morning Dr. Argyll looked in on him.

CHAPTER 16

At the governor's house, the guests, most of them much the worse for wine, had departed one by one until only little Dr. Argyll was left. He was too unsteady on his feet to walk and Esthonie would have packed him off home in a wheelbarrow in care of a servant but that Gauthier stopped her. Dr. Argyll, he told her sentimentally, needed them on this—he waxed flowery, like the voluble Frenchman he was—"occasion of his bereavement."

"Bereavement?" cried Esthonie, scandalized. "Why, he's better off without her! The woman was nothing but a trollop—worked in one of those awful houses down by the quay." She gave her husband a hard look. "I don't see how a decent man could stomach such trash!"

Gauthier, who was well aware that his wife was speaking not of Dr. Argyll's errant sweetheart but of his own light of love, Josie Dawes, cast about for a diversion, for he was well aware that he was about to be called on to endure one of Esthonie's famous tongue-lashings.

"We owe it to him," he insisted. "Don't you remember when Virginie had the fever two years ago how kind he was to her?"

"*And* well paid for it!"

"Nevertheless, he got her through it. Come back, we must sit with him for a while until he is a condition to go home."

"I wonder if I gave Virginie enough advice," fretted Esthonie. "Jean Claude dawdled away and then he took her upstairs so *quickly.*"

"If you haven't, it is too late," said the governor firmly. "The time for advice is past, Estie. Jean Claude will take over from now on." Even as he spoke he was urging her from the hall where they had been quarreling back to the drawing room, which the recent festivities had left in a shambles.

Muttering, Esthonie accompanied her husband back into the big empty room full of drooping flowers, guttering candles and a pervasive odor of fresh paint. There on a tall-backed chair sat Dr. Argyll, dignified and straight as a poker but leaning slightly to windward as if he might at any moment topple from his perch. There was a long smear of lavender paint down one of his sleeves and another on his white ruffled cuffs.

"Have some coffee made," said the governor quietly and turned a cheerful face to his guest. "Well, well, Dr. Argyll, do you think that Layton fellow will be coming soon to pick up his sons?"

"I hope so, I hope so." Dr. Argyll shook his muddled

head. "Wouldn't want them to go astray on Tortuga. Not under my care."

Esthonie, having ordered the coffee, came back and sat down, settling her black and gold skirts about her. She was looking at Dr. Argyll, but her ear was cocked alertly toward the bridal chamber upstairs where Jean Claude had just escorted a blushing Virginie.

She hoped Virginie would heed all that she had told her, for just before Jean Claude held out his hand to escort his bride upstairs her mother had leaned forward and whispered a last admonition in her ear. "Don't let yourself be dominated! If you do, you'll become a doormat!"

Thoroughly confused, and with both Georgette's and her mother's advice ringing in her ears, Virginie was in a near hysterical state when at last she faced Jean Claude across the bridal bed. Jean Claude, who had had a bit too much to drink of the governor's excellent Canary, stumbled but once as he rid himself of his boots and regained his feet with dignity.

He swayed before her in his blue satin suit, a marvel of French tailoring that had been a last gift of his embattled family, bestowed on him with the admonition to marry the wench or face debtors' prison. The effect of his splendor was but slightly dimmed by the fact that the lace at his throat was askew from being clawed at in the heat, and he had lost one of the rosettes from his cuffs.

All evening Jean Claude had been feeling extremely sorry for himself—forced suddenly into marriage on the lure of a wedding gift that had turned out to be but a dozen silver goblets and not a chest of buccaneer's treasure. And now in this heat he must face the exhausting task of deflowering a virgin! Ah, well, better get on with it. With intense concentration, he addressed himself to removing his blue satin doublet.

Across from him, Virginie, standing like a statue in her lace-overlaid taffetas, did not move.

Jean Claude flung aside his doublet and began unfastening his white shirt.

Still, Virginie continued to stare at him.

Jean Claude looked up. He thought Virginie was looking exceptionally fiery as she stared at him across the bed. He had not considered her a particularly good-looking wench but now he could see that she had a certain shimmering magnetism. . . . Somewhat befuddled by drink, he thought she was excited at being brought to bed for the first time.

"Aren't you going to undress?" he hiccuped, noting that while he was down to his trousers and smallclothes that she was still standing there completely bedecked in her bridal finery, even to her veil.

"*Not* until we come to an understanding," said Virginie fiercely.

Jean Claude blinked. It had been a long time in truth since he had bedded a virgin but he did not think they could have changed *this* much. " 'An understanding'—about what?" he managed manfully, half expecting her to demand the whole thing be put off until tomorrow. Or perhaps she only wanted to demand a particular side of the bed. He waited.

"I will not be overcome—I mean overwhelmed," cried Virginie, her words getting tangled up in her excitement. "I mean *dominated*!"

Jean Claude was getting a new view of femininity. He

stood stock-still in amazement and blinked at his bride. "Have I—tried to dominate you?" he hiccuped.

"No, but you will!" accused Virginie. She was warming to her subject. After all, she had had a harpy for a model. "First you will try to dominate me *in bed*," she declared vindictively. "Mamma says so! And *then* you will try to take over my life! Because I am a woman!"

Jean Claude gave her a slightly woozy look. "Well, that is the way things are," he said pleasantly.

"Not in *my* house!" Virginie stamped her bridal slipper on the floor. Its soft sole made almost no sound but the imperious toss of her dark head gave sufficient emphasis to her words.

"You mean *my* house, don't you?" corrected Jean Claude haughtily. "When we are settled in Paris, it will be *my* house that I take you to." All this defiance was beginning to sober him.

"*Any* house where I am mistress is mine," said Virginie so impressively that he burst out laughing.

"I don't know where you got your ideas but you will soon lose them in Paris," he assured her. "Here on Tortuga you may be allowed to run about wild, but *there* my mother will take you in hand. And 'tis plain you need it."

"No, I refuse to live with your family. I have thought about it and we must have our own apartment."

"Oh, very well." Jean Claude supposed that Virginie's father would foot the bill for this extravagance since his daughter was so set upon it.

Virginie looked at her bridegroom in some surprise. She had set out to quarrel with him and was amazed that he should give up so easily. Even papa had *some* spirit! Look at the way he continued to buy shipments of wine against Mamma's orders. It occurred to her suddenly that if she handled this right, she could end up lording it over Jean Claude. Her eyes gleamed.

"I intend to assert my rights," she told him airily.

"What rights?" This was beginning to wear thin with Jean Claude. To his mind a wife had no rights.

"Why, my rights as your wife, of course!"

"Good. Then begin now. Undress."

Virginie stood her ground. Without her clothes she would have no dignity at all—and, anyhow, she was afraid to take them off.

"I will have you know," she cried, suddenly veering to Georgette's way of thinking, "that I am no green girl you can order about! I am an experienced woman!"

Jean Claude's jaw dropped. "And what does that mean?" he inquired irritably.

"That I am—that I am—" Virginie sought for another word and did not find it. "*Experienced.* I am no timid virgin that you can order about!" she finished haughtily.

She had meant to emphasize the word "timid" but had choked on it. Jean Claude had caught only "virgin." *I am no virgin*—and the wench was bragging of it, facing him down across the bridal bed.

When he said nothing—although she should have been warned by his excessive quiet—she went a step further. Her last words had seemingly made no impression on him, for he was standing stolidly before her with a blank expression on his face. She would penetrate that thick skull of his, she would get the whip hand! ''I have had many lovers,'' she bragged. ''So do not think you can order me about.''

By ''lovers'' Virginie meant ''suitors,'' but to Jean Claude, fresh from Paris, who had leaped out of many a boudoir window when the husband arrived home too early, the word had an entirely different connotation. So she was bragging of her exploits, was she?

''Undress!'' he commanded in a shaking voice. Although why life should see fit to hand him a virgin at this point in his checkered career he did not know, still he had been led to believe by one and all that Virginie's maidenhead was still intact. At that moment he was damning his father who had made the match, Esthonie who had catapulted him into the ceremony ahead of time, and his dark-eyed angry-looking bride who seemed to be standing there daring him to prove himself a better lover than his predecessors.

''Undress!'' he cried harshly again. And when Virginie only sniffed and stuck up her nose, he strode over to her and attacked the gown she was wearing. Entirely sober now, he snatched away her veil, ripped away hooks, tore at ribands, entirely ignoring Virginie's angry cries as she slapped at his hands and twisted and turned to escape him.

When he had fought his way down to her chemise, he pushed her unceremoniously onto the bed and leaped upon her. In the heat of the moment he had quite forgotten that he was still wearing his trousers. And when he scrambled up to rid himself of them, struggling because they were indeed abominably tight, Virginie bounced up indignantly.

Jean Claude, now completely naked, gave his bride a

fiercely lowering look. He had enough energy now to subdue a brace of virgins.

"Come back to bed," he growled.

But Virginie stood riveted, staring at him in dismay. She had never seen a naked man before and she found the view disconcerting. She stood there with her arms wrapped around her breasts. Surely he wasn't going to—to—

Her shivering reverie was interrupted as Jean Claude seized her by the forearm and hurled her to the bed. Thus propelled, Virginie landed on her back, sinking into the soft yielding feather bed like a stone in water. A moment later Jean Claude's long form had descended on her and he was asserting his marital rights.

Bragging she wasn't a virgin, was she? Well, he'd let her know what it was to be made love to by a *real* man! (For Jean Claude had endless—and misplaced—confidence in his prowess.)

Thoroughly aroused now, he thrust within her strongly— and was rewarded by a sharp scream from the squirming Virginie. In bewilderment he drew back—the tricky wench had lied to him! She was a virgin after all.

While Jean Claude considered this amazing new factor, Virginie, feeling herself the victim of this frontal assault, clawed at his chest and tried to push away from him.

"You're not doing it right!" she accused—for she remembered seeing the cats, and Esthonie had absentmindedly agreed with her that yes, that was the way it was done. It *couldn't* be right—it hurt too much!

Downstairs, Esthonie and Gauthier, who had not yet gone to bed and who were still sitting with Dr. Argyll as they plied him with coffee, had heard sounds of minor warfare from upstairs. Now they heard Virginie's wild, "You're not doing it right!" and froze into stillness.

They looked at each other in dismay as Dr. Argyll muttered pleasantly, "Who's not doing what right?" and without waiting for an answer began to topple from his chair.

The governor forgot his "bereaved" friend. He forgot the coffee cup in his hand, which went crashing to the floor. He leaped up and was making for the stairs when Esthonie pulled him back.

"Gauthier, Gauthier," she cried. "It is their wedding night, you mustn't interfere!"

The little governor fell back panting and both husband and wife looked at each other in fear as Virginie shrieked again, "*You're not doing it right!*"

"How would you know, you damned virgin?" came a roar from Jean Claude.

And then a loud crack as if a hand had slapped a face.

This was followed by a yowl, a scuffling sound, and a crash as if a heavy piece of furniture had been tipped over.

Gauthier's face was white. He had visions of his little girl up there, lying unconscious on the floor while that savage young Jean Claude (he had up to this point considered Jean Claude mild to the point of being a milquetoast sort of person) raped her! He gave Esthonie a wild look.

"I'm going up there. God knows what is going on!"

"*Mon Dieu,* you must not!" Esthonie clutched at his arm and he charged forward, dragging his ample wife. They skirmished at the base of the stairs and Esthonie lost several gold tissue ruffles from her dress during the battle. Unmindful of the gold brilliants that were showering from her dress at this rough treatment, she clenched her fingers firmly in her husband's trouser top and managed to drag them entirely from his bottom as he charged upstairs. Halted by her weight and by the uneasy feeling that his trousers were departing his body, Gauthier turned and expostulated with his wife.

"No, no," she was hissing. "You mustn't go up there. All marriages have their little adjustments, Gauthier!"

"Adjustments?" cried the governor, incensed. "He is killing her!"

Together, floundering, they surged up the remaining steps and crashed together into the door at the top. It was of heavy oak, hewn by sweating Spanish captives working out their ransom time on Tortuga, and it stood placidly firm against the impetuous assault of the governor and his lady.

Even at this noisy heralding of their approach, there was no sound from the other side of the door.

Both Gauthier and Esthonie held their breath.

"Are you going to ask, or shall I?" growled Gauthier in her ear.

"Virginie!" trilled Esthonie nervously. "Are you all right, *ma chère*? We thought we heard something fall over."

There was no answer.

"Dead, I tell you!" Gauthier gave the door a violent kick with his boot. "Answer me, Virginie!"

"Yes, papa?" came a dreamy voice from within. "Did somebody say something?"

Gauthier's shoulders slumped down in relief. At least if someone was dead in there, it was not his daughter. Let Esthonie's relations bury Jean Claude if Virginie had found it necessary to slay him on their wedding night and then gone mad as a result!

"Virginie, dear, are you *all right*?" Esthonie's more insistent chirp rose beside him.

"Why, of course, Mamma!" And then a low giggle and a sound as if a pair of bodies might have fallen off the bed and another giggle and—

"Come along, Gauthier," said Esthonie firmly, seizing her husband by his satin-clad arm. "I think Virginie can handle the rest of the evening by herself." Well, not *quite* by herself, she thought with a twinkle. Doubtless Virginie had been sensibly putting Jean Claude in his place, just as she had instructed her. She did hope he was not too bruised—it would make a scandal if he went about sporting a black eye or a bandaged nose. Of course, she reflected, any wounds would have plenty of time to heal before he and Virginie sailed away to France.

Together, looking a little the worse for wear, for the governor's trousers were torn and Esthonie was trailing some defeated-looking ruffles that had been ripped from the gold tissue overlay of her brocade gown, the Tourailles returned to their drawing room, where Dr. Argyll, roused by the racket upstairs, had tottered to his feet.

"Can I be of some assistance?" he asked with enormous drunken dignity.

"No, I think we are past the need," Esthonie assured him, and under her breath suggested to Gauthier that they order out a wheelbarrow to cart the doctor home.

But all the excitement prevented either of the elder Tourailles from noticing that both Veronique and Georgette were conspicuously absent.

PART TWO
The Spanish Vengeance

What would he give to get her back?
All that he has, and more
And now his vengeance is at hand....
Death settles every score!

The Caribbean, 1661

CHAPTER 17

Van Ryker would have been stunned to know that *La Belle France* had been taken by Spaniards her first day out from Tortuga.

Diego Navarro was equally stunned. It seemed to him as he stared at the approaching galleon, coming in majestically out of the dusk, that ill fortune had dogged his efforts from the first in this venture. He had found Veronique in Cartagena without difficulty of course and had persuaded her to accompany him on the *flota*'s return voyage to Spain only because the captain of the *Delgado* was a cousin of his, and a romantic, and when Diego had presented his impassioned plea of love for a lady to his cousin, the cousin had agreed to take Veronique on board in the role of a French captive, who would be allowed fortuitously to "escape" when the ship reached Spain.

But the cousin and the ship had died together in a hurricane that swept over the Antilles.

And then there had been what seemed an enormous stroke of luck when, to Diego's astonishment, the buccaneer van Ryker had offered to help them, and had indeed arranged this voyage to France at no little expense to himself.

But that escape had lasted but a day.

Diego felt at that moment that God was against him. He cast a baleful look at the sky—and then came down to earth. If he was to save this woman who meant everything to him, he was going to have to do it without divine intervention.

He was thinking fast.

Was it best to continue to pose as Monsieur and Madame de Jonquil, he asked himself, and become prisoners of the Spanish and transported to Spain for ransom and there attempt to arrange an escape? Or to admit their real identities at once and chance on an escape of opportunity when they reached Spain? He decided on the latter, for their position as French prisoners with no hope of ransom would be untenable, and if either he or Veronique were recognized in such a deception—as he felt was bound to happen—there would be hell to pay.

No, he would tell the captain of the *Maravilloso* who they were at once and brazen it out. Who knew, if the captain turned out to be a good fellow and inclined to bend the rules—and perhaps he would also be impoverished as such good rule-bending fellows were prone to be—Diego might try a little bribery. There would be plenty of time on the voyage to ingratiate himself. He bethought him of his handsome estates in Valencia—estates he would be glad to sign away to the *Maravilloso*'s captain, if only he would allow Veronique to fake a suicide, or arrange some likely "accident" that would allow the lovers to escape.

He would have to play it by ear, he knew, but his was a stout heart, and now in this desperate case the courage that van Ryker had admired in him came to the fore and made him put a brave face on things. He would get his woman through this yet!

When Veronique had said with fear in her voice, "They will take us—*to Spain*," Diego had gripped her arm to give her courage.

"Perhaps not," he said with a lightness he did not feel. "We do not know yet where the *Maravilloso* is going. She may be headed for some Spanish port in the New World. I have friends in Cartagena—if she takes us there, we will escape. If she carries us to Panama, we will escape if we have to cross the Isthmus on horseback!"

Veronique gave him a smile that lit the dusk like a candle—but it was a heartbreaking smile to Diego, for he knew that although she loved him, she had no faith in what he was saying. The chains she had so lately managed to shrug off had come back to shackle her again.

"We will say nothing at first while I size up the situation," he muttered. "And I will later explain my silence by saying that for all I knew, we were being taken by pirates disguised as Spaniards. Such things are done, I'm told! Trust me, *querida*."

"I trust you, Diego," said Veronique steadily, but her gaze was distant, removed from him.

If Diego died of this venture—as well he might—she did not intend to survive him.

The transfer of the passengers from the fat merchantman to the haughty galleon was marked by only one tragedy, for the captain of *La Belle France*, outgunned and outmanned, when faced with this formidable Spanish man-of-war, had given up without a fight. But one of the passengers had chosen not to accompany them on board the *Maravilloso*.

Mademoiselle Pernaud, sister of the French governor of Martinique, had no intention of spending the last days of her life in a Spanish prison. She walked with stately grace to the rail—but instead of allowing herself to be handed into the waiting boat, she suddenly threw herself over the side into the sea.

To their credit, the Spanish officers made a gallant effort to rescue her. They were not so rash as to leap into what were well known to be shark-infested waters, but they threw her a line and shouted to her in broken French to seize it, they would pull her to safety.

Mademoiselle Pernaud, afloat only by reason of the bulk of her billowing skirts, for she was making no effort to save herself, ignored the line they had thrown her. She ignored the cries of the Spanish officers and the passengers alike, as they called to her urgently to take the line and save her life. She looked out upon a dark and shadowy sea and felt the tug of her heavy skirts as they became wet and saturated with seawater. But a moment more and she would be dragged down and down by their very weight.

Mademoiselle Pernaud looked her last upon a world that had not been kind to her—that had given her the gift of beauty and position, yet kept her from achieving her one desire. Drifting there, just before the dark waters closed over her head, she whispered but half a dozen words—and those spoken to a lover dead these dozen years past.

"Andre," she whispered. "I am coming, *mon amour.*"

And let the sea claim her.

Veronique felt a lump rise in her throat as she saw the fragile Frenchwoman sink below the sea's dark surface. It was a lesson in courage, she told herself. Mademoiselle Pernaud was showing her the way.

But Mademoiselle Pernaud's untimely death had struck terror into the huddled passengers. Colette was openly sobbing. Only Diego and Veronique stood apart, cool and watchful. Veronique meant to follow his lead as she had promised and give Diego's plan, however slight its chances, every chance to work.

But Diego's plan had no chance to be put into effect. Even as they boarded the *Maravilloso*, the Spanish captain's eyes lit up at sight of Veronique and her silent lover.

"Make way for the duquesa of Sedalia-Catalonia," he said, shouldering people aside. "How are you, Diego? We have been scouring the seas, looking for you both. Word had reached the duke in Madrid that while you were escorting the duchess home from her visit with relatives in Cartagena, you were both taken when that devil of a buccaneer seized the plate fleet. It is good to see you both looking so well. Suitable cabins will be prepared at once. I hope that you will both do me the honor of sharing a bite of supper with me—once I have got this rabble taken care of.''

''Thank you, we have both eaten,'' said Veronique distantly. She recognized Captain Garcia as someone in her husband's retinue that she had met once or twice.

''It is good to see you too, Ferdinand,'' said Diego. ''I did not know that you had become captain of the *Maravilloso*.'' He could hardly keep the gloom out of his voice.

''Since just after you left for Cartegena,'' Captain Garcia assured him.

''She is a worthy vessel, Ferdinand.''

''Aye—a better one than I had before!'' Ferdinand laughed. He was in fine spirits. His master would be delighted with him and he might next be given a ship with tall castles at stern and bow, such a ship as his heart yearned for!

But Diego's heart had sunk into his boots. Ferdinand was a friend, yes, a drinking companion. But he was also totally incorruptible. Ferdinand would be shocked should Diego offer to bribe him—nor would he be moved by Diego's plea that the lady loved him. With his dying breath, the loyal Captain Garcia would carry out his instructions to the letter. Whatever hope there was for spiriting Veronique away would have to come on shore, for it would not come aboard this vessel!

''Where are you bound, Ferdinand?'' he asked his friend.

''For Spain, I hope, as soon as we make rendezvous with—'' Captain Garcia turned irritably to an officer who had just come up and muttered something to him. ''Yes, what is it, Ramon?'' And then, ''I am sorry, Diego. There are some problems with these passengers, it would seem. I will see you presently.''

·But he did not return presently. The problems with the passengers must have proved enormous, for Captain Garcia did not return at all. As they waited, Veronique and Diego were ushered into adjacent staterooms.

Disregarding the danger, Veronique insisted that Diego come in and talk to her.

"I remember seeing this Captain Garcia only once or twice," she told Diego frankly. "And then when he came to see my husband on some matter or other. But he seems to be a friend of yours—at least he greeted you warmly. Do you think you can trust him?"

"In some things perhaps, but not in this matter. Not as regards us." Diego shook his head and his strong jaw hardened. "Ferdinand would as soon slash off his sword arm as be derelict in his duty to Don Luis. His is an unswerving loyalty that knows no shades of gray."

"Then we are lost!"

"No, he said that we were making rendezvous—with another ship, no doubt. Perhaps we can find some reason to be transferred aboard her. And her captain may prove more amenable. You still have your jewels?"

She nodded.

"You may need them. But with luck," he promised her, "we may yet buy our way out."

He had but little belief that that would happen, but he wanted to give his lady hope.

"Diego," she said, touching his arm. "You will stay the night?"

He gave her a haggard look. "I dare not, *querida*. Ferdinand

315

said he would see me presently. He may come looking for me at any time. I should not be here even at this moment."

"Diego." Her low wail tore at his heart. "Do not deny me! This may be the last time you will ever hold me in your arms!"

"No," he said hoarsely. But it was with a wrench that he managed to back away from her, for all his being wanted to seize her and hold her and never let her go. "I will not be the immediate cause of your death," he said harshly. "If Ferdinand were to report to Don Luis that we had spent the night together on board his ship, Don Luis would not wait for trial—he would run you through with his sword."

"He will kill me, anyway!"

"No, he will not," he told her stubbornly. "I, Diego Navarro, promise you that. I do not know how I will manage it, but manage it I will." *Even if it is with my dying breath*, he promised himself. "Good night, Veronique."

"You can call me Maria again," she told him disconsolately.

"Better I call you *duquesa*," he muttered.

"Diego." She called to him softly at the door. "If you do not stay with me, I promise you that I will come to your cabin. I will sigh at the door and beat upon it until you relent and let me in!"

His feet had dragged him to the door and now he turned with a groan. "Veronique, it is for your own safety."

She was taking off her clothes even as she had spoken, and now the sight that greeted him was of a wine red velvet bodice half shrugged off, of creamy olive skin, ripe and smooth and inviting, seen through the black lace of her chemise—and of a reckless and beautiful aquiline face half obscured beneath a cloud of dark curls.

"I do not want to be safe, Diego," she said quietly. "I want to be loved."

Her wistful words struck a note in him and made him remember. . . . Skin of silk and eyes of amber. The first time he had ever seen her, the very first, he had been but a stripling lad and she a child with a challenging face peering out at him from behind her duenna's severe black skirts as they circled the Plaza del Mercado. He had felt strangely exhilarated even then. And when next he had seen her, very proper, dressed all in white with a lacy mantilla over her dark hair on her way to church, he had not been able to take his eyes from her. Afterward he remembered that he had dashed through the park of his father's estate, leaping over stones, hurdling bushes in a most unseemly way.

After that he had set out to win her favor—in boyish ways. He had near broken his neck riding recklessly to get her attention. And then, as a man, he had come courting. His father, knowing his son's passion for the lovely Dona Maria, had—when Dona Maria's father had confided that the great lord Don Luis was interested in the girl, the marriage as good as arranged—prudently sent Diego away so that he might not disgrace himself and his family by attempting to storm her balcony and elope with her. He had judged his son shrewdly, for that was exactly what Diego would have attempted.

Hair of ebony, skin of silk, and mouth of velvet. Her golden eyes rested on him beseechingly and Diego was instantly reminded of everything he had ever loved about Spain: the green waxy leaves of the orange trees, the fragrant blossoms, the soft winds that blew north out of Africa, the flashing skirts of flamenco dancers, the merry *fiestas* with laughing young girls in billowing ruffles riding through town in gaudy carts, the brilliant snapping banners, and the towering *alcázars* and the bells that chimed through the dusk. And the promise, ever in his mind, that one day he would take this lovely lady home with him.

As if bereft of reason, he felt himself melt. He moved toward her like a man beset. She held out her arms to him and her smile would have moved the devil to tears.

"Oh, Diego," she murmured, pressing her lithe slender form against him, letting her soft breasts move maddeningly across his chest. "Do not deny us this last evening together. Captain Garcia may knock on your door, find you gone—but you can make some excuse, tell him that you were walking about on the deck and missed him. He will believe you. But for us . . ." they were falling upon the bunk even as she spoke ". . . there can be no other time—only this moment."

Diego forgot reason and sense. He let his wild love for this passionate beauty carry him along as if there were no tomorrow. His lips found hers eagerly, hungrily. And he could feel as well as hear through those lips the little moans and gasping sobs of passion that his nearness engendered. For them this night of love became a night of fury, of passion that crested and peaked and crested again. A night of bliss, of surrender, of madness, of torrents of sighs and sweetness too ecstatic to be believed.

Tomorrow would carry its own burdens—they had tonight. And they cherished and caressed each moment as if it were to be their last.

It was early when Veronique left the cabin. She had been loath to leave it, holding out her white arms to him, but Diego had been adamant.

"You must go out and tell me when there is no one in the corridor," he told her urgently. "I must not be seen leaving your cabin."

To please him, she had dressed—again in the low-cut red velvet, although all her things had been brought aboard. She gave him a rueful smile, and went out and beckoned to let him know that there was no one there. He came swiftly out.

"Go up on deck," he told her. "I will join you—after I have made the bunk in my cabin look slept in."

She touched his cheek with light caressing fingers, her eyelids still heavy with sleep—and desire. Then she moved with that light floating walk that was so distinctive, away from him.

When Diego hurried at last to the deck, he found Veronique standing by the rail in the morning sunshine. She turned and acknowledged him gravely. "Diego, I hope you slept well."

He realized then that Captain Garcia was standing nearby, studying the horizon intently through his glass.

"Very well, thank you," he told her in an expressionless voice, for Ferdinand must not be allowed to suspect. He tried to keep his eyes from devouring her. "Would you care to take a turn around the deck?"

"Captain Garcia has asked me to wait while he studies the sea," she explained, giving him a wistful smile. "He thinks he sees something out there that will interest me."

They stood there facing each other. They seemed suspended in space and time, these two who had so lately been locked in each other's arms. Captain Garcia continued to stare through his glass while they made polite conversation as if they were casual strangers, people meeting for the first time.

The French passengers from *La Belle France* had been allowed the freedom of the deck. They passed by in huddled little groups—and in passing gave Veronique and Diego suspicious looks. Why were *they* being treated so royally? Not put in with the rest but given special cabins, they had heard! And what had Captain Garcia called her? A *duchess*? They kept their distance watchfully.

Veronique noted their frightened looks but she had no reassurance to give them. She felt as lost as they.

After a long time, Captain Garcia turned to Diego with a broad smile on his jovial countenance.

"I thought I would have a surprise for you along about now," he said merrily. "Take a look through the glass, Diego, and then let the *duquesa* have a look. I will have a bottle of good Canary sent to my cabin and we will all celebrate there presently." He bowed and left them.

It was with reluctance Diego had taken the glass, and with reluctance that he looked through it now. He studied the horizon—and the ship that rose and fell on that horizon.

Approaching them at a leisurely pace was a true castle of the sea. Her lofty bow castle and her mighty stern castle rose stories high, gilded and sparkling—tall keeps built high for battle. She was an imposing and terrifying sight as she marched toward them under a mountain of white canvas. He studied her for a long time.

"What do you see?" Veronique asked him impatiently. "What is this surprise the captain speaks of?"

In silence Diego handed her the glass.

She looked through it and he could hear the sudden intake of her breath. She gave him the glass with nerveless fingers and sagged against him.

"It is the *Alforza*—the *Scar*," she whispered. "It is Don Luis's flagship—and see that flag, it is his personal flag. He will be aboard her!"

Diego looked wistfully at the advancing seven-hundred-ton Levanter and his arm went around Veronique's trembling shoulders and tightened. He knew that he was looking at one of the greatships of Spain. Her menacing gunports counted fifty-two and her admiral, Don Luis, duque of Sedalia-Catalonia, was no less formidable.

Diego had diced with Fate and lost the toss. There was no future for him anywhere now. But—he looked down tenderly upon those shining dark curls that had for a little while lain on his pillow—he could yet save her life. If only she would let him.

"Veronique." Very gravely, Diego wheeled her around to face him. There was no time now for love or pity—only for survival. They would soon be aboard that seagoing castle, facing Spain's most formidable grandee.

Veronique had hold of herself now. Her natural dignity had come to the fore. Still, something in his voice tore at her heartstrings as he spoke her name.

She lifted her head and met his grave, steady gaze. For a moment the lovers looked at each other with a wild surmise.

"Now listen to me, Veronique," he said quietly. "This is what you must do. I will go aboard as your captor escorting you back to the husband you deserted. And you will go with humility, you will humble yourself before Don Luis."

"No!" She would have torn herself from his grasp, but that his fingers bit into her flesh. "I hate him!"

"Pretend you do not! He has been careful to hide your defection—to save his pride. Even the captain of this ship does not know of it! And he must not learn of it from us. What passes between you and Don Luis will be said in private. None will know or care what Don Luis says to his wife in the privacy of his cabin. Meantime I will be acting strangely. I will say a strange-tasting wine was served me aboard the French ship. And when Don Luis comes out of his cabin I will appear to have a hallucination. I will cry out that I see demons and I will draw my pistol and inadvertently shoot him. Through the heart."

Veronique drew a long shivering breath. "So you will make me a widow to save my life. But what about you?"

"Do not think about that," he said gently. "It is enough that I have loved you."

"*I will not let you do it!*" she cried in a heartbroken voice. "Diego, I will not let you die for me!"

"Very well." His face was harassed. "Then we will try another tack. He is a religious man, you have told me?"

"Deeply." Her voice was bitter. "But I think it is not God but the devil who claims his soul!"

"Then you will tell him that you had a vision in that *alcázar* where he imprisoned you in Castile. You will tell him that the Virgin appeared to you and told you to steal away and go to the New World, there to rebuild your spiritual life in some holy place—a convent, perhaps. Tell him you desire to become a nun. Tell him you have repented and seek salvation. Tell him anything, swear it on your knees—but manage to survive this journey. When we reach Spain, I will find a way to rescue you.''

She gave him a fond sad look. There was a farewell in that look, for she was already certain of the course that he would take. He would rid her of Don Luis—and die in the doing of it.

"Of course," she said mechanically. "I will do as you say, Diego." *And then I will die with you.* It was a pact unspoken, made between herself and God.

Beside her, Diego squared his jaw. For he knew what he must do.

CHAPTER 18

Esthonie learned about the *Sea Rover*'s sailing and Veronique's disappearance at almost the same time. Clad in an enveloping pink dressing gown, she was seated with Gauthier at breakfast—a late breakfast, since the entire household was exhausted from last night's festivities. Virginie and Jean Claude, understandably tired from their exertions, were not yet down. Georgette, she supposed, still lingered in her room. Gauthier, who had been up earlier, brought her the news about the *Sea Rover*'s disappearance from the bay just as one of the servants came in to report that Veronique's bed had not been slept in.

"Well!" Esthonie set down her spoon and forgot all about her porridge. "Do you think there could be something to the gossip, after all? Do you think van Ryker actually *took her with him?*" Her eyes gleamed at how furious Imogene would be if he actually had.

"Of course not," said Gauthier energetically. "She is probably out riding. She often rides in the morning."

"Well, of course you can check with the stableboys and see if the horse is gone too," said Esthonie regretfully. "But wouldn't it be amusing if he *had* taken her with him?"

"You would do better to make your arrangements to move into his house if they are really gone," advised the governor briskly. "For you will not wish to leave it vacant and there will be much to do."

"Oh, yes, I am sure there will be," said Esthonie in a vague voice. She was more interested at the moment in scandal than in moving her household. "I must say they might have *told* us they were leaving," she said in an injured tone.

"'Tis understandable. There's word about that there are those who may seek to corner van Ryker when he sails. I hope he has escaped their net."

"Yes, of course," said Esthonie absently. To her mind, buccaneers were quite capable of taking care of themselves. She looked up as Virginie, followed by Jean Claude, sauntered into the room.

Virginie was looking sleepy-eyed—and kittenish. She was wearing her pink organdy and she moved seductively, swinging her hips, obviously to fascinate Jean Claude who followed. His eyes, considering the amount he had had to drink last night, were exceptionally bright and he was watching his young bride's languorous approach to the breakfast table with relish.

Obviously, despite its unpropitious beginning, the wedding night had been a success.

Gallantly Jean Claude pulled back Virginie's chair. Virginie smiled and leaned against him lovingly before sitting down. The submissiveness of her daughter's gestures made Esthonie want to throw up. She gave Virginie a frown.

"Did you sleep well?" she inquired tartly.

Jean Claude favored his new mother-in-law with a broad smile. "Never better, madame!"

Virginie simpered and chose not to answer at all. She hardly took her adoring eyes from Jean Claude's face. Esthonie decided suddenly that she did not like that face; she wondered what she had ever seen in Jean Claude.

"Captain van Ryker may have run away with Veronique," she said in an attempt to startle Virginie into more rational behavior.

"With Veronique?" gasped Virginie. "Then that explains why Georgette—" She stopped short.

"Explains why Georgette *what*?" demanded her mother impatiently. "Where *is* Georgette, anyway? She should be up by now."

Virginie considered her answer carefully before she spoke. "That explains why Georgette dressed up in Veronique's clothes last night. I suppose Veronique gave them to her before she left."

"*Gave* them to her?" Esthonie half rose from the table. "Georgette!" she shouted. "Georgette, come here this instant!"

There was no answer from Georgette but there was instead an insistent knocking on the front door. It was opened to reveal a panting Dr. Argyll, his eyes bloodshot but determined. He had hold of Andy Layton—in fact, he had him by the scruff of the neck and was propelling the protesting lad forward.

All the company at the table considered the little doctor in astonishment. None of them had ever seen him so aroused, for his teeth were actually bared. Esthonie was about to ask him if he had taken leave of his senses when he gave Andy a sudden shake.

"Speak!" he commanded.

Red-faced and embarrassed, Andy squirmed but he was held in an implacable grip. "I—I happened to be outside the house last night," he began haltingly.

"You were lurking in the bushes. Admit it!" roared Dr. Argyll.

"Well, why didn't you come inside?" demanded Esthonie tartly. "After all, we sent word to Dr. Argyll that both you and your brother were invited to the wedding."

Andy gave the little doctor a hurt look but found no comfort there. In fact, he felt himself being shaken impatiently.

"And Mademoiselle Fondage came out and met Captain van Ryker," he blurted out. "And they went away and then they came back."

"She *did* have a rendezvous with him!" marveled Virginie. "She said she did, but I didn't half believe her."

"Veronique?" Esthonie didn't understand. "What's this about Veronique and van Ryker?"

"Well, he brought her back and he left her here. Then she went into the courtyard and there were a dozen men waiting—I think they were buccaneers because they had cutlasses and pistols and—well," he finished lamely, "they *looked* like buccaneers. And they took her away."

"Carried her away in a sack!" roared Dr. Argyll, giving the young culprit a shake that rattled his teeth. "And *you* didn't report it! Instead you slunk home and pulled the covers over your head!"

"Veronique? Taken?" cried Esthonie. "Then you mean she didn't run away with Captain van Ryker?" She stopped suddenly for Virginie had clapped a hand over her mouth. Her eyes were wild. "Whatever is the matter, Virginie? You look ill!"

"That wasn't Veronique who was taken," gasped Virginie. "It must have been Georgette *dressed up* as Veronique! She said she had a rendezvous with Captain van Ryker and he was going to give her a string of pearls. She said he was going to get rid of Imogene and they'd have a buccaneer's marriage. Oh"—she wailed—"why didn't I believe her?"

The governor sat thunderstruck but Esthonie didn't wait to hear it all. She was already running to Georgette's room.

The bed, she saw, had not been slept in. And a quick check revealed that all Georgette's clothes were there. If she had left, she had certainly left in other garments—very possibly Veronique's, for a search of Veronique's room revealed only two items missing: her riding habit and the black satin gown she usually wore in the evening.

"Oh, you don't think Imogene found out about Georgette's flirtation with van Ryker and arranged to have Georgette kidnapped?" cried Virginie in a tragic voice.

"No, I do not!" snapped her mother. "I think that van Ryker, long planner that he is, arranged it all to make us *think* that! I do not know what else is afoot but oh, Gauthier!" She turned with a wail to her husband. "Captain van Ryker has made off with Georgette!"

At that very moment a meek and very penitent Georgette was slumped beside the rail of the *Alforza*, for Don Luis himself had engineered last night's "raid." It had been carried out by Spanish officers who had come ashore in a longboat dressed as buccaneers to snatch from the "governor's palace" a woman with a heartshaped birthmark on her arm—and they had brought her back as planned to the tall-castled Spanish ship. Georgette was slumped there because Don Luis had not yet decided what to do with her. She was still wearing the black satin gown she had donned so proudly last night. It had seemed such a great lark at the time. Now in the bitter light of morning, with the gown hopelessly rumpled from having been carried about and slept in—if you could call it sleep, that frightened catnapping that Georgette had engaged in—she was looking hopelessly out to sea. Her elaborate hairdo was rumpled and undone, the carefully contrived heart-shaped birthmark smudged past recognition.

Her flesh still crawled as she remembered being dragged into the great cabin where Don Luis, handsomely garbed in black and gold, as became a grandee of Spain, had risen to his full height, and then seemed to rise higher and higher in his fury as he exclaimed with a bitter oath in Spanish, "This is not my wife! What deception is this?"

Georgette had shrunk back in her fright, not understanding what he meant. Don Luis, white with fury, had waved away the man who had brought her and, once he was gone, tried her in English.

"This is my wife's doing, don't deny it. Where did you leave her?"

"I don't know," stammered Georgette. "Captain van Ryker asked me to put on Veronique's dress and—"

With an angry gesture, Don Luis seized her arm to see for himself. The heart-shaped birthmark was plain.

"So she has tricked me," he said more quietly. "Again. And she has used *you* to do it."

Georgette fell silent in confusion.

"Who are you?" he asked at last.

"I am Georgette Touraille, daughter of the governor of Tortuga," she told him in a quavering voice.

"So? The French governor of that buccaneer island is your father?"

Georgette nodded dumbly.

"And where is this—this Veronique, as you call her?"

"She is staying at my father's house."

"I knew that," he interrupted, for his intelligence was excellent and he had spies at work in Tortuga. "But where is she *now*?"

"She was not there when I left. She did not attend my sister's wedding last night. Mamma thought she was angry about something. I slipped into her room and borrowed her gown—"

"Without asking her? So you are not only a fool, you are a thief as well!"

Georgette sank back in fright before the whiplash fury of his tone. "I don't know where Veronique is," she mumbled. "And I didn't know she was your wife. Who are you?" she ventured.

331

Don Luis ignored the question. He was pacing up and down. The heavy gold chains he wore around his neck clashed as he walked and then swung softly back against his black velvet doublet. In the froth of lace at his throat was the largest ruby Georgette had ever seen, and the appointments of this cabin were breathtaking. The furniture was heavy and carved and inlaid with ivory and jade and shell. An almost oppressive air of opulence prevailed. Unfortunately Georgette was too terrified to appreciate it.

"What has she done?" she whispered fearfully. "Veronique?"

Don Luis gave her a sharp angry glance. "Her name is not Veronique and you will not call her that! She is my wife—the *duquesa*."

Georgette's eyes widened to saucer size. Veronique was a duchess! And married to this Spaniard who must then be a duke!

That fashionable flatness, thought Georgette, wide-eyed. She might have guessed! For she knew that aristocratic Spanish girls were forced as children to wear iron stays that flattened their burgeoning young breasts and made them—if they survived the torture—as flat as Veronique. But Veronique's passionate will to live had surmounted even that. For a brief moment Georgette both envied her and was sorry for her.

Don Luis gave a pull on a velvet cord. The door opened and a young officer came in.

"Take her away," sighed Don Luis with a gesture of dismissal. "Let her stay on deck until I decide what to do with her. If she really is the daughter of the governor of Tortuga, it may be that an exchange can be arranged—my wife for this impudent child."

332

Georgette had been on deck waiting ever since, fighting sleep or taking short catnaps from which she snapped awake, frightened, half expecting to be thrown overboard to feed the fish. She was almost the last to see the sleek *Maravilloso* come alongside and she struggled up only long enough to see that it was a Spanish ship before she slumped back.

Thus it was that she was almost the last aboard ship to see Veronique and Diego come aboard.

Veronique gave Georgette a surprised look as she swept by her, but she gave no smallest gesture of recognition. Georgette, who had started forward hopefully, now crouched back in a disconsolate heap, too tired even to wail.

Diego accompanied Veronique to Don Luis's cabin. He did so ruthlessly, brushing aside the ship's officers who would have stayed him. If Don Luis showed a disposition to draw his sword and bring speedy justice down upon his erring young wife, Diego intended to kill him here and now, regardless of the consequences. He was loosening his sword in its scabbard even as the door was ceremoniously opened for them.

This was the same sumptuous great cabin into which a shrinking Georgette had been ushered earlier. The rich dark red velvet hangings embroidered in gold made a dramatic backdrop to the ivory inlaid furnishings. Don Luis himself sat behind a large oaken table inlaid with jade and abalone shell. He rose as they entered, a dark commanding figure.

Veronique swept into the room with all the aplomb of a queen. Diego was proud of her. She swept back into Don

Luis's life as if she had never left it, and inclined her head gravely toward her husband.

"Don Luis," she said coolly.

Diego bowed.

The frown that had only hovered between Don Luis's thin dark brows deepened as he studied the gorgeous expanse of pale olive-toned flesh that was displayed in Veronique's lush decolletage.

Diego caught that look.

"We donned these clothes to make our escape," he explained quickly. "We were taken, along with the plate fleet. Our only recourse was to pretend the *duquesa* was French. We were taken to Tortuga, where she was a guest of the French governor."

"Guests of the French governor, you say?" Don Luis demanded sharply.

"Yes," said Veronique. "I see you have his daughter aboard. She will verify what I say. Until yesterday I was a guest in her father's house."

"And you, Diego?"

"I fought the buccaneers as they stormed the beach in the Antilles," said Diego truthfully. "And was wounded. A buccaneer doctor treated my wounds—and yesterday I managed to engineer my own escape and the *duquesa*'s."

"She came willingly?"

"I came willingly," said Veronique, answering for herself. Her amber eyes glinted. If only she dared tell him *how* willingly!

"I knew you were there," Don Luis said with a slight sneer. "My intelligence is excellent—even on Tortuga."

Veronique and Diego exchanged glances.

"I sent a force in to get you—but they netted the governor's daughter instead. Dressed, surprisingly enough, in your clothes and with an identical birthmark etched on her arm. She said van Ryker asked her to wear your dress. Can you explain that?"

Veronique shrugged. "I cannot explain it."

"And you still maintain you came willingly?"

"Yes."

"You have come to your senses, then?" Don Luis's voice was blunt.

"I went to Cartagena—for my sins," said Veronique carelessly. "I found it hard to pray for redemption in Castile while I was shivering on my knees on the cold stones. I thought—some warmer place." Her bland smile was infuriating.

Don Luis's evil answering smile told her hell would be a warmer place and he might well send her there.

Veronique stood her ground. Diego trembled for her.

"I would know where I stand with you, Don Luis." She faced him fearlessly. The only sign of emotion she gave was the slight rising and falling of her elegant velvet-clad breasts. "Do not ask me to grovel on my knees, for I will not do it."

"You will be kept in this cabin," he told her tonelessly. "You will not leave it. If you attempt to do so, I will have you chained to the bed. You will be returned to Spain there to await my disposition of you."

She half expected Diego to shout, "No, by God, she will not!" as he ripped out his sword. But a sudden diversion came in the form of a knock on the door and an excited ship's officer who burst in and muttered something in Don Luis's ear.

Don Luis leaped to his feet. "Keep her here!" he ordered Diego, and took off at a gait hardly commensurate with his dignity.

Alone in that sumptuous great cabin the lovers faced each other.

"We are lost," she told Diego expressionlessly. "He will interrogate the passengers and crew of *La Belle France*. He will wring from them the truth—about us."

"No, he will not," said Diego fiercely. "His pride will not let him do that. For he cannot bring himself to admit publicly that you fled from him, that you have been living on a buccaneer island."

"For that alone," said Veronique, "he would kill me."

"*Not* if you do as I tell you! Don Luis is most devout. You will tell him that you had a vision, and that vision led you to Cartagena, there to repent. That you had intended to incarcerate yourself there, to find some nunnery and wall yourself away from the world."

"Don Luis will wall me up soon enough!"

"No, no, listen to me. You will tell him that you have changed, that you have forsaken the world. You will beseech him to send you to some nunnery near your home in Valencia. There *I* will find you, we will make our escape there."

"It will never work," sighed Veronique, casting a glance down at her revealing red velvet gown. "He knows that I am worldly, he will not believe me."

"It is our only chance," said Diego desperately. "He will lose face if he refuses you a retreat among the nuns to weigh and consider your many sins!"

"You are beginning to sound like him!" she said with a

twisted laugh. "He told me of my sins so often that I was burning to be out and sinning! But he also told me that I would live out my life in his *alcázar*, entombed there living— like Juana la Loca." Diego repressed an inward shudder, for Mad Juana, the unfortunate wife of Philip the Handsome, had spent the last forty-six years of her life incarcerated at Tordesillas. "He is inflexible and will never change. Diego, give me your dagger."

"No!" In terror lest she would plunge the knife into her young breast, Diego seized her arms in his strong hands and whirled her about to face him. "That is not the way, Veronique."

"It is the only way," she said stonily. "For I will not go back to him."

"We must play for time."

"Time?" She gave a short derisive laugh. "Our time has run out, Diego."

"Perhaps not," he said desperately. "Oh, Veronique, listen to me. Do not despair."

Her proud aquiline face softened. She loved him so much, her Diego. Without him she would have despaired long ago and plunged a knife into her heart, ending her war with Don Luis.

"For your sake," she said in a sad voice, "I will not despair."

CHAPTER 19

Another man, faced with Imogene's defiant refusal to sail on the *Goodspeed*, van Ryker knew, might have resolved it differently. Another man might have handled her roughly, might have dragged her aboard the *Goodspeed* and left her there locked in her cabin until the ship sailed. Or put something into her wine and carried her aboard unconscious. But dragged or drugged, van Ryker knew his spirited lady too well to think that she would speedily forgive him for taking such stern measures. So he had chosen another course.

Imogene would know a few moments of fury, he had guessed, as she dashed aboard the *Goodspeed*, she would shake a mental fist—and perhaps a physical one as well—at the *Sea Rover*'s sails in the moonlight, and she would undoubtedly rip to shreds the note that told her how he had tricked her. And then—ruefully, of course—she would begin to calm down, and to laugh. And in a day or two she would be asking the captain to slow his ship and signal a message to the *Sea Rover* and suggest that van Ryker take her on board for supper as he had done when first he met her and she was sailing to America. . . .

Thus reasoned van Ryker, in his fool's paradise aboard the mighty buccaneer vessel cutting cleanly through the blue waters of the Caribbean. He never dreamed that Imogene had not received his note, or that she had misunderstood his careful arrangement of her cabin. His face would have gone pale with dismay if he had thought for an instant that she believed herself cast out, that even now she imagined him to be standing with his arm around a dark triumphant Veronique as the *Sea Rover* breasted the blue waters of the Caribbean.

Still, foolproof as his plan had seemed last night, van Ryker was having second thoughts about it today.

The lean buccaneer frowned and ran his fingers restlessly through his dark hair. He was having regrets about the agony—brief though it was—that he must have put Imogene through. He had rightly guessed her proud nature, that she would impulsively fling away from him, seek passage aboard the departing *Goodspeed*.

Arne had reported that she had taken it badly, storming aboard crying out her real name.

"I done what you said, lied about the jewel case, brought her back here." He shook his grizzled head, looked with disapproval at van Ryker. "'Tweren't right," he muttered, and spat.

"But you did give Captain Bagtry my note?"

"Put it in his hand," affirmed Arne.

Arne was reliable. So why then did van Ryker feel this nagging stir of alarm? As if somehow he was communicating with Imogene, and felt wild rage and passion flaring toward him from those white sails far away. . . .

His frown changed suddenly into determination. He would satisfy his fears for her once and for all; he would catch up with the *Goodspeed* and send Barnaby over. And Barnaby would bring back word that all was well.

He was about to give the order to put on more canvas when there was a shout from above. In the distance another sail had been sighted—no, there was a pair of them, just looming over the distant horizon.

Intently van Ryker studied those fast-approaching ships through his glass. Spaniards! One a sleek galleon, "race-decked," or *rasa* as the Spanish would call her, for she was all on one level, lacking a raised forecastle and having but a relatively low poop deck and aftercastle. But she was fast and weatherly and he counted fifteen gunports down her side—a ship of thirty guns, a worthy adversary.

But the other ship—van Ryker drew in his breath and his strong fingers tightened on the glass in his hand. *That* castle of the sea moved toward him ponderously, like a juggernaut— and he knew her by description. Stories high her lofty castles at bow and stern rose above the water. Yes! She was the *Alforza*—the *Scar*! And now he squinted his eyes and leaned forward, trying to make out that flag, and when he finally identified it he put aside the glass and a cold smile lit his ice gray eyes.

That flag was her admiral's personal banner. Fortune had

smiled on him this day. Don Luis Alvarez was aboard the *Alforza*—and bearing down upon him.

Now he turned his glass toward the *Goodspeed*, noted with satisfaction that she was slipping away, her sails fast disappearing to the east.

All was activity aboard the buccaneer vessel now as more canvas was piled on and the *Sea Rover*, like the lean wolf she was, raced forward to intercept the Spanish warships.

Van Ryker gave swift orders, for he meant to engage, but he cast a last look at the *Goodspeed*'s white sails before she disappeared from view over the horizon.

He had been right, he told himself grimly, and gave thanks in his soul that he had not yielded to temptation and let his lovely lady accompany him aboard as she had so wanted to do. It was always chancy, taking on two such warships, for one was a vessel of thirty guns and highly maneuverable, and the other a leviathan of men and guns deemed almost unsinkable—with fifty-two brass cannons to his forty. And in the case of the *Alforza*, Don Luis bore the *Sea Rover* and her captain a special grudge, and those aboard her could expect no quarter if the battle went against them. And what would it avail him to vanquish these two stout ships, if some chance musket ball or shot killed or wounded Imogene? He told himself that his scheme had been justified, his lustrous lady would forgive him for his deception, and turned to argue with de Rochemont.

"What madness is this?" The French doctor's face was red with conviction. "We are all of us rich now. Why should we do battle with two such monsters? And shorthanded as we are? Let us be prudent for once and show them our heels!"

Many aboard the buccaneer vessel agreed with de Rochemont. They were rich men now, their plunder safely stowed aboard, and they had no particular quarrel with these two Spaniards. The *Sea Rover* was one of the fastest ships afloat, she could easily outsail that big Levanter, the *Scar*. And if the *Maravilloso* chose to give chase—and with her racier lines she might be able to catch up—well, so much the worse for her, they'd blow her out of the water! Do as de Rochemont suggested, show the Spaniards their heels, they counseled. But van Ryker, well aware that the fat wallowing *Goodspeed* could not outsail the Spaniards, and with a burning desire at last to confront his hated adversary face to face, held firm.

They would engage.

But first—since all battles were unpredictable—he would lead the oncoming vessels away from the *Goodspeed*, back toward Tortuga and prowling coveys of buccaneer ships that might finish off the Spaniards even if he failed. Moving under a mountain of canvas, while Barnaby and the crew fretted and de Rochemont swore a torrent of French oaths, van Ryker led the Spaniards on a tantalizing chase ever deeper into Caribbean waters, and at last—just when Captain Garcia had decided scornfully that this particular buccaneer did not choose to fight—turned suddenly on the pursuing *Maravilloso* with a burst of fire from his culverins that shot away her masts.

With the element of surprise on his side, and with the *Alforza* firing ineffectively from too great a range, van Ryker followed up his advantage with a close-in broadside that near shattered the facing side of the *Maravilloso*, came about and repeated the maneuver. The *Maravilloso* seemed to stagger.

She was shrouded in smoke—and suddenly a great explosion ripped her. Van Ryker had got in a lucky shot. He had breached her powder magazine, and her supply of fine-corned powder blew up, making a great surge of fire over the water.

With the *Alforza* coming into range, van Ryker left the *Maravilloso* in confusion and afire, turned gracefully away and contented himself with long-range fire with his culverins. The *Alforza* came up to her sister ship to give assistance. From the poop deck of the *Sea Rover* van Ryker watched grimly. He had had time to observe the *Alforza* being handled as he sailed and although she was a solidly built Levanter of seven hundred tons and fifty-two guns, he knew her now for an awkward, ungainly sailer, clumsy and hard to handle—and she had obviously been long at sea and was barnacled and in need of careening and tallowing. Now he took advantage of that knowledge gained by observation. Sailing up swiftly in his fast-running *Sea Rover,* he panicked the gunners of the *Alforza* into firing on him while he was still out of range, ran swiftly in abreast of them and gave the lofty castle-ship a rending broadside with his heavier, ship-smashing guns, and was gone before they could reload. Their fire ripped the water twenty yards from his stern.

In the sudden confusion, the great ship fouled her rudder and drifted aimlessly. Van Ryker fired his culverins at will and raked the decks with shot. The *Alforza* was hard put to avoid the fiery holocaust of the *Maravilloso* drifting toward her like a fireship, and he got in broadside after broadside with his ship-smashers. Staggering broadsides that—although she still roared her defiance from her fifty-two cannons, some of which overheated and exploded—were bringing the mighty

Alforza to her knees. She was entirely out of control now, and van Ryker at his pleasure could glide abreast to rake her with a broadside, come about and give her another, and while Barnaby and an excited de Rochemont cheered, he crossed her stern to pepper her with half-musket shot. On board the *Alforza*, when Don Luis was knocked to the deck by a falling spar, a frightened second-in-command seized that opportunity to strike her colors.

Van Ryker himself led the boarding party. De Rochemont thought that he had never seen him look so determined—or so dangerous. He wondered what the Captain had in mind.

He had not long to wait to find out.

Van Ryker ignored all aboard save three. He gave a slight start as he saw that Veronique and Diego were on deck and facing him. Triumph shone in Veronique's amber eyes.

But it was on Don Luis that the buccaneer's implacable gaze was focused.

Don Luis, his face gone pale from the blow the spar had dealt him and the added blow of the loss of the battle, was standing on his feet when the boarding party set foot on the *Alforza*'s deck. As he stepped forward, an elegant figure in velvets still, despite a smudge of black powder on one high cheekbone, the tall buccaneer came to a halt.

"You are Don Luis, duke of Sedalia-Catalonia?" he inquired almost pleasantly.

"I am he." The old grandee spoke fearlessly. It irritated van Ryker to see how old he was. He had hoped for a younger man. . . . "And you are—?"

"Van Ryker."

The old grandee studied him haughtily from top to toe. "I

345

had hoped to meet you—under other circumstances," he murmured.

"I don't doubt it," said van Ryker ironically. "Preferably in chains?"

"Preferably," was the cold reply. Flint-hard, Don Luis's harsh countenance returned van Ryker's cold surveillance. "What are you going to do with me?" he demanded of van Ryker. The question was asked proudly but it was met by a savage smile.

"I have not yet decided," said the buccaneer with the wintry eyes. "Perhaps I will be able to find suitable housing for you on shore in Tortuga—a dungeon such as the one in which you kept my father, suitably furnished with rats."

Don Luis's elegant shoulders gave a slight start. "Your . . . father? You say he was in my dungeon?"

"Hauled off his own ship, which was peacefully plying the seas. Stowed in your dungeon, and ransom demanded. That ransom was paid but the man you returned to us was dying of starvation and maltreatment. For that, Don Luis," van Ryker said silkily—and he was loosening his sword in its scabbard as he spoke—"*I hold you personally accountable.*"

Comprehension was dawning over the Spaniard's olive features. "Then you seized *El Cruzado* because she was mine?" he cried. "And not because she was Spanish? Your war is with *me*, Señor, and not with Spain! I am an accomplished swordsman and will be glad to grant you a meeting!"

Van Ryker thought of his father—dying a cruel death, of his mother wasting away of a broken heart. He cast a look at Veronique standing silent and proud in her wine red velvet dress.

346

"Do not press for such an engagement, Don Luis," he said in a low savage tone. "For I would be tempted to castrate you!" Before the Spaniard could reply, van Ryker turned to Veronique. "Duquesa, is it your desire to speak to this man alone before I make you a widow?"

Veronique nodded silently. Her eyes were very bright. Diego made an abortive movement but she pushed him away.

Van Ryker personally escorted them to the great cabin, flung open the door and made Don Luis a mocking bow.

"Allow me to restore you to your wife," he said ironically. "In this extremity she asks nothing more than to be by your side." He reached down and dexterously removed the handsome dress sword Don Luis wore at his side, tossed it to de Rochemont, who caught it with a grin. "Put a guard on the door, Raoul," he said, and strode away to survey the damage.

Inside that handsomely appointed cabin, which had now changed ownership, Don Luis flung himself into a tall carved chair and groaned.

"You are pale," observed Veronique. "Have some wine." She went over and poured wine from a big decanter into an ornate silver goblet studded with emeralds—a goblet, she thought wryly, that would be in buccaneer hands ere nightfall.

She watched him as he drank it. Her manner was most composed.

"Now that Diego is not with us and we can speak freely," she asked lazily, "do you not wish to know what I have been doing while I have been gone?"

Don Luis looked up sharply. He was very pale about the lips.

"Did you see that buccaneer up there?" Her smile was

sweet. "I have been his mistress! Ah, yes, the stories you no doubt heard about me were true. *His* mistress—and a dozen others. *Think on that,* Don Luis, locker-up of women!"

The duke staggered to his feet. He took a step toward her but now he halted. It was unthinkable—could it be true? "Swear that you are lying," he cried in a trembling voice, for he was thinking of his sullied honor. *"Swear!"*

"I swear that I am telling you the *truth!*" she flashed. "I have made up in this short time for the months and years you took from me!"

Don Luis tottered back. He believed her—as he had not believed the stories that had filtered to him from Tortuga. "I will cut this dishonor from your body!" he cried hoarsely. He reached for his sword—and found it not.

"No, you will not," she cried. "Not even if you find a sword to do it. For even now you are dying. I have given you a slow poison in your wine. Did you not taste the manzanillo in your wine? Or was it too cloaked, too diluted? No matter, it is honey-colored and deadly and available on Tortuga. And this particular manzanillo I have kept for you for a long time."

She pulled from her sleeve a small vinaigrette and waved it at him, noted with satisfaction his expression of spreading horror, as he stared down at his empty goblet.

"And if you are still alive tonight," she promised sweetly, "you will have yet another treat in store. For you will see me dance for these buccaneers, tossing off articles of my clothing as I dance. You will see me take off my clothes and dance naked before them all, Don Luis, my husband—it is a sight I would have you see before you die. My vengeance will be

348

complete when, completely nude and with men all about me cheering, I make my final bow and sweep the floor with my long hair and then invite—who knows which one?—but *one* of them to bed with me!''

Don Luis's lips had gone ashen. His face was working. He fell backward, clutched at his throat and made pawing motions in the air. He looked as if he were drowning. His lips formed words but no sound came out.

Veronique glided toward him with that gait peculiar to the women of the Spanish court—she seemed to float on air, her wine red velvet skirts swirling.

''You will die unshriven,'' she said softly as she bent over him, her luminous amber gaze fixed upon his ashen face. ''This is my parting gift to you—the gift of hell.''

She thought—or was it only that she *hoped*—that she read terror in the old grandee's eyes before they closed for the last time.

When she was very sure he was dead, she left him and went out into the corridor, stood pensively for a moment. Van Ryker was striding toward her. With great composure she took a little of the perfume from the vinaigrette she carried—for it had never held anything deadlier than perfume—and dabbed it behind her ears.

''There is an emerald-studded goblet in there that you might like to have as a souvenir, a memento of your triumph,'' she told van Ryker. ''For it is the last thing Don Luis touched in life.''

Van Ryker stared at her. Conflicting emotions warred within him. She had robbed him of his revenge—a revenge he had waited for for all these years. Still—he was not sure he would have been able to bring himself to kill the proud old man. His very age was an armor.

"You and Diego will come with me," he said brusquely. "All the rest will remain here."

He would take them as near to Havana as he dared. There he would put them in a longboat and bid them row ashore. He would watch to make sure they made it.

For Veronique and Diego it was over. There would be a period of mourning—and van Ryker guessed it would be brief. And then Don Luis's striking widow would marry Don Diego and go to live on his lovely neighboring estate.

They would win through to their orange groves after all.

The *Alforza* was taking on water from a gaping hole in her hull. To everyone's surprise, van Ryker made no effort to repair her. Instead he was towing her fast toward Cayona Bay.

He was about to leave the ship when a thin wild scream deterred him. A shame-faced young Spanish officer came forward—and with him, her face white and grimy and her eyes dark spots of terror, for she had been certain she would be killed in the battle, was Georgette.

Van Ryker could not have looked more amazed.

"How," he demanded, "did *you* get here?"

"I was seized in the garden at home after you brought me back to the house," cried Georgette, aggrieved. "And a gag was stuffed in my mouth and I was brought here by force! Oh, Captain van Ryker, it is all your fault because they thought I was Veronique!"

Van Ryker was taken aback. He had not realized Don Luis had actually sent a shore party to Cayona. So the old sea wolf had come for his erring wife—and got a half-grown French pepperpot instead.

"I am sure you disabused them of the notion," he said ironically.

"But not till after I was aboard," wailed Georgette, for with the resilience of youth, her good spirits were returning to her. She was saved! "They were going to take me to Spain"—her imagination danced ahead of her—"to be *martyred*."

A slight smile played around the corners of van Ryker's stern mouth. "Ransomed more like," he said.

"You should have kept your rendezvous with me in the town instead of at your house," she whispered conspiratorially. "I could have stayed out till morning and *then* I would not have been kidnapped and you would not have to save me now!"

"You deserve a spanking," said van Ryker. "I am torn between giving it to you now—or feeding you some supper. Since I have time for neither, I will leave you aboard."

Georgette gave him a reproachful look. "But I really *do* need to lose my virginity, Captain van Ryker!" she complained. "Else how will I ever gain experience and *flair* like—like Veronique?"

"Veronique was born with flair," said van Ryker, his lips quirking in amusement. "*You* have something else. I'm not quite sure what it is. At the moment I think I would call it impudence. When you are older it may turn into something else. *I wouldn't want to meet you then*," he muttered under his breath.

Georgette's keen ears caught that last. "You are right,"

she declared happily. "I will be quite *fatal*, will I not?" She began to look alarmed as she saw he was leaving. "You—you aren't going to leave me here on a Spanish vessel?" she quavered.

Van Ryker's smile became a broad grin. "That lad hovering in the background, is he a friend?"

Georgette blushed. "He hid me when the fighting started," she admitted with a provocative smile at the worried-looking young Spanish officer. "He promised to protect me with the last drop of his blood!" she declared dramatically.

Van Ryker guessed that Georgette was making up that rather melodramatic statement but that the young officer had indeed gallantly tried to put himself between a child-woman and harm.

"Soon we will reach Cayona Bay," he told her. "And all there know who you are. The buccaneers will not harm you. You will be sent ashore on one of the *Alforza*'s longboats, and your young Spaniard may choose his own crew to take you there. When you arrive, tell the governor how he aided you during the battle and you may yet find yourself a suitor, Georgette!"

She pouted. "You promised me a string of pearls," she reminded him.

"And when you arrive, you shall collect it. Arne has instructions to pay for them." And as her face cleared, "You have gained something else, Georgette—a story to tell your grandchildren."

A cloud of smoke had hung over the battle and was duly noted on nearby Tortuga, where a number of ships had hastily put out to see what was afoot.

They came upon the scene when the battle was already over, the flaming *Maravilloso* burned to the waterline and sinking, the mighty *Alforzo* riding low in the water. She was taking water steadily into her hold as van Ryker towed her ruthlessly toward Tortuga.

When he sighted the line of approaching buccaneer ships, van Ryker stopped towing the *Alforza* forward and let her drift aimlessly. Well he knew those hastily launched ships out there would be shorthanded, low on shot, unprovisioned—but they were a pack and packs are always dangerous.

He watched as a longboat put out from the *Alforza* with Georgette preening in the prow and a full complement of Spanish officers, watched it as it went through the first of that line of ships. She was safe now, he thought, heading toward Cayona and that strident mother of hers.

Now he stood upon the rail, holding on to a ratline, and hailed the nearest ship. His whole ship's company were in fullest agreement with what he was about to say, for he had discussed it with them and they were, to a man, eager to get on.

"Brethren of the Coast!" His voice drifted out to the nearest ring of buccaneer vessels—some of whose captains itched to attack van Ryker and take his gold from him. "We of the *Sea Rover* have taken this fine Spanish vessel and need it not. We know not what stores are aboard her, but rest assured they will be plentiful for this is the flagship of the duke of Sedalia-Catalonia. We are of one mind—to give this prize to a friendly captain of the brotherhood—that he may ransom her crew and spend her gold and have money to dice with! That he may refit her and careen and tallow her and let her carry him to harry the might of Spain wherever it may lie! And that he may take the rivers of wine that lie in her hold and drink the health of the men of the *Sea Rover*! So sail in with your grappling hooks at the ready and board her—she is yours. We give her to you freely.''

''To whom do you make this gift?'' came a foghorn of a voice.

''To the strongest!'' replied van Ryker instantly. ''Decide among yourselves who that is. And drain a glass to us for the gift!''

As van Ryker stopped speaking, for a moment there was a dead silence. Then a mighty roar of approbation went up from the buccaneer ships. Hearing it, Flogg and the others who had hoped to bring this pack to harass van Ryker, to surround and capture him, looked at each other in balked impotent fury. And then abruptly they reconsidered, every man for himself, for here before them was treasure too— treasure in the great hold and in the cabins of the *Alforza* —the great ship herself was a treasure!

Pandemonium broke out among the ships of the buccaneer fleet. The great prize riding majestically before them belonged to the captain who could take it! Van Ryker had correctly judged his men.

Fear was struck into the hearts of the Spaniards on board the *Alforza* as the buccaneer fleet of Tortuga streamed out to board her. Iron grappling hooks were tossed and scraped against wood. Barefoot and cutlassed buccaneers stormed over the side to take possession.

But victory was short.

Van Ryker in the distance saw it happen. He watched,

grim-faced, that first puff of smoke. They were fighting over possession of the *Alforza* now, that wild convoy that was escorting her into Cayona Bay. Soon there was a steady rattle of gunfire as the fleet broke up into groups, having at each other in fury over who should have the lion's share of the loot. "Share and share alike" did not count that day.

And the *Sea Rover* sailed away from it. It was probably the first battle van Ryker had ever sailed away from, and he left it with a grim smile on his face.

He wondered how the little governor of Tortuga was going to handle his unruly daughter—and now his unruly buccaneers.

But in Tortuga, when the battle was over—and by then but half the ships were in condition to sail, and none of a mood to pursue the *Sea Rover*—they patched up their wounds and drank van Ryker's health in the taverns. For he'd done handsomely by them, hadn't he? Even if the *Alforza*, victim of furious if uncertain gunnery, did sink even as they fought to possess her in the middle of Cayona Bay, what did that matter? When buccaneers sailed over that spot where she lay like a jewel at the bottom of the brilliant blue bay, she would be called forever after "van Ryker's gift to the Brethren of the Coast."

But the battle had taken a toll on them too. The captain of the *Maravilloso* had got in a lucky shot before the *Sea Rover*'s deadly accurate guns had struck his powder magazine and near blown him out of the water. The *Sea Rover* was taking on water; she had taken a pounding and needed repairs to her sheets and rigging, as well as repairs to a gaping hole in her hull.

Van Ryker knew he could not cross the Atlantic with his

ship in this condition. With reluctance, he put ashore on an unnamed island, a mere group of rocks and beach with a fringe of palm trees, and made his repairs.

And then he set sail again. He knew there was no hope of overtaking the *Goodspeed,* even with the reckless amount of canvas he piled on in the effort, but he had no doubt her captain had observed through a glass how van Ryker had drawn off the Spaniards. Captain Bagtry, he told himself, would linger off Plymouth—and there the *Sea Rover* would rendezvous with the *Goodspeed* as planned.

It was with confidence that van Ryker headed his prow into the broad wastes of the Atlantic.

With misplaced confidence for he had no knowledge of the despairing thoughts that now consumed his young wife.

CHAPTER 20

Imogene never knew van Ryker had sailed the *Sea Rover* away to divert the Spanish. Indeed, none on the *Goodspeed*, including her captain, saw the *Sea Rover* come about and lure away the Spanish vessels—for the little Miller lad, with his mother in full pursuit, had collided with one of the cookpots and scattered fire all across the deck. Captain and crew and passengers had come running, for fire was the dreaded enemy of all voyagers.

By the time the fire was got under control, and the Miller lad soundly spanked, there was not a sail to be seen in any direction. So what reached Imogene was a somewhat different version of the truth.

"I thought Captain Bagtry said that damned buccaneer was protecting us," grumbled a man in a high unfashionable sugarloaf hat to another who was crouched over the rail

357

studying the sea through a spyglass. "And now you say there's no sight of him?"

"Right you are." The linsey-woolsey-clad fellow with the spyglass turned his glass to give the empty sea another sweep. "Dumped us, he did. Unless he's dropped back over the horizon."

"Sailed back to Tortuga, more likely! And yon's the reason for it, I've no doubt." Sugarloaf gave Imogene an unfriendly glance, letting his voice rise so she would be sure to hear. "They'll have had a fight and she ran off—and he don't want her back! So he followed us until he made sure the wench hadn't persuaded the captain to turn back and leave her in Tortuga where she'd be a trouble to him. Now he's seen us plowing straight ahead, he knows he can rest easy and forget her. So we won't see *his* sails no more!"

Imogene pretended not to hear but pain knifed through her heart. She wanted to scream at them, but she held her anger in check. For it was even possible. . . . Van Ryker *could* have sailed back to Tortuga, where he could exact an even more galling revenge on Don Luis by letting all the world know Veronique reigned there as his mistress.

She felt cut to the quick and turned a stony face toward the stares of the curious—and that brought out baleful looks from some of the women. And relief on the faces of some, for by now everyone knew that she was the wife of the notorious buccaneer and there had been rumors flying about that she had escaped him and that he was sailing fast to retrieve her—and who knew what he would do in anger to those on board the ship that had carried her away?

Now word spread rapidly that she was the discarded mistress of a buccaneer—a woman to be despised and laughed at discreetly behind one's hand. As the day sped by and no sails were sighted, that was regarded as clear proof that the buccaneer van Ryker had cast off this resplendent creature who had come running aboard in a ball gown and still wore it, like someone demented.

There she was, alone and silent as a ghost by the rail, still ablaze with topazes and diamonds, flaunting her illicit wealth in their disapproving faces. Did she think they were going to hold a ball in her honor? some tittered. Or was she going to wait there forever for van Ryker to catch up? Certainly she looked calm enough now.

It was a facade that had cost Imogene much, but at least it kept her pride from cracking. She stood silently at the rail because she did not want to go back to her cabin and face the specters of memory that would rise up to confront her— memories of another ship and a great cabin that had burned with love.

In the days that followed she was made aware, by many slights and drawn-away skirts, that the women passengers disliked her. The men, sober merchants for the most part, watched her covertly, yearning secretly for her delicious body but prudently keeping it to themselves. For there was a brooding emptiness in those beautiful delft blue eyes that told them they would get nowhere with her. That lovely expressive face had assumed a masklike quality that told the beholder nothing of what she was thinking or feeling.

Only one passenger, a small wrenlike woman named Gert, made any overtures of friendliness toward Imogene. At her vigil by the rail one day, Imogene heard a voice behind her say, "Would you not like to share a bit of my porridge, Madame van Ryker? For I've gone again and made too much and 'twill only be wasted?"

Imogene turned gravely to look down into that small pert face. "I'd like that," she said gently. "And indeed I've some leaves of the new China drink, which would go well with it. If you've some hot water to brew it?"

The expensive new China drink! Gert was delighted. Imogene fetched the metal tin of black tea leaves and a pillow and sat and watched her newfound friend brew tea on the open deck. Around them other passengers, as was the custom, had built small careful fires on the deck and were making porridge. They watched curiously as Imogene and Gert shared the tea.

"You know why nobody talks to you?" Gert asked conspiratorially.

"No. Why?" asked Imogene indifferently.

"They be eaten up with envy," pronounced Gert. "Especially *them*. The Osgoods." She bobbed her head meaningfully at a large family of sallow-faced Puritans. "They's going back to England for good. Said the Colonies was a Godless place. Full of *your* kind."

Imogene turned to look at the nearby family clad in sober black. The woman's back was ramrod straight and she returned Imogene's inspection truculently. To gaze into their sallow faces, Imogene could not help remarking, one would have supposed their disapproval extended to sunlight itself, for all were notably pale.

Gert choked on her tea at that remark. The hot drink had warmed her bones and loosened her tongue. "Their children have names like 'Sorry for Sin,' 'Penitence' and 'Lament Thy

Thoughts,' " she told Imogene, giggling. "Their father calls himself 'Bare Bones'. Imagine!"

Imogene shuddered. She turned to watch the children scurrying around with hunted pointy faces, trying to escape the notice of their dour, black-hatted father.

As if incensed at this obvious attention from a sinful buccaneer's woman, Osgood's wife leaped up, overturning a pewter bowl with a clatter. She had sharp features and an even sharper tongue, had Bare Bones's wife—indeed she had narrowly escaped the pillory for some of her remarks made in the New World. She could not forgive this "pirate's wench," as she dubbed Imogene, for combing her hair at the rail day after day with a silver comb, whilst she, Godfearing woman that she was, was forced to comb her own dull locks with a wooden one.

"Gert Tyler, you are accepting tea from this pirate's woman!" she shrilled. "I would think it would stick in your throat! And," she added balefully, "there are those of us who'll remember it of ye back in England!"

Gert dropped her cup at this outburst. Imogene would have risen to confront her detractor, but Gert, busying herself cleaning up the spilled tea, tugged at her skirt to pull her back.

"They's vengeful, these Puritans," she muttered. "You'd best look to yourself. That pack there"—she nodded her head without looking up—"are going to Plymouth same as me."

Imogene settled back with a sigh. She understood Gert's fear of reprisal later. It did not surprise her that from then on Gert ducked her head and scuttled away when she passed. There were no more tea parties.

After that Imogene proffered nothing to the other passengers—not her friendship nor the fine claret and Canary that van Ryker had had put aboard for her use—although she did covertly pass out oranges among the children. She sat on deck alone, nibbling the excellent Cheshire cheese and the puddings and other dishes that were prepared for her by the ship's cook and served by an eager cabin boy—both of whom had been overjoyed to receive as payment for their services golden links from the heavy money chain that lay in the bottom of her trunk. Around her on deck the other passengers gathered in little groups, cooking their oatmeal and dried pork and pease and munching dry ship's biscuit. They washed down their food with beer and muttered as Imogene drank fine wine from a silver goblet that had, along with table cutlery and plates, been packed in the trunk that had been put aboard for her.

"Thinks she's too good for the likes of us," she heard more than once, but any overture she made was turned down with a sniff and a toss of the head as the *Goodspeed*'s passengers banded together against her.

Imogene was a woman who loved life and good times and their treatment of her was a further burden. She was bereft—and lonely.

In time she found a friend—the ship's cat.

His name was Nicodemas and he had thick short black fur and four white paws and a purr loud enough to wake the dead. He leaned blissfully against the legs of the passengers, purring for all he was worth—but it was with Imogene that he found a home.

It happened on a particularly unhappy day when Imogene

sat on deck waiting for Nat, the cabin boy, to finish preparing her dinner. She spent the time looking pensively at the pen of green turtles, waiting patiently above deck for the day when they would be cooked and eaten. As Nat brought her a platter, from a nearby group gathered around their little cookfire a head turned spitefully.

"Pirate's woman!" spat a voice. "No wonder nobody will eat with her."

At that moment Nicodemas loped up, stared intently up into Imogene's face with enormous earnest green eyes, and tentatively extended one furry white paw. He was hopeful of receiving a bit of succulent meat from her plate but Imogene, driven to fury by the constant ill will of her fellow passengers, accepted it as the paw of friendship.

"Nat." Her clear voice rang out, drawing everyone's attention. "Prepare another plate, if you please. I am to be joined by a gentleman."

Bewildered, Nat did as he was told, looking uneasily around him.

"Set the platter down there beside me," directed Imogene. She pushed it under the nose of the now excited Nicodemas. "Nicodemas is better company than anyone here," she remarked casually to nobody in particular and there was a general mutter around the deck.

Nicodemas did not care about murmurs. Enraptured, he demolished his chine of beef, purring away, and afterward followed Imogene to her cabin, where he jumped to the foot of her bunk and sat happily licking his paws.

After that the black and white cat and the buccaneer's woman were inseparable. And if there were those on board who complained that the ship's cat had lost interest in the ship's rats now that he was dining elegantly on silver platters, the captain—who valued Nicodemas—ignored such grumblings.

Day followed endless day on this voyage across the ocean. Isolated, cold-shouldered, Imogene felt she would have gone mad had it not been for the company of her staunch furry friend, Nicodemas. But in spite of that, her spirits sagged.

For Imogene the storm was, in some ways, a godsend.

She had been slipping down of late, down into despondency. Not even Nicodemas with his friendly purr and his habit of curling up and sleeping on the foot of her bunk with his furry chin propped trustingly on her ankles, and his way of strolling up the blankets and touching her cheek with his warm pink tongue when he felt she should wake up and feed him, could pull her out of it. It seemed to her that her life, so turbulent always, was finally shattered past all repair. If she could not count on van Ryker, who could she count on? Oh, why had he not let her slip over the side of the ship to oblivion on that long-ago night when he had pulled her back from self-destruction—if he was going to do this to her?

She began to pace the deck through the long days, brooding on that. She ignored the frowns of the women passengers and how they averted their faces and passed by her with a contemptuous flirt of their skirts. She saw instead the cool deep water in whose depths one could float endlessly, those depths that made all human problems irrelevant. . . .

With every day those waters looked more inviting to her.

She began to spend more and more time at the rail, staring in fascination at the gray green sea. The passengers remarked it—and shrugged. Did this foolish woman expect her buccaneer to rise suddenly from the sea like Neptune from the waves? They tittered to themselves and nodded their heads wisely. Imogene was far past caring. She was teetering on the brink of self-destruction.

Live without van Ryker, without him. . . . It pounded in her head, sapping her will to live. Half crazed with grief, one gray day she leaned into the mist far over the rail. It would take only a moment to go over the side and it seemed to her that it would solve everything.

She had actually started to climb over when the first drops struck her face. They did not fall gently but landed like a handful of sand dashed in her face. She flinched back from those cold drops that turned swiftly into a sheet of rain that drenched her.

The shock of that cold water, the misery of standing there wet and bedraggled, brought her painfully to her senses. Not only did it restore her to sanity—it made her realize she was a woman wronged. She had been mourning her loss—now she turned a bright-eyed, resentful face into the rain.

Nothing would please Veronique more than to have her rival do away with herself—well, she would not give the Spanish woman that pleasure!

How *dare* van Ryker profess his love for her when all the time he was deceiving her with Veronique? Wrenching as it was to believe in her heart that he well might be at this very moment lying recumbent in his bunk in the *Sea Rover*'s great cabin toying with the ribands of Veronique's black chemise, running his hand down through the spiderweb black lace to stroke the creamy olive skin below—instead of driving her over the rail, that thought now made her furious.

Ah, if she but had him before her once more! What she would do to him! Her blue eyes blazed.

And—knowing him—what would make him angriest? Her eyes narrowed thoughtfully. Jealous fellow that he was—despite the fact that he had taken a mistress—nothing would gall him more than for Imogene to take a lover.

Unfortunately, there were no likely candidates aboard. . . .

She looked down and saw that Nicodemas had run up to her through the rain. He was rubbing against her long skirts, swishing his tail expectantly in anticipation of his dinner. She swept him up in her arms and looked into his knowing green eyes.

"I'll *find* someone, Nicodemas," she whispered to the cat. "Wait till I get ashore!"

Nicodemas purred blandly and shook his head and ears to fluff up his fur and dislodge drops of water. Like her, he was getting soaked.

But as she marched off toward the cabin with him, with the rain pouring down her face, her fair hair wet and sticking to her forehead and her clothes rapidly becoming a sodden mass, her sinking heart admitted something else: *She still loved van Ryker, she would always love him.*

Dear God, what she would not give to have him back! No matter what he had done! She would forgive him all. . . .

A bitter laugh drove raindrops into her mouth. It was doubtful she would have the chance to forgive him. Veronique would see to that!

Back in her cabin she changed her clothing and dried her wet hair—and dried an unhappy and bedraggled Nicodemas with the same towel. Then she climbed into her bunk and hugged the damp cat.

"Nicodemas," she whispered. "We may need our courage. I don't like the sound of that wind."

The captain, frowning on deck, did not like the sound of it either.

North of the Azores the storm had caught them, and now it drove them before it willy-nilly. For four days and four nights the bleary-eyed captain had hardly slept, trying to guide his ship before the lashing wind. Now with another night drawing on, great sheets of rain beat against the *Goodspeed*'s torn and straining canvas and cascaded down like a waterfall onto her slippery wooden decks. Had the *Sea Rover* been near, van Ryker would surely have taken Imogene off before the storm broke to the greater safety of the *Sea Rover*'s massive hull. But the *Sea Rover* was far away, beating its way toward them across the broad wastes of the North Atlantic.

First there had been a mist so thick that Captain Bagtry could not see where they were going, and then this storm had come out of nowhere, blown the mist away and replaced it with driving rain and seas that rose ominously high, great walls of water that seemed intent on breaking open the *Goodspeed*'s fat sides.

It was a terrible time for the passengers, most of whom were seasick and groaning. During storms like this one, Captain Bagtry heartily despised them all, complainers that they were, but against Imogene he would forever nurse a special grudge, for at the storm's height she had done something that had ruined her in the captain's estimation forever.

At a terrible cracking sound that meant to her that a mast had snapped, she had raced to the deck. Great dark waves were roaring at them out of sheets of rain that slapped like the crack of a mighty whip. And in a wild bolt of the almost continuous blue lightning that raged around them, Imogene saw the last two survivors among the green sea turtles that had been taken aboard in Tortuga as fresh food for the journey. With the reduction of their numbers, the pen had been abandoned and the two turtles had been bound securely against the day when they too would be served up. But now they lay pitifully in the wash of the waves, being battered back and forth against timber and rigging. At any moment one of those great waves might sweep the deck clean and they would drown!

Imogene, who loved living things, fought her way toward those helpless gentle giants through the wild crashing seas. The captain saw her and bawled at her to get below. When she continued her course, he moved toward her, bellowing. She could see the knife at his belt—a knife he always wore, ever since that long-ago day in the Bahamas when a crazed sailor had leaped upon him unaware with a long sharp knife and carved a scar upon his arm that would be with him to his grave. Imogene's gaze fixed on that knife—if she could but reach it! Ah, he was very near now, he was within reach! Before the captain could guess her intention, her hand snaked out and snatched the knife from his belt.

He saw the knife in her hand and fell back in alarm. "Gone

mad!'' he gasped, and had a wall of water dash into his face and choke him.

When the water receded, he saw that Imogene was leaning over the turtles, slashing at them.

The captain, not comprehending her intent but being in no mood to defend the turtles in such a gale, tottered back to the helmsman. "Gone mad!" he bawled. "Trying to kill the turtles now!"

Intent on trying to keep the ship headed into the wind, the sweating helmsman—the better for his peace of mind—never heard that comment. He was grunting with the strain, for he could not hold the course, and Captain Bagtry, turtles forgotten, threw himself forward to add his own weight to the cause. Meantime Imogene hacked away and watched, exhausted but triumphant, as the green sea turtles, on their backs but freed, slid across the slanting deck and disappeared into the sea with the next wave. Exhausted by her efforts, she drove the knife into what was left of the mast and staggered back to her cabin. When the captain looked back, after a hard ten minutes during which it seemed the ship could not survive another mauling wave, he saw neither turtles nor woman.

"Gone over the side," he mused. "And just as well. Can't have a madwoman rushing about—" He leaped forward again as another great wave threatened to collide with them from the side. "Hold her!" he yelped. "She'll turn over!"

Battered, leaking at every seam, somehow the *Goodspeed* still managed to hold together. And at her helm the captain now cursed his luck, for they were near England now and these mountainous seas and violent wind-driven rain were sending the *Goodspeed* with a broken mast hurtling toward the Cornish coast.

Desperately he turned his ship south, trying to find his way around Land's End to Lizard Point and thence into the English Channel.

But it was not to be. The gale that had dogged them since the Azores was now about to dash them upon the Western Rocks of the Scillies—that archipelago of "fortunate isles" that lay off England's southern tip.

Imogene was down below, huddled with Nicodemas, trying to snatch fragments of exhausted sleep, for the beating of the gale and the ship's tossing and the imminent danger of capsizing or being swamped by the enormous waves had battered both passengers and crew alike almost into insensibility.

She woke to the wild tossing of the ship—woke indeed when the vessel almost turned over and she was flung violently against the wall. She came to groggily in the damp darkness, trying to collect her scattered wits. She was aboard the *Goodspeed* and van Ryker and the *Sea Rover* were far away.

Pray God that he be safe, she thought treacherously. And then turned her face to the wall and lay there, wracked with silent sobs.

A wave breaking against the hull nearly tossed her from her bunk and she sat up, hanging on to the bunk, listening to the loud protesting creaking as tortured timbers tried to ride out the storm.

She knew they were near the English coast. She had heard the captain say so, shouting it through the gale at one of the passengers. They seemed to have been traveling interminably across a fierce and endless ocean. Lifetimes, eons might have passed, but in her heartbreak Imogene had hardly noticed the passage of time. Gradually she had made a hard peace with herself. Van Ryker, she had told herself stonily, was gone. Out of her life. Completely.

But she had all of her life to live out. Without him.

Somehow she would do it.

Nervously, in her rocking bunk, she twisted the ring on her finger. It was a square-cut emerald set in heavy gold—a mate to the one van Ryker always wore on his little finger. Imogene was wearing hers on her middle finger for the jeweler had made it too large and there had been no time to have it cut down. She touched it with bitterness. *If ever you need me,* he had told her, *send me this ring.* And even then he had been lying, planning his future without her.

The ship shuddered again like a creature in pain. Most likely they were foundering. Horrified by the thought of being trapped below with the dark water rushing in, Imogene fought her way on to the deck, being tossed bruisingly against wooden walls as she did so. Once there, the rain struck her like a solid blow and she winced back as a sudden wide bolt of blue lightning lit the scene.

She would have edged forward, hanging on to whatever was available, but that vivid lightning bolt brought her to a staring halt—for it had illuminated a scene with which she was all too familiar.

She knew those rocks! The ship was not out upon the North Atlantic's broad face, where she had confidently believed it to be. Somehow in the night they had careened past Land's End, somehow missing the rocky monolith that rose menacingly from a cauldron of waves, soaring to a height of some sixty feet. While she lay tossed about in her bunk, they had passed that scramble of weirdly shaped tiny islands with picturesque names like Spire and Shark's Fin and Armed Knight and Irish Lady. Those sharp sawtooth rocks just ahead that the blue lightning had illuminated, those upthrust rocks with their grotesque shapes sculpted by a thousand such storms, were the Western Rocks of the Scillies! A notorious graveyard of tall ships!

Slipping in panic over the wet careening deck, clinging to ropes—to anything, she clawed her way to the captain's side.

"You must turn hard to starboard," she screamed at him, "or you'll end up on the rocks!"

Through blinding sheets of rain, she saw him turn, saw him start, saw his face turn livid. *Up from the dead!* he was thinking, and then his careening senses righted themselves. He got hold of himself and shook his gray head.

"Nay, mistress," he bawled. "Ye see those lights over there? Them's shore lights!"

Her wet hair, come loose, whirled about in the gale and struck her in the face like a wet hand. She pushed back that curtain of wet hair and peered forward. The captain was right. Lights danced in the distance. Lights where there should be no lights. She dashed the water from her lashes to clear her shimmering vision and the lightning came again. It showed her a two-humped landmass rising out of the boiling cauldron of waters that seemed about to engulf them.

"But that is St. Agnes Isle!" she cried. "Those must be wreckers' lights! They seek to deceive you, to wreck you. See, that larger mass is the main part of the island and that other smaller part is called the Gugh. Oh, listen to me," she pleaded, seizing his arm. "I am from these islands, I have sailed these waters!"

"Go away, mistress!" cried the beleaguered captain, who was having all he could do to avoid the rocks that seemed to come at him from all sides like great snapping fangs.

"No!" she screamed in panic as she saw a great rock rise up ahead. She made a lunge for the wheel and the captain sent her spinning away from him with one hand. She lost her footing and would have gone overboard with the next onrushing wave save that she managed to seize the rail and cling to it, half into the sea.

The great sea that had washed over the ship subsided as the *Goodspeed* wallowed in the trough of the next wave. A sailor saw Imogene hanging helplessly half over the side and pulled her back, shoved her toward some ropes on which her hands closed thankfully. He was moving toward the captain when the next wave struck—and caught him on the clear deck. It was a fatal error. Imogene's scream was lost in the shrieking wind as she saw the wave go over him, lift him—then the spray smashed into her face, blinding her. When she opened her eyes, choking and gasping, he was gone, washed somewhere out into the fury of the sea.

Saving her had cost him his life.

But Imogene knew—if the captain did not—that their sands had run out anyway. Surely no ship could make it through this patchwork of jagged rocks, thrown as they were this way and that by the violence of wind and wave. And even if they did—St. Agnes waited. Rocky St. Agnes Isle that had ground up so many good ships and left the broken bones of men and ships to litter the pounding sea.

But there was no use, she realized, trying to tell the captain anything. He had made his choice and, like a man demented, he was driving the *Goodspeed* through rain and rocks and screaming ocean. After four days and nights of storm he had lost faith in nearly everything. He *had* to believe in those lights. Somehow, magically, the ship still survived.

Imogene's gaze, as she clung to the ropes, was still riveted in horror at the sight ahead and those dancing lights that beckoned to the captain. The ship, she knew, had but minutes to live. And the passengers seemed to know it. On deck now, they swirled around her in a screaming mass, dragging their children and their possessions, clinging to whatever offered, crashing into each other. About her all was confusion.

But one pair of blue eyes was calm now, fatalistic. For Imogene clung to the ropes, watching those giant rocks rise up and disappear beneath the waves with frightening regularity.

Growing close now was the awesome sight of St. Agnes's rugged shores, the massive cliffs towering above the breakers. Lightning flashed again and she traced in her mind that landscape she knew so well. Up there on the main part of the island was the cottage where Clara, Elise's sister, had lived. And down there was St. Warna's Bay and the tall standing stones men called Adam and Eve, that she had asked on summer nights to send her a lover. . . .

Fate, that deadliest of hunters, had brought her home to the Scillies—to die.

BOOK III
The Shipwrecked Beauty

His hot gaze scorches her burning cheeks
As his long strong arms enfold her,
But her future would be a life of shame
If she stayed and let him hold her!

PART ONE
The Wreckers

The waves that pound upon the beach
Have many tales to tell.
They've dragged her back and now they'll teach
This lass the ways of hell!

The Scilly Isles,
1661

CHAPTER 21

It is said that in life's last breathless moments one's past passes before the mind like some vast roll unfurled.

It happened that way to Imogene.

As she waited fatalistically for the ship to strike and break apart, for those sturdy wooden timbers to shatter and the dark wild seas to break over them and drag them down, down into the wet depths, Imogene looked with steady eyes out through the sheets of wind-driven rain and saw St. Agnes Isle once again as it had been for her on that last day there. . . .

She saw again the copper-haired lover who had seduced her on the night-glamoured beach below Star Castle on nearby St. Mary's Isle. Her first lover, Stephen Linnington, a man she had thought so true. . . . She felt again the wild wet surf pour like white lace around her naked thighs and froth like bridal lace around her shining naked breasts. All that she had felt that night, when in her heart she had pledged her troth to him, washed over her again and she was dizzy with remembering, shaken with the wonder of that first awakening.

It was Stephen who had known her first, loved her first. Indeed, it was Stephen who had been making love to her on the hot beach at St. Agnes that day they had stolen away from Ennor Castle where she had been visiting her best friend, Bess Duveen, and sailed to St. Agnes . . . that terrible day when Giles Avery had followed them to bring to Imogene her guardian's decision that she was to wed not Stephen but Giles. And come upon them suddenly, stiffening in shock as he saw them lying naked together, bodies entwined upon the sand.

It was a remarkable betrothal announcement delivered as it was as maddened Giles drew his sword and plunged over Imogene's prone body in a mad attempt to run Stephen through. Instead Giles had tripped and found himself impaled on Stephen's hastily drawn blade.

They had tried to save his life, to bring him aid—but Giles had died there on St. Agnes. Stephen and Imogene had looked at each other with a wild surmise. They had both known even then that if they claimed Giles's death was an accident, they would not be believed. They would not be believed, in Imogene's view, because her wild nature had prejudiced the gossips against her. But Stephen had known something else, something he had not told Imogene—he had not dared let his own wild past catch up with him.

So he had fled, and left his love on the Scillies.

Imogene had been so sure he would come back, she had meant to wait for him. Forever if need be. But Giles Avery's family were certain Imogene had contrived in Giles's murder. And her guardian had realized her danger and packed her off to Amsterdam.

She had not seen the Scillies again. In Amsterdam she had met the Dutchman and made a disastrous marriage from which she had been rescued by van Ryker.

She had loved him so.

And he too had proved false.

Her romantic past with all its glory and bitterness rose up before her like those towering black rocks that reached their fangs up from the sea to devour the ship. Imogene waited stoically for the sudden grinding shock that would presage the ship's wooden timbers bursting apart.

Life was exacting a price from her, she felt. She would pay for her recklessness, pay for it dearly—even if by some miracle the ship survived these treacherous rocks uprising from the sea's vast churning cauldron. Even if she survived the wreckers whose lights danced up ahead.

For she knew fatalistically that Giles's family would never cease to hate her. They would see her hanged.

For such as she there was no way out. She would pay for those other days when she had thrust reason and sanity aside and taken—with Stephen Linnington—the lovers' path to doom. Pay for them dearly—with her life.

Like a great tolling bell, fate's hammer had sent forth yet another peal. The familiar sawtooth rocks of the Scillies lay dead ahead welcoming her to death.

Imogene stood braced, waiting for the ship to strike. But when it struck at last, she felt unprepared. There was a sudden grinding lurch, and a great shudder that shook the hull from stem to stern. Great spumes of foam shot over them, competing with the sheets of blinding rain.

For a few moments she could not see. And then—as if it had achieved its purpose by piling them upon the rocks—the rain slackened suddenly and in the lightning's flash she could see exactly where they were. They were almost on St. Agnes Isle and below the gnarled rock masses and massive towerlike boulders and curtain wall of cliffs were dancing lights—the lights the captain had pointed out. Lanterns.

Wreckers, she thought and was surprised to find, even in this extremity, a chill of fear course through her. But it is one thing to pit one's self against the sea, implacable as it seemed tonight, and quite another to drag one's self exhausted from the surf and be clubbed to death.

Wreckers . . . she had heard enough stories about how they operated.

There was a nasty but quite rational reason why the wreckers killed so mercilessly. Under the law, if anyone survived a shipwreck, those salvagers from the shore who had risked their lives to save the cargo could not claim their loot. If no one was left alive, the law tended to shrug. To a wrecker the logic of that was simple—and deadly.

Under the circumstances, it was a rare soul who survived a shipwreck upon these forbidding shores.

But even this new horror bursting upon her was fleeting, for she expected in that instant to be dragged down by some great green sea oversweeping the deck, some final catastrophic wave that would force them to the bottom—and turned in surprise to find that it had not happened yet.

They had, she realized after a moment, crashed onto the

jagged rocks in such a way that the ship remained suspended on those stone fangs, like some helpless little sea creature waiting to be devoured. On either side of them the seas beat, slowing grinding the hull to pieces, but for the moment they were perched there drenched in plumes of sea spray.

People were running about the slanted deck, slipping, shouting. Some of them staggered under possessions they had clawed from the rapidly filling hold. Soon the deck was filled with a jumble of trunks and boxes and valuables, all slithering this way and that, knocking down the hysterical running passengers.

At the height of the storm the ship's boats had come free from their lashings and been washed away by the same wave that had snapped the *Goodspeed*'s mainmast like a toothpick and sent it overboard to be lost in the massive seas—all save one.

Now amid the wild panorama of the ship's tilted deck, Imogene saw that the crew was trying to launch it—and having trouble doing it.

As she watched, the set-faced Puritan woman, dragging her crying children, scrambled into it. Little Sorry for Sin gave a howl as her shins were bashed against the wood of the boat. Beside her Lament Thy Thoughts was crying lustily. Gert Tyler, the little wrenlike woman with whom Imogene had shared tea and porridge, tried to clamber in but was knocked back sharply by Bare Bones himself. His face was contorted with fear as he leaped in and gave a mighty push against the hull, designed to send them away from the ship's side and down into the sea.

It was the wrong move. At this added insult, the ropes

broke and the boat overturned, spilling the shrieking family into the sea. The boat, dangling now by a single rope, crashed down on top of them. Gert Tyler, leaning far over the side and screaming in horror, toppled over after them, made a wild grab at the boat, which bobbed tantalizingly away from her, and disappeared shrieking into the wild sea not to be seen again.

Wild pantomimes were taking place around her as desperate men and women struggled in vain to save themselves.

Imogene felt mesmerized by horror.

Now from the rail someone, a member of the crew, was beckoning.

Numbly following his gesture, Imogene saw what he intended. A moment later he had dived overboard.

She struggled to the spot from whence he had plunged. And now she saw what he could see. The hull of the disabled ship, helpless as it was, still made a kind of bulwark against the advancing waves and behind it the route to shore was relatively clear.

It was a difficult—but possible—swim.

But at the end lay the lights of the wreckers.

As she peered at those dancing lights, the blue lightning lit up the shore again. Was that a boat being launched?

Fear raced through her.

A *wreckers' boat*, she thought, and had a sudden wild vision of men clambering over the side of the wrecked ship, of being seized by her long fair hair and clubbed senseless and tossed into the sea.

Instinctively she removed the topaz and diamond necklace from around her neck. It was not valuable like the van

Rappard diamonds, of course, but it was a trophy one could be clubbed to death for. She coiled her long hair tightly against the swim so that it would not sweep over her face in the waves, blinding her and causing her extra effort to dislodge it. The earrings might well be lost in the sea, but she worked the necklace into her tightly coiled hair. If it stayed there, it might be something to bargain with, to buy her life perhaps.

More people were going overboard now. A man dragging a woman in a sodden purple dress shoved by her and she recognized them as a dour couple from Glasgow who had muttered and turned their heads every time she passed. The woman clawed at the railing and hung back but the man heaved her over. The woman screamed as her purple dress described an arc toward the water. Her husband jumped in after her and Imogene saw him fighting valiantly to keep her head above the water, but she was terrified and clutched him around the neck, dragging him down. The little Miller lad took a running jump and dived in; Imogene saw him come up and swim strongly toward shore. A woman went over holding hands with her two children. They struck a floating board and went under, hands gripped. They did not come up again.

Imogene took a deep breath. There was nothing for it but to give the sea a try. At any moment the hull might go and this spot where she stood would become a foaming cauldron full of flying debris. It was now or never.

Quickly, bidding herself not to think, she shucked off her shoes and stockings and tore off her wet dress and petticoat. Driven by desperation, she ruthlessly ripped off all the lower ruffles of her chemise and the big sheer sleeves so that only a scrap of cloth remained, enough to cover her breasts and reach to her hips. Modesty no longer mattered—it was survival that counted.

She took a last look at those lights on shore and braced herself for the plunge into the dark water. She was about to go over the side when she remembered Nicodemas, trapped in the cabin, for she had thoughtlessly shut the door. She could not leave him there to die!

The captain, who was beckoning to her now as the last to leave, saw her turn back and watched agape as she headed back toward her cabin. He gnawed at his beard for a moment, scowling, and then went over the side himself. Be damned if he'd drown for a madwoman who'd no doubt be screeching and clawing at him if he tried to bring her back to the deck! And who knew if the ship could last another second, impaled as she was on these blasted rocks?

But Imogene, on her way to the cabin, had found what she was looking for: a keg well wound with rope with two handholds for lifting it. The keg might once have contained something heavy but it was empty now. She kicked it among some ropes, where it lolled back and forth, and went to fetch a terrified Nicodemas.

It was no easy matter getting the cat to the keg. He was in a frenzy of terror and she had to drag him, spitting and howling, from the bunk. When she fell at last with him onto the keg, his slashing claws ripped her chemise up the side and gave her a long gash. But once his claws fixed into the thick ropes, they stayed there with fiendish determination. Nicodemas was not to be wrested from his rocking perch by anything human. His green eyes were wide and staring, his furry black coat entirely soaked, his ears lay down flat and his mouth was wide open and wailing imprecations against all oceans and all ships.

He looked thus as she staggered to the rail with him and threw cat and keg out as far as she could.

The keg made a clean landing. Nicodemas went under with it, but so fierce was his hold that he came up out of the water still clinging to the keg, his hold intact. He remained anchored there, bobbing in the water. Imogene feared he would be dashed back against the hull, the keg would shatter and Nicodemas would drown.

Now nearly naked and with her fair hair as tight as a cap, she took a last brooding look at those lights on shore and plunged over the side, trying to reach Nicodemas. As she floundered toward him a wave caught her, tossed her. And then another. She had almost despaired of reaching the cat when a playful wave suddenly smashed the keg right at her and she seized one of the pair of rope handholds and let the keg take her with it as it went by. A moment later she had the other rope handhold in a good grip and by a mighty effort kicked her feet.

She had chosen the right moment. A wave just crashing off the *Goodspeed*'s hull hurtled back toward shore carrying her with it—and before her Nicodemas, crouched down flat, wet as a seal, mouth grimly closed against the salt water, staring into the darkness with wide terrified eyes.

Like the figurehead of a ship, Nicodemas rode the keg to shore. Fighting exhaustion, breaking her hold now and again to use one arm in a short powerful stroke, Imogene—fine swimmer that she was—brought him there. She shoved the keg up into the surf and in a single bound Nicodemas sprang to the wet sand and disappeared from view. Imogene saw him go and sagged against the keg.

Excellent swimmer that she had always been and accustomed to these waters, she still had almost drowned as she fought her way through the battering waves toward shore and those dancing lights. Her one hope on reaching it was to lie apparently lifeless in the surf until those lights danced away, then struggle out and scamper to safety over the rocks.

It was not to be.

As she reached the shore she could see what was happening to those stronger male passengers who had arrived before her. They were being dragged out and clubbed to death and their howls of rage and pain and despair poured through her consciousness like a scalding bath.

There to her right in a lantern's swinging light she saw a wet staring face disappear in a splash of blood. Over the pounding surf she could hear agonized grunts and bones snapping and one wild agonized wail as someone—she thought it was Captain Bagtry—staggered back into the sea to die.

The wreckers at their fearsome work. . . .

Later on, boats would be put out to save the cargo. There would be real acts of heroism as the tough wreckers fought the seas to save the *Goodspeed*'s goods.

But now was the time of killing.

Stunned by the ugly brutality of the scene, Imogene too would have staggered back into deeper water but that a lantern bobbed suddenly beside her.

"Here's another one!" came a hoarse shout and as she turned in panic a man's fist delivered a glancing blow to the side of her head that dropped her on her hands and knees into the surf.

She only half heard the woman's scream nearby. Blinded momentarily by pain, she never saw the bludgeon the man who had struck her now lifted to finish the job.

But a woman in worn homespun who had been shivering among the wreckers with a shawl wrapped around her now plunged forward over the wet sand of the beach.

"No!" she cried piercingly. "Don't hurt her, Lomax—*she is one of us*!"

Her words gave pause to the giant whose bludgeon was already raised to dash out the brains of the stunned woman in the surf at his feet. As the woman in the shawl clutched his arm he dropped his bludgeon and even assisted her to drag Imogene, reeling, from the water.

"There'll be the devil to pay if this wench talks," he grunted.

"Oh, she won't! She'll say nothing, Lomax—*not ever.* You have my word on it."

Unbelieving, Imogene looked dizzily into a face she knew so well. It was Clara, sister of her old nurse, Elise Meggs. She had somehow assumed that widowed Clara had long since left her little cottage on St. Agnes Isle. Seeing her now was doubly shocking, for it had never occurred to her that Clara would herself be standing amongst the wreckers, conversing with them!

"Clara," she faltered. "Is it really you?"

At her words, the uncertain giant who stood studying the two women in the lantern light, relaxed. The wreckers needed Clara. On this almost uninhabited island she fronted for them—and was not Bowes Granby her lover? Bowes would not appreciate it if Clara were to become angry and attempt to turn him out. Lomax decided he could wait a bit and talk to Bowes before he slaughtered the golden-haired wench. After all, this half-drowned creature he had struck down had no way to leave the island. The wreckers were in control here. And, anyway—he gave her now a more comprehensive inspection in the lantern light—could be they'd have some fun with her later—*before* they disposed of her.

Imogene's blood would indeed have run cold had she known what was in big Lomax's mind.

Clara was pulling her away, but Imogene was still only half-conscious as she stumbled along, leaning on Clara and being urged on vehemently at every step.

"I—can't believe it's you, Clara."

"Yes, 'tis." Tears coursed down Clara's weathered face, tears more for the life she was leading than over this meeting. "I've often thought about you, Imogene, but I never thought you'd return *this* way in a broken-up ship." Her voice was entreating. "Elise isn't with you, is she? I mean, not out there on that ship?"

"No." As she stumbled along, Imogene's head was clearing. "Elise is dead, Clara."

A little cry broke from Clara and her hand went over her mouth. "I knew it, I knew it," she wailed. "For many's the night I dreamed about her and always she looked pale as death and wearing a winding sheet! Tell me, how did it happen?"

"She and—and my baby, little Georgiana"—Imogene choked

over the words—''went down on the *Wilhelmina* when the Spanish sank her.''

Another moan from Clara. Imogene could feel the older woman's shoulders rock as they stumbled through the dark. She felt herself caught up by some terrible nightmare—the darkness, the surf beating, her scanty wet clothing sticking to her, and penetrating her shocked consciousness, retreating now as they went farther from the beach, the screams of dying men.

There was a sudden yowl as something wet ran over their feet.

''Oh, Lord!'' cried Clara. ''What's that?''

Imogene looked down. She could see Nicodemas's eyes, two spots of shining green gold in the dark. ''It's Nicodemas,'' she said. ''He was shipwrecked too.'' She bent down and picked up the bedraggled cat, huddled him against her. It seemed to her a miracle that he had survived.

''Oh, it's a cat,'' sighed Clara in relief. ''I thought there for a minute something *had* me!''

Imogene said nothing. She buried her face in Nicodemas's wet fur and found it strangely comforting in a terrible world.

She was fully restored by the time they reached the stone cottage. Her head still ached where Lomax had struck her but she knew where she was and what was happening. She was on St. Agnes Isle and this was Clara, sister of her old nurse Elise, and down below them somewhere on the beach the wreckers were killing her shipmates.

As full comprehension of their situation came to her, she came to an irresolute stop. ''We must go back and help them,'' she muttered. ''We must get help.''

"There's no help for them now." Clara was urging her on. " 'Twas all I could do to save *you*."

"Then I must go back alone," protested Imogene. "I can't let them—"

"No!" Clara's hold on her tightened in desperation. " 'Tis death to go back—death for *you*. Anyway, 'tis all over. Do you hear anything? *Listen!*"

Imogene paused in her effort to break away from Clara's frantic grip and lifted her head. There was only the roar of the sea and the occasional shouts of the wreckers and the sound of the waves breaking on the rocks.

The time of the killing was past.

"They're all dead," Clara assured her. "And if you go back down there, that's what *you'll* be. Dead."

Imogene's slender form shuddered in that sturdy clutch. Dead . . . all those people she had sailed with such a short time ago. Still half-stunned by this night's terrible events, she let Clara propel her through the cottage door.

"Here, dry off," said Clara gruffly, thrusting a towel at her.

Automatically Imogene began to rub Nicodemas's wet fur. "Clara," she whispered, "how do you stand it? Why don't you go away from here?"

A single candle was burning on the room's single wooden table, and Clara flushed and turned away from its light as if she could not bear for Imogene to see her tormented face. " 'Tis lonely here on St. Agnes," she muttered. "And so silent—after my man died."

Imogene's gaze fled in the flickering light to the long musket above the mantel that Clara had kept polished in memory of her dead husband.

"But—*wreckers*, Clara!" She still couldn't understand how someone as straitlaced as Clara had been could tolerate this life.

"I—I got friendly with one of them," Clara admitted, hanging her head. "His name is Bowes Granby. I met him in Helston and then he sailed over to call. And one thing led to another and he moved in with me. I thought we'd be having the banns called but . . . Bowes weren't the marryin' kind. And then his friends came and 'twas then I learned Bowes's true profession. They're wreckers, and they'd kill me, I do think, were it not for Bowes. And then too they need me to keep up the appearance of respectability when boats and fishermen chance by the island. Here, dry yourself with this. I'll take the cat." As if glad to be doing something, Clara tossed Imogene another towel and took Nicodemas from her and toweled him energetically. "There, you want a bite to eat, puss?" she crooned. "Here, set your little teeth in this!"

She reached into a round iron pot that hung from a tripod at the hearth and pulled out a piece of meat, proffered it to Nicodemas who seized it with a purring growl and ate greedily. Pensively she watched him eat. " 'Tis a wonder you managed to swim through the surf," she told Imogene. "You're the only woman who did."

CHAPTER 22

So the other women had been lost to the sea. . . . Imogene shuddered, and then told herself bitterly that it was a better death than their men had met, believing themselves saved and then as they reached the shore, dragging themselves out of the surf to find they faced a new and implacable enemy.

Imogene was toweling her dripping hair, rubbing life back into her wet body, still clad only in the remnants of her chemise.

"Why don't people stop them, Clara?" she demanded. "They *must* know about them."

Solemnly, Clara shook her head. She bent down to stroke the cat. "They're not locals, and they pretend to be a religious sect seeking quiet and sanctuary. Big Lomax—he's the one who struck you down and would have finished you had I not screamed at him to stop—can talk very pious when he's a mind to. He can convince anyone, big Lomax can, nice as pie when he wants to be. And, besides, they don't sell the stuff local. They take it somewheres else, to the mainland—Helston, I think. Move it by night, they do. About twice a week a boat sails over."

"And you mean no one even notices all this?" demanded Imogene indignantly.

"Why should they?" shrugged Clara. "Lomax arranges the lights and after the"—her voice trembled a little—"the killing is over with and the stuff is on shore, we sorts it and arranges it in piles, and spreads things out to dry. And then the boat with the red sail comes and takes the stuff off."

"Red sail? I'm surprised they'd be so conspicuous."

"They're not afraid," said Clara bitterly. "Because none suspects them, you see."

"Who is it who comes?"

"There's never but one man in the boat and they keep me away those times so I never seen his face. But I heard him calling to Lomax once or twice and he sounded like gentry to me."

Gentry! Indignation fired Imogene. *Mainland gentry stooping to this!*

"He puts up that red sail to say all's well on the mainland. And when Lomax sees that sail he lights a fire on the rocks if all's well. If 'tis not lit, then the boat sheers off."

Well planned, thought Imogene bitterly. *And well manned* —these men were professionals, luring in and stripping wounded ships, falling remorselessly upon the passengers. She shook her head to clear it of the dying screams that still echoed there.

"But *you*, Clara," she demanded passionately. "Once you knew what they were, why didn't you run away? They're not keeping you here against your will, are they?" she asked appalled.

Clara hung her head. "'Tis because of Bowes," she admitted reluctantly. "I ain't never known nothing like it, the way I feel when he holds me in his arms. Not even when my man was alive, it weren't never like it is with Bowes. All warm and lovely. I'd do anything for him, I would." She sighed gustily.

You already have, thought Imogene sadly. *Out of loneliness, out of lust. . . .*

"Your wreckers won't let me live," she told Clara quietly.

"They *will*!" Clara stuck out her lower lip. "I'll talk to Bowes about it." Her eyes burned fiercely into Imogene's. "But ye must swear to say nothing that will endanger us if I get ye out of here."

"Clara," sighed Imogene as she toweled her hair, "you never even approved of me, and now you're risking your life for me. Why?"

"I do it for Elise's sake," Clara admitted frankly. "Because she loved you like her own child." Clara dashed away a tear. "She'd want me to do it. *Swear* now."

"I swear I won't bring the law down on them, Clara—but only because you're here and they might kill you."

"There's Bowes too," Clara reproved her.

Imogene held her peace on that; she had her own opinion about Bowes, a man who would ingratiate himself with Clara and drag her into this hell.

"I'll tell them ye used to live with me and there was

wreckers here before," Clara told her briskly. "They'll believe me."

Imogene doubted it, but she surrendered her towel to Clara, who said, "Now I'll get ye some dry clothes—hush, someone be coming. In there—quick!" she muttered, pointing to the tiny curtained alcove where she slept of nights with her wrecker lover. And the urgency of her whisper drove Imogene behind the curtains and into the feather bed in a bound.

"What brings you back, Bowes?" Imogene heard her ask in an altered tone and even had Clara not admitted it, something in that tone, some warm shivery quality, would have told her that Bowes was Clara's lover.

"Some fellow from the ship give Lomax a knock on the head," Imogene heard a surly masculine voice say.

"Did it kill him?" Clara sounded indifferent.

"No," snarled Bowes. "It didn't kill him. But it laid his head open and I come up here to tell you they'll be carryin' him up here as soon as we make sure there's nobody left alive from the ship. It'll be up to you to clean and bandage his wound."

"He can die for all of me!" Clara flared. "He called me a Cornish whore and not worth spit, he did!"

There was a cry of pain and Imogene guessed that Bowes had seized Clara roughly to emphasize his words. "You'll take care o' him!" he raged. "And you needn't worry about him sayin' nothin' to you. He's out cold and who knows when he'll come to?"

She heard him stomp off and a moment later Clara jerked open the curtains. "They'll be puttin' Lomax in this bed," she said. "But 'twon't be for a while yet. Here, drink this hot soup—ye look about to fall down." She ran to the tall hearth and from the heavy iron pot that hung there suspended on a chain, ladled out soup into an earthenware bowl and proffered it to Imogene.

Wavering on her feet, her own head still ringing from the blow Lomax had given her, Imogene accepted the soup gratefully and drank it all before she spoke again.

"What now?" she asked, feeling some strength return to her limbs.

"Now we'll change our plans," declared Clara energetically. Seeing Imogene seemed to have drawn her away from the wreckers and back into the old respectable life she had once known. "Lomax is the only one as knows you're here. None of the others saw you"—and as Imogene started to demur—"even if they *did* see you, they'll have given you no mind, they'll have thought Lomax finished you off. They didn't see us slip away in the dark. And if Lomax can't tell them—"

"But he *will* tell them, Clara, when he comes to!"

"No, he won't!" Clara shook her head grimly. "Here. You take these." She had been working as she spoke and now she thrust upon Imogene a hastily filled linen square containing a slab of cheese, some brown bread and apples. "And this." She gave her a bottle of wine. "Bowes will never miss it. And take this kirtle and bodice—they won't fit, but leastways they'll cover you up. And put this over your head." She was tossing a big brown linsey-woolsey shawl over Imogene's head as she spoke. "It will keep you warm. 'Tis best not even Bowes knows you was saved," she decided. "You go down and hide among the rocks till I come for you."

Imogene stared at the older woman, moving so competently—

and with her own life at stake if things went wrong. Clara had never liked her much, she was doing this for Elise who was dead. . . .

Silently she uncoiled her hair and held out the topaz and diamond necklace. The earrings were long since gone, snatched away by the angry sea.

"Lor'!" Clara's eyes glittered at the sight. " 'Tis a good thing Lomax didn't see *that*—he'd have split your skull for sure! *Or* that ring." She cast a look at the emerald on Imogene's finger. "He must have missed it."

Imogene moved the hand away from her. That ring was all she had left of van Ryker. She didn't want to think about him but she wasn't going to part with the ring easily, either.

"Take the necklace, Clara," she said quietly. "It's yours, you've earned it. Hide it and if you get a chance to get away from here, *do so!* You can find a new life somewhere else, a better man than Bowes."

"No, I—I couldn't go nowhere else." Clara flinched away from the necklace, as if she felt that leaving here was a condition of the gift.

Imogene sighed. *We all made our own beds*, she supposed— *Clara as well as she. And then we had to lie in them, uncomfortable or not.* "Take the necklace anyway," she said. "Maybe Bowes will have a falling out with these people and want to run away. This will give you running-away money."

Clara's eager fingers closed clawlike around the glittering topazes and diamonds. She stuffed the necklace down her bodice. "I'll find a safe place for it later," she promised.

"Can you get word to Ennor Castle?" wondered Imogene. "I know Hal would sail me across to Ennor. No matter what he thinks of me—and he's probably bitter, for I did jilt him once—he'd do it for Bess's sake.''

''Yes, ye'd be safe could I but get you to Ennor,'' agreed Clara with a frown. ''But I don't know how soon I can get word to them nor where Hal's at these days. Mayhap I can find a way to go over to St. Mary's myself on some pretext.''

Imogene wondered if she could really do that. It was plain Clara was out of touch with life outside this tiny island; would the wreckers trust her enough to let her wander abroad? She paused uncertainly in the doorway. ''When they begin to search for me—''

''They won't search for you, not till big Lomax comes to,'' Clara told her with a grim look. ''And I don't mean he should come to at all.'' She nodded significantly at the lye-pot that she was about to use to make soft soap. ''I mean to pour *that* onto the gash in his head as soon as they leave him to me and go back to the beach. He won't call me names no more nor take off after you, neither! He won't never wake up—this stuff'll eat his brains out!''

Imogene shuddered and went like a shadow through the doorway. She felt as if she were in hell. Clara had always been a decent, unimaginative woman. Now suddenly she had taken a wrecker to her bed and was calmly planning murder.

It came to Imogene with force *whose* murder Clara was planning—a man with the blood of the *Goodspeed*'s passengers and crew on his hands, and who knew how many other innocent victims? She hardened her heart and silently wished Clara luck with the venture.

Moving stealthily, for she did not know if the wreckers had by now fanned out or were all still at the beach, she made her way into the concealing rocks, found a familiar cleft where she could hide concealed even in the daytime. She donned the rough linsey-woolsey clothing Clara had given her—too short and too full but welcome enough over the rag of her chemise. Wearily she wrapped herself in the shawl and even in this extremity—perhaps because of it, for the dangers she had just undergone had washed her mind clear of everything but survival—slept.

Alone in the cottage, true to her promise, Clara poured lye-water on Lomax's head wound—with unexpected results. The pain brought the giant to himself with a howl and he fetched Clara a blow that rendered her senseless. For a moment he stood over her with murder in his little piglike eyes, but the pain in his head drove him away from her to the washbowl where, groaning, he managed to rinse the lye-water from his head before it killed him.

With a mouth afroth with curses, he charged back down to the beach. He was just in time to see the triumphant—and totally dry—removal of Imogene's trunk from the ship. A howl of delight went up from the wreckers as the trunk was opened on the beach and displayed not only a sky blue velvet gown with an amethyst clasp and other feminine garments, but a silver goblet and two silver trenchers and silver toilet articles as well.

"And lookee here!" came a shout as one of their number reached down a gnarled hand and brought up the heavy gold money chain, each glittering link of which would be worth in another century a hundred-dollar bill.

"We're rich!" bawled Bowes. "Must've had royalty aboard!"

"Naw!" Still in pain, big Lomax lumbered down to the

group. "That trunk must've belonged to that wench your slut wouldn't let me kill!"

"Wench? What wench?" On his knees as he rummaged in the chest, Bowes turned to him in astonishment. "Clara didn't say nothing to me about any wench."

"Clara dragged the wench away with her," shrugged Lomax. He groaned again as pain bit into his head. "That was afore she tried to kill me by pourin' down fire on my head!"

Bowes gave him a scathing look. "Probably whiskey," he said. "I told her to clean out your wound. At least it brought you to!"

"Brought me to?" bellowed Lomax. "It near finished me. I knocked her across the room for it. May have done for her," he added indifferently. "I didn't wait to find out."

"Done for—!" Bowes stumbled to his feet. Impelled by fury, he seized the larger Lomax by the throat. "If you've done Clara in," he yelled, "I'll do for you myself! You know she's our safety! The locals round here know her, and she fronts for us!"

Lomax growled and flung Bowes away from him. He moved away grumbling and let Bowes retrace his steps to the cottage, where he found Clara moaning with a concussion and unable to answer him coherently.

The wreckers held a council of war. They decided that whatever had happened to the woman, it was of small account—she could not get off St. Agnes Isle. Clara was walking around dazed and would be in no position to help her, and the only ship that would probably visit in the near future was the wreckers' own boat, which would visit by night when signaled by lights.

So suppose there *was* a woman wandering around the island? Hunger would drive her to them, or if her fear was too great, she might finish herself off in the sea, trying to swim to some safer place. They'd search for her at their leisure. Meantime, there was more flotsam to be searched for, found and salvaged, and all that stuff to be hauled away from the beach lest some passing fisherman see it and get suspicious. By the time anyone called, they'd be back in their brown robes walking around piously with their heads bent as if in prayer.

This decision gave Imogene precious time.

Although Clara was in no shape to aid her, in the dusk of the next evening, a little recovered by her day's rest and by eating bread and cheese and apples, Imogene made a discovery. One of the ship's boats—perhaps the one that had overturned as they tried to launch it—had been beached by the waves. It lay now overturned in the sand, almost hidden beneath a shelving outthrust of rocks.

She knew now what she was going to do. . . .

It was two days before she could put her plan into effect, two days in which Clara could make only muddled answers to Bowes's angry questions as he glared down into her glassy eyes, two days in which the wreckers hauled away and sorted out their loot from the *Goodspeed*, two days in which the sea quieted so that great waves did not boom against the cliffs of St. Agnes.

But on the evening of the third day, Imogene, from her rocky hiding place, saw the sails of a fishing boat approaching.

She guessed that it was not coming here, but merely passing by on its way home. She timed its approach and hurried down through the dimness to the beach and the rocky overledge. It was only a short struggle to launch the boat through the now quieter surf. She seized the stout barrel stave she had found to serve her as an oar and bent her back to the task. She doubted her ability to row all the way to St. Mary's, indeed she knew she could well be overturned. But she headed, struggling with all her might with her makeshift oar, toward the small fishing craft. She could see a man aboard that boat now, a small figure peering toward the island, and she waved the big linen square that had contained the food Clara had generously given her.

She was sure the fisherman saw her, for he was coming about, heading toward her now.

Someone else saw her too, for she heard a hoarse shout from the cliffs behind her. The wreckers had discovered her! And if the fisherman discovered a jumble of boats putting out to sea behind her and rowing fast toward him, he might well turn tail lest he be mixed up in something he didn't understand.

She had to prevent that, to keep him from sheering off. Her heart lurched—*was his course wavering?*

With a wild cry that she hoped would carry to the approaching sailboat, Imogene stood up in the boat. She tore off the homespun kirtle and bodice Clara had given her and left them in the bottom of the boat. Wearing only the thin fragment of chemise in which she had swum away from the *Goodspeed*, she stood poised for a moment—a beautiful white and gold figure shining in the late afternoon sun.

Then she knifed over the side with her gold hair blowing back and swam toward the fishing boat.

The fisherman had seen her. Indeed he had been all but struck dumb by the sight of this near-naked beauty, her white flesh gleaming in the sun. And had she not waved to him— nay, *beckoned* him with her scarf? For such he considered the linen square to be. Predictably, he tacked toward her.

Imogene, always a strong swimmer, gave a sigh of relief as she cut the water with long clean strokes. She was sure that even if the wreckers set out now, the fishing boat would reach her first.

From the cliffs of St. Agnes, the brown-robed members of the ''brotherhood'' were running about distractedly. Bowes rushed inside the stone cottage and seized Clara by the throat.

''That woman ye've set upon us,'' he roared through his clenched teeth. ''She's getting away! D'ye know where she be going?''

Clara, thus rudely handled, looked dazedly up at Bowes. ''Woman?'' She tried to clear her muddled head. ''Oh—you mean...'' Snatches of what had been happening came back to her. ''She won't hurt us,'' she mumbled. ''I made her promise she wouldn't bring the law down on us.''

Bowes's expression was ludicrous to observe. A wench's promise! And their lives were to depend on that? He was past speech.

That expression frightened Clara. Her jumbled mind remembered something else. ''If she's gone,'' she declared vaguely, '' 'tis only to her friends at Ennor Castle over on St. Mary's.''

The change on Bowes's face was immediate and—to frightened Clara—amazing.

"To Ennor Caslte," he repeated in a blank voice, relaxing his grasp on Clara. "She's gone to Ennor Castle, you say?"

"Aye," repeated Clara, slumping away from his grasp. "She's got friends there," she mumbled.

"At Ennor Castle?" With a wild guffaw, Bowes flung away from her and went out the door laughing, stood there with his legs wide apart looking triumphant. "Lads, we've naught to worry about," he called to the others. "The wench is on her way to Ennor Castle!"

CHAPTER 23

The bearded fisherman who hauled Imogene into his boat was a man she had never seen before in the Scillies. His pale watery eyes gleamed as he threw her a line and his gnarled hands hauled her over the side.

What a catch! he was thinking. A near-naked mermaid clad in a scrap of cloth that would soon come off!

"You've all my thanks," gasped Imogene, with a look back at the cliffs where brown-robed figures now watched impassively. "I might have drowned but for you."

The fisherman's naked sun-browned chest expanded. "That ye might," he agreed affably. "Name's Tate." And then, his curiosity overcoming him, "What caused ye to leap from your boat?"

"I wanted you to take me aboard for I'd never have made it all the way to St. Mary's—my strength would have given out. I lost the oars and the barrel stave was too awkward for me to handle."

"Ye were doing well enough for a while there," he grinned. "When I first seen ye, ye were making good time!"

"And already wearing out," she sighed, smoothing down her wet chemise around her hips, for she saw that his eyes were roving up and down, studying her through material that—now that it was wet—was practically transparent.

"Be ye from around here?" he wondered.

"I was once, but I've been away a long time."

Away a long time . . . He digested that, stroking his beard. "And have ye relatives here, then?"

"No, not anymore. Could I—could I have something to put on? Anything will do."

He sighed. "I'll look for something." But he made no move to do it.

Imogene tried to crouch low in the boat. Her legs were pressed tightly together and her crossed arms hid her breasts. "Anything—even an old piece of sail," she said desperately.

Tate frowned. He was fooling with his nets, marking time while St. Agnes Isle grew smaller in the distance. "No people at all?" he muttered and straightened up. "Then what be ye doing here?"

"My father and I sailed here from Helston," Imogene improvised—for to tell the true story was to get Clara hanged. "Our sailboat overturned at the beginning of the storm and I made my way to shore—like this." She indicated the remnants of her semitransparent chemise. "For days I waited in the rocks in hopes my father had made it ashore and would find me but I fear he is lost."

"What be your father's name?"

"John Sims," she said quickly, hoping she would be believed. "I am his daughter Janet."

"There be some religious sect living on St. Agnes now. Why did they not give ye clothes or a blanket to put over your nakedness?"

"I—I didn't want to ask them." Imogene cast her eyes down modestly. "All those men . . . Oh, can't you find *something* for me to wear?"

"But they'd have returned ye to Helston."

"I suppose so—but I found a rowboat and when I saw your sails I thought an honest fisherman was just the one to drop me off at St. Mary's, which is not so far."

Tate stood staring down at her. Now he smiled. St. Agnes Isle had drifted far off their bow. Around them was empty water. Above them a couple of gulls screamed and circled.

" 'Tis all a lie," he said softly. "Ye're running from the law, lass. Most like ye stole something from those brown-cloaked fellows and they tore off your clothes to give ye a taste o' the cat and ye escaped them—to me."

"No, it wasn't like that at all! My father and I—"

"Ain't no John Sims in Helston, leastways none with a daughter Janet." Tate's smile broadened. "*I'm* from Helston."

Imogene's heart sank. Of all the bad luck, she had selected the very town this man lived in!

"I'll thank you to deliver me to St. Mary's," she said coldly. "I have friends there."

Tate's derisive laugh chilled her. "*Ye've* no friends there!"

"I have! And they'll pay you well to take me there safe."

"Oh, I'll take you there. And they need not pay me a penny. All I ask is a wee bit o' fun on the way there."

Imogene shrank back. This burly sailor who smelled of fish, with a beard that stank of his morning meal, repelled her. The thought of his flesh was revolting.

"I'm not prepared to pay you in that coin," she said quietly.

Tate was chortling now. "Are ye not? That's funny, that is. For there's no way for ye to reach St. Mary's except to swim it, save I take you. Is there, now?"

"Surely you'll listen to reason." Imogene was tense as a spring now, her wet body ready to leap up and evade him should he dive for her.

Tate saw her tense up. She'd be slippery as a mackerel if he tried to take her now. Let the wind dry her a bit more and she'd be easy to catch. His hard horny hands would close down on that soft body. Oh, she'd squirm frenziedly, like a fish trying to escape her fate—and in the scuffle her chemise would come off. He licked his thick lips. And *then*—then he'd have her down in the bottom of the boat, crushing down those soft hips as he worked his way, squeezing those breasts that seemed to wink at him whenever she turned, trying to keep his gaze away from her.

"Oh, I'll listen to reason," he drawled, admiring his catch.

"No, no, you must hear my story first." Imogene had to keep that rapt gaze fixed on her. For over his shoulder she had seen what he had not: a sail, coming up fast on the horizon. In a little while that sail would be close enough. "I wasn't always bad," she whispered.

Bad? Her captor took a deep happy breath, sucking the air like wine into his lungs. Street wench, no doubt, in spite of her fine way of talking and her delicate aristocratic loveliness.

Oh, she'd know all kinds of cute whore's tricks! He was going to have a fine time.

"You must remember that I—I was only thirteen when I tried out for the theater," Imogene rushed on, babbling out any lies she could think of to keep Tate's gaze on *her* and away from that oncoming sail. "I was selling oranges and I never thought when this fine gentleman took me to an inn because he said I looked thin and needed a good meal to put flesh on my bones, I never *dreamed*—"

"That he'd bed ye?" chuckled Tate.

"That he'd tear my clothes off before I'd even sampled the duck," cried Imogene indignantly. "Of course," she added caressingly, as if she toyed with happy memories, "he was far gone in drink—else he'd never have invited his friends in."

"Oho, so he gave a party with you as the main course?" Tate was delighted, for fishing was a lonely life and a good story was almost as good as a good lay, he reasoned. He'd be telling this one about the taverns of Helston for a long time! "And what did they do to ye, lass?"

"Oh—you wouldn't want to know!" gasped Imogene. "They stripped me naked and threatened me with hellfire."

"With *hellfire*?" Tate was riveted.

"Yes," sighed Imogene, thankful to have his full attention. "One of them claimed to be a preacher and he said the others had lost their sweethearts and unless I gave them comfort I'd be condemned to hell forever!"

Fascinated, Tate shook his head at the strange antics of the gentry. "And did ye fall for that?" he wondered. If she said she had, he meant to try that line on the next innocent lass who wandered his way. Could be he'd learn something here.

"Oh, I—I thought about it, " admitted Imogene. "But they were taking off their *clothes* as they talked and I was so *shocked*—"

"Never seen a man before!" Tate slapped his thigh. "What then?"

"Well, then they said we must all drink wine—and anyone who didn't drain his glass must lie down on the floor and pretend to be asleep. And of course I didn't want to lie down on the *floor*."

"So they got ye drunk?"

"I—I'm afraid so." She gave a hunted look about her that amused Tate mightily. "At least I don't remember anything till the next morning when I woke up on a cart, without a stitch! And I must have been there a long time because the sun was beating down and my body was sunburned. We were heading out into the country. It was some branches that woke me up—the leaves tickled me. Oh, you don't think they paraded me through all of London like that, do you?" she entreated.

"Most likely they started out afore dawn. Where was you headed?"

"They had sold me to this carter and he was hauling me out into the countryside like the baubles he peddled!"

"Quite a bauble he'd picked up!" Tate's brows shot up.

"Yes, and *then*—" She leaned forward conspiratorially and Tate bent forward too. "While we were going through the woods I leaped off the cart into the grass and he never noticed." The sails were coming very near now. "I was floundering through the woods stark naked and I got stuck in *quicksand*—''

'' 'Quicksand'?'' He came alert.

She nodded, apparently as rapt in her story as he. ''And I began to scream, 'Help, help!' '' She threw back her head and screamed the words with all her might.

''Here now!'' Tate cried, darting a look about him—and saw the approaching sails.

But it was too late. His prey was already on her feet, running about the boat screaming ''Help! Save me! Oh, help me!'' And as he plunged after her he could plainly see the man on the other boat run to the side and peer over.

That stranger was in time to view a wild scene as Imogene dived overboard while Tate cursed and leaned over the side, trying to throw a net over her.

''Stand off there!'' came a sharp command from the other boat. And there was the sudden crack of a heavy pistol.

With a howl Tate dropped the net and betook him to sailing his boat fast away from this armed enemy.

Imogene trod water until another line was dropped and she was hauled—more gently this time—aboard another boat manned by a single sailor.

The face into which she looked when her bare feet landed on the deck was a laughing face. The eyes that smiled into her own were blue and merry. The hair that blew around that boyish face glowed red against the setting sun but as he turned she saw that it was actually as dark as van Ryker's. He was as tall as van Ryker too and the naked chest against which she slid to the deck—for his arms had clasped her, hauling her up into the boat—was pleasantly masculine and the wet fabric of her chemise hewed to it, hauling up her already too short skirt.

Quickly she snatched down her skirt, smoothing it nervously around her hips—for she was afraid it might have ridden up above her hips and she had no desire to inflame yet another man this day!

"Welcome aboard," said her newfound friend. "That fellow who's scudding away from us as if the devil was after him didn't look to be the type for a wench like you!"

"He wasn't," she agreed, stepping back. For all that his accent was genteel, she eyed him warily.

"What were you doing with him, then?" Arms akimbo, bare feet planted wide on the swaying deck, clad only in dark trousers in the belt of which was stuck a large smoking pistol, he considered her.

"I thought he had rescued me," she said pensively. "But it seemed I had gone from the frying pan to the fire."

"Oh?" His brows shot up. "Tell me about it."

There was something commanding in the way he spoke. She had the uneasy feeling he might toss her back if he liked not her answer.

"I became lost from my party," she improvised. "Six of us from Helston had decided to go picnicking to St. Agnes. We meant to climb Kittern Hill and see the Old Man of Gugh, and near the cairn, St. Warna's Well below where her hermitage once stood."

"You came to view antiquities," he mused.

"Yes," she said eagerly. "And most especially the two tall standing stones they call Adam and Eve—above St. Warna's

Bay. Do you by chance have a coat? Or even a bit of sailcloth? I'm freezing.''

'' 'Tis a warm night,'' he smiled, eyeing her appreciatively as she stood before him in the bit of blowing chemise.

"But I'm wet and the wind is cold,'' she complained.

Obligingly he proffered his own shirt, of fine cambric, draped it around her. "You were saying—?''

"We landed on the beach and ate our lunch.'' She was struggling to get her wet arms into the shirt sleeves as she spoke and he reached out to help her. His touch was light, caressing. She backed off warily. "Afterward I thought we were going to climb to the stones but we had seen this wreck—''

"Wreck?'' he interrupted alertly.

"Yes, a broken-up hull of a ship. *I* was not interested in it—'' She watched his face because much as she yearned to tell him that the wreck was the *Goodspeed* and that she had been aboard and only just barely escaped the savagery of the wreckers, she knew that Clara's life depended on her keeping silent.

"But the others—''

"Wanted to explore this wrecked hull that was clinging to the rocks. I elected to stay and go swimming instead.''

"You could not have swum all this way,'' he said softly.

Something in his tone alarmed her. "Of course I did not! But I went swimming in—in this.'' She indicated the bit of semitransparent chemise now hidden by his fine cambric shirt that fell halfway to her knees. "And when I came back my clothes were gone.''

Something in the tall man before her seemed to relax. "So your friends stole your clothes? What then?"

"I thought it was a very mean trick," said Imogene hotly. "And I thought that men who would do that would—do other things!"

"And well they might," he murmured.

"So I found a beached rowboat and when I saw a sail, I rowed out in it and called out to the fisherman to take me aboard. He was ready enough to do so."

"But once you were aboard he had other ideas?"

She nodded. "I suppose I could have expected as much."

"Was there no one on St. Agnes to help you?" he asked carelessly. "I am told a widow lives there in a stone hut, and that some religious order has taken up residence on the island."

"I saw no woman," lied Imogene. "And the others must have been at their prayers, for I would certainly have enlisted their aid rather than chance a stray sail!"

"Won't your party worry about you?"

"I doubt it. They were far gone in drink before they decided to explore the wreck. They'll to Helston before they'll miss me! Could you but take me to St. Mary's, I've friends at Ennor Castle."

"It's a fine night—I could sail ye all the way to Helston."

"No, I—I can't arrive like this. In a scrap of chemise and a borrowed shirt! My father would disown me! But at Ennor they'll give me a fresh dress to replace the one I've lost and I can go back to Helston saying I stayed over to visit my friends on St. Mary's."

"And thus suffer no loss of reputation," he agreed sunnily.

418

"Exactly. And since I'm betrothed to a magistrate in Truro"—Did she imagine it, or did he stiffen a bit when she said "magistrate"?—"and he's not one to let his betrothed be spending her time with a wild crowd, I'd take it as a kindness if you'd not mention in what condition you found me?"

The last rosy glow of the setting sun bathed her in its soft light as she spoke. The ruffled white cambric shirt that blew against her delightful figure was turned to strawberry, her golden hair to flame, her fair skin to coral pink, and her delft blue eyes to deep sparkling pools of rosy violet. She was a sight to dream upon, and the man's face softened.

"I'll sail ye to Ennor," he agreed. "Who is it ye seek there?"

"Any of the Duveens," she said carelessly. "Hal, if he's about. Or Ambrose."

That seemed to satisfy him and he brought the boat about and set sail across a claret red sea.

"I haven't asked your name," she said. "Or yet thanked you for saving me from—I know not what."

"It's Harry," he said carelessly. "And I think we can both guess what I saved you from." He grinned.

In spite of herself, Imogene had begun to relax. At least they were sailing in the right direction! And Harry was right, it was a warm night. Her long wet hair was beginning to dry in the breeze, her long bare legs were already dry. If only she could toss off all her clothes for a few minutes, she could arrive dry at Ennor. She yearned to ask Harry to turn his back, but surely that would be asking too much of human nature! A stranger, even with such an angelic smile as his, could hardly be expected to keep his back turned on a naked woman all the way to Ennor Castle!

"You know the Duveens?" she asked.

"Oh, yes." Still carelessly.

"You live on St. Mary's?"

"No, just visiting."

"I did not think your accent was local."

"No, I'm from Oxford originally, but of late I've been living in London."

They sailed for a while in silence. The red glow had left the sea, leaving it bathed in mysterious darkness. Now the moon came up and cast its silvery path across the dark water.

"I've never been to London," she said a little sadly. For it had been van Ryker's promise that he would take her there.

"Ye've not missed much." Did she detect a shade of bitterness in Harry's tone? The sails above them billowed. A night-flying bird cast its silhouette briefly across the moon.

She yearned to ask him why he had said that, but she could feel him studying her. The moonlight bathed her face and hair, but cast him in shadow.

In silence they sailed to St. Mary's and he beached his craft below Ennor. She could see the castle's familiar crumbling mass rising above her. How often she had visited Bess here in the old days! She had even, for a short time, been betrothed to Bess's older brother, Hal. And Ambrose, Bess's younger brother, had been devoted to Stephen and had not wanted Stephen to fight a duel for her.

It had all seemed so far away and now she was about to tread the familiar path up to Ennor once again....

"I'll carry you ashore," Harry said gallantly. "No need to get your feet wet in the surf."

She would have protested but she was bone-tired and hungry from her recent experiences and was more than grateful to have him vault over the side and catch her as she came over.

"I can't stay," he said as he deposited her on shore. "For there's a wench waiting." He grinned. "Will you be all right if I leave you here?"

Imogene nodded. She gave him back his shirt and as she did so, he leaned forward suddenly. "If I had more time, I'd do this properly," he murmured. And of a sudden his mouth pressed down on hers. Ruthlessly. Their lips met and held for a long reeling moment.

Imogene had felt his arms go round her with a kind of shock. They were not so hard and sinewy as van Ryker's arms, but they were pleasant arms. The mouth that sought her own so greedily was a smiling mouth.

He let her go and grinned that boyish smile.

She stood there dizzily, wondering why she had not tried to ward him off.

And then he was gone, leaping back into the boat. He turned to call, "What's your name?"

"North," said Imogene instantly, for wasn't that the direction she'd eventually head? With luck she'd make her way to Bath—and then possibly she'd try London. "Imogene North."

"Take care, Imogene North!" His smile flashed.

She smiled back, then stood and watched him go, saw him wave as the boat receded from view. She couldn't know how she looked to him, standing there near naked, bathed in moonlight with her long fair hair streaming pale gold and the bit of sheer chemise whipped by the wind. Like a vision, a goddess. He watched her as long as he could make out her figure standing there on the rocks.

And Imogene watched his receding sails and wondered about him: who he was, where he was going and why? And . . . treacherously . . . *would he be back?*

Then she turned and began walking up the familiar path toward Ennor Castle.

PART TWO
The London Rogue

He swore he loved the London wench
Who knew his every haunt,
But he's a liar—this woman of fire
Is all he'll ever want!

Ennor Castle,
The Scilly Isles,
1661

CHAPTER 24

Imogene was but halfway to the castle when she heard running feet. Instinctively she stepped into the shadow of the rocks but when she saw the face of the woman who was running down the path, she gasped and stepped out from their cover.

"Bess!" she gasped. "Bess, is it really you?"

The young woman who came to a sliding halt before her had thick dark hair and gray eyes and a face that was at the moment bereft of its usual calm. "Imogene! I looked out the window and saw you standing there on the rocks. I thought I must be dreaming! What are you doing here—and in *that*?" Bess stared at the scanty bit of half-transparent chemise that seemed to emphasize her friend's nakedness in the moon's pale light.

" 'Tis a long story, Bess."

"Then you'd best tell it inside—but we'll slip in a side door. For you'd create a sensation among the servants if you arrived in the great hall in your chemise!" It came to Bess how often by merrily tossing away her whisk, lustrous Imogene had created a sensation merely by baring the top half of her pearly breasts. And in *this*—!

"I never dreamed you'd be here, Bess—I thought you were living on Barbados."

"And so I am. I've a fine plantation there and it's prospering. But Ambrose's letters never mentioned mother, and I feared for her health. So I came to see for myself and found her in bed recovering from a broken hip but otherwise cheerful and in good health."

"And your father, Bess?"

There was a catch in Bess's voice when she answered, "He's been dead these two years past, Imogene. 'Twas his heart—it just gave out one day."

"Oh, Bess, I'm sorry, I didn't know." How forcibly that brought to Imogene how very out of touch she had been with the Scillies!

"No, of course you didn't. We never correspond any-more. . . ." Bess's voice dwindled away, for both of them knew the reason *why* they didn't correspond: Stephen.

"Bess"—it had to be said—"is Stephen with you?"

"No. I left him back on Barbados." Bess stopped in her tracks. "No one here knows I'm married, Imogene."

"Not even your family?" Imogene was amazed. She peered searchingly at Bess. "Why not?"

"Everyone in the Scillies believes Stephen dead," said Bess carefully. "And it's better so. There's that old murder charge against him and—"

"But it was false, you know that!"

"Yes, you know that and I know that, but if Stephen came back they might hang him all the same. So I'm Madame Linnington on Barbados and old-maid Bess Duveen here at home."

"I can't believe you're leading a double life, Bess!" gasped Imogene. "Not you!"

"Well, I am. I mean to keep Stephen safe." The moonlight showed Imogene the worry on Bess's usually calm face. "I—I know you loved him once, Imogene."

"That was a long time ago," said Imogene hastily. "And best forgotten. He's married to you now."

"Yes, and a changed man you'd find him. Even though he was deep in love with you, Imogene, I do believe he now loves me best of anyone in the world." Bess's face glowed with pride.

"Oh, I'm so glad for you, Bess." Sincerity rang in Imogene's voice and Bess felt something tight ease within her. She pushed aside the thought that she was delighted that Stephen had *not* accompanied her to the Scilly Isles. She'd not have relished having old memories roused in Stephen by the sudden appearance of Imogene Wells, half-naked, with the moonlight gleaming on her slim legs and long fair hair!

They had reached a rarely used door of the castle now and Bess struggled to open it. " 'Tis dark in here," she said breathlessly as it finally creaked open. "But we can feel our way by the walls as we go up these stairs."

Gratefully, Imogene followed her friend.

They emerged at last into a wide hall, lit by moonlight from a window at one end. They turned a familiar corner and were in Bess Duveen's room.

Imogene felt she would not have known it. The single candle burning there illuminated new damask draperies, a new coverlet, and a Turkey carpet that had never graced this square shabby room in the days when Imogene Wells had been a frequent visitor at Ennor.

"I'll find you some clothes—"

"Just a night rail for the moment, Bess. I couldn't face everybody's questions tonight."

"No, of course you couldn't. Have you eaten?"

"Not since yesterday. I ran out of food then."

Bess looked surprised but she did not push it. That was one of the nice things about Bess; she didn't try to drag things out of you, she let you tell your story in your own good time. Now she held out a filmy night rail to Imogene.

"But that's lovely! Are you sure you can spare it?"

"I've a dozen like it," declared Bess proudly. "My fortunes have improved since last we met! But you'll be wanting a bath first." She pulled at a big velvet-covered rope.

"Those bellpulls didn't work when I was here last," laughed Imogene.

"A lot of things have changed since I've been back. I've had men swarming about repairing the roof and—" she went to the door, spoke through it. "I'll be wanting a bath brought up right away, Maysie. And supper on a tray.'' She turned back to Imogene. ''Do you like the new drapes and coverlet?''

''I've been admiring them.''

''They're from materials purchased cheap in Tortuga,'' laughed Bess. ''It could be your buccaneer 'lifted' the very damask that's hanging on these walls.'' She indicated the viridian and gold drapes with a nod. ''How is Captain van Ryker, Imogene? Stephen told me about him.''

Imogene had dreaded that question. ''I've left him.'' Her voice was curt.

Bess's indrawn breath spoke volumes. ''I can't believe it,'' she whispered. ''Stephen told me Captain van Ryker was madly in love with you. He said it was a driving force with him—I remember his very words, *driving force*!''

''Well, it isn't any longer. There's—someone else.''

From her knowledge of impulsive Imogene, who had led all the lads a chase, Bess followed that to its natural conclusion. ''You've found someone else?'' she demanded incredulously. She was thinking, *It didn't take long!*

''No. *He* has.'' Bitterly.

Bess's expression took on a kind of awe. Here was a man who had loved Imogene enough to do all the things he had done for her—and he was casting her aside? It wasn't credible. ''I don't think I understand men,'' she said at last, troubled.

''I do. They're polygamous brutes.''

''No. Neither of us thinks that.''

''I think I hate van Ryker. No''—impetuously—''that isn't so, Bess. If he came through that door this minute, I think I'd forgive him. Everything. But—I'm not sure I'd be faithful to him now. Can you understand that?'' She gave her friend a wistful look.

''I think I do,'' said Bess softly. ''You're angry with him, but without van Ryker you're like a ship without a rudder, swinging this way and that wherever the winds take you.''

''Yes,'' Imogene whispered. ''Like that.'' She marveled that her friend should know. ''Bess,'' she said impulsively, ''you're so wise. You always were.''

''Hardly that.'' Bess gave a rueful laugh. ''I was fearfully jealous of you and Stephen. I wanted to send you to the ends of the earth.'' She stopped short, for Imogene, she felt, *had* gone to the ends of the earth.

''*You* didn't consign me to the ends of the earth, Bess.'' Imogene's smile was warm and forgiving. ''I consigned myself. And now I know what it is to watch your man being won away by someone else.'' She went on, speaking almost to herself. ''Now I know all the joys of jealousy, Bess. All the sleepless nights . . . now I know the pangs I must have caused others. All the pangs I must have caused *you*, Bess. For I didn't know how you felt about Stephen at the time.''

Bess smiled her sweet, forgiving smile. ''I didn't want anyone to know,'' she said softly. ''I wanted it to be right— when it happened. And it was, Imogene. *So right*.''

''I am truly glad, Bess,'' Imogene said tenderly. ''I wish you and Stephen all the happiness in the world.''

''Oh, we have that,'' Bess assured her proudly. But she was still glad, looking at Imogene, whose glowing beauty lit up the room like a torch, that Stephen had not accompanied her to the Scillies. Old passions sometimes flared up like embers from a dead hearth. She wouldn't want to chance it. "I hear Maysie coming. Quick, in the dressing room."

Imogene stepped quickly into the small room she had remembered as so barren and found it newly decorated with French blue wallpaper, silvery in the moonlight. Bess had indeed worked miracles here!

With the servant gone, it was a delight to soak the sea salt from her body in the comfortable hip bath, sponging the warm water over her shoulders and letting it run down delightfully over her breasts and body.

"But you're hurt!" Bess cried, seeing the long gash down Imogene's side.

Imogene winced as the soap hit it. "Would you believe it, Bess, that was done by a cat?" *A cat I hope is faring well on St. Agnes.* "Bring me up to date on your life, Bess."

"I wrote you I was being sent out to marry a man I'd never seen. And on arrival, I found"—her laughter tinkled—"that he'd up and married somebody else. My Uncle Dicken was quite put out, and when he died he left me his plantation. Idlewild was losing money when I took it over, so I set out to improve things—not in the grand ways my uncle improved things, by adding paneling and plate and liveries and such, but in plain commercial ways. I found my bondswomen were quite accomplished and now I have a small lace industry flourishing at Idlewild and I import flax for my own weavers, and I have modish clothes made up, which are sold in the Colonies as Parisian imports!" She laughed again.

"And you visit Tortuga to buy fabrics and goods?"

"No, I send my own ship to call there now," said Bess gravely.

"I wondered that I had not seen you, if you buy there."

"You have been on Tortuga then, all this time?"

"Most of the time." The big sponge seemed to hesitate. Then she rose, drying herself off with the big linen towel Bess tossed her. She noted that it was monogrammed with a large "D" for Duveen.

"It's one of a vast number I had monogrammed for my mother," Bess smiled, realizing Imogene wasn't ready to speak about Tortuga just yet.

"I never asked about your brothers, Bess." Imogene slid the sheer night rail over her head as Bess rummaged about and found her a light blue dressing gown, then waved her to a table where a silver tray supported cold capon, thin-sliced ham and bread, apricot and quince preserves, olive pie, a large pasty and a slab of Cheshire cheese. "How are Hal and Ambrose?"

"Hal is married and gone," Bess told her blithely. "Living in York now and writes that he hates the weather, especially last winter when they had heavy snows."

Imogene was abruptly reminded of the Hudson—her only experience with heavy snows. That white world had been a tragic one for her. She sympathized with sturdy Hal, stuck inside with a blizzard blowing—Hal, who had been wont to sail barefoot through the foaming wind-whipped channels of the flower-filled Scillies.

"Hal wasn't able to sell his boat before he left but I sold it for him," declared Bess proudly. "To a man who's such an indifferent sailor he managed to capsize and swamp it!" she added ruefully.

"Did he drown?" asked Imogene dispassionately.

"Oh, no," said Bess. "Indeed, he's bought a new boat

just today and is trying it out. But Hal will be brokenhearted to think that boat he loved so is at the bottom of the sea even though he can well use the gold pieces it brought!''

"She was a fine craft," murmured Imogene. Her face grew pensive as she recalled how noble Hal had looked, standing by the mast with the sun glancing off his impassive chiseled features—back in the days when he was courting her.

"You were right to jilt him, Imogene," said Bess tolerantly. "Hal would never have approved of you and you'd soon have lost patience with him."

"That's true enough," agreed Imogene with a rueful smile. "And Ambrose, what of him?"

"Ambrose wrote me he wished to marry a girl in Sussex— a girl so sought after that there could be no question of a dowry, indeed he must needs raise a settlement to satisfy her father. I advanced him the funds, but then it occurred to me that there was no point in getting Ambrose married only to starve later. So, can you believe it, I've turned one wing into an inn!''

"I can't believe it!"

"Wait till you look about you in the morning," chuckled Bess. "Part of this old heap is too ruined to repair, of course. But the 'inn wing' has three guests already: a vacationer from Lincoln, and a gentleman and his sister who say they are looking for a suitable location in these islands to raise flowers to be transported to the mainland for sale. Because of our fortunate climate, of course." Bess's gray eyes twinkled. "I'm persuaded the lady is not his sister, but that he was too embarrassed to admit she's his doxy!'' She gave Imogene a merry look. "They all take their meals with the family, for the repairs to the common room aren't complete.''

"How is your mother taking all this?"

"Very badly at first," admitted Bess. "She wonders why, since I'm wealthy now, I don't marry some likely lad and settle down here at Ennor."

"Not knowing you're already married," murmured Imogene.

"It does have its difficult side, this charade," sighed Bess. "Perhaps it's just as well she keeps to her room, she'd start throwing suitors at me! Anyway we warred over it for a while—starting an inn, I mean. But now she's quite resigned to it. At least, she will be when she sees how happy Ambrose will be to be making a living doing something he likes. He always hated fishing, you know, has no talent for farming, is not literate enough to teach, and not religious enough by half for the cloth. He had thought to try for a military career but then he smashed his foot and that was out of the question."

"I'm sorry to hear that," exclaimed Imogene, remembering how stuffy Ambrose had enjoyed dancing.

" 'Tis mending," said Bess. "Soon he will be walking as well as ever. Here, have some more of the West Indian drink." She proffered Imogene more hot chocolate. "I wanted the family to see what we drank in the West Indies," she laughed, indicating the specially made covered cups in which it was served. "So I brought not only a supply of chocolate but my cups as well."

"I haven't seen food like this since I left Tortuga, Bess!"

"It's just some leftovers from dinner. Except for the chocolate, which Maysie was already making for me."

"Then Ambrose could still pursue his military career when his leg mends."

"Ah, but in between he met this girl from Sussex! And *she* abominates everything military—mainly, I expect, because

434

she was practically left at the church by a major who couldn't raise the settlement, either. Ambrose caught her on the rebound when she came to the Isles to 'recover' from that event. She was visiting her aunt, Lady Moxley, and Ambrose lost his heart at once, wrote me twelve ridiculous pages describing her myriad virtues!'' Bess's laughter pealed again. ''He's in Sussex now—although I do expect him home soon. I've warned him that he must learn his trade as an innkeeper before he embarks on married life and a cloud of joy! No, this is the answer for Ambrose, I'm convinced. He's a natural-born innkeeper. He has the right manner for it—courteous but not too ingratiating. And a liking for people that should eventually help him fill the common room. I think he'll make a first-rate living here.'' Seeing Imogene had finished her meal, Bess tossed a chemise and a gray voile dress over her arm. Imogene noted that beneath it was a white petticoat embroidered in a design of black lacy vines. '' 'Twill fit well enough,'' Bess promised, ''and we can make any needed alterations tomorrow.''

''Those clothes *do* have a Paris look to them,'' said Imogene. ''I can't believe you had them made up in Barbados.''

Bess nodded, pleased. ''They are my own designs,'' she said complacently.

''Bess, you surprise me. You never showed this flair when we were girls together!''

''I never had a penny to spare,'' sighed Bess ''I used to think if only—well, you know how things were with us.''

Imogene knew. Bess had risen steadily to the heights, like a solid hearth log catching fire, beginning to glow and then burning long and steadily. While her own fortunes had flamed like a candle, flaring up, flickering, burning brilliantly—and now guttering out and choking her with the smoke. . . .

"I'll bring you some shoes tomorrow," Bess promised. "Do you think you can keep those floppy slippers on your feet? My shoes are all a size too large but somewhere I have a pair that's too small—I'll look for them tomorrow."

"You've done far too much for me already, Bess."

"Nonsense! You're the best friend I ever had."

"And I took your man from you," sighed Imogene.

"But you didn't know then that I cared for him," pointed out Bess reasonably.

"No, I didn't know that." *But would it have made a difference?* Imogene asked herself bitterly. She had thrown herself into Stephen's arms with all the impetuosity of first love. Would she even have considered Bess?

Bess seemed to divine what she was thinking. "It's over now," she said in a sensible voice. "And it all worked out fine for me. I'm sorry it didn't for you. Come, I'll light you to your room." She picked up a dishlike silver candleholder and moved ahead.

"I could sleep on a cot here, Bess," Imogene demurred. "No need to trouble you to make up a room for me."

"No, there's a room already made up. For Lady Moxley's coming over tomorrow afternoon to call on Mother—as she does weekly, now that Ambrose is to marry her niece! And since on both of her last visits she had the vapors and had to be put to bed complaining vastly of her liver and her joints and all else, I thought this time to be prepared! And a good thing I did," she twinkled, "for now 'tis ready for *you*." She smiled at Imogene as she led her down the long corridor in the flickering candlelight, their long shadows wavering on the plastered walls. "But I *am* sorry she's coming, for I know you can't abide her!"

" 'Tis Lady Moxley could never abide me," remembered Imogene with a faint smile. "She never could forgive me for appearing in public without my whisk!"

"I know." Bess laughed. "Although you used to remind her airily that was the way court ladies dressed!"

"I did give everybody a hard time," sighed Imogene. "Elise said I'd be the death of her, and Lord Elston . . ." Her voice drifted off.

"I know how you must miss them," said Bess sympathetically. She threw open the door of another big square room, which she had freshened with rose hangings and a rose coverlet.

"Is this one of the rooms you've fixed up for guests?" wondered Imogene, noting the richness of the room. "If so, 'twill be a noble inn, indeed!"

"No, this is still the family wing," said Bess. "I couldn't ask Mother to have strangers walking down her corridor. It would have been too much for her, even to get Ambrose settled! But if you notice the place is a bit sprucer, Imogene, that's because I've hired a cook and a brace of chambermaids." Imogene looked up sharply at the complacency in Bess's voice, and realized that Bess was having the time of her life in her role of Lady Bountiful at Ennor. "But there's something we must speak about before morning when most like one of the maids will wake you up and ask questions. How came you here, Imogene? Don't you know it's dangerous for you to be here where the Averys can have at you? They'll never forgive you for spurning their son, you know."

437

"It isn't spurning Giles they hate me for," sighed Imogene. "They believe I killed him—or aided in it."

"At least *I* know you didn't. Stephen told me all about it."

Imogene's face was sad. "But who would have believed us, Bess?"

And it was that fact that had driven Stephen from the Scillies and Imogene to Amsterdam and other arms. Dark-haired Bess was well aware that her legacy of love was hard come by.

"Who will believe you now?" asked practical Bess. "Still . . ." She grew thoughtful. "Why face it?"

Imogene gave her a blank look.

"I mean, who's to know you're here? The servants are new. Mother keeps to her room. When Ambrose gets back, I'll explain to him and he'll be no bother, either. You can take some new name—"

"But then there's always Lady Moxley," said Imogene dryly.

"That's right, I'd forgotten her."

"I could keep to my room till she's gone?"

"Oh, no need for that," said Bess quickly. "You'll be perfectly safe for breakfast—there's no chance she'll come till afternoon. If you just disappeared for the afternoon, you'd be safe to come down to dinner—Lady Moxley always takes dinner with Mother. And then she'll have the vapors, which is really just indigestion, so we'll put her to bed and she won't stir until the following morning. And since she's up early and takes only tea in her room before leaving, there's scant chance you'd meet."

Imogene felt as if her eyes were closing. She nodded tired agreement, but Bess was going busily on with her plans.

"You can take some new name—Imogene whatever-you-like. I think we'd best keep your first name intact because I for one am sure to slip and call you by it. Unless"—Bess frowned—"you've already been seen and the story is already out. Who brought you here?"

"A stranger dropped me off here. I told him a wild tale about living in Helston and being betrothed to a magistrate in Truro."

"What—really happened?" asked Bess hesitantly.

Imogene thought of the wreckers, of her promise to Clara. "I can't tell you, Bess, because there's someone who will suffer if I do. Could you just trust me?" Her gaze on her friend was wistful.

"Of course I can!" Bess's maternal instinct was aroused. "It's Helston, then." She hesitated. "This stranger, did you give him a name?"

"Yes, I told him I was Imogene North."

"Then that's established," laughed Bess. She picked up the silver candleholder. "Sleep well, Mistress North."

"Bess, there's no one like you," murmured Imogene. She could feel sleep stealing over her even as Bess softly closed the door behind her.

Dazed with fatigue, she climbed into the big square bed. The moon showered its sliver light upon her, just as outside it silvered the old lichened stones of Ennor. But, tired as she was, memories were crowding in on her tonight, and when sleep came it brought with it disturbing dreams.

She was fifteen again and back on St. Agnes Isle, looking

up at those tall standing stones men called Adam and Eve, asking them breathlessly to send her a lover. In her dream the answer was immediate—they sent her a copper-haired lover. But—because the Fates never give you everything—they snatched him away again. Restless, she tossed in dreams in a fragile sailboat over great dark seas. The sails of her fragile craft were ablaze in blood red sunsets, blown day after day over an endless ocean, while the thrashing waters turned wine red. Her nights were beset by demons through which, endlessly distant, she seemed to hear mermaids singing of bright isles far away. Then—still in her dream—she woke to a brilliant unreal morning when even the air seemed to glisten. Every breath was soft and fresh and the sea strummed beautiful music. Before her lay an enchanted shore—no, it was Ennor Castle, but somehow the old standing stones men called Adam and Eve had become displaced and wandered down to Ennor. They stood frowning down at her before its entrance and she hesitated to walk between them, for something told her that if she entered she would be forever lost.

In her dream, she lifted her head, threw off her tremulous mood, and went inside. She was wearing something gossamer that seemed made of moonlight and that glittered with golden points of light. Her hair streamed down behind her like a skein of golden silk and her bare ankles wore delicate anklets of gold. The old stones rang with the sound of boots, and hearing them, she tried to walk faster, but each step was harder to take. She looked down and saw that attached to her anklets was the heavy golden money chain that van Ryker had packed inside her trunk aboard the *Goodspeed*. Something seemed to be tugging at that chain, pulling her back.

In panic—for she feared to look behind her—she tried to run, and the links of the delicate anklets snapped. The money chain slithered away and she burst into the great hall of Ennor—a transformed great hall all hung with red sails and roaring with the wind from the sea. And standing before her, laughing, was Harry, her friend of the night who had rescued her from the sea and stolen a kiss. With his reckless boyish face, he stood before her—laughing.

She ran toward him and then she saw that standing behind him was somebody else. A pair of eyes looked at her over his shoulder, endlessly evil, and she saw a knife raised.

She woke with a short sharp scream and sat up, looking about her in fright to see that the sun was streaming in through the windows.

And then she remembered. She was back at Ennor Castle and the sun was shining and downstairs Bess was busy transforming the place into an inn.

She got up, shaking the sleep from her eyes. But the dream, so vivid had it been, was still with her. That something that had glided behind the man with the laughing face, the cold malevolence of the pair of eyes that had regarded her over his shoulder. . . . Even now, wide awake, she recoiled from that memory in horror.

It was to prove a strangely prophetic dream.

CHAPTER 25

"Mistress North." Imogene woke to a servant's voice calling. "If ye be wantin' breakfast, my lady says ye'd best come down."

Bess's way of telling her she'd best eat now if she didn't want to run into Lady Moxley! Imogene stumbled out of bed with her eyes shut and felt around for her clothes. She yawned and stretched, then opened her eyes and smiled as she saw the pair of gray satin slippers that had been left just inside the door. She must have been asleep when those were left. It was a relief to slip into an entire chemise, instead of the ruinous remnant she had worn for days. A relief to feel the delicate lawn fabric slip down around her body caressingly, to don the stiff white petticoat with its handsome embroidery of black silk and slip on the light gray voile overdress with its band after band of black braid outlining the hem of her voluminous skirt and the big flaring sleeves through which her chemise ruffles cascaded about her elbows.

Chuckling, she arranged the modest white lawn whisk Bess had provided and slipped her feet into the gray satin slippers.

The slippers fit remarkably well.

Realizing full well they might be waiting breakfast for her, she hurried out and down the hall. Hardly had she set her foot upon the top step of the lovely carved Jacobean stairway when she faltered.

There was someone standing in the hall below. She could not quite make him out in the dimness, but as he turned, hearing her step above, a shaft of light came from a high window behind him and made his hair flame and his broad shoulders assume an impossible width.

Still under the influence of her turbulent dream, she caught her breath. For in that dream she had asked the great standing stones to send her a lover—and for the space of a single heartbeat she thought it was van Ryker standing there below. Then she realized that while this man was tall and dark, he was certainly not van Ryker.

But here below her was indeed a tall fellow, his booted feet planted firmly on the old stone flooring, devouring her with hot blue eyes.

It was Harry, the man who had rescued her last night. His thick dark hair was combed this morning, whereas last night it had been tumbled by the wind. And instead of being clad merely in breeches and boots, he was dressed like a coxcomb. Natty sky blue satin breeches molded his long lean legs, and his matching doublet sported gold satin revers and a profusion of gold buttons. A dandy was Harry, and he had a jaunty stance. Somehow she guessed he had been waiting for her.

The man who gazed up at Imogene so appreciatively had had a lifetime love affair with a succession of golden blondes. As a child he had associated them with angels—his mother, who had died when Harry was six, had been always gentle and loving and sublimely fair. In his early teens he had associated blondes with mermaids and with Circe-like temptresses who lured men to their death. His first stormy joining had been with a yellow-haired scullery maid who had teased him into following her out behind the great stone stables and giggled as she took his virginity. His first mistress had been a taffy-haired schoolgirl—and his downfall had been a strawberry blonde who had firmly intended to marry him. Faced with her angry father and her three gigantic brothers, Harry had run away. Afraid to return to his disapproving family, he had sunk to the depths in London: thief, cutpurse, pickpocket—Harry had tried them all.

And then he had met Moll and she had changed his life.

Moll was self-assured, bold, a product of the London streets. Her father had been a tough, flaxen-haired thief, her mother a red-headed dockside whore. Born in a bawdy house, Moll had been an accomplished pickpocket from the time she was six, a prostitute at eleven, mistress at thirteen of a famous highwayman who was hanged at Charing Cross. She had gone on to become a celebrated fence and the acknowledged queen of London's crime—but that was after she met Harry. It was the golden mane of her hair that had first called Moll to his attention.

When she met Harry, Moll had fancied him—and Harry,

with his acknowledged weakness for beautiful blondes, had felt himself really in love. Earnestly he had set out to change Moll into a creature more to his liking—and his opening gambit had been to rename her "Melisande." Harry worked hard to knock the edges off his rough diamond, to refine her—and though in the end it was Harry who was changed the most, Melisande had been quick to realize the advantages of polish, for she was nobody's fool. She had streetwise ways and big melting brown eyes and a face that men turned in the street to look at; if she could also pass for a duchess at will, to what might she not aspire?

Patiently Harry had schooled her, patiently tried to give her the outward veneer of the aristocrat. Inwardly he had never been able to change her, for Melisande had an inborn toughness and street logic that Harry was never able to share.

Her friends distressed Harry—and secretly terrified him. A fellow called Taz Wheats, built like a Boston bull, had nearly strangled him one fine night in Soho in a quarrel over Melisande. Melisande had settled the issue herself by slipping a dagger into Wheats's ribs and claiming Harry did it.

It had given Harry stature among the rough men with whom she rubbed elbows.

Next, Melisande had engineered a clever robbery and claimed Harry had thought it out. *That* had given Harry stature of another sort. *A good man to know, was Harry,* muttered the bully boys. *Had ideas—some of them good.*

Although it grieved Harry to have some of Soho's bull-like, barrel-chested brutes refer to him contemptuously as "Spindle Shanks" (for leanness was a trait that ran in his family), Melisande shrugged.

"Ye're better than all o' 'em, Harry," she'd say with a friendly cuff to his shoulder.

"Better than 'all of them,'" he'd correct her absently.

"As ye like," grinned Melisande. "I can't be a duchess all the time, Harry—not even for you!" She edged against him so that her supple hip rubbed against his groin. "And you be the best lover o' the lot, Harry, my lad!"

Despite his careful, bookish upbringing in Oxford, which tended to make him shrink from such as Melisande, Harry could not but feel a glow of pride. Melisande was beautiful and strong, like some prowling lioness—and she was his.

And he was *hers*. Somehow Harry had not quite counted on that, being a possession. He had always run from commitments, but with Melisande the task had become harder. Impossible, perhaps.

And now they were guests at Ennor Castle.

"Mistress North," said Harry softly from the foot of the stairs.

But even as Imogene stood poised to take that first step, mesmerized by the sight of the man below her, there was a movement behind him in the dimness. Someone who had been bent down, perhaps taking a pebble from a shoe—someone she had not noticed with her surprised gaze riveted on Harry—rose up and a pair of cold, cold eyes considered Imogene from over Harry's shoulder. There was a flash as an arm went up. A flash of—was it metal?

No—it was a fan. Imogene controlled that little shiver of fear that had gone through her and acknowledged her rescuer with a gracious nod. Then she lifted her head and went gracefully down the long staircase. From below she seemed a woman of light with her sheer pearl gray voile dress floating mothlike around her and the delicate black markings of the braid and of the stiff white petticoat making her seem to be a butterfly of note.

At the bottom she paused to extend her hand, for Harry was bowing from the waist.

"Harrison Hogue at your service." Gallantly he kissed the hand she proffered. "And this," he straightened up, "is my sister Melisande."

Imogene acknowledged Melisande. In fact, she gave Harry's "sister" a good look. Golden hair almost a match for her own met her gaze—except that Melisande's was excessively curled and pomaded. A pretty face, on the thin side with high cheekbones and deep startling brown eyes that looked like deep pools of swamp water. *Mud puddles*, she thought, and laughed at herself. *It's the dream*, she told herself. *It's made me dislike a total stranger!* For the fact remained, as she accompanied the others into the long dining room, that she had formed an instant and intense aversion to Melisande.

"You shouldn't have waited breakfast, Bess," murmured Imogene as Melisande settled her wide black and white striped taffeta skirts across from her and toyed with the black rosettes in her bright hair.

"I don't know why not," laughed Bess. "Mother takes her breakfast in her room. Mr. Robbins is out bird-watching. Nobody else was down until just now. Did you want me to sup alone? I see you've met Harry and Melisande."

"I told Mistress Bess we'd met last night," said Harry lazily.

"Yes, so you did," laughed Bess. "It was good you took

your new boat out, Harry, because from what you tell me you may have saved Imogene's life.''

"Or at least her virtue." Harry gave Imogene a humorous look.

Imogene gave him back a sunny smile. "I am beholden, sir," she said. Indeed she was glad to be diverted by Harry, even though Melisande was giving her black looks, for the hurt van Ryker had given her was still very fresh and it was good to look into a man's eyes and see herself reflected there gloriously. "You're a wretch for dropping me off and not telling me you were staying here," she accused. "Why did you let me make such a fool of myself?"

"Because you made such a delightful fool of yourself," he declared coolly. "You were so certain I was going to rape you—at the very least."

His "sister" gave him a furious look. "Don't speak so, Harry!" she said with a false simper.

"Ah, here's one who knows me for what I am." Harry turned an affectionate smile toward Melisande.

"You do talk too wild," complained Melisande. "Don't he, Mistress Bess?"

"I don't know—I enjoy the way he talks," laughed Bess. "Imogene, any wild tales you've told him are justified. Harry is always pulling our leg!"

Imogene saw that Harry was gazing thoughtfully at the square-cut emerald she wore on her middle finger. For a violent moment, remembering van Ryker's treachery, she wanted to fling it away from her. Instead she moved her hands gracefully so that Harry might be dazzled further. She saw

Melisande studying it too, looking out from under her thick lashes in a furtive way.

Mr. Robbins did not turn up at breakfast, and Bess determinedly guided the conversation. In the course of that conversation Harry and Melisande learned that Imogene was indeed from Helston and a longtime friend of Bess's.

"But being betrothed to a magistrate in Truro was a lie," laughed Imogene. "I said that only to intimidate you!"

A somewhat steely light appeared in Harry's blue eyes. "It didn't have quite that effect," he murmured, and the toe of Melisande's shoe connected with his shin beneath the table.

"Will ye walk with us?" Harry asked Imogene as they rose from the breakfast table. "I know Mistress Bess is too busy with her carpenters and her beams, but 'tis our custom to take a stroll around the castle grounds after breakfast."

Imogene bethought her of Lady Moxley, who might choose this inopportune moment to be early. "No, I'm still tired from last night's dip," she smiled. "I think I'll nap till dinner. Will you have someone call me, Bess?"

"Of course." Bess watched her go gracefully from the room.

Harry watched her go too. He was seized with a sudden desire to go up and nap with her, only sleeping was not quite what he had in mind.

"Coming?" His "sister" gave him a sudden dig with her elbow.

"What? Oh, yes, of course, Melisande."

The two of them strolled away.

"What did you mean, ogling her like that?" demanded Melisande as soon as they were out of earshot.

"I wasn't ogling her," objected Harry. "I was trying to appraise that emerald she's wearing."

"Bah! That's not an emerald—that's glass." Melisande sniffed. "The color's wrong."

"Maybe not—if it came from the Inca mines."

Melisande considered that. She could always be diverted by the mention of jewels and money. Melisande adored both.

"How d'ye intend to find out?" she asked suspiciously.

"Why, I intend to get close enough to get a real look at it," said Harry in a suave voice.

"Ye could have done that when ye kissed her hand this morning—as if she was some duchess!"

"She was wearing it on the other hand and the light was bad," said Harry coolly. "Besides, I wasn't aware of it then."

"You pulled her out of the sea and didn't even notice her ring?"

Harry could have explained that it wasn't Imogene's hands that had occupied his attention on that occasion but the whole glowing length of her, but he thought it best to leave well enough alone. "It was getting dark," he said mildly.

"I don't want ye getting that close to her, Harry!"

"Why not?" asked Harry, surprised.

"I never seen you look at nobody that way before," countered Melisande sullenly.

Harry gave a shout of laughter. "Melisande, you're jealous!"

"My name's Moll," she flashed. "And I'll thank you to remember that when we're alone!"

Harry turned to her, his laughter quenched. "You'd best

remember that it's Melisande," he said quietly. "If you don't want us both to end up on the gallows."

"C'mon, Harry!" Melisande gave him a light rallying blow on the shoulder with her fist. "Don't be so dramatic! Everyone winds up on the gallows someday." Her careless shrug dismissed it as unimportant.

That was a near truth, reflected Harry gloomily. A goodly number of their circle *did* wind up on the gallows—and weren't the rest candidates?

"See that bunch of yellow flowers over there?" Melisande tugged at his arm. "Thicker'n a Turkey carpet! I've a mind to lay me down on 'em and—" She was pulling Harry down with her as she spoke, letting her skirts ride up so that her white legs flashed.

Harry reminded himself that he was gallows bait like the rest of them, and he'd best drain the glass while wine was still being poured. He grinned down at Melisande as he fell upon her, noting as he tore aside her whisk and pulled down her bodice, how white her breasts were—not weathered like the skin on her forearm. Noted, too, as he planted a kiss on one throbbing breast, the nasty scar on her bosom that came from a scuffle at Newgate with a black-eyed witch they'd called Dirty Emma—it was that scar and not modesty that made Melisande wear a whisk. The scar brought a softer light to Harry's eyes, for he had a real affection for Melisande— and sympathy too, did she but know it. "They'll see us from the house," he chuckled, running his impudent hand up her leg, pushing her chemise up her squirming thigh and squeezing one cheek of her round bottom while she made mock efforts to evade him.

Melisande gave a sudden lurch that rolled them both over, laughing, and got strands of grass in Harry's hair and hers. "Won't no one see," she gasped.

But Imogene did, from her window, and turned away feeling suddenly bereft. It seemed to her as she flung herself face downward upon the bed that everyone had someone to love—everyone but her.

And far below in the grass, when Melisande and Harry had finished their brief tumultuous lovemaking, Harry lay beside her with the golden mane of her hair cascading over his shoulder. He chewed thoughtfully on a grass stem and let the fingers of his left hand run along Melisande's throbbing body, making her gasp now and then as his fingers grew impudent again.

He felt good and complete and for the moment he had almost forgotten how desirable was the woman who lay in the castle above them, napping.

"Could be I've figured out a way to find out if the emerald is real *without* getting close," he murmured.

But although Melisande teased him, and near tore his clothes off demanding he tell her what that way was, Harry refused. "I'll show you at dinner," was all he'd say, no matter how she baited him. And Melisande had to be content with that.

"While I was out sailing this afternoon, I was hailed by a fisherman," he told them at dinner, watching Imogene. "He had a woman's dress on board that he said he'd found. It was so pretty I bought it on the spot for my sister, but then I remembered, you said you'd lost yours when you went swimming on St. Agnes. Could it be yours?"

453

"It could if it's blue," said Imogene calmly, remembering the dress van Ryker had stowed in her trunk aboard the *Goodspeed*.

Harry smiled into those calm blue eyes. "I'll bring it," he said, pushing back his chair. He strode from the room, ignoring Melisande, who had half risen from her chair in indignation, and Bess, who had lifted her hand as if to ward off something.

As they waited, Mr. Robbins, the bird-watcher, leaned forward. "Swimming? Did you say you were *swimming*?" he asked incredulously.

"Without my dress," said Imogene in a clear voice.

Melisande gave her an evil look. Bess repressed a shudder.

All eyes were on Harry when he came back into that long cavernous room. He was walking briskly with that slight swagger that he always affected when he felt he had a good-looking woman's attention, and it gave him a certain jauntiness that, combined with his boyish smile, brought a soft light to every feminine eye at the table. Over his arm he carried a sky blue velvet creation that, when he spread it before Imogene, caused her to exclaim, "It *is* mine. But . . ." She studied the neckline regretfully. "The amethyst clasp is missing." The wreckers were getting more reckless, she thought. Selling goods locally to such as Harry.

" 'Amethyst clasp'?" Harry, consummate actor that he was, turned a blank look upon the lady. "Oh—amethyst clasp. Lost in transit, I suppose."

Melisande had been looking at him stormily. She had snatched the amethyst clasp and was in no mood to part with it.

Bess leaned forward. "A couple of hooks sewn in, a rosette to cover it and it will be as good as new, Imogene," she said briskly.

"My friends must have left it for me on the shore when they left the island," said Imogene carelessly. "Was anything else of mine found? My shoes perhaps? I am missing a pair."

"Your *friends* took your *dress*?" cried the bird-watcher.

"And my shoes and petticoat as well," said Imogene.

Bess hoped this conversation never reached Star Castle or Lady Moxley; no one at Ennor would ever hear the end of it if it did.

Harry looked surprised. "Indeed, dear lady," he said tolerantly, "there was no real reason to believe even this dress and petticoat might be yours. Except"—his tone grew caressing, it raked over her senses with gentle claws—"that you'd mentioned you lost yours and this seems to complement so well the color of your eyes."

"And seeing it you thought of me?" Harry felt himself squirm under that level blue gaze. "I am beholden to you, sir. But then you are out of pocket for—?" She gave him a questioning look.

Harry's chest expanded happily. "Accept it as my gift. The debt will be more than paid if you will but wear the gown," he declared gallantly.

"Indeed I *shall* wear it—tomorrow! That is, if Bess is able to work her magic with a needle so that it does not fall open in front!"

"Will you be here in September, for the pilchards?" interrupted Bess, for the bird-watcher was looking shocked.

Harry looked blank. " 'Pilchards'?"

" 'Tis a great sight. Men called *huers* watch from the headlands for the first tinge of purple on the sea—"

"That's a French word," explained Imogene. "It means 'to shout.' "

"All along the western coast of Cornwall in September you'll find the *huers* watching. And when they see the telltale purple on the sea that tells them there's a great shoal of fish out there, they cry out '*Heva, heva!*' "

"That means 'found, found,' " explained Imogene.

"And then everyone is away in the seine boats and they all wave calico-covered wooden frames called bushes, and they take the fish in the great seine nets. Sometimes they take thousands and thousands of them."

"Millions," corrected Imogene.

"It's very exciting," said Bess. "You must stay for it."

"Fishing never interested me much," admitted Harry.

"Always angling for something else, Harry was!" put in Melisande sarcastically.

"Millions, you say?" said Harry as if Melisande hadn't spoken. "There must be lots of *huers*!"

"And lots of pilchards," smiled Imogene.

"Perhaps we will still be here," said Harry, kindling to that smile.

"Ha!" Melisande tossed her head. "Wintering someplace else we'll be, and on our way by then." Her truculent expression dared Harry to deny it.

"Where will you go?" asked the bird-watcher politely.

"Someplace else!" snapped Melisande in such a belligerent tone that the whole table fell silent, addressing themselves to what Imogene believed to be the most elaborate meal ever served at Ennor Castle, for it featured a delicious green sallet, fricassees, baked "cheewits," a chine of beef, "stewed" broth, jiggets of mutton, and a bewildering assortment of breads and preserved fruits.

And through it all, Harry Hogue's speculative gaze seldom left Imogene, while Melisande smoldered.

After supper, the bird-watcher wrote to his brother in Kent:

These people here at Ennor most remarkable I've met. Odd crowd, prickly as pears. Woman named North seemed to be missing a gown which she'd lost while swimming in the sea. Quite beautiful—woman, that is. Turned up on the arm of a fellow at dinner—gown, that is. Saw vast numbers of cormorants today, kittiwakes, terns. Fine long necks—cormorants, that is. Visiting island of Annet tomorrow, where I'm told millions of puffins breed. Should abandon your roses, come down here. Yrs, R.

Meanwhile Melisande stormed into her bedroom and turned on Harry. " 'Accept it as my gift!' " she mimicked savagely. "You *gave* her my dress, Harry! How could you do it? I wanted to snatch it back and scratch your eyes out!" She struck at him wildly.

Harry caught her arms and grinned down at her. "Cheap at the price!" His voice was exultant. "An emerald like she wears will buy you a dozen such dresses—and now we know it's real." Before Melisande could refute that, he added softly, "Besides, you still have the amethyst clasp."

While the bird-watcher was writing his garbled letter, and

Melisande and Harry were working out their differences, Bess was pacing up and down in Imogene's room.

"Do you think it was wise to claim the dress?" she demanded in a worried voice. "Grant you it's beautiful and with a rosette stitched on it you can wear it again, but it makes *talk*. You saw how scandalized Mr. Robbins was! Suppose word reaches Lady Moxley? Do you think she won't descend on us and demand to see the infamous Mistress North?"

Imogene sighed and ran a hand through her hair. "Stop pacing about. Don't you know by this time I'm seldom wise?" She strode restlessly to the mirror, frowned at her reflection as if to chide herself. "I don't know why I did it—or, yes, perhaps I do. It's been a very long time since I wore blue and it's my best color!"

Bess regarded her with open-mouthed astonishment. *Her best color*! As if that mattered when perhaps one's life was at stake!

"As for Lady Moxley, I could hear her snoring as I came down the hall."

"She must have left the door ajar. I'll go close it."

"Oh, later, Bess. You said yourself she'll be gone in the morning. And how's she to hear? Robbins will be on Annet poking around in the sea pinks for puffins' eggs!"

"I suppose you're right." Bess stopped pacing and picked up the blue dress. "I'll sew a rosette on this right now and you can wear it tomorrow," she declared energetically.

Imogene watched her work with a hunted look on her face. After a moment she walked to the window and looked out. Down below she could see a man running and she squinted her eyes to see him better. Why, it was Harry! Running barefoot and unshirted, clad only in his trousers, down toward the water. Escaping from Melisande, she'd no doubt! As she watched, he climbed aboard his boat and cast off.

"Here, now it's ready." Bess bit off the thread with her teeth and turned to Imogene. "Come try it on and see if it holds."

Imogene turned away from the window. If she had stayed there it would have altered the course of events.

She had turned away a moment too soon. In the golden rays of the setting sun Harry had unfurled another sail, a small one. And the sail he had unfurled was red.

Clara's "boat with the red sail" was heading for St. Agnes—and the man at the helm was Harry Hogue.

CHAPTER 26

So Imogene slept well that night, unaware that Ennor Castle was currently harboring the brains behind the wrecking operations on St. Agnes Isle.

She woke to brilliant sunlight flashing through the castle windows. After so much sleep yesterday and the night before she felt refreshed. She stretched luxuriously and sprang up, ran to look out the window at a beautiful new day. Yesterday had been cloudy but today the very air sparkled. Below her was spread out Bess Duveen's small walled garden and it was bursting with narcissus in full bloom and a host of other plants that crept over the ground or climbed over the granite walls or simply burst forth in glorious profusion like the golden narcissus.

There was no one about.

Lured by the outdoors, Imogene did not even stop to comb

her hair. Pulling on her blue dressing gown, she peered out into the corridor. No one there either. She stole down a side stairs and found herself in the little garden Bess had worked so hard on years ago. Now she saw that it was bursting with new additions that Bess must have brought in recently.

Imogene leaned on the low stone wall and looked out to sea, drinking in the clear cool salt-laden morning air, looking out into the blue distance at a pair of great wheeling cormorants.

The shipwreck, hiding in the rocks on St. Agnes, shivering through the dark hours, dreading the coming of each day's light—all that was now forgotten. This was the Scillies as she remembered them: a glorious place. Her gaze left the cormorants and swung around to the windbreak hedges planted to soften the bite of fierce Atlantic gales, colorful flowers massed against dark ivied walls, and where there was no ivy covering the granite, yellow lichen splashed against the castle's proud old stones.

She looked up again at the wild cry of a group of black-backed gulls. Huge and white with long black wings, they circled above her, then sped away, swooping out over the brilliant blue emerald of the sea. Now another great flock of seabirds flew over, filling the air with their wild sounds, for it was spring and they came to these islands in the millions. At sunset, she guessed, that flock would stream back toward the little island of Annet to their nests, burrowed under mounds of enormous sea pinks.

And they would find Mr. Robbins, the bird-watcher, crouched there staring at them, she thought amusedly.

The ghost of a smile was still on her face when she turned

462

at a sharp exclamation behind her and found herself looking into Ambrose Duveen's startled countenance.

Ambrose had changed a bit, she saw, since the old days. He was a good twenty pounds heavier and much better dressed than he had been the night he had taken Stephen Linnington to a ball at Star Castle and warned him—futilely, of course!—to beware of Imogene Wells, for she was the wildest girl in the Isles and had jilted his brother! Imogene wondered if Bess had been fitting him out, for his bright yellow doublet and trousers rivaled the daffodils, and the lace that spilled from his neck and cuffs was more expensive than he could have afforded in the old days. But the look he gave her was just as disapproving. The priggish youth had grown into a sententious man.

"Imogene!" he gasped. "How come you here?"

"By way of the stairs yonder, Ambrose," she said blithely, ignoring the fact that she was standing there in her dressing gown, a fact that could not fail to scandalize circumspect Ambrose. "It's been a long time!" And when he still hesitated. "Come now," she coaxed, holding out her hand, "aren't you glad to see me?"

Ambrose wasn't in the least glad to see her for he'd always deplored Imogene's influence on his sister Bess, but courtesy forbade him to say so. "Of course I am." He stepped forward and with some difficulty made a leg. Still it was more graceful than the last time she'd seen him do it, she thought— he must have been practicing. No doubt for the bride-to-be who must needs have a settlement!

"I hear you're to be married, Ambrose."

"Aye," he said stolidly. "To Marcy Dane, Lady Moxley's niece. You met her once. We're to marry in the fall."

Imogene looked puzzled. Anyone so sought after she would surely remember! Then she reminded herself that four years had passed and that Marcy Dane might not have been sought after *then*—she might have been a schoolgirl sewing samplers! "I do hope you'll be happy, Ambrose," she said warmly.

Ambrose acknowledged her sentiments with a solemn nod and would have brushed by her but he paused suddenly and frowned. "Bess wrote us you'd married a pirate."

"Buccaneer," corrected Imogene automatically. "Yes, I married him." *And lost him*. . . . She didn't feel she had to add that.

"Is he here with you?" asked Ambrose bluntly. She noted he looked perturbed.

Imogene shook her head carelessly and Ambrose's young face cleared. "Well, 'tis good to see you, Imogene," he said with more heartiness. "Will you be staying long?"

"No, not long."

"I'm sure Bess is pleased. She was always fond of you. Well, I must be off. I've a message from Marcy for her aunt at Star Castle that won't wait."

So Lady Moxley had already departed—well, that was good news!

Ambrose's parting glance showed Imogene plainly that he hoped she would put some proper clothes on before anyone else saw her, but he bowed most correctly and went on his way, self-important and dignified as always.

Imogene watched him go, trying desperately to conceal his

limp and maintain a smooth gait over the uneven ground, and all the old life here surged back upon her. She was Imogene Wells again, fighting off the unsuitable suitors her guardian, old Lord Elston, so determinedly thrust upon her. Falling in love with Stephen on a moonlit night on the parapet of Star Castle. Finding ways to elude her chaperon and meet him during the long lazy days. Lolling with him on white beaches, making love recklessly in the shade of tall and ancient standing stones that frowned down eternally.

It was all so different from her life with van Ryker.

She sighed. Why had she never missed it? she wondered. Was it because the lean buccaneer had filled her life so completely?

But he was gone now and she was alone.

She *felt* very much alone as she retraced her steps back to her bedchamber.

She put aside the gray voile dress, which she could now return to Bess, and told herself recklessly she would not let loneliness spoil her morning. She had a whole life to live without van Ryker and she might as well get started! But as she dressed herself in the sky blue velvet gown, she was reminded that this had been van Ryker's choice for her. Or perhaps, she told herself bitterly, it just hadn't suited Veronique. And it would have been Stephen's choice for her as well, she told herself perversely as she turned back and forth before the mirror—that deep, square-cut neckline, that bodice that molded her round breasts and emphasized the slimness of her waist, that great flaring skirt that billowed out over a blue silk petticoat embroidered in shimmering silver. A faint perfume from some bottle that must have spilled in the chest during the storm rose from it, and the wide blue velvet sleeves allowed a froth of white ruffles to spill out gracefully over her elbows.

It was a dramatic dress of great beauty, and Imogene, looking narrowly at the reflection of a golden woman clad in blue and silver in the mirror, remembered the days when she had shocked Lady Moxley by tossing away her whisk. With a sigh, she picked up the white lawn whisk Bess had provided and tucked it in demurely to conceal her white breasts against that shocking low neckline. On Tortuga she would not have done it, but she felt she had done enough to shock Bess yesterday.

There was a discreet knock on her door, and a servant's voice saying Mistress Duveen said she was to come down, breakfast was being laid.

With a last pat to her golden hair, which she had dressed simply but stylishly, Imogene strolled downstairs to breakfast, where everyone was waiting.

The effect of her sky blue gown on the company was immediate and electric.

Not until he saw her floating toward him, a vision of blue and gold and silver, did Harry Hogue realize his real reason for giving Imogene the dress—he had wanted to see her wearing it; it was as simple as that. And now there she was—ravishing! In the gown that *he* had given her. No matter that it had been hers in the first place; it was he, Harry Hogue, who had restored it to her. He drew in his breath at the dazzling sight of her as she moved gracefully across the dining room—and across from him Melisande's brows drew together sullenly. Mr. Robbins regarded this blue vision with stupefaction as he might some new and remarkable bird of plumage.

"Why, you look lovely, Imogene," cried Bess. "Suits you much better than the gray."

"Thank you." Imogene sank into the chair Mr. Robbins sprang forward to pull out for her. She rather enjoyed the sensation she had created, basking in Harry's obvious admiration and watching Melisande squirm. They were a pair of wandering rogues, she'd decided, but of the two Harry was far the better! "Ambrose has put on weight," she remarked to Bess.

"Ambrose?" Bess blinked. "Where did you see *him*?"

"You mean you didn't know he was back?"

"No, I was with the carpenters—"

"Oh, there *was* a short gentleman arrived looking for you," put in Harry. "I told him you were probably in the garden at this hour, and he told me if he missed you, not to wait breakfast. He had an errand."

"He found *me* in the garden," said Imogene. "And after half a dozen words, he was off to Star Castle to deliver a message to Lady Moxley from Marcy Dane."

"But Lady Moxley just left!" cried Bess. She got hold of herself. "I suppose they won't meet," she said. And then because both Harry and Melisande were favoring her with curious glances, she added weakly, "Lady Moxley is sure to pry the wedding plans out of Ambrose and advise against everything. I had so hoped to catch him first before he could agree to anything. She's Marcy's aunt, you know."

Imogene nodded. She was beginning to remember a ten-year-old gamin who had visited at Star Castle and been forever tearing her petticoats climbing about the rough stones of the castle walls.

"Yes, you met her, I'm sure. She was visiting here from Sussex and—" Her voice dwindled away at a noise outside in the hall, the clatter of boots.

Flush-faced from exertion, his limp much more pronounced than it had been earlier, and with his golden-plumed hat awry, Ambrose Duveen swept into the room.

At sight of his anguished expression, Bess dropped her spoon. "What is it?" she cried, white-faced.

Oblivious of the others, Ambrose burst out, "Bess, Lady Moxley's carriage caught up with me on the road. When I told her I'd just been speaking with Imogene Wells"—Bess held up a warning hand but it was too late to stop Ambrose— "she was so incensed she turned her carriage around and insisted on driving back." He turned an angry glance on Imogene. "You might have warned me Bess was keeping your visit a secret!"

"But we aren't!" cried Bess in an agonized voice. She was only too aware of the dead silence that had greeted this pronouncement.

Even that did not stop Ambrose. "Anyway, she's outside and will come storming in at any moment. She says she's going to tell your mother it's being kept from her who's visiting in her own house, and what's more—"

He fell silent. Behind him, her large girth surging inexorably forward in a sea of lavender ribands, Lady Moxley had entered the room. She seemed to fill it.

"Lady Moxley." Pale but composed, Bess rose and went

to greet her returned guest. "I didn't expect you back so soon," she said on a note of irony.

"Dear Bess," trilled Lady Moxley, setting every riband aflutter as she came to a sudden halt. "I clean forgot my shawl—and on such a windy day too! It must be in your mother's room."

Bess, who remembered very well seeing Lady Moxley off in that shawl, maintained a discreet silence. "I believe you have met all my guests. And of course, you remember Imogene?"

"Ah, yes." Lady Moxley's disapproving gaze passed over Imogene with distaste. "Who could forget Imogene Wells? Although it is Imogene something else now, if reports are correct?"

"Van Ryker," said Imogene clearly.

Bess winced, for she had but recently introduced Imogene all around as "Imogene North." But Imogene felt as if she were a rebellious sixteen again, falling under the shadow of Lady Moxley's disapproval every place she went. She wanted to shock the older woman.

"Lady Moxley," she said on a note almost of derision. "I don't find it at all cool. In fact, it's terribly warm in here. So warm I feel no need of my whisk!" In a moment she had pulled it free and sat fanning herself with it.

Six pairs of eyes fled to the lovely expanse of white bosom bared by that swift gesture, the pearly tops of two round breasts that were suddenly displayed to their surprised view.

Mr. Robbins straightened up and cleared his throat awkwardly. He would write his brother he'd had something more than fowls to observe today! Bess gave a small gasp and looked worried at this obvious taunting of a powerful adversary. Ambrose reddened resentfully. Lady Moxley drew herself up with a lavender quiver and said, "Well!" in an affronted tone. Melisande bit into a piece of bread so hard her teeth clashed together, and turned to look at Harry. Harry controlled a chuckle. He was gazing in delight at this luxuriant display.

"I'll remind you, Imogene, that you're a married woman!" said Lady Moxley tartly. "And not some long-haired girl of sixteen!"

All the slights she had endured from Lady Moxley over the years crowded in upon her. Smiling into Lady Moxley's pale snapping eyes, Imogene reached up and pulled the pins from her long hair and shook it out. She moved quite deliberately and her smile was insulting.

Lady Moxley drew in her breath sharply and then surged forward. "I intend to speak to your mother, Bess!" she called over her shoulder as she disappeared from the room.

"Imogene, how could you?" muttered Bess and fled after Lady Moxley.

"Imogene North–van Ryker–Wells?" said Harry lightly. "Pray, in what order do your multiple surnames appear?"

"She's Imogene Wells who married van—I thought it was Rappard," exploded Ambrose, who was hot with shame over the incident. "At least, there was a name like that in there somewhere, but there isn't any North unless she's thrown van-what's-his-name over and married another one!"

"Thank you for supplying my background so well, Ambrose," said Imogene silkily. She was feeling reckless today and her encounter with Lady Moxley had only heightened that feeling.

"And from whence *do* you hail?" wondered Harry. "Surely not from Helston?"

"No, I'm from Penzance originally. But after my parents were killed in the civil wars, I went to live on Tresco with my guardian. Bess and I have been friends for years."

"Ah, so you live on Tresco?"

"I used to. I've been . . . living abroad."

"Van Ryker," he mused. "A Dutch name. You married a Dutchman, I take it?"

"Yes," said Imogene shortly. "I married a Dutchman." But she was thinking of her tragic first marriage to Verhulst van Rappard and not of van Ryker.

"Van Ryker," pondered Harry. "An uncommon name that. The only van Ryker I can recall is—" His eyes twinkled as he studied Imogene.

Imogene was tired of keeping up this charade. "The only van Ryker you can think of is the famous buccaneer, Captain Ruprecht van Ryker, who seized the Spanish treasure fleet," she said dryly.

"Ah, yes, that is the one," said Harry instantly. "Good of you to remind me. Is he any relation, then?"

"My husband," said Imogene.

You could have heard a pin drop at that table. The birdwatcher choked. Melisande was staring at Imogene fixedly. Her jaw had dropped and it had given her a stupid expression. Even Harry, who had begun his inquiries with such aplomb, looked startled. Bess had come in and was beckoning to Ambrose, but she too froze at this sudden announcement.

"Is it really true?" ejaculated Harry. "Or are you having us on again?"

"It is true," said Imogene calmly.

"Then where is he?" cried Harry. "Are we about to meet this famous individual?"

"No, you are not," said Imogene. "I am visiting Bess alone."

"Ambrose, mother wants to see you—right away. Please keep Lady Moxley from upsetting her any further, if that's possible." Bess had regained her composure and now she resumed her seat at the table. She turned to Harry without breaking the flow of her conversation. "Imogene came down from London to visit me. She did not want a great fuss made over her or wild stories flying about, so we decided to call her 'Mistress North' and say she came from Helston." The story sounded thin even to her own ears.

Melisande's gaze now raked Imogene up and down. No jewels, save for that single square-cut emerald ring set in heavy gold. Surely a buccaneer's woman—and such a buccaneer! —would have come in with a blaze of diamonds.

Imogene continued to eat in desultory fashion. She was uncomfortably aware of Melisande's appraising inspection.

"Tresco is the right place for your flower plantation, Harry," said Bess, desperate to change the subject. "Everything grows there—it's a tropical paradise. Ask Imogene if it isn't true—cinnamon and bamboo, prickly pear and citron, belladonna lilies and ferns—even palms and bananas."

"Everything does grow there," affirmed Imogene.

"You must take me there," smiled Harry. "I'm impressed."

Bess tossed her a warning look and Imogene was again

reminded that on Tresco—and St. Mary's as well, indeed throughout the Scillies—even though she had never been formally charged, she might yet be implicated in a "murder." For it was doubtful that time had healed the hurt the Averys had felt at Giles's death, or dulled their vengeful feelings toward her.

"I don't wish to go back," she said in a blurred voice. "It would remind me of my guardian, who's dead and—other things."

"But *you* must go," Bess told Harry. "It really *is* the best place to start a flower plantation. And even if you decide it's not, there's so much to see. You can follow the road around the western side and pass Hangman's Island and reach—"

"'Hangman's Island.' That's appropriate," said Melisande to no one in particular.

Bess gave her a surprised look. "And reach Cromwell's Castle," she said. "It was built just below King Charles's Castle—and I'm afraid they took down most of *that* to build the Lord Protector's stronghold!"

Melisande was watching Harry with an unpleasant look in her brown eyes. Imogene thought they looked more like swamp water than ever before. Melisande's full lips curved into a slight sneer as she took a last bite of plover's egg and wiped her mouth inelegantly with the back of her hand. "Yes, Harry," she drawled. "*You must by all means go there!*"

And later, when the disastrous breakfast had ended and Bess had fled upstairs to intervene between Ambrose and Lady Moxley and her mother, when Mr. Robbins had gone off whistling on his bird-watching expedition to Annet, and Imogene had strolled outside to let her long hair blow in the

473

sun and think, Melisande caught at Harry's arm and dragged him back down the endless corridor that led to the "inn wing," as Bess now called it.

"Do you believe Imogene is really van Ryker's wife?" she asked him excitedly.

"No," mused Harry. "But if she is . . ."

Melisande sniffed. "If she was, she wouldn't be *here*. She'd be with *him*, wouldn't she, livin' off the fat of the land?"

"They might have had a falling out," said Harry softly.

Melisande made a derisive sound. "She wouldn't be livin' in no rundown castle like this one, she'd be off to London or somewheres and rentin' her a fine town house!"

"But she *did* claim the dress—and it fits her like it was made for her," he pointed out.

"She saw it and she wanted it! Same as I did! And Bess altered it overnight—you heard her say Imogene was down from London."

"I heard it, but I didn't believe it. And besides, she knew about the amethyst brooch. Melisande, there was a trunk found on the wreck full of silver plate and at the bottom was a heavy gold money chain worth a fortune. And the blue dress was in that trunk. If that trunk belonged to *her*—"

"It didn't!"

"But if it did . . ." Harry's face had grown dreamy. He was remembering the sight of that golden woman with the delft blue eyes in that sky blue and silver gown. What buccaneer would *not* want her? "If the dress is hers, then the money chain's hers, and if she left Tortuga with that much gold, there's a fair chance her buccaneer wants her still—and will pay to get her back.''

At last Melisande's murky brown eyes held an answering gleam. ''I take your meaning, Harry,'' she said, giving him an exuberant slap on the back. ''We'll ransom her!'' She did a little jig and threw her arms about him.

Harry winced inwardly. Ransom was not really what he had had in mind for glamorous Imogene. He had been merely thinking out loud and Melisande had seized upon it.

Now she drew away from him. She was pouting. ''Oh, come on, Harry, you don't really believe she's van Ryker's wife, do you?''

''No,'' sighed Harry. ''But if she is, we're wasting our time with these wrecking operations.'' Smoothly, he followed up her thought. ''For van Ryker would pay more in ransom than we could make in a year just to get her back. But if she doesn't belong to him''—he gave her a wry smile—''then we'd be wasting our time to take her at all.''

''How can we find out?'' wondered Melisande, frowning.

''There's no other way—I've got to get to know her better.'' Harry sounded pleasantly resigned.

Melisande drew in her breath and gave him a sharp look. Then she clapped him playfully on the shoulder and laughed. ''I guess you've got to at that, Harry, you fox!''

Harry, looking at her thoughtfully, hoped this mood would hold through the ensuing days, for Melisande was given to sudden rages. She could ruin everything.

''You must give me some time with her,'' he said harshly. ''She's not apt to confide in me in the presence of witnesses!''

Leaving Melisande discomfited, he strode away. He found

Imogene strolling in the garden, pensive, wondering what she should do now. She started as he called her name, for she was lost deep in her own thoughts. She tossed back her long fair hair and waited for him.

"I saw you out here this morning, leaning on the garden wall, looking like a blue angel," he told her with a grin.

So not only Ambrose but Harry as well had seen her in her dressing gown! The corners of her mouth twitched with amusement at what Lady Moxley would have to say about that! "I was looking out to sea," she said frankly. "I didn't see you."

"No, I expect you didn't. I was watching from the walls and looked down and there you were." His tone was caressing. "You should always wear blue, you know that?"

Two other men had told her that . . . her first love and her last. But she had married, in between, a man who had loved her in yellow and called her his golden bird of love.

"No, I don't know that," she said perversely. "In fact, I thought the gray voile suited me very well."

"Oh, anything would suit you," he drawled lazily. "With a figure like yours! I was talking about what suits you *best*."

"I am surprised Melisande lets you out alone," she said ironically.

Harry was taken aback. "D'ye think me tied to Melisande's skirts, then?"

"Aren't you?"

"Only so much as brotherly piety leads me to be," he said in a bland voice, and took hold of her wrist.

Imogene gave him an impatient look. "You are a fake, Harry," she said.

"Oh?"

"Yes. And I know your secret."

His hand, which had been caressing her wrist, now closed over it. He was holding her lightly still but at any moment his strong fingers could clamp down. *Was she telling him,* he wondered, *that she knew that he and Melisande were the brains behind the wrecking operations on St. Agnes Isle? If so, she could be dangerous to him.* "Then share it with me," he said steadily.

Imogene laughed. "You are traveling with your doxy and because you are staying in a respectable house, you have passed her off as your sister. No, do not bother to deny it because I saw you rolling about with her yesterday in a great clump of yellow flowers!"

Harry relaxed. "My secret is out," he said charmingly. A sudden shadow of embarrassment passed over his cynical countenance. "Does Mistress Bess suspect me as well?"

"'Suspect'?" laughed Imogene. "She is certain of it! But have no fear, Bess is of a serene nature. She does not believe in meddling in other people's affairs."

"I am glad to hear it." His face cleared. "And what does Imogene van Ryker believe?"

She took back her hand from his grasp and resumed her stroll. "Imogene van Ryker believes in the truth," she flung over her shoulder.

Harry fell into step beside her, his dark head bent slightly over her own. From that position he could inhale the slight lemony perfume that emanated from her hair, and watch the sun shimmer its golden strands. "And what truth would ye have me admit?"

Imogene shrugged. "No more than you've a mind to!"

"Is that what your buccaneer did?" he challenged her.

"My . . . buccaneer," she said in an altered voice. She had been trying not to think about van Ryker. She cast a hunted look about her. Past the yellow-lichened stones she could see clouds of purple heather, sea holly and bracken and foxgloves and huge golden mounds of gorse. And past all that a lonely cormorant was diving upon the glittering sapphire surface of the sea. She took a careful step to avoid a wayward white and gold narcissus that had invaded the stones of the garden walk. "I do not wish to talk about van Ryker," she said distantly.

"Nor do I," agreed Harry with a sincerity that surprised him. "Indeed, I'm glad he's far away! Even though I think him a fool to let you wander so far. . . ." he added, leaning a trifle closer to that bright head.

Imogene lifted her skirts to avoid another clump of narcissus. Plainly, Bess had not been able to bring herself to move the plants at this time of year, fearing they would die. "Watch out there," she said sharply. "Your boot near did for some of Bess's flowers."

The only flower that interested Harry at that moment was the flowerlike woman swaying beside him, fragrant, desirable, remote—but he removed his boot from the spot with alacrity. "You make me regret . . . many things, Imogene." The honesty of his tone made her look at him sharply.

"Regret nothing for me," she said with a small discordant laugh. "My life is none so perfect!"

"Yes, but you have come through it unscathed," he murmured. "You have come through it—well." *Clean*, he was thinking and marveled that it should be so. *Shining*,

unsullied, and—a phrase he had not heard since his childhood—
pure of heart.

"You must be speaking of some other woman," she
scoffed. "Surely not of me."

"Only of you, Imogene." He thought of Melisande, so
damaged by life, so hardened—and contrasted her with the
woman beside him. He halted, caught her by the elbows and
turned her to face him. "I'll change your mind about me, you
know," he promised her in a rich-timbred voice. He smiled
caressingly and the sun flashed on that smile, making it
blindingly brilliant.

"You're a rogue," she laughed, but there was a catch in
her voice.

"Perhaps we're a pair?" he suggested impudently. "Well
matched?"

She shook her head. "Never a pair . . ."

"Why not?" he asked softly. "I'd change to suit your
pleasure. D'ye wish a wandering life, Harry's your man!
D'ye wish to sport silks and gauzes and dance at Whitehall,
Harry's your man!"

That last made her laugh. "You? At Whitehall? I'd give
odds you've never set foot there!"

"Aye, and you'd win," he agreed instantly. "But for *you*,
Imogene—" He reached out and tenderly ruffled a tendril of
her fine fair hair that had come free and blew lightly in the
breeze. "For you I'd make it happen."

She was studying him, grave now for she recognized
something real and earnest in that timbred voice. A commitment. "I almost believe you would," she murmured.

"Oh, I would do it." His self-assurance was contagious; it

led her to believe that Harry would do great things—if only she'd join him in the venture. "For *you* I'd do it." He sounded suddenly melancholy. "But then . . . you're not planning to give me the chance, are you?"

She caught her breath. How well he had guessed what was in her mind! And now she looked away from him quickly lest his hot blue gaze penetrate to the very depths of her—and find there a woman tempted.

"You have Melisande," she pointed out in a breathless voice.

"Ah, yes, Melisande . . ." His hand stroked her hair for a moment. "There's always Melisande. But Melisande has a dozen rogues back in London eager to take my place." *And some on St. Agnes too if the truth be known, but Harry wasn't willing to admit that just yet!*

"You're saying she wouldn't miss you?" Imogene gave him a level look. "Then perhaps you're saying *I* wouldn't miss you, if later you were to leave *me*?"

Harry's blue eyes widened. He hadn't expected such a challenge to be flung at him—or that she'd see him for what he was, a rover with a rover's way with women. He respected her the more for saying it and now he looked at her anew. Not only desirable—she had honesty and spirit. Behind those level eyes that now considered him there stood a woman *worth* winning, worth—he had almost said to himself, *worth dying for.* But of course that was nonsense; no wench was worth dying for—not even this one.

"I'd never leave you," he declared gallantly.

Imogene favored him with a mocking smile. "You say that now."

How well she divined his faults! Plainly here was a lass who had known many rakes and knew their ways. "How can you say that?" he complained. "When you know so little of me?"

"I know your kind, Harry. Charming, attractive—and false."

"Then tell me if this is false!" he said harshly. And of a sudden he seized her and whirled her into his arms. His blue eyes burned into hers. "You believe you know the truth when you meet it. *Tell me if this is false!*"

His lips—for she made no move to stop him; indeed her heart was beating like a butterfly's wings—crushed down upon hers, warm, demanding, willing her to love him. For a moment the ocean's deep rumbling became a torrent in her ears, a clamorous rush of sound. And with it her reserve broke and she melted in his arms, unresisting, passionate, giving him back kiss for kiss.

It was an impassioned moment and it lasted for a long time.

When, finally, Imogene burst free, she was panting and her face had gone two shades paler.

Harry too was pale. He looked almost appalled, as if he had encountered some great revelation about himself.

"We're too much alike," she said bitterly. "We would only bring about each other's ruin!"

"How can ye say that?" cried Harry. He had kept hold of her hand and now his grip tightened. " 'Twas not what your lips told me just now!"

"My lips are no concern of yours. They have their own treachery." She ran a trembling hand over her mouth as if to erase the memory of his lips. For she had fought that wine of freedom that had stolen rapturously over her, even as Harry had fought it—because, like him, she feared commitment.

Harry stared down at her in tormented fashion. He felt as if his senses were drugged with some new sweet perfume. A kind of enchantment was stealing over him and he shook his head to clear it.

"I'll make you mine," he predicted hoarsely. "Faith, you're mine already—'tis just you have yet to admit it!"

Imogene shook off his hand and flung away from him. She felt confused, endangered. A girl could break her heart for the likes of Harry—and be thrown away carelessly, like some broken toy. He was no good, some sure cold instinct told her that. And yet for the space of a heartbeat or two, her whole being had responded to him wildly.

The ice on which she trod was treacherous at best—and now it was beginning to break up. She could find herself dragged down, down into some deep desperate pool, drowning in love for Harry . . . and break her heart again.

Her slender back stiffened. Harry, who stood silent, watching her blue velvet skirts swish away from him, noted that change.

She is fighting me, he thought. And then reluctantly: *That speaks well of her, does it not?* He tried to laugh off that sudden reckless feeling that had washed over him when he held her in his arms. At that moment he would have done anything, promised anything, and perhaps—it was only a "perhaps" but it nagged at him—*kept that promise.*

If he made a commitment to this golden woman—and at the moment he had no intention at all of doing that—he sensed that it could well be for life. For under the calm blue pressure of those level eyes, what would he not attempt?

It was a new and frightening thought to Harry and it was a shaken man who sauntered back to the castle and stood looking from its old gray walls across the turquoise sea where other men led other lives, respectable untarnished lives . . . men who basked in the pride of their women. Did he want to reform? To be like those other men?

These were new questions that Harry asked himself, still caught up by the remnants of that enchantment that had shaken him to the core. This newfound passion that tore at him, threatened to destroy his comfortable roving ways—it never once occurred to him to call it love.

CHAPTER 27

It had been a stormy week at Ennor Castle—a week no one at Ennor would soon forget. A week during which Imogene had fought off the strong attraction she felt for Harry, a week during which he had sought her out at every opportunity, teasing her, cajoling her, begging her to love him. And after she turned him away (each time, he told himself, more reluctantly), he would go back to Melisande, gloomy and dour, and tell her that the wench was mighty cagey about van Ryker and he still couldn't quite make out how matters stood.

Melisande was beginning not to believe him. Suspicion showed in the pout of her full lips and in the way she'd turn swiftly when Imogene came into a room, or watch her balefully out of the corner of her eye.

All week low, scudding clouds had skimmed over the horizon, promising rains that did not fall. In between, the sun broke out for brief periods, bathing everything in its glory. But inside the old walls of Ennor Castle a tempest more violent than any that was likely to beat down upon its ancient battlements was building up.

It had begun the afternoon of Lady Moxley's abrupt return. Bess had knocked on Imogene's door, very pale, and informed her that Lady Moxley had "talked it over with her mother" and intended to stay all week.

Imogene gave her hostess a tormented look. "Shall I stay in my room, Bess? Would that help?"

"Of course not," said Bess with dignity. "I just wanted to warn you that she's apt to be very unpleasant. Oh, Imogene, you shouldn't have baited her so by tearing off your whisk and letting down your hair."

"I'll tear it off again," said Imogene through her teeth, pulling off the whisk she was even then arranging. "I'll go without one the entire time she's here!"

Bess sighed. She had known it would be like this. Imogene and Lady Moxley were old antagonists, and Ennor Castle was merely a new setting for their continued combat.

"I wonder why she hates me so," puzzled Imogene.

Bess gave her a startled look. "I thought you knew. Your mother took the man Lady Moxley loved away from her and then jilted him to marry your father. Her rejected suitor drowned a week later—oh, it was a very ordinary accident, his boat capsized, but Lady Moxley persists in believing he committed suicide because your mother wouldn't have him. She was convinced that if he had lived he would have turned to her, and has told everybody so. Your mother escaped her wrath by moving to Penzance, where you were born. But

Lady Moxley never forgave her. And since you look so strikingly like your mother, everybody says, it rubs an old wound every time she sees you."

"Who told you all this?"

"My mother. Long ago."

"I wonder why I wasn't told?"

"I suppose everyone thought you knew."

Imogene frowned out the window. *So it wasn't just the whisk, Lady Moxley was nursing an old enmity. . . .* Somehow that put a different light on things.

"I really think you should leave here," said Bess frankly. "Escape while you have the chance. There's no telling what the Averys will do when they hear you're back."

"But they won't know until Lady Moxley leaves, will they?"

"I suppose not."

"Unless she sends her driver to them with a message?"

"Oh, she won't do that," Bess assured her. "She has a positive dread of being left without a servant. The poor fellow hardly dares stray out of earshot—didn't you see him hovering about the halls wondering if he was wanted?"

"No, I didn't, but then my mind was on other things. So you think I'm safe here until Lady Moxley leaves?"

"Not *safe*," said Bess reluctantly. "But safer." She gave her friend a tormented look. "Oh, you know how much I'd like you to stay," she burst out. "It's like old times having you here. I feel like a girl again. But I could let you have some money and I'm sure Harry Hogue would be glad to sail you to the mainland."

"I'm sure he would," sighed Imogene. "Indifferent sailor

that he is...." Why *didn't* she leave? she asked herself honestly. When to stay was so dangerous? Was it because the hull of the *Goodspeed* might still be clinging to the rocks and that would tell van Ryker when he passed this way to look for her here? For she'd little doubt but that he'd keep to his intention to sail to Amsterdam, if only to put his treasure in trusty Dutch banks. It would be so easy to go away and let him believe her dead...and *then* he could go in good conscience with Veronique, she thought, her face twisting. *No, she would not make it that easy for him! She would stay right here and face him down when he came this way at last!* "I will leave if you want me to, Bess," she said quietly.

"No, no—that isn't what I want. It's just that that woman's up there with Mother, raving on about you. I could wring her neck! And Ambrose's too sometimes."

Bess was thinking of what Ambrose had said yesterday. He had caught her on her way to her room and blocked her way. His face had been red and earnest. "Lady Moxley says you should be more careful about who you take in, Bess. She says that woman with Hogue is not his sister, couldn't be. She says—"

"Ambrose," Bess had cut in, in a dangerous voice. "I have been listening all day to what Lady Moxley says—first from Mother, and then from the lady herself. I will not listen to her second-hand from you! You would do well to realize that you are soon to become an innkeeper and your very livelihood will depend upon your getting along well with the public. It is not for you to decide who is moral and who is immoral, who is just and who is unjust! It is for you to feed them, house them, and be pleasant to them. Can you take that in, or is it too much for your feeble brain to digest?''

Ambrose looked nonplussed. Gentle Bess had never spoken to him so in the old days. Barbados had certainly changed her—no, it was Imogene's influence. Resentment flooded through him.

''You aren't the same since Imogene is back,'' he accused. ''You've taken her side of things. She was always a wanton and if you take up her ways—''

''Ambrose, read me no sermons!'' Bess's voice rose. ''I have been to great trouble and considerable expense to set you up in business and—''

''Don't throw that at me!'' cried Ambrose, in a passion. ''Nobody asked you to do it! I could have taken a turn at the military, as well you know!''

''And how would that have suited your intended?'' asked Bess sweetly, ''since you tell me she is so set against all things military. Do you think she would have married you then?''

Ambrose had dug the pit himself and now as he fell in, he tried manfully to claw his way out. ''Ah, Bess,'' he said placatingly, ''let us not quarrel. I miss Marcy and it makes my temper short. And Lady Moxley plagues me with all manner of things she says Marcy would take exception to!''

In spite of herself, Bess had begun to feel sympathy for her crestfallen brother. ''I'm sure she does, Ambrose,'' she sighed. ''But remember that after you're married, it isn't Lady Moxley who'll be meeting your bills, but you yourself. And if Marcy is as spirited as I remember her, she'll probably have a falling out with her aunt, Lady Moxley, the first week she's here. So you'd do well to master the art of innkeeping, for there'll be no help for you from Star Castle."

Bess felt somehow trapped between them all, all these warring factions. She realized again how glad she'd be to get home to Barbados—and Stephen!

Meantime, here she was and she must make the best of it. She took Imogene's arm companionably. "Come down to the dining room and help me arrange a centerpiece."

On the way downstairs they ran into Ambrose, who was airily waving a letter that had just come. "Finest vellum," he reported with pride. "Marcy is used only to the best. She pomades her hair with—"

"Indeed?" cut in Bess tartly, who didn't want to hear what Marcy pomaded her hair with. She could pomade it with crushed pearls for all Bess cared. "I had not imagined Marcy's family to be so wealthy. I remember when she visited as a child at Star Castle and was forever tearing her petticoats, little tomboy that she was! Lady Moxley told me then that she was having to finance a new petticoat herself, for Marcy's family wouldn't be up to it!"

A slow flush spread over Ambrose's face. Barbados had been a coarsening influence on Bess, he reflected gloomily. She would never have said that in the old days—and before Imogene!

"Oh, I'm sorry, Ambrose." Bess saw his dismay and her natural kindliness rose to curb her tongue. "But 'tis a bit thick, is it not, that Sir Launceford should claim such a high price for her?"

"Not a 'price,' Bess—a settlement!" Ambrose's protest overrode her voice.

"Very well then, a settlement." Bess sighed. "But it seems to me that it is very like selling sheep, this selling of daughters."

"You'd not have thought so had it been a dowry I'd been receiving!" he said hotly.

"Wrong." Her voice was firm. "I think as badly of dowries as I do of marriage settlements. Marriages should be for love and not for gain!"

Ambrose's flush deepened. He jammed on his hat. He was barely able to control his voice as he muttered, "I'll be taking my supper at the Thaxtons. Indeed, I may stay the night with them." He limped out angrily.

Bess watched him go. She seemed to wilt. "I shouldn't have said those things," she sighed.

"Why not?" said Imogene. "They're true."

"I know, but people don't like to hear the truth. Especially Ambrose. And"— she smiled wistfully—"I *am* fond of him, you know. For he's got many good traits underneath all that stuffiness."

"Of course he has," said Imogene, who was in a mood to be generous—even with priggish Ambrose. "That little tomboy will make a man of him!"

"If she doesn't ruin him first." Bess's rueful glance through the window followed Ambrose, stomping through the gorse on his way to pour out his troubles to the Thaxtons—as he had been doing ever since Hal left. "I hear she's most extravagant. Like her father. 'Tis said the reason he's selling his youngest daughter—instead of giving her a dowry as he should by rights—is because he built a new wing to the hall.

And that in the face of bad crops and illness among his tenants!'' She shook her head at such bad management.

"You'll straighten her out," predicted Imogene indulgently.

"I won't be here to do it. I'm back to Stephen and Barbados as soon as I can straighten things out here. I miss them now." Bess gave her a homesick look.

Imogene chuckled. "Don't let your mother see you moping. She'll connive with Lady Moxley to find you a suitor!"

"*That*," agreed Bess cheerfully, "would be the worst. Can you imagine my having to sit through the attentions of some pompous lad or senile gentleman they dredged up?"

They both laughed—and forgot Ambrose and his vexations as they moved on toward the dining room.

It was a mistake they would both come to regret.

It was quiet and pleasant in the big familiar dining room, and Bess found herself falling into a mellow mood and humming ''Greensleeves'' as she strolled about its long cavernous length, setting things to rights here and there that the serving girls had missed.

But Imogene grew silent and sad as she helped Bess arrange big bunches of yellow flowers. Somehow they reminded her of the Cups of Gold that had bloomed so prolifically on Tortuga—those flowers had been the opening gun in the barrage that had shattered her world.

"You're mourning Captain van Ryker, aren't you?" asked Bess softly. She gave Imogene a slanted look through her lashes. "You know, I think Harry Hogue is interested in you."

Imogene gave a strangled laugh. "I've *no doubt* he is!"

Bess looked puzzled. "Captain van Ryker may come looking for you," she said tentatively.

"But do I want him back?" Imogene gave Bess a tormented look. "Oh, Bess, are all men no good?"

"Of course not! You mustn't think that!" Bess looked shocked and then her face went dreamy.

She is thinking of Stephen, guessed Imogene. *Yet he was false to me too!*

They both swung around as Lady Moxley entered the room. Lady Moxley ignored Imogene as if she wasn't present. She spoke to Bess exclusively—looking down her nose. "Your mother and I," she said heavily, with a significant look at Imogene, "feel that you need a chaperon."

"Lady Moxley," said Bess in a somewhat shaken voice, for she yearned to tell Lady Moxley she was a married woman, "I am well able to chaperon myself, I assure you."

Lady Moxley sniffed. "That is your opinion. *We* do not agree."

Bess faced her tormentor with a very level gaze. "If you intend to follow me about, I will tell you now that you will find it tiring in the extreme. I am now going to the 'inn wing' to give the carpenters further instructions. After which I may do a bit of weeding in the garden."

"*Yourself?*" gasped Lady Moxley.

"Certainly, myself," said Bess grimly. "If you want a thing done well—" She did not finish because Lady Moxley cut in with "I shall certainly not follow you around, no matter how unladylike your pursuits. I but came to tell you that I will be taking my suppers in the dining room."

"Will Mother not miss your charming company?" demanded

Bess. Imogene was amazed at the irony in her voice; the sweet yielding Bess she had known so long ago was certainly changed.

Lady Moxley's shoulders jerked. "You will put yourself beyond respectability if you spend too much time with *certain* people," she warned. "And then *none* of us will be able to find you a husband."

"I might prefer that side of respectability to this," said Bess irrepressibly. "And I do not need *you*, Lady Moxley, to find me a husband!"

Lady Moxley wheeled away from them, a gigantic lavender figure moving ponderously, every riband atremble with wrath.

"She will report to Mother," said Bess in a shaking voice, "that I am no longer the sweet child everyone loved, so biddable, so yielding. She will say that I am being *unsuitably influenced*. And Mother will tell me for half an hour that I was wrong to plague her! And Ambrose will agree!"

"Perhaps I *should* leave," said Imogene quietly. "I'm causing you so much trouble."

"No, I won't have you driven out! I won't let that terrible old woman rule my life! If only—oh, why did you say all those things at breakfast? It was madness!"

Imogene's head was bent, "I think I was striking back at van Ryker," she said in a muffled voice. "For deserting me." Then she lifted her chin, and her bright hair, which she still wore defiantly unloosed, fell back like a long twisting scarf down her back. "Oh, God, Bess, why must I always think of him?"

"You love him," said Bess gently.

"Sometimes love isn't enough," choked Imogene. "There's pride too."

Bess sighed. She had to admit she had felt the same way once.

"But I can tell you this, Bess." Imogene dashed the tears from her lashes. "If van Ryker comes this way—and oh, he will, Bess, he will!—I'm going to wait for him and see him and ask him why. I have to know." Her voice broke. "You see that, don't you?"

"Yes, yes, I see that." Bess's gentle arms went round her and she comforted her friend. The world, thought Bess, was a strange paradoxical place. Her gaze caught sight of a dark head through the window. "Oh, there's Harry," she said. "He's strolling about alone. Why don't you go out and join him, Imogene? He's sure to cheer you up."

"I think I will," said Imogene, for she was feeling rebellious. Van Ryker had Veronique, why should she not have Harry? She went outside and saw that he was looking very dashing in amber silks that must have been tailored in London. His smile flashed at sight of her.

"I am fortunate indeed," he said warmly, waving a gold snuffbox. "Will you walk? Or would you rather sit with me on yonder stone bench?"

"I'll sit with you awhile, Harry." She smiled, as she settled her blue velvet skirts. "And we can stare up at the castle and conjure up its ghosts."

"Are there so many of them?"

"There must be, for Ennor Castle was the main residence of the constable of the Isles, Bess tells me, back in 1300. I imagine it was a bit more formidable then."

Harry gazed up at the old lichened walls appreciatively. "Amazing that it's still standing if 'tis as old as that!"

"Oh, now that Bess has taken it in hand, it will rise from the ashes," laughed Imogene. "She improves everything she touches."

"As you enchant everything *you* touch." He was looking into her eyes as he spoke and his voice had a mellow ring. Around them the breeze blew softly, filled with the fragrance of flowers.

"Ever a seducer," she said lightly. "Doubtless you've left broken hearts from here to—the Humber?"

"The Thames." Harry fell in with her mood. It had been a long time since he had entered into lighthearted dalliance with a lady of quality; the woman and the beauty of the day were not to be resisted. He leaned back lazily on the stone bench, long slender fingers clasped about one amber silk knee and considered her rakishly.

She looked back in amusement. "Harry, you're a mountebank! The stage should have been your calling! I'll warrant," she added wickedly, "that it was because of a woman you fled Oxford!"

"A strawberry blonde with kisses sweet as honey," he said ruefully. "Determined-to-be-married kisses."

"We each have our cross to bear," she teased him, leaning back and letting the breeze ruffle her hair. "And have you forgotten her or will you"—she placed one hand dramatically over her heart—"carry her memory with you to the grave?"

"I almost did," grinned Harry. "Her brother took a shot at me."

They both laughed. It was the most *companionable* moment Imogene had known since she had left Tortuga. And then they fell silent, a pensive pause in which they considered each other.

Something might have come of that, for Imogene felt a stirring of her heartstrings—something about this smiling rake reached her, moved her. But Melisande chose that moment to stride blithely through the garden, overdressed as usual in brilliant pink satin larded with black braid. She was humming as she sailed by them and to Harry's chagrin, the hum became words:

> *"Oh, Harry Hogue was a merry rogue*
> *And all the girls adored him,*
> *But it was Flo, Queen of Soho,*
> *Who was the first to floor him!"*

Harry's face had turned livid but Imogene murmured after Melisande had passed them with a careless nod, "What was she singing? Something about a rogue?"

"'Twas naught," said Harry in a strangled voice. "Melisande picks up street ditties and affixes other names to them. 'Tis a trying habit of hers and tests my patience."

"Oh, I'm sure it does." Those delft blue eyes whose regard he sought so ardently were gazing at him in amusement. "Perhaps she will favor us with some of her verses after supper? Bess could accompany her on the harpsichord."

Harry felt smothered. Damn Melisande! She'd be the death of them both. "Perhaps," he said vaguely. "But they're not songs for a lady's ears."

"Oh, that's to their benefit," Imogene assured him. "For

there's a vast want of entertainment here." She was thinking of how Lady Moxley would take such a song and the thought brought an impish grin to her face, but Harry felt she was making fun of him.

He rose stiffly. "Excuse me, I must speak to Melisande."

Harry caught up with Melisande around the corner of one of the gray stone walls. With a ripped-out oath, he spun her around. He was trembling with anger. "Why d'you mock me?" he demanded.

"By singing, you mean?" she mocked. "Ye should not have friends who are poets, Harry, if ye don't wish to be sung about! Roge must have made up a thousand verses about you in London and you didn't mind it then!"

Harry gave her an angry shake that bade her forget drunken Roge and his rhymes. "Have ye lost your mind, Melisande? Do ye want these gentry to know who we are? *What* we are? Why d'ye tempt fate like this?"

She shrugged, but her smile was contemptuous. "Because you're making a fool of yourself, Harry. Over that woman. You're falling in love with her, Harry, and I warn you—I won't have it!"

"You . . . won't . . . have it." He repeated the words slowly, in wonder. Did this street wench think she owned him? He flung her away from him, so violently that she stumbled and fell to the ground. "Now hear me, Melisande. If you keep on like this, I'll tell Lomax about it and let *him* silence you."

From the ground she stared up at him. "Afraid to do it yourself, Harry?" she mocked. "Afraid you'll weaken?"

She looked beautiful and angry there on the ground with her pink skirts riding up. Harry had seen her fall thus once before, felled by a London whore in a dispute over territory. But Melisande had risen with a long bodkin and driven the bodkin into her tormentor's throat. Harry had been proud of her.

Now he stared down at this woman who had shared so much with him, who was after all only fighting for her own. And then he took a step forward and bent down and helped her up.

"Melisande," he said in an altered voice—and for the moment he felt truly penitent. "Ye know where my heart is. With you."

Melisande was brushing herself off. Her eyes were snapping. "Wherever your heart may be, Harry, I know where you eyes are—on *her*."

"She may be useful to us, Melisande," Harry soothed. "She may make us rich."

Somewhat mollified, Melisande fell into step beside him. "I'm tired of being gentry," she grumbled. "Taking little mincing sips of wine when I could drink them all under the table! Having to say, 'La, Mr. Robbins, I don't play cards!' when I could win all his money in a trice!"

"We're playing for bigger stakes, Melisande," Harry reminded her.

"And having to keep my skirts down prim when I'm dying to toss them over my ears and kick up my heels in a dance with you!"

Harry laughed. The storm was over. Like a lightning bolt, Melisande had washed her skies clean with her sudden rage. Her eyes were deep brown inviting pools as she grinned up at him. "Come on, Harry, let's have us a swim!"

"We can't, Melisande," he demurred. "They'd see us from the castle. And I know you—you'd swim naked!"

"O' course," said Melisande sturdily. "Any other way, I'd drown! Well, then." Her gaze was restless. "Let's sail over to St. Agnes and drink a few rounds with the lads. Unless," she rallied him, "you think you're like to sink this boat like you did the last one?"

Harry frowned. "That was bad luck, Melisande. The wind caught me and the cargo shifted. And we'd best stay away from St. Agnes. Remember, if Lomax and the others get caught, we've still time to show the law our heels and get away clean!"

A slight sneer crossed Melisande's strong features. "Aye, we'll show them our heels again, Harry," she said scathingly.

"And what else would you have us do?" he demanded hotly. "Swing from a gibbet with the rest of them?"

Melisande sighed. "No, I guess not, Harry." She was thinking how Harry had taken to his heels and left her father to battle off the law alone—and her father had died of it. She'd forgiven Harry then because she was deep in love with him, but it would always rankle. Full of excuses Harry had been, but she knew the real reason he'd fled—fear. Harry hadn't wanted any part of this wrecking operation, but she'd pushed him into it, knowing he could sail a boat. He'd been some help with that, delivering goods to the contacts she'd made in Helston. But she'd doubted his story about losing the boat, guessing that a sail had come too near in the night and Harry had thought it was the law and sunk the boat not to be caught with the cargo. Harry, she told herself contemptuously, was always running. The real leadership was *her*. She'd inherited leadership of the gang of thieves and cutthroats her father had led—but because she was a woman, Harry must front for her. Harry didn't know it, but it was Melisande who was the true leader of the pack, Melisande to whom the men turned for advice. She was canny and she was bold. And she was experienced, she'd grown up in crime. On the streets at eleven. In Newgate at thirteen. Bought out by her father and a successful whore at fourteen. And at fifteen, still fresh-looking and pretty, she had met Harry and fallen in love with him. She was nineteen now, although she looked older. Despite her deceptively vacuous expression, Melisande had a keen and decisive mind. She had known instantly that she wanted Harry—and she was still willing to take him as he was, with all his flaws.

Now her gaze on him softened. Harry, she knew, was irresistible to women. They loved his wildness, his ready laughter, his gambling, his insatiable lovemaking, his mad pursuit of any wench he wanted.

Harry grinned back at her. He felt a kinship with Moll—his Melisande. All his life Harry had taken long chances. It was in his blood, his scholarly father had told him mournfully— the hot blood of those rakish cavaliers that had been introduced into his own bookish strain courtesy of the aristocratic young wife who'd died when Harry was a child. He had complained that Harry never fretted over anything. Harry enjoyed the best of everything—and when it came time for the piper to be paid, Harry took to his heels. His father had viewed Harry's undoubted popularity with a long face. Did you want to take a long chance, he was wont to say, Harry was your man!

It had puzzled his father, why women had always adored his son. It had never penetrated the old man's consciousness that Harry, like another great lover, Don Juan, was blindingly sincere. He loved with absolute passion—but only for the moment. Harry had unshakable faith in his own romantic prowess and when he wanted a lady nothing else counted for aught.

It would be the death of him. Everyone had always said so. To none of the gorgeous blondes of whom he had been so wildly enamored had he stuck—only to Melisande, and that was not so much a hot love affair now as a companionable business arrangement.

Perhaps she was the only one who really understood him. She worked through Old Isaac, a goldsmith in London whose real profession was that of master fence. When Isaac had decided to widen his scope to include the southern tip of England—the Scillies, graveyard of a thousand ships—Melisande had seemed the perfect front for his operation: tough, resourceful, a survivor—and she had Harry. Isaac considered Harry too soft but that didn't matter, for Melisande was there to stiffen his backbone. Melisande was ruthless enough for two. Harry, a gentleman born, was the perfect front for them and Harry had taught Melisande enough that she could pass under casual inspection as a lady of wealth and breeding.

They were a dangerous pair.

Imogene had guessed but half of Harry's story—that he was a rogue, traveling with his doxy. Had she known he was part of the gang of wreckers, she would have recoiled in disgust.

Harry sensed this—and feared it.

For it was fast coming to him that Imogene was the one woman in all this world whose approval he most desired.

And Moll—or Melisande as he had rechristened her—was threatening that approval.

She threatened him even more that night at supper, for she came down dressed flamboyantly in bright orange and black striped taffeta with enormous black and orange rosettes artfully planted at strategic points to accentuate her sensuous figure. Harry ground his teeth. He had warned Melisande about looking like a flaunting London whore in conservative Ennor Castle. Indeed, before they arrived he had personally stripped—while Melisande heaped him with abuse—rosettes and spangles and dangling ribands and all manner of decorations from her striking wardrobe. Somehow this dress had escaped his notice and now Melisande was swaggering toward him with jet earrings dangling from her ears and a golden lovelock falling down upon her white shoulder and an expression on her hard face that boded no good for anyone.

"Harry." She minced him a charming curtsy as he growled a greeting. Imogene and Bess had just entered the room. There was nothing for it but to offer Melisande his arm and take her in to dinner.

Conversation languished under Lady Moxley's frowning surveillance. Ambrose, vexed at Bess's refusal to get rid of Imogene, had been dining out of late, so the only person at the table of whom Lady Moxley wholeheartedly approved was Mr. Robbins, the bird-watcher, who chirped gratefully about auks and puffins and kittiwakes and petrels under her insistent prodding.

Dinner was excellent and Harry said so heartily.

Bess smiled kindly on him. "But now you must sample cook's crowning achievement—gooseberry cream. For it is made from a recipe that I was told in Barbados came from the old Lord Protector's wife. And even if she was a hypocrite and wore all the fine laces and brocades her husband banished for the rest of us, I think you'll find this seasoning of nutmeg and mace and rosewater delicious."

"What else is in it?" asked Melisande, whose mother had worked briefly as a pastry cook and let her precocious daughter sample everything.

"Oh, cinnamon and eggs, garnished with sugar," smiled Bess. "I do think you'll like it. And do try a bit of this cake as well."

Melisande took a spoon of the gooseberry cream. "Why, 'tis as fine as anything in London!" she declared almost indignantly.

But not so fine as Tortuga, thought Imogene, remembering the gilt icings and crystallized rose decorations and delicious marchpane that Esthonie Touraille had served at her last party. Not to mention the sit-down dinner for fourteen that she had herself given that had featured some thirty-two dishes, including the popular carbonados—meat broiled over hot coals— and complicated compound fricassees made of fritters and tansies and quelque-choses (the tansies themselves were an elaborate dish made of scrambled eggs blended with cream and wheat-blade juice, strawberry and violet leaves, walnut tree buds and spinach, mixed with grated bread, cinnamon and salt and nutmeg, and all of it sprinkled with sugar before serving). "A princely feast," van Ryker had called it, and Esthonie had been green with envy.

The smile Imogene turned toward Harry was bittersweet, pensive.

He thought her the most enchanting woman he had ever met and ignored the black looks Melisande was giving him.

"Imogene tells me you sing." Ever the gracious hostess, Bess swept forward after supper when she had brought her guests into the drawing room. It was not necessary for an innkeeper, nor had she invited her paying guests into her drawing room before, always allowing them to return to the "inn wing," but tonight she was smarting under Lady Moxley's obvious disapproval and yearned to shock her. "This harpsichord is sadly out of tune, but I'll try my best to give you an accompaniment."

Harry opened his mouth—and closed it again.

Melisande tossed her head at Harry and sauntered arrogantly to the instrument. "Do you know this one?" She leaned against the harpsichord:

> *"Come, all you stout fellows and drink*
> *up with me!*
> *For I've a fair lassie from over the sea—"*

"No, Melisande, no!" Harry was on his feet, his face scarlet, for the next two lines were unprintable.

Imogene had covered her face with her hand to hide her laughter. That was a song she'd heard sung, from her windows, in Tortuga, by passing drunken buccaneers, and it was very explicit indeed. She took her hand from her face. "Try the song you were singing as you passed by today," she suggested politely.

Melisande gave Harry a withering look. She was in no

mood to be stopped. "Don't mind if I do," she said. She began to clap her hands and sway and tossed over her shoulder to Bess, "Try to play this one:

> "Harry Hogue was a reckless rogue,
> Whose plans all went awry!
> And Harry, if he don't watch out,
> They'll hang poor Harry high!"

"I think I have the lilt of it now," cried Bess, and began to tinkle the harpsichord keys.

Convulsed, between watching Melisande's arrogance and Harry's obvious dismay, Imogene sat through another stanza, beside a gradually stiffening Mr. Robbins.

Melisande, her brown liquid eyes glittering, was beginning again.

> "Harry Hogue, that London rogue,
> He stole the gentry blind!
> But it was Moll, queen of them all,
> Who was really Harry's kind!"

Lady Moxley's eyes bulged. She seemed past speech.

Melisande went recklessly on with a verse on which she'd collaborated with Roge one day when she was mad at handsome Harry. Roge had been in love with her and glad enough to lance at Harry's pride. She missed Roge, who'd had his throat cut in a brawl over a tavern wrench just before they left

London. Now she smiled into Harry's furious face and sang out:

> *"Handsome Harry's in command,*
> *His hot gaze seems to tease her!*
> *But she stands in awe of a man with a flaw—*
> *A coward, if you please, sir!"*

She was about to go on when Harry leaped to his feet.

"Stop!" he cried in a smothered voice. And as Bess's fingers faltered to a halt and Melisande gave a contemptuous shrug and let her hands, which she had been waving for emphasis, fall to her striped taffeta hips, he turned to Imogene. "You must understand that those verses are about a highwayman called Jack and a woman called Flo. Melisande has a perverse sense of humor. She has chosen to make mock of me and thereby dragged herself down!"

Melisande sniffed, but Imogene leaned back in amusement. "Why don't we hear a song from Bess, then? 'Greensleeves,' perhaps?"

Melisande sauntered back to flounce into her chair beside Harry. The look they gave each other had daggers in it, but Imogene forgot them both in the lure of the lovely love song, 'Greensleeves,' as Bess's sweet voice rose clear and high to peal into the castle's old rafters.

" 'Twas said old King Harry himself wrote that song," Bess smiled as she finished with a soft chord. "To his love, Nan Bullen." She sighed. "Wooed like that, no wonder she became Queen Anne Boleyn!"

"And lost her head," Harry said warningly to nobody in particular, but beside him Melisande took the hint.

She bridled. "Queens 'ave got nothing to do with me," she declared stridently. "Whether they lost their heads or no!"

All in all, it was a grim evening and it ended with Lady Moxley tottering away to her room, wondering if she could warn Bess's mother with sufficient force of the bad company her daughter was keeping.

Harry had excused himself early and taken Melisande in an iron grip and escorted her upstairs. Melisande, looking impish and glad to have his full attention at last, had skipped along beside him.

Harry pushed her into the bedroom and closed the door hard behind him. Then sudden fury had washed over him and he dragged her across the room and flung her on the bed, stood there shaking with rage.

"What did ye mean by doing that, Melisande?" he demanded. "They're onto us now!"

"No, they aren't," said Melisande sulkily. "They're puzzled that such as you took up with the likes of me—that's all."

"I'm puzzled about it too," he grated.

Melisande laughed and arranged herself sinuously on the bed. When Harry stood and watched her with a wooden expression, she gave another laugh. Finally, seeing he was not going to join her on the bed, she gave him a look that scorched, rose and stretched, and moved to the window and began to hum. After a while it was not humming but low-voiced, insolent song—a bitter verse Roge had made up the day Melisande left him for Harry:

> *"Harry Hogue was a dandy rogue,*
> *Who sets girls' hearts aflutter,*
> *But Harry's character was flawed—*
> *He was destined for the gutter!"*

"I reached the gutter when I found *you!*" Harry grated.

"No, you didn't." Melisande gave an arrogant twitch of her shoulders. "You were already in the gutter—'twas I got you out of it!"

Harry gave a ragged sigh. "Cut it out, Melisande," he said roughly. He came up to her and clamped a hand down on her shoulder. "Try to remember that's all behind us. We're gentry now."

She was laughing up at him. "We'll never be gentry, Harry. No matter how much gold we garner. We'll always be us, headed for the gallows!" She began to sing again, *"Harry Hogue was a dandy rogue—"*

Harry's teeth were clenched and suddenly his other hand slapped her face hard enough to snap her head back.

Melisande was used to blows. She'd taken many a one from her drunken father—and given some herself to ensure her position as queen of the London streets. She gave Harry a dangerous look from her murky brown eyes but her lips formed a reproachful and seductive pout.

"I want you for *me*, Harry! I don't want to share you."

"Melisande, you don't understand—"

"Don't I now, Harry? Don't I, though?" Her seductive

body was pressed against his, her breasts crushing softly against his chest, her hips moving gently against his thighs. "Tell me about it, Harry."

With a groan, Harry looked down at this iron-willed woman who could turn all to softness at his touch. "You'll be the death of me, Melisande!"

"And you'll be the death of me, Harry," Melisande sighed, knowing she had him now. "But we'll go out together, you and me!"

Trancelike, moving sinuously as one person, they made it to the bed and fell upon it like two strong young animals. And Harry, to his discredit, closed his eyes and pretended that it was Imogene he held in his arms, golden Imogene who responded to him with such amorous violence.

If Melisande knew this, she gave no sign. She was content to take Harry as he was—and sure she could hold him.

Melisande did not come down to breakfast the next day. Harry came down, announcing that Melisande had twisted her ankle and when Bess offered to call a doctor, he said it was no great matter, a couple of days' rest in bed would cure it, he'd take her meals up to her.

In the turmoil that surrounded Lady Moxley's presence, Bess was rather grateful that the servants—who were being ordered about on the run by Lady Moxley's trumpeting voice—would not be further burdened.

In point of fact, Melisande had left. Her clothes remained, so Harry presumed she'd be back. His Melisande had left him before—but never for very long. Always she came back smiling and full of schemes to take the world. The boat was gone too, so he presumed she'd sailed to St. Agnes to consult with Lomax. Harry sighed. He wished he hadn't taught Melisande to sail. Still, Melisande had the devil's own luck; he was confident she had made it to St. Agnes.

Now with Melisande out of the way, Harry set about his pursuit of Imogene in deadly earnest.

"Come away with me," he urged. "I could take you anywhere. We'll start a new life—together."

"And Melisande?" she mocked.

"Melisande can find her own way," he said shortly.

"I don't think she'll let you go so easily, Harry," warned Imogene.

But Harry, who lived for the day and never gave tomorrow a thought, brushed that off with a careless, "She'd have no choice."

Imogene gave him a brooding look. In a way it would be tempting to disappear with Harry, to find a new life, to walk in the glow of this man's eyes, which told her more strongly than any words how very much he wanted her.

Still she hesitated, holding him off.

Another day passed. Melisande stayed away and Bess, fully occupied with Lady Moxley and her mother's exhortations, paid little attention. Her concern was for Imogene.

"I'm sorry Ambrose is staying with the Thaxtons," she said. "I'd hoped he would help me control Lady Moxley and soothe Mother. She's almost too much for me, I confess. And—I'm afraid for you, Imogene. There's something spiteful in Lady Moxley's tone when she speaks of you. She might do anything. Indeed, I now believe we've got to get you away from here."

"I have decided to stay, Bess," shrugged Imogene. "That

is, unless you cast me out. Van Ryker will pass this way eventually, I presume, and I intend to flaunt in his face a new lover. Just as he flaunted his mistress in mine!''

''A new lover! Oh, you can't mean—''

''Harry Hogue.''

''But that woman with him isn't his *sister*! She's his doxy! She'll tear your eyes out once she's up and around!''

Imogene gave her a Circe-like smile. ''Do you think Harry will let her?'' she asked tranquilly. ''Besides,'' she added contentedly. ''I think she's left, Bess. For good.''

''But—where would she go?'' Bess gave her a blank look.

''I don't know, but I noticed the boat is gone. Harry told me some story about it but I didn't believe it. I think Melisande may have sailed right out of his life.''

Bess received this new information with shock. Imogene had always moved too fast for her. Hers was a settled nature, meant for tranquillity, while Imogene seemed always destined for passion and danger and unsettling events. ''I would never turn you out, you know that,'' she said.

''Yes, Bess.'' Warmly, Imogene clasped her friend's arm. ''I know that.''

Frightened, for she knew Imogene's impetuous nature, Bess waited for something to happen. With each day Imogene's blue eyes had grown more luminous, her manner more carelessly flaunting. Bess did not like the way she smiled at Harry—it was an invitation, that smile.

Things came to a head the very next night. It was a beautiful night and Bess felt in her bones that something was going to happen, for Lady Moxley was entirely silent, studying Imogene balefully, and Imogene reacted by flirting outrageously with Harry at supper. She had entirely abandoned Bess's gray voile and was wearing the sky blue velvet dress with the shimmering blue silk petticoat alight with silver. She looked stunning. Bess, watching the reckless abandonment of her gestures, was afraid for her. She remembered another night four years ago at Star Castle when Imogene's voice and smile and gestures had had the same reckless quality.

The reckless girl had become a reckless woman, Bess thought sadly. And once again she might crash on the hidden reefs of love.

She watched as, after supper, Imogene let Harry lead her out into the garden, although Lady Moxley protested that they should stay to hear Bess play the harpsichord.

"No, let them go," sighed Bess. "They wouldn't hear me, anyway," she added in an undertone.

For Imogene, as she walked beside Harry through the familiar castle halls, there was a magic in the air tonight. She felt its touch like gentle fingers as they strolled out into the softness of the night.

On such a night, she thought idly, *a girl could fall in love.* But she was no longer a girl, of course. She was a woman, but she knew, ruefully, that she lacked a woman's wisdom. She would follow her heart—wherever it led.

And tonight it led her dangerously in Harry's direction.

Harry led her to the garden wall, glamoured by moonlight.

"The gorse is springy as a bed—and as soft," he said wistfully, flexing her fingers in his. "Would you not like to try it?"

Imogene's light laugh had a little catch in it. "I'm still

making up my mind about you, Harry. I know you're a rogue—don't deny it. But would you be true to me?"

"Forever," he declared gallantly—and at that moment he meant it with all his heart. And that heart leaped within him as he spoke, for she had never said anything so serious to him before.

"I doubt it," Imogene sighed and gave him a rueful look.

"You give me no chance to prove it," he complained.

"No, I don't, do I?" His arms were around her waist now, his face rubbing gently against her hair, his warm breath now brushed her ear like a feather. "I've not been lucky for the men who've loved me," she added soberly, trying halfheartedly to pull away.

"I'd chance it," he said, his arms tightening. His lips traced a hot tingling path from her delicate jawbone down her slim neck and over her shoulder and down the smooth white flesh of her bosom. "I'd make you love me, Imogene," he murmured. "I'd make you care."

Little waves, little ripples of emotion went through her, like the frothing surf as it struck the beach and receded—back and forth, rhythmically. She could feel his words striking her heart, soft and heavy and comforting. Her senses responded to him, and his touch seemed to her like the wild waves striking at the rocks. His very maleness seemed to pour over her, surround her, claiming her, *owning* her as his own.

She lay back lazily in his arms, drifting, feeling her body's sense of release, of surrender. The magic of the night had claimed her. In a few moments she would let him lead her from the garden to one of those clumps of springy gorse that rose up everywhere, and there beneath the stars of Cornwall she would take a new lover.

So rapt were they, so intertwined were their emotions, that neither seemed to hear the sounds about them. Then:

"She's there, she's out there!" screamed a triumphant voice that penetrated Imogene's bewildered senses as Lady Moxley's.

There was a sudden pounding of feet that seemed to come from everywhere. She heard Harry's low curse and felt rather than saw him leave her arms and vault over the low wall, disappearing around a corner of the castle.

And now rough hands had seized her.

"In the name of the law!" cried a hoarse voice. "I arrest you for complicity in the murder of Giles Avery four years ago."

BOOK IV
The Legend

Fortune smiles on fools and knaves,
They need her or they'll fall,
But those who break the rules each day,
They need her most of all!

Cornwall, England, 1661

CHAPTER 28

It was a glorious day in Penzance and the town had the look of holiday about it. Hawkers were out on the village streets, crying their wares, for people had come from everywhere, on foot and on horseback, gliding along in carriages or creaking in on carts and wagons, all of them converging on the stone building where a great event was taking place. There in a makeshift courtroom (actually a ruined hall, but no place else in the town had been adjudged large enough to hold the crowd) the most beautiful woman in all of Cornwall was on trial for her life. Something to tell your grandchildren about, people muttered, how you watched Imogene Wells tried—and hanged. For the Averys were the most powerful family in this part of Cornwall, and had Imogene not been implicated in their son's murder? Punishment, they predicted, would be fierce—and fast.

Now in the heat, lords and ladies, hostlers and chamber-maids, coachmen and cooks, jostled and craned for a better view as the lovely accused, conducted by the bailiff, walked gracefully into the courtroom. A murmur went through the crowd at the sight of her.

No quailing prisoner this! Erect and regal in her sky blue gown, Imogene's delft blue gaze swept the assemblage and not a man there but was stunned by her beauty.

But to Imogene, coming in off the hot cobbled streets, seeing her last of the sunshine, and now emerging into the dimness of this high-walled ruined hall, into this press of people all staring, it seemed incredible that she should be here on trial for her life.

It had all happened so fast she still could not believe it. She had been seized, charged, and—over Bess Duveen's tearful protests—carried away to jail in Penzance on the mainland. Harry had disappeared somewhere; Bess had promised to do what she could.

Imogene had sailed in silence from St. Mary's, crouched in a boat with her captors, watching the island world recede in the darkness and with no real hope in her heart that she would ever see it, or Ennor Castle, or Bess Duveen ever again. Dawn had broken as they reached the shore of the Cornish mainland, but Imogene had scarce taken notice of the wrecked village of Penzance, devastated as a loyalist stronghold during the civil wars and just now rising from the ashes. Due to that destruction, she found herself quartered in a makeshift jail—actually a small barren room in a private house—but what did that matter? She was locked in, without hope.

A day passed, uninterrupted except by food and water,

brought by the jailer's surly wife. And another. The sun was up on the third day, and still she did not bestir herself. She felt as if she had been overtaken by fate—as if she had been given a whimsical four-year reprieve and now she must pay the piper, not for murder—she was not guilty of that—but for an indiscretion, for taking a lover four years ago when she was sixteen.

Through the roaring in her mind she seemed to hear Bess Duveen's anxious voice. It *was* Bess. She was being let in by the jailer, who locked the door again as he left.

"Oh, Imogene, I can't believe this has happened to you!" Bess quickly set down the basket of food and wine she was carrying and embraced her friend.

"What news, Bess?" asked Imogene in a tired voice.

Bess sank down on one of the two three-cornered stools the room sported. "I sent a note to the Averys entreating them—but there's been no answer."

"Nor will there be. You'd best stay out of it, Bess," Imogene counseled wearily. "You could make a slip of the tongue and they could get wind that Stephen is still alive. They'd be after him like bloodhounds—all the way to Barbados."

"I know." Bess shivered.

Imogene's lips twisted. "It would seem that Lady Moxley has done her work well."

Bess hung her head. "'Twas not Lady Moxley who betrayed you, Imogene—although it *was* at her instigation. It was Ambrose. He claimed he was protecting the family name!" Her voice grew scornful but her gray eyes were beseeching.

Imogene was taken aback, but she felt Bess had suffered

521

enough on her behalf. She patted her friend's hand. "If Ambrose hadn't, Lady Moxley would have."

"Yes, that is what he said. She kept at him, it seems. Told him no niece of hers would marry into a family who shielded a murderess!" Her hand flew to her mouth. "Oh, I'm sorry, Imogene!"

"It's all right," said Imogene stonily. "I'm sure that's what she considers me. Like mother like daughter," she added in a wry voice.

"Anyway, Ambrose was so terrified she'd prevent his marriage to Marcy that he sent word to the Averys that you were staying with us. And the rest"—Bess shrugged helplessly— "you know as well as I. I couldn't believe that my brother would do such a thing—and to a guest in our house, someone we grew up with, someone he knew I held in such affection! But I have told Ambrose"—her tearful voice hardened—"that if the trial goes against you, I will abandon any further restoration of Ennor and go back to Barbados!"

"Well, let us hope that Ambrose's first commercial venture does not die aborning," said Imogene with feigned lightness, for it grieved her to see gentle Bess in such disarray.

"Oh, don't make light of it, Imogene," cried Bess. "It was a terrible, inexcusable thing to do!"

"Yes, it was, Bess," soothed Imogene. "But remember he's your brother and you do care for him."

"If the trial goes against you, I shall never forgive him! I have told him in that event he can no longer consider himself my brother, that I will refuse to receive either him or his bride and will return all letters unopened!"

Imogene thought privately that that would be a protection for Stephen, but she refrained from saying so.

"The jailer told me the trial is day after tomorrow," she told Bess.

"Yes, and you must eat and look your best," said Bess, indicating the basket. "And appear downcast and submissive. *Then* perhaps—"

"But I am innocent!"

"I *know* that, Imogene, but—" Oh, how could she tell Imogene the terrible rumors that were running like wildfire through the town? She had heard them as she arrived. They were saying that Imogene Wells had never really left Cornwall, that she had turned into a witch these four years past and was to blame for all the ills that had befallen them. That old woman who'd been struck by lightning at the foot of the great standing stone called the Blind Fiddler—Imogene was to blame for that. And the child who had died of a stone in its throat—had not a big white bird flown in through the window, crashing through the leaded panes and dying at the doctor's feet, at the very moment he pronounced the child dead? *Her* spirit had been in that bird! And those three women, *huers'* wives, who had been raped and strangled near Boleigh (which, as everyone knew, meant "a place of slaughter") and their bodies found in the ancient *fougou*, or underground passage— *that* was not done by foreign sailors, as had been thought, but the women had chanced upon Imogene's lair, the cavern from which she wrought her evil! Bess had been shocked at the rumors, and now she could not even bring herself to speak of them to this steady-eyed woman before her. "Judge Hoskins is coming back from Bath to preside at your trial," she told Imogene.

"*That* old lecher?" said Imogene contemptuously.

"Oh, don't, I pray you, take that attitude!" wailed Bess. "And Mr. Allgood undertakes your defense, I understand."

"He has already been here," said Imogene shortly. "He has undertaken my case for the notoriety, it would seem." Her lips curled. "He does not care for the truth, but wishes me to fabricate a new story more to the liking of delicate ears!" Her teeth closed with a snap.

"Well—perhaps you should listen to him," worried Bess. "For any delay, Imogene, works in your favor."

Imogene flashed her a keen look. *What did Bess know?*

"I do not wish to raise your hopes up too high, but Harry says the *Sea Rover* was sighted by a fast sloop, and if that's true—"

Imogene's heart leaped. If that was true, then van Ryker was nearby. He must be informed of her predicament and at once! For whatever future he had envisioned for her when he tricked her into storming aboard the *Goodspeed*—whether it was a *ménage* for three, or a different wife for each of his plantations, or just to be rid of her—whatever his intent, van Ryker was not the man to let the authorities hang a woman he had once held in his arms!

"*If only it be true* . . ." she whispered.

"Harry told me he would be willing to take his boat out and scour the coast watching for him—that woman Melisande has come back to him, Imogene, and with her the boat!—but he was uneasy about facing up to a shipload of buccaneers, I think, and he wondered if you might not give him some sign so that van Ryker would know he had indeed spoken with you? Your ring, perhaps?"

"Yes, of course, that would be just the thing!" With shining eyes, Imogene tore off the ring and deposited it in Bess's hand. "Harry is right, he will know the ring! Indeed, it will exactly match the one he wears upon his little finger, for he had mine made to match it!"

"Then I must be about it!" Bess rose and smoothed down her gray skirts. "I hope to have good news for you soon, Imogene—news that van Ryker is coming." She gave her friend a last embrace for—like Imogene—she felt that if van Ryker did not reach her, Imogene was as good as dead already.

Until the night before the trial, the news that van Ryker's ship had been sighted sustained Imogene. She ate heartily, she drank the wine Bess had provided, she was filled with hope.

But as the long hours dragged on and there was no word, she found herself pacing restlessly in her cell. And at midnight with her trial set for the next day, she faced the fact that they had somehow missed van Ryker, that he had not seen the *Goodspeed*'s hull sticking to the rocks—if indeed it was still there—that he had sailed on to Amsterdam . . . without her.

And with Judge Hoskins presiding, she was now bereft of hope.

People were supposed to compose themselves for impending death, she had heard, and she little doubted that she would be taken from the courtroom to a place of execution and there strung up on a gibbet, but she could not even seem to arrange her thoughts. Her past life beat at her stormily, all the good and all the bad seeming to weigh her down equally.

But when on the morrow the bailiff took her through a muttering crowd to the courtroom, she was calm as ice. For it had come to her in those last hours of tossing and turning on the narrow pallet in her cell, that *she wanted to die well*. They would get no mawkish protestations from *her* at the end! She would face them down, every one!

It was as well for her peace of mind that the beautiful prisoner did not see the tall leathern-clad man and his homespun female companion who edged into the courtroom behind her, and far better for her peace of mind that she had not heard their conversation of two days' past when Bess had brought Harry Imogene's ring.

" 'Twill identify you to van Ryker,'' Bess had explained urgently. "Imogene tells me he wears a similar ring.''

"And so do you now, Harry,'' quipped Melisande when Bess had left and Harry was inspecting the square-cut emerald that now flashed from his little finger. Her voice harshened maliciously. " 'Twill be something for you to remember her by, Harry—after they've hanged her!'' She laughed. "I told you if you made up a story about van Ryker's ship being sighted and asked for the ring, you'd get it!''

Harry's jaw hardened. "They may not hang her, Melisande. Remember, she grew up here. She'll have friends who'll use their influence.''

Melisande shrugged. "And plenty of enemies too, I hear. In any event, 'tis time we left Ennor Castle, Harry. If she is *not* convicted, public vengeance may strike somewhere else— there may be an investigation of those at Ennor. And we wouldn't like that, would we?''

Harry winced. "We would not,'' he agreed. "Still . . .'' he

cast around for some reason to stay near golden Imogene, and decided to appeal to Melisande's greed. ''If Imogene goes free, should we not seize her and ransom her? 'Twould bring us more gold than we could make in a year from wrecking.''

In the end, that was the course they agreed on. They told Bess they were off to find van Ryker. Actually they went only as far as Penzance, for if Imogene was hanged they meant to come back to St. Agnes and make plans to meet Lomax and his group in London. They'd find some new game to bring in gold.

But it was a changed pair who entered the courtroom that day. Harry was not so resplendent as usual—nor so conspicuous. He was wearing a wide-brimmed dark hat, serviceable boots, and a leathern doublet and trousers. Melisande wore indeterminate gray homespun and looked like some serving girl on holiday with a scarf tucked neatly around her golden hair.

They found seats as far away as they could from Bess Duveen and Ambrose and ducked their heads lest someone recognize them. For theirs were faces known all over England as cutpurses and cheats and they wished desperately to escape attention.

Harry's gaze was on the woman standing in the dock. She stood proudly, facing her accusers with a level gaze. A shaft of sunlight through a broken corner of the roof beamed down upon her head, haloing its gold fierily, and striking sapphire lights from her delft blue eyes.

The barrister Allgood, with his wig slightly askew, was ponderously addressing the jury. The tale he wove was a fanciful one, for the recalcitrant accused had stonily refused to testify to such a concoction. The two men, he declared impressively, pursued by Imogene—airily he left out how she would manage to pursue them—had repaired to St. Agnes to duel. And Imogene, noble character that she was, had entreated them on her knees to desist.

"More like she told them she'd marry the winner!" came a derisive voice from the crowd and there was a ripple of laughter from the gentry in the front row and loud guffaws all around the room.

Judge Hoskins banged for order. Allgood frowned and continued. Now he held forth on her beauty—he was indeed stunned by it—even though he had known her for less than forty-eight hours he was half in love with the maddening wench.

"*Look at her*!" he finished raptly. "Could any man *not* desire her?"

As one, the courtroom turned to consider her. A soft sigh swept the crowd.

Harry dreamed with the rest. The thought that she could be his—by fair means or foul—filled the room with a dark perfume.

He was roused from his reverie by a dug-in elbow from Melisande, who was nudging him. There had been a sharp interchange between the accused and the judge. The accused was about to speak.

The courtroom was totally silent as Imogene fixed them with her blue gaze. Her voice rang out.

"I know that in this court it is useless to protest my innocence," she said calmly. "For you have all condemned me in your hearts long ago. Not for the death of Giles

Avery—of which I am innocent. No, you have not condemned me for that—you have condemned me for taking a lover.'' Her voice rang out contemptuously. ''It is for *that* I must die!''

''God, she's magnificent,'' muttered Harry. His eyes shone as he watched her. Melisande kicked at his boot to silence him.

''But none of this matters,'' Imogene added bitterly. ''There is another, *more compelling reason* why you will set me free!''

Here Judge Hoskins caught the infuriated eye of Mortimer Avery, sitting crouched in a front seat, and lifted his brows derisively as if to say with this last exhortation the young accused would surely hang herself.

Everyone held his breath, waiting for her next words.

''I am wife to the famous buccaneer Captain Ruprecht van Ryker, who loves me more than he loves his life, and I am told his ship of forty guns now stands off the coast of Cornwall.''

A murmur went through the courtroom.

From the dock, leaning forward with her weight resting on her hands on the railing before her, the glorious expanse of her bosom and the pearly tops of her breasts in full view, Imogene was speaking again, more softly, in a low deadly tone.

''Good people of Cornwall, I urge you to reconsider before you pass sentence upon me. For whether I am guilty or no, I am wife to the Caribbean's deadliest buccaneer. And I warn you that as surely as the sun rises in the morning, van Ryker will come for me. If he finds that you have harmed me, he will level Penzance to the ground and put everyone in it to the sword! He will lay waste to the Cornish coast and ravage the Scilly Isles! Do you take in what I am saying? If you harm me, you will surely die!''

His face convulsed with rage at the temerity of the accused, Judge Hoskins brought his fist down upon the table before him with a force that shattered the inkwell and spattered those in the front seats with India ink.

''Silence, woman!'' he roared. ''You dare to show contempt for this court?''

''Indeed I have every contempt for it,'' replied Imogene calmly. ''For I have always understood that, though born in wedlock after Hoskins's death, you were in truth Mortimer Avery's bastard brother, and therefore uncle to the man I am accused of murdering! Guilty or no, you are bound to bring me down as a sop to your blood relations!''

The courtroom erupted into uproar, for that story, though much denied, had long been rife in Cornwall.

''And to think I had thought she would plead for her life!'' marveled Ambrose.

''Oh, be quiet,'' pleaded Bess in anguish. ''She will soon wish she had!'' After this outburst, they were sure to condemn Imogene!

''A jury of your peers will decide your guilt or innocence,'' thundered Judge Hoskins, his face mottled with wrath. ''*I* will decide your sentence.''

''And we both know what that sentence will be,'' rejoined Imogene in a cold voice. She turned dramatically to the jury box. ''It is to you I appeal,'' she cried. ''Not for my life but for yours! For I promise you that van Ryker and his buccaneers will destroy you all if you harm so much as a hair on my head! Find me innocent and he will spare Cornwall and take me away. You can forget Imogene Wells and go back to your own lives again!''

It was all very brave, thought Bess, shivering. And very foolhardy—but then Imogene had always been reckless. And very futile, for from her vantage point Bess could see clearly the furious uncompromising face of the judge.

''Silence, wench! I tell you, *be silent*!''

Before Judge Hoskins's strident bellow, Imogene at last fell silent. She stood pale and waiting.

''The accused has finished her statement. The jury will deliver its verdict.''

Shaken, the jurors bent their heads together and whispered.

''I have one more thing to say,'' cried Imogene irrepressibly. '' 'Tis a pity I am to be judged entirely by men. Not a woman in this courtroom but could understand my situation, how I did not know I was betrothed, how it was done behind my back—oh, that I could have had women jurors!''

Her last words were all but drowned by a roar from the judge. ''If the prisoner opens her mouth again,'' he howled at the bailiff, ''I charge you to put a bag over her head. Has the jury reached a verdict?''

''We have, Your Honor.'' A meek-faced, worried-looking fellow stumbled to his feet. ''We find the accused not guilty.''

Harry gave a gasping laugh, Bess sank back with a long sigh and buried her face in her hands, Ambrose choked. Imogene stood marveling. She had not really hoped to buy back her life with her impassioned speech; that she had, dazzled her.

"What?" Judge Hoskins was on his feet. He leaned forward. "I can scarce believe my ears! How came you to such a conclusion?"

"There's no real proof she done him in, Your Honor! Mayhap 'tis as the lass says, and she's innocent! And beggin' your pardon, Your Honor, but we all of us have homes here and families. And we don't want some great crew of buccaneers to fall down on us with their cutlasses and chop us to pieces!"

"Cowards!" the judge flung at them. He mopped his forehead. From florid, he looked pale and dizzy now, as if he might have a stroke. " 'Tis a great miscarriage of justice, but we are ruled by laws which must not be broke. Release the prisoner, bailiff."

Through the pandemonium of the courtroom, Bess fought her way to Imogene and enclosed her friend in her arms.

"You take your reputation in your hands when you acknowledge you know me, Bess," said Imogene shakily.

"Oh, what care I for that?" Bess hugged her. "You're free, Imogene. *Free!*"

"Now we must make our move. I'll join you later, Harry. You know what to do," breathed Moll and scurried away as Harry edged forward through the crowd.

"Imogene." It was barely a whisper in her ear.

Bess Duveen was trying unsuccessfully to clear a path for her. Imogene looked up into Harry's face.

"Van Ryker isn't coming," he said simply.

The shock of that stopped her forward momentum. The crowd swirled about her. "How do you know?"

"No sails were sighted. I sent word—to give you hope."

And it had worked! She gave him a crooked smile. "I must join Bess, Harry."

"No." His arms stayed her. "That is exactly what you must not do." Again he leaned close to her ear. "Word's out that the Averys have a second plan if hanging failed. They'll descend on Ennor Castle tonight, I've no doubt."

And in the Averys' effort to kill her, sweet loyal Bess might die in the crossfire!

"You've something in mind, Harry?" she murmured.

He nodded. "Come with me. I've a boat waiting." He took her hand.

In the crush, Bess had not noticed Harry. "Come along, Imogene," she cried happily. "We'll celebrate your victory!"

There were black looks all about at this comment, for the terrible rumors that had been circulating had now reached staggering proportions—Imogene was being blamed for half the crimes in the county.

"Bess." Imogene put her lips close to Bess's ear. She knew that loyal Bess would never let her go now, she'd insist on standing by her and it would be her ruin. "I'm off to meet van Ryker," she whispered, and Bess's face lit up.

"He wants you back?" she breathed.

"Yes." Imogene felt bittersweet emotions surge through her at Bess's heartfelt joy. Bess hugged her.

"Then I wish you well, Imogene," she cried.

"Sh-h-h, remember the Averys," muttered Imogene. "They could still have dirty work afoot."

She saw Bess nod as they were jostled apart. She glimpsed Bess going over to collect Ambrose, who was standing, puzzled and dismayed, beside a furious Lady Moxley. Then she melted into the crowd with Harry, and soon found herself—by Harry's clever maneuvering—out of town and hurrying down a grassy slope toward a narrow gully that led down to the sea.

Harry was following Melisande's plan, which was to bring Imogene along this path—but there was another plan that interested him more. Tempting as the thought of a long stay in London with Imogene, while they arranged for her ransom, might be, shucking off Moll and running away with Imogene at once was even more appealing.

"I've come to take you up on that notion you had, Imogene—that I should go away from here, change my life," he said.

He was holding her hand caressingly in a light grip. Around them birds were singing. The air was salt and fresh for they were very close to the sea. Grassland went clear to the tops of the gray granite cliffs that faced the ocean. But into this low hollow in which they were going they could not see the ocean; instead, rounded grassy hills lay before them and behind them.

"That is"— he smiled that boyish winning smile of his— "if you'll go with me, Imogene."

Imogene looked at him. A man with a bad past. But then hadn't *she* a bad past? Who was she to judge him? And hadn't he said that he wanted to change?

"Harry," she said softly. "Do you think you really could— *change*?"

There was a flicker in Harry's eyes and he stood straighter. She was going to accept his offer! This lustrous wench was going to sail away beside him! Who cared what way they went? Straight path or crooked, it was all the same to him. Just as he'd always followed the path any of his women took, he'd be content to follow Imogene anywhere she went—indeed, to take her where she wished to go.

"For *you*, I could change," he said, and now that they were down in the gully and out of sight of any who might have followed—for he was well aware that Imogene was now a celebrity of sorts and he'd had to duck around corners to escape those who would have pursued them in town—he moved to take her in his arms.

"Only you won't, Harry," said a hard voice behind him and Harry swung around to see Melisande standing there with a pistol aimed at his heart. "You ain't never going to change, and you ain't going nowhere with *her*. Not unless *I* go along!"

CHAPTER 29

Harry's arms fell to his sides. He stared apprehensively at Melisande—and at the gun, which never wavered and which was pointed straight at his chest.

"Harry," directed Imogene in a steady voice. "Go with Melisande. 'Tis to your best advantage." For she knew in her heart this jealous woman with the pistol, driven but a step farther, would shoot him through the heart.

Harry knew it too. He winced as Melisande mimicked Imogene. "'Go with Melisande, Harry. 'Tis to your best advantage!'"

"Harry loves you, Melisande," said Imogene. She was fighting for Harry's life.

"Does he?" Melisande's voice rose in fury. *"Does he?"*

"Yes," sighed Imogene. "I think he truly does— in his heart." Sadly she realized that it was probably true. "Take

him along with you, Melisande. So he once had a passing
fancy for a girl in a blue dress—what can it possibly matter
when you're far away?''

Melisande studied Imogene from under lowering brows.
For a moment she seemed to vacillate. Then, ''Now that you
mention the blue dress, you can take it *off*!'' she ordered
contemptuously.

Imogene's startled gaze fled downward to her blue velvet
gown. ''Why?'' she demanded.

''Because it's *mine*,'' was the insolent answer. ''Harry
took it away from me when—''

''Melisande!'' The words were torn from Harry. ''Melisande—enough!''

Melisande laughed. For the moment she seemed to be
enjoying herself. ''Do you think you're the first wench I've
had to rid Harry of?'' she flung at Imogene. ''There was a
dishwater blond tavern maid in York, name of Emma. Harry
was so tender of her, you'd have thought 'twas his first time
with a wench! So I got big Logan to rape her and get her
pregnant and told her Logan'd kill Harry if it came to a fight.
So she kept her mouth shut, and when she was too big to
ride, what do you think I done? I told Harry we was leaving
and what do you think? Harry went with us and left Emma
there to rot! Take off the petticoat too,'' she added sharply as
Imogene, having shed her blue dress, recoiled from the story.

''Melisande.'' Harry's face was red with shame and embarrassment. ''You've said enough.''

''Not quite!'' The gun was still pointed at him steadily.
''There was others too—worse stories than that I could tell

you about Harry here. But maybe one'll be enough. You know when I first decided I wanted this dress?''

"I have no idea," said Imogene coldly. "But it's ridiculous to claim it was ever yours!" She was standing there in har chemise with the wind blowing the light fabric about her and she felt resentful. Resentful at Harry that he didn't do something, didn't wrest the gun away from Melisande. Van Ryker would have! Hot shame flooded her that she had so nearly run away with this man.

Melisande saw the change in her expression and gave a scornful laugh. "Know our Harry a little better now, don't you? Don't like what you're learning, do you? But I'm not through yet. How do you think Harry got that blue dress, my fine lady?''

Imogene felt cold creeping down around her. "I don't know but I'm sure you'll tell me," she said crisply.

"Melisande!" The protest was torn from Harry.

"Harry got it from Lomax, and Lomax got it from a chest on board a ship he wrecked. A chest with a money chain in it. We wanted to know who owned that chest, Harry and me. And Harry thought the way to find out if it was yours was to offer you the dress and see if you noticed the brooch was missing." She reached in her pocket and tautingly held up an object. With an indrawn breath, Imogene recognized the amethyst brooch that had once held the bodice together at the top. Her accusing gaze flew to Harry. "Then you're one of the—''

"Wreckers," finished Melisande for her. "Only he's not just *one* of the wreckers, like you puts it. Harry and me, we run this wrecking operation, we do! 'Tis Harry and me who arranges everything, we takes the loot and gets rid of it.''

"Then you were sailing to St. Agnes the night I met you," said Imogene in horror. "*You* were the man who'd unfurl a red sail and wait for an answering light!"

His shamefaced look told her it was all true.

"Oh, Harry," she whispered. *"How could you?"*

It was Melisande who spoke for him. " 'Twas easy for Harry," she said coolly. "He needed the money! And when Harry Hogue needs money, he gets it—don't you, Harry love? And now I'll just put on this blue dress, which was mine by rights anyway, seein' as how Lomax took it! And *you'll* put on these gray weeds I'm wearin', and we'll take you to a boat we've got waitin' down below the cliffs." She nodded in the direction of the ocean. "And we'll sail away with you to somewheres nice and safe where Lomax and the others can join us. And we'll *keep* you there until your buccaneer pays a fat ransom for you!"

"No!" cried Imogene, forgetful of the gun, forgetful of everything but her disgust for the pair of them. "I won't do it! I won't go with you!"

Her voice died as Melisande struck her a blow on the side of the head with the barrel of the gun. She crumpled to the grass, a slight figure in a sheer chemise. In a daze she heard Melisande say, "You're well shut of her, Harry, in spite of anything you think now. She'd have got you killed, sooner or later, and you know it as well as I do!"

There was an unrecognizable sound from Harry and then Melisande's voice again. "Here, help me with these hooks. There ain't no time to lose, Harry. I seen a big crowd headed this way—come to see the hangin', I guess, only there ain't goin' to be no hangin', so's they might start lookin' around and some o' them might happen to recognize us. Ain't as if we was new at this game, Harry. There's those as would recognize us for havin' picked their pockets or cut their purses for them. Or maybe even held them up on the king's highway!'' Her laughter pealed.

Imogene's head was ringing, but she managed painfully to sit up and open her eyes. She saw that Harry was helping Melisande with the hooks of the blue velvet dress. The pistol lay on the grass. Absorbed in getting Melisande dressed—and quickly—neither of them was watching her. She felt a wave of blackness stealing over her but she crawled toward the pistol.

"Ouch, Harry, that hurt!" Melisande was scolding him. "You caught those last hooks in my hair!"

A resentful mutter came from Harry's lips that sounded vaguely like "I'm sorry."

"You should be! Are you sure you've got it hooked up right in the back there? I don't want to be lookin' like I've been rollin' in some hayloft, Harry!"

"Stand still, Melisande! How do you expect me to—there!"

Imogene reached the pistol, felt her fingers close around it. She rolled over and from her prone position on the ground, pointed it at them.

"Harry," she said quietly.

Harry turned in surprise that her voice was coming from the wrong side of him. She saw his eyes widen. "Imogene," he said. "Imogene—don't."

"Why shouldn't I kill you?" she asked dully. "You killed so many others. People who never hurt you."

Melisande had glided behind Harry. She was using his lean body as a protective shield, her blue velvet skirts blowing around his thighs, between his legs. "Talk to her, Harry," she muttered anxiously.

Harry moistened his lips. His eyes were on the gun, held there, riveted. "Look here, I didn't take part in the killing, Imogene. I never killed anyone in my life!"

"No, but you profit from it, you see that it's done," she sighed.

Sweat had broken out on Harry's brow. "I told you I'd change," he cried.

"How? By taking me captive and holding me for ransom?" she mocked him.

"He won't do that now." Melisande jabbed Harry with her elbow. "Will you, Harry? He'll be true to you. *Promise her, Harry!*"

"I'll be true to you, Imogene!" cried Harry in an anguished voice. And deep with hurt, torn from the heart of him, "God help me, you know I will!"

"Like you were true to Emma and all those others?" Imogene's voice sounded remote. There was a roaring in her ears. Suddenly she realized that the roar came not from within but from without.

"Oh, my God, what's that?" cried Melisande. She stuck out her head from behind Harry's shoulder. Harry too was staring forward.

Imogene inched to a sitting position. A quick glance behind her showed a number of men running downhill toward them. They were making an enormous noise. "*Heva, heva!*" came the roar.

And suddenly, without being told, she knew what had happened. Knew with inner certainty. The Averys had decided to make certain that their dead son was avenged. They had managed to set the *huers* on her and now they were bearing down the hill hard upon them, shouting "*Heva, heva!*" which meant "Found, found!" Unaware of the rumors that had been circulating, Imogene wondered briefly what lie the Averys had invented to set them against her. No matter, she told herself, almost tranquil now at this anticlimax after the agony of her trial, she would soon be dead—just as dead as if that Cornish jury had convicted her!

It amused her that first these *huers* might strike down Melisande by mistake simply because she was wearing the blue dress.

"They're after *me*," she told them, pleased that she could strike terror into Melisande's cold heart. "And at this distance they think you're me—because you're wearing my blue dress."

"I'll get it off!" cried Melisande in panic. She began ripping at the bodice.

Imogene's voice stayed her. "I'll shoot you if you try it," she told Melisande amiably.

Melisande's hands fell away like lifeless things. She began to whimper. "Harry," she pleaded. "That mob is after Imogene because they think she's a witch—you heard the talk in town. *Do* something, Harry! Don't you see, if they get her, they'll get *us*? Even if they kill her before she can accuse us, they'll ask us questions we can't answer because we're *with* her!''

Harry was trembling. ''Imogene,'' he whispered hoarsely. *''For the love of heaven!''*

''Heaven doesn't love you, Harry,'' mocked Imogene. *''How could it?''*

He stiffened at her mockery. His boyish face was gray with fear, but now a spark of desperate courage kindled in his eyes. ''We're going to make a run for it,'' he said. ''Melisande and me. There's no point our dying with you!''

Imogene laughed. She was surprised she could still laugh, when anytime now her life would be ending. ''No point at all,'' she agreed. She cocked the gun.

''I *loved* you, Imogene!'' The words were wrenched from Harry. ''You'll not shoot me,'' he added with strangled bravado and turned away from her.

Imogene lifted the pistol. And then she remembered how she had felt about this rogue, how he had amused her, kindled desire in her, made her want to live again. She remembered how for a moment there he had wavered, wanting to go *her* way. Why *should* he die with her after all?

With a sob she let the pistol barrel fall. Harry might be as bad as she now believed, but *she* could never be his executioner.

Casting a look of triumph behind him that he had correctly judged his woman, Harry had already taken to his heels and Melisande was sprinting along beside him.

The roar had increased to a mighty tower of sound and those vengeful feet were pounding ever nearer.

Suddenly a hand went over Imogene's mouth. ''Quiet,'' grated a low voice and she felt the gray homespun petticoat

Melisande had left on the ground flung over her head. Imogene struggled indignantly. "They went *that* way!" roared the voice above her, obviously addressing the tumult that was bearing down upon them. "Tried to steal this poor woman's clothes to get a disguise! Held a gun on her!"

The roar increased as pelting feet sheered off and passed them by but Imogene had gone limp. For she had recognized that voice.

"Now!" came a low-voiced whisper close to her ear and she felt herself swept up and carried in strong arms. Arms she knew. Arms she loved. Arms she should never have left.

The gray petticoat was still thrown over Imogene's head like a hood, obscuring her golden curls, but the face that looked up from beneath it was alight and starry-eyed.

"Van Ryker!" breathed Imogene. "How did you ever find me?"

CHAPTER 30

Van Ryker was running now, holding her lightly in his arms, sprinting down the grassy gully that led to the sea. The torrent of men had gone on past them, through the shallow valley. They were running up the long slope after Harry and Melisande—in pursuit of Imogene, as they believed the woman in the blue dress to be. Herding them upward toward the cliffs, toward the sea.

"I'd come ashore looking for you." The dark, loved face that smiled down upon Imogene's split into a wide grin. "At first I thought 'twas you standing there beside the tall fellow in leather, for I recognized the blue dress. I was dashing toward you with my boots making hardly any sound on this soft grass, for 'tis damp the way I came up, as you can tell by how quiet we're going, not hard like that ground over which that great body of men is pounding. Who are they and what do they want? Do you know?''

''They're *huers* and they want me,'' said Imogene composedly. She would have been content to lie in these arms forever and be carried along.

Van Ryker quirked an eyebrow at her.

''Like you,'' she murmured, ''they've been fooled by the blue dress. They think they're pursuing me. But never mind about that,'' she added impatiently. ''Go on. Start at the beginning.''

''I left the ship far out,'' he said, ''with orders that when Barnaby received my signal, he was to sail in and start bombarding the town. I would lead the attack from the land side.''

Imogene felt a little thrill of joy go through her. She had not lied to the jury. Van Ryker had sailed in ready to do battle for her.

''I left a force of men below the town and came in to reconnoiter—I had to locate you. I reached Penzance just as you and the fellow who just ran away were leaving. Or escaping. I couldn't tell which. He appeared to be removing you from harm, so I followed, not daring to attract attention to you by calling out or giving chase. When I saw he was leading you into that gully, I began to suspect his motives. About the same time I sighted far off a great body of men running this way. I didn't like the look of any of it, especially since he seemed to be leading you into the concealment of some trees. So I decided to circle around and approach you by way of the gully from below, under cover of the trees. At least that way I'd have blocked his path to the sea. I was out of sight for a short while and when I got there I thought it was you standing there in the blue dress—and then I saw that you were lying on the ground holding a gun on the pair of them. The woman seemed to have materialized out of nowhere."

"She stepped from behind a tree," said Imogene.

"I was about to spring for him when the pair of them broke and ran. It occurred to me then that *you* might be the quarry when I saw the men running downhill toward the gully were all pointing at the woman in the blue dress and waving each other on—and when I realized that you were lying on the ground in your chemise with your dress on the other woman's back and naught but a pile of gray homespun on the ground. Fabric," he chuckled, "that you would *never* wear by choice! So I seized you before you could cry out, threw that petticoat over your head to conceal your identity and called out to your pursuers to draw them off."

She owed her life, she realized, to his quick thinking. It brought home to her how narrow her escape had been—if escape it was, for they were not out of it yet.

The gully had narrowed to a steep rocky ravine down which he ran, light-footed in his wide boots as a mountain goat. That narrow defile had now led them far down to the base of the cliffs, where they could see the whole wide panorama of the sea and the mighty cliffs rising tall on each side of them in their granite march along the Cornish coast. At last van Ryker slowed his breakneck pace and found a concealing cleft in the rocks.

"We'll wait here a moment," he said, looking about him keenly. Her senses quickened for she knew he sensed possible pursuit and was quietly loosening his sword in its scabbard.

"Put on the petticoat," he flung over his shoulder. "I'm afraid I left the dress in my hurry. But this"—he pulled out a scarf—"will at least conceal your hair, which is too conspicuous for comfort."

Quickly, still feeling that all this could not be happening, that van Ryker could not really have appeared out of nowhere, she did as she was bid. The scarf was of heavy gray silk and long; it covered her hair and fell down over her breast, hiding the fact that the top of her garment—above what was in reality a petticoat but appeared to the onlooker because of its homespun serviceability to be a kirtle—was not a sheer bodice but indeed a chemise!

He looked at her when she had finished.

"You will do," he smiled, and the caressing way he said it made hot color rise into her cheeks.

Over the roar of the crashing surf as they crouched there, listening to it break rhythmically against the cliffs, she said puzzled, "I still don't see how you knew to look for me *here*?"

"'Twas chance mostly," he admitted. "From the *Sea Rover* we spotted the wreck of the *Goodspeed* still hanging to the rocks and went ashore on the island there."

"St. Agnes," she supplied breathlessly.

He nodded. "I had neglected to paint some other name on the *Sea Rover*'s hull." He did not add that it was anxiety for her that had caused him to neglect it, but she guessed as much and smiled gently at him. "Someone on shore recognized her as a buccaneer ship and men in brown robes poured down toward the beach. One of them tried to sell me this." He reached inside his doublet and pulled out the topaz and diamond necklace Imogene had given Clara for saving her from the wreckers.

"But I gave that to Clara for saving me!" she exclaimed in alarm. "What happened to her?"

He frowned. "There was no woman. They told me there were only men on the island."

"They lied!"

"I recognized the necklace as belonging to you and offered a large price if the fellow who had it could tell me where the golden-haired wench who owned it was to be found."

"And they told you?" Surprise made her look blank.

"They were eager enough to tell me," van Ryker told her sardonically. "They told me the golden-haired wench was being tried for murder in Penzance and would probably have been hanged before I could get there. As you can surmise, I wasted no time in setting out for Penzance!"

"And found me!" she marveled. "I still cannot believe it!"

"I have a strong force of buccaneers just down the coast," he told her grimly. "Barnaby and de Rochemont and all the rest were almost as eager for this venture as I—you are popular with them, Imogene."

"I am glad," she said, smiling. "For I have an affection for them too—" She broke off, her gaze suddenly riveted on a sight farther down and above them, atop the gray cliffs where a long ledge of overhanging rock at the top pointed a finger out toward the sea. The top above was grassy and must have looked safe enough to a stranger, but anyone local would have known better than to run out upon it, for it seemed supported by nothing—almost to hang in the air like a snow bridge.

But a pair of strangers *had* run out upon it: a tall dark man and a woman with long golden hair—for Melisande's hair had come loose as she changed clothes with Imogene. Her sky blue skirts were blowing.

"It's Harry and Melisande!" she cried—and clasped her hand to her mouth in horror at what she was witnessing.

The cliffs were old and gnarled—they had waited for centuries for this moment, it seemed. Year by year, little bits of the cliff's body had crumbled away, battered by the fierce Atlantic gales, the boulders rumbling down to crash upon those other sawtooth rocks far below, rocks that as the tide came in would be covered by the sea. Even now that tide was surging in, each wave licking farther toward the tall cliff's ancient face.

And now it was as if the old cliffs had grown restless and with the rhythmic shouting of the *huers*, some inner resonance along the cliff's fault lines was set up and the ground swayed for a moment beneath the panicky feet of Harry and Melisande.

Swayed—and rent asunder with a sound like a great cracking cough as the old cliff cleared its throat and straightened its granite shoulders to stand sentinellike and watchful once more in its timeless role of guardian of the land against the hungry prowling ocean.

As the ground beneath their feet gave way, a terrified shout from Harry pierced the forward-pressing onlookers' ears and a wild scream from Melisande rent the air, silencing those shouts of "*Heva, heva!*"

Their screams continued eerily to reach the *huers* as they and the very patch of earth upon which they had stood disappeared from the *huers'* view, and those who leaped forward, daring annihilation to get a better look, saw their crushed bodies lying in the foam upon the rocks below. But Imogene, from her vantage point, saw Harry and Melisande describe a long arc, falling downward, ever downward, on their long, long drop to crash on the sawtooth rocks below. Rocks that waited like an endlessly open mouth filled with big shark's teeth—to destroy them.

Together, screaming, they fell—together landed.

And so perished Harry Hogue, the London rogue, and the doxy he had christened Melisande.

Together. As Melisande had predicted, they would always be together.

Imogene had heard their screams end abruptly as the rocks found them and broke their bones. A cry would have risen in her own throat had not van Ryker swiftly clasped a warning hand over her mouth.

With a convulsive shudder, she hid her face in van Ryker's doublet. Gently he removed his hand from her trembling mouth and his arms went round her warmly, cradling her, murmuring to her soothingly. She had been through so much, his lady. He wanted to care for her, to protect her, to shield her from harm.

"They—couldn't have survived it?" she whispered.

"Not a chance," he said cheerfully. "No, don't look—nothing to see, anyway. That last wave washed what was left of them out to sea. No one will find them now—not for a while at least. You're free, Imogene—because those men up there believe that woman was you.''

''It's horrible.'' She shuddered.

''Yes,'' he said, stroking her hair. But he was remembering that they had had her, might have killed her . . . van Ryker was not sorry for the pair who had plummeted to the rocks. ''We must wait a while,'' he told her. ''For you'd be conspicuous in a crowd of men. But soon the townsfolk will arrive in abundance—and the curious from other parts. We can make our way through them like ordinary citizens—you in your homespun and myself an inconspicuous stranger.''

''You could never be inconspicuous, van Ryker,'' she protested in a tremulous voice, thinking of his height, the mighty wingspread of his shoulders, the majestic commanding look of him.

''Well, I'll hunch my back a bit,'' he grinned, ''and try to look humble. Now tell me, Imogene, what brought you to this pass?''

The story poured out of her then—about the shipwreck, the wreckers, the trial, about Bess and Ambrose and Lady Moxley, about the Averys and the *huers*—but not about Harry, not about Melisande. Van Ryker listened raptly, holding her close to him there in that sheltering cleft in the rocks.

When she had finished, there were tears on her lashes, and very tenderly he kissed those tears away.

''I've men and a longboat waiting down the coast,'' he told her softly. ''We'll to the *Sea Rover,* Imogene, where you can forget all that's past. We'll to Amsterdam and thence to London—and Ryderwood.''

Imogene remembered then what in the trepidation of the last few minutes she had clean forgot. She pushed him away.

"I'll go with you to the *Sea Rover*, van Ryker," she said, giving him a scathing look from her smoldering blue eyes. "But *not* to make a future. You can drop me off at any safe port—say in Amsterdam, if that wouldn't be putting you out!" And to his shocked expression, "For I'll not spend my future sharing you with Veronique!"

"Veron—?" His astonishment was almost as unsettling to her as had been his calm assumption that she'd spend her future with him on any terms at all. "But didn't you get my note, Imogene? Arne told me faithfully he had put it in Captain Bagtry's hand! That note explained all!"

She shook her head. "Captain Bagtry lost it overboard when he leaped forward to rescue a child from the railing."

Van Ryker's expression changed to one of remorse. "Then all the time you thought—"

"That you had taken a new woman," she said steadily. "As indeed you have. And don't bother to deny it—I saw you together on the long divan with my own two eyes!"

"Imogene—"

"And all the notes in the world couldn't wash *that* away!"

He would have put his hands on her shoulders but that she shrugged him off.

"Imogene," he said earnestly—but there was a twinkle of mirth in his gray eyes, swiftly controlled at her gathering rage. "The woman you saw on the divan was not Veronique— it was Georgette."

"Then you are not only a lecher but a cradle robber," she gasped.

"No, no." He reached out to catch her for, unmindful of the crowd atop the cliffs, she was flinging away from him. Holding on to her trembling shoulders, he told her how it had been.

"Then Georgette impersonated Veronique?" she began indignantly. "Oh, how could she lend herself to such a charade?"

Van Ryker pressed an unexpected kiss on her lips that cut off her words, left her breathless with her heart pounding. Then he lifted his head. "Georgette would do anything to own a string of pearls." His voice was suddenly overborne by laughter—and a note of triumph too, for had he not found his woman, saved her, was she not clasped here safe in his arms? "And now she owns such a string."

"I wonder," murmured Imogene, falling in with his lightsome mood, "how she explained them to Esthonie?"

"Said she found them in the street, I shouldn't wonder, the little minx—knowing Esthonie would never say 'La, we must look for the rightful owner!' "

It was true, Imogene knew. Esthonie was at heart more of a buccaneer than any of those scarred and cutlassed gentlemen who purchased letters of marque from her plump, perspiring husband. She leaned against van Ryker's deep chest, hearing the strong steady beat of his heart.

"But it was a cruel thing to do, van Ryker," she murmured reproachfully. "Didn't you know I'd suffer the agonies of the damned over your defection?"

"I thought you'd suffer only long enough to clear the harbor," he explained frankly. "And after that I expected you'd be shaking your fist at the *Sea Rover*'s sails and wanting to get your hands on me to straighten me out for tricking you!''

"Your sails?" she asked blankly. "But you were nowhere in sight! I stood on the deck all night, and when dawn came I couldn't have missed seeing them."

He frowned. "Didn't Captain Bagtry explain that I was shadowing the ship?" he asked sharply. "Didn't he lend you his glass so that you could see for yourself?"

She shook her head. "He told me nothing. Perhaps he was diverted by the fire when that little boy knocked over one of the cooking pots on deck."

"*Fire*?" he said. "Good God!"

"It was soon put out. And after that there was talk aboard that you'd sailed only far enough to make sure the *Goodspeed* had not turned around and headed back for Tortuga—at my instigation. They said you had rid yourself of me and were making sure that I was not returned!" *And in my despair I believed it*. It was there in her voice like frozen tears.

"Did you really think me of such little account, Imogene?" He looked searchingly deep into her eyes.

"I was too confused to think," she muttered, dropping her gaze before his deep probing one. "And after what I'd seen. . . . The thought that you had taken another woman melted my brain!" *And made me easy prey for such as Harry*, she realized—but left the words unspoken. "So it was none of it true," she mused. "And to think, I left Esthonie my lovely marquetry standing clock to thank her for telling me lies!''

"You did not leave it," he said quietly. "The clock is aboard the *Sea Rover* at this moment. I told Gauthier of your decision to leave the clock and he said that his wine cellar was low in stock and he would much better appreciate some of my fine Canary. I left him beaming, with bottles stacked up around him, and took the clock with me."

"Oh, van Ryker!" Imogene burst into wild laughter—a relief after all the emotional turmoil she had been through. "Can you imagine Esthonie's face when she discovers Gauthier afloat in a sea of wine and the marquetry clock she coveted has sailed away?"

"She'll get over it," he said, ruffling her hair. "Esthonie complains but she always accommodates herself to circumstance. I think she could get over the loss of anything. But *you*..." his voice deepened. "I would never have gotten over the loss of *you*."

Her heart strummed happily at the rich tenor of his voice, at the tenderness reflected in his gray eyes. Someday she would tell him how she had challenged the jury, frightening them with *him*, how she had threatened everyone in the courtroom with loss of life—at his hands! He would throw back his great head and laugh—and then his face would become sober and thoughtful, for what havoc might he not have wrought if they had killed her, if he had come ashore only to find her lifeless body swinging from some high gibbet looking out to sea?

The threat had been real enough and they had understood it, those twelve good men of Cornwall. They had traded a buccaneer's fearless woman for their lives and property—and would be to the end of their days glad of the bargain.

"I was right about one thing," he said. "Two great

Spanish galleasses were waiting for me off Cayona Bay and had the battle gone otherwise, you might have been taken.''

"As it was, I was merely shipwrecked,'' she said crisply. "Seized by wreckers, and finally tried for my life on old trumped-up charges.''

He winced. "I did not foresee the storm,'' he admitted. "Nor could I know you would not receive my note explaining everything.''

She gave him a cold look. For, perversely, now that he was here—this man she had desired so ardently with the whole of her being—she was determined not to let him off so easily. Faith, he had put her through a real hell! That it had all been a mistake counted for nothing—it had all been of his contriving. She gazed at him accusingly. "You almost drove me into other arms!''

Van Ryker studied the hot-blooded woman before him. Her beautiful flushed face was stormy with conflicting emotions.

"I set a trap for you, Imogene—and trapped myself,'' he admitted with a sigh.

"Yes. You did!'' Resentfully.

"And these other arms,'' he said steadily. "Were they so tempting?''

Hot color flooded her face as she remembered Harry and all that she had, so briefly, felt for him. But for the intervention of the law's long arm, what might not have happened on that soft scented night in the garden at Ennor Castle when he had clasped her to him urgently and she had felt surrender flowering within her? "I—do not want to talk about that,'' she said in a suffocated voice.

"I don't doubt it!'' His face hardened.

"After all, I thought you were with Veronique the whole time. You had given me reason to believe it!" she flashed resentfully. "I imagined you making love to her in the *Sea Rover*'s great cabin—after all, Esthonie had told me you gave her the great cabin on the voyage from the Antilles to Tortuga!"

"True—and bunked in with de Rochemont." He nodded urbanely. "But more to the point, where is this fellow—my rival?" His voice was nonchalant but he was loosening his sword in its scabbard as he spoke.

"You have no need to kill him, van Ryker." Her voice saddened as her gaze flew involuntarily to the broken cliff face. "The world—and his own folly—have already done that." For a moment Harry's face rose up before her, merry and roguish. He'd had lighthearted winning ways, had Harry— and one fatal flaw: he never faced up to anything. But—she had been on the brink of falling in love with him.

"Then he was the man who fell when the top of the cliff gave way?"

She nodded.

"A fellow you were holding a gun on when I found you? A fellow who ran away and left you to a mob?" He sounded incredulous.

"It's—a long story."

"And the woman?"

Imogene shrugged. "Some London wench who had dragged him down. I think Harry might have made it, had it not been for her. She wasn't right for him, even though he loved her."

"And I suppose you were?" He snorted.

The face she turned to him was stripped of artfulness or

pretense; it was grave and sad. "Perhaps. But Harry wasn't right for me. For me he filled a need, a void, a—oh, haven't you ever felt like that, van Ryker? I couldn't love him, but I—I tried to. I wanted to. God, how I tried!"

"I didn't know women felt like that," he admitted thoughtfully. "I knew men did."

"And so, in a way, I failed you," she said in a small voice. "Nothing happened but—something *would* have happened had I not at that moment been seized and dragged away to jail. I wasn't entirely true after all." She forgot Harry, who had been, after all, but a romantic interlude and never meant to last, she forgot everything but the tall stern man before her looking down at her with such love and understanding. "Van Ryker . . . can you ever forgive me?" she asked wistfully.

And her tall buccaneer answered her as he had once before, the night they had plighted their troth. "Imogene, Imogene, how could you ever doubt it?" And gathered her into his arms.

He was thinking how true she was, that she could suffer over what had never been but only might have happened. His lady, his peerless Imogene, there would never be anyone like her. Faith, her near-miss with infidelity might trouble *her*— but it would never trouble him. Good God, had he not thought about it himself once or twice? And resisted, of course.

And holding her, he swore a great oath to himself: that she would never have cause to doubt him again. Nor would she ever again wander unprotected through the world. By God, he would never leave her side!

After a time of sighs and touching, of lingering kisses that took the breath and caught at the heart, of murmuring promises and soft regrets, a time when they wished themselves aboard the *Sea Rover* and lost in the magic of its great cabin, lying in the big bunk looking out at the stars through that bank of slanted windows in the stern, after all that had to be said urgently was said and all the cobwebs and misunderstandings cleared away, van Ryker put her gently away from him.

" 'Tis time to go, Imogene. There'll be enough people wandering about these slopes now that we can mingle with the crowd and not be noticed. My buccaneers may become uneasy and strike out to find me. Best we not keep the longboat waiting."

For a moment Imogene hung back. "But first shouldn't I find Bess and thank her for all she did?"

Van Ryker cast a speculative look at the broken section of cliff that had tumbled down carrying Harry and Melisande to their death. "That pelting crowd of—what did you call them? *Huers*? They believed they were chasing *you*," he pointed out. "And now, for the time at least, until they find the bodies of those two, they believe they did you in. Let's leave it that way. Safer for you."

"But Bess—she wouldn't tell anyone!"

"She might be tricked into it. By her brother, perhaps. You said he bears you no love."

"Yes, that's true, but—"

"You can let Bess know your fate later—on Barbados. Although"—he gave the dazzling woman beside him a sardonic glance—"you might be doing Bess a favor to let her think you were no longer in the land of the living!"

She caught his meaning: *So that Bess need never have a qualm about how she stood with Stephen . . . yes, perhaps that would be a gift, a silent way to show her gratitude. To let Stephen and Bess think that she was dead.*

She gave van Ryker a look of silent appreciation. No one would ever suit her as he did. And to think, she had been on the verge of leaving—with Harry!

Panic over that narrow escape made her throw herself against him again, burying her face in his deep chest. There was a wonderful haven here, listening to the strong beating of his heart throbbing in her ears.

She cast a look back at the cliffs, at the broken shelf from which Harry and Melisande had plunged to their death. He had been very enticing, had Harry. And had it happened slightly otherwise, she might even now be in his arms sailing away to an uncertain future. Or perhaps on a fast horse heading for London, with Melisande and the wreckers in full cry after them—and van Ryker a part of her past.

"It was foolish of you to deceive me," she said softly, touching his lips with gentle fingers. "It was dangerous—and reckless."

"But then I was ever so," he assured her, and seized her fingers and kissed them. "As are you, Imogene. Perhaps 'tis why you please me so." He held her off from him and his voice was deep and rich. The glow in that voice promised her everything.

She smiled up at him. Then, trustingly—for he was worthy of her trust—she gave him her hand and let him lead her over the grassy slopes and through the milling people, down the coast toward the longboat and his waiting buccaneers. Somehow she seemed to have walked this path before, she thought dreamily as she sat beside van Ryker in the prow, with strong oarsmen bending their backs to carry them to the waiting *Sea Rover*.

Van Ryker's arm was around her and her long bright hair, loosed now from the gray silk scarf and shimmering like the *Sea Rover*'s golden hull in the afternoon sun, was blowing over his shoulder. It blew across the saturnine features of the man who looked down on her so tenderly. He brushed it away, then bent to press a gentle kiss upon those shining strands and rub his cheek against her fair head.

"All our lives lie before us, Imogene," he whispered, and she knew thrillingly that it was true.

Tonight there would be a celebration aboard the *Sea Rover*. Her decks would be dancing with lights, the air filled with music and song. They would paint the name *Victorious* across her golden hull and drink fine captured wines and congratulate one another on the world that they had won.

Then they would depart the Scillies forever and sail away toward their destiny. And as the great ship beat its way into the English Channel, she and her lean buccaneer would have their own celebration in the luxurious great cabin with only a low-hanging moon to watch them. They would toast the future and then—because they had been so long apart—an impatient van Ryker would not even let her finish undressing. When she was only down to her chemise, he would sweep her up and carry her to the big familiar bunk where so much had happened, and lay her down upon it tenderly and there divest her of her remaining garments, while little shudders of feeling coursed through her.

And then he would shed his own clothes. She would marvel for a moment at the wondrous vibrant masculinity of him, standing broad-shouldered and dominating and lean-hipped in the moonlight—but only for a moment would she marvel, for he would move swiftly to join her, lowering his long hard body gently onto hers, and all the past would be forgotten in his arms.

Her woman's body, her throbbing heart, her very soul would respond to him, soar with him, become one with him. And all the misunderstandings, all the troubles, all the dangers would be blotted out. Their naked limbs would intertwine—and tremble with the joy of it. Their bodies would lock sinuously, their lips meet and hold. Ardently, urgently they would embrace and the passion that shook them whenever they touched would engulf them once again. Soaring and honest and real, that passion would thunder through their veins like an earthquake—it would swallow them up and leave them shaken and amazed. As it always did.

In the prow of the longboat, Imogene leaned against van Ryker, blissful and content. Harry and the Scillies were already fading from her mind. Van Ryker was working his magic on her once again and she was lost in happy dreams of bright tomorrows.

EPILOGUE

They scrambled down the cliffs, those *huers*, seeking their quarry. But by the time they reached the place where Harry and Melisande had fallen, the pounding waves had carried the bodies out to sea. It was three days later that they were washed ashore—and by then they were unrecognizable: their faces were smashed—and the woman's hands as well, where they had struck the rocks.

Bess was dragged, trembling, to the beach and asked if this was the buccaneer van Ryker and his woman, who had once been Imogene Wells.

Bess took one look at that streaming golden hair, the rags of a sky blue velvet dress that even after three days in the ocean was unmistakably the one that Imogene had been wearing. No one, not even Bess who had known her, would have dreamed that she was looking, not upon Imogene, but upon Melisande, queen of the London streets. Bess's tortured gaze flew to the tall man with wet dark hair and a smashed face lying there in clothing she had never seen Harry wear. Dark hair—Stephen had said van Ryker was dark. And tall. This man was tall. And on his hand a ring exactly like the one Imogene had given her to send to van Ryker. Bess never dreamed it was the identical ring that she herself had entrusted to Harry!

"Is it van Ryker? And his woman?" came a harsh voice beside her.

"Yes," she whispered almost inaudibly. "*It is van Ryker—and Imogene*." And when, insistently, they made her look again to make sure, she reeled on her feet and added, "Those are the clothes she was wearing at the trial and that emerald ring on the man's hand—Imogene told me that van Ryker always wore a ring like that on his little finger. And"—her voice was hoarse—"I know he would have come through hell to rescue her."

They would have asked her more, but she fainted.

Grim-faced, those men of Cornwall buried the lovers—that pair of opportunists who had sought fortune the wrong way and found death waiting. None save Bess wept for Imogene and her buccaneer, none save Bess mourned them. And there were many scathing remarks passed among the crowd of curious about the graveside that van Ryker's buccaneers had not come back to save their leader or even to rescue his body. Then the skies opened and the rain poured down.

No honor among thieves, it was agreed damply.

Bess wept. And looking up, blinking into the pouring rain,

she thought God wept too. Wept for doomed lovers passing into history.

Bess sailed back to Barbados and in the savage brilliance of the tropical sun beating down, she took a deep breath and looked around her at the blowing palms of her island world. And realized with force that, shocking as the thought now seemed to her, she was glad that Stephen had not seen Imogene again, that the love so deeply imprinted on his memory had had no chance to flare up from the ashes. Bess flayed herself for thinking that, but the thought was lurking in her mind even as Stephen flung his arms around her when he met her ship in Bridgetown.

Van Ryker had been right—by "dying," Imogene had given kindly Bess peace of mind.

The coarse gray homespun dress Melisande had worn that last day was found at the spot where Melisande had flung it at Imogene. That was proof, wasn't it, said the townsfolk. Proof that Imogene Wells had been planning to change into more sober garments and slip out of here to safety—after all she'd done! The poor woman who owned that dress, frightened by all that had happened, must have run away! They asked about, exhibiting the dress, and finally a hard-faced serving wench from Mousehold claimed it. It gave her stature in the taverns to tell how Imogene Wells and her buccaneer lover had caught her out walking on her way to visit her brother and forced her to disrobe. The story was always good for a free tankard of ale.

And it tied the events all up neatly. For she had been at the trial and could describe Imogene very well.

No one doubted her. No one at all.

Some few, talking it over in taverns and alehouses, voiced their puzzlement that the men of the *Sea Rover* had not stormed ashore at Penzance, plundering and killing as they went, to avenge the death of their captain and his bride. Strangely enough, they had not done that. Instead they had poured ashore on St. Agnes Isle and killed every man on the island. Some religious sect—nobody local knew anything about them, but it was strange the buccaneers had chosen St. Agnes for their vengeance. Even poor Clara who had lived there so long, the only resident until that religious group came, had been found in a half-concealed shallow grave. When someone pointed out that the body they exhumed there had been dead some days, only shrugs greeted the pronouncement. Those pious recluses who had moved onto the island wouldn't have done that, would they? So it must have been the buccaneers! And when someone, prying Clara's still-clenched fingers apart, found a link of what must once have been a diamond and topaz necklace, they shook their heads learnedly and agreed that proved it was the buccaneers who had done her in.

But the *huers* and the townsfolk had not searched well enough. They had searched the sea—but not the shore.

They had not noticed the tiny cleft between the rocks where Imogene and van Ryker had crouched and waited. They had completely overlooked the tall man with the saturnine face and the very serviceable-looking sword and brace of pistols, and the woman with him who wore a plain homespun kirtle. She had kept her head bent in its flowing gray silk scarf and her eyes modestly downcast. And though some had noticed her pretty face, none had more than a passing glimpse of it as the pair hurried through the onlookers. Nor did anyone, among all these people milling about, wonder where this pair of strangers went, as they disappeared over a grassy rise, heading down the coast. None ever guessed that the pair they had glimpsed was van Ryker and his woman, strolling away to rendezvous with a waiting longboat.

They did not see a great golden-hulled ship, anchored far offshore, sail away into oblivion.

The *Sea Rover* was said to have perished in a great storm that swept the North Atlantic that year, for she never made port in Tortuga again. And in Cayona the buccaneers mourned van Ryker in their fashion—by telling of his exploits and downing great amounts of rum to his memory. And Esthonie Touraille sighed irritably over Imogene's passing—if she was going to die in Cornwall anyway, why must her trunks have gone down with the *Sea Rover*? Why couldn't she have left some of those gowns and jewels in the house on Tortuga where they could be made good use of by herself and Georgette?

Esthonie glared at the plain lantern clock that graced the spot where the handsome marquetry long-case clock *should* have stood—and sighed that it had gone down with the *Sea Rover* as well, traded for a lot of Canary wine that had since disappeared. The governor insisted obdurately that it had been stolen, but Esthonie had reason to doubt it. She railed at her plump husband, the governor, about the wine, about the climate, about his personal habits. Why had he been such a fool as to pay cash for this great barn of a house when, if he had but bought it on credit, there'd now be nothing to pay, since van Ryker was dead?

The governor met all these verbal onslaughts equably—as he had over the years. He was far more worried over the pearl necklace his daughter Georgette had inexplicably "found" than over the rantings of his wife. Esthonie would soon realize that she had the best house in Tortuga and that, now that van Ryker was dead, the Spanish were unlikely to deign to send a fleet to destroy it. Esthonie would come round—she always had. But Georgette! He was not fool enough to believe the girl's story of "finding" the necklace even if Esthonie chose to swallow it. He put her in Virginie's old room and told himself he must get her married before she became a trollop!

And none on Tortuga guessed—for if Arne knew, he did not tell it—that a battered ship with a golden hull and the name *Victorious* painted across that hull, had limped out of the great Atlantic storm that was said to have claimed the *Sea Rover,* into the mouth of the Cooper River in Carolina, and that buccaneers turned pioneers were even now carving out an empire whose capital would one day be called Charles Towne and later Charleston.

They never guessed—in either Cayona or Carolina—that the tall Englishman, Branch Ryder, and his lustrous lady, who came down to Port Royal from their plantation called Gale Force upriver toward Spanish Town and dined with the governor—Branch Ryder with a huge sandy periwig and his blue-eyed lady with a wig black as ebony and almost as large—were the fabled van Ryker and his golden Imogene.

The governor of Jamaica knew. He chuckled as he lounged back and clinked glasses companionably with them as they toasted other days and other places. For the governor of

Jamaica was a London rake reformed by love of this same lustrous lady who lounged beside her ex-buccaneer and whose delft blue gaze challenged him above her silver goblet of port. The governor of Jamaica thought it all a great joke—but he would never tell.

"You should marry," Imogene told him bluntly, smiling beneath his glowing gaze. "And stop ogling married women!"

"I *would* marry," agreed the governor idly, "if I could find a woman like you. Why do you not send this great fellow out to sea again so that he may chance upon some mishap? Then I will pay you court!"

The "great fellow" shrugged. "I am afraid to let my golden lady out of my sight," he admitted with a grin. "For she has a knack of getting into trouble and must needs be saved from it."

"True," sighed the governor, his wistful gaze playing over Imogene. "But then, she's so very worth saving. . . ."

Van Ryker lifted his glass in silent acknowledgment of the truth of that remark. He thought so too.

Word spread across the western world that the tall buccaneer was dead. And women sighed who remembered him. And men who had envied him his seizure of the Spanish plate fleet grew thoughtful as they drank their wine, for he had lived so short a time after winning it—and lost it all for a woman.

But those who remembered golden-haired Imogene could understand that he would throw away his fortune for her, and his life as well. For not a man on whom those delft blue eyes had rested but had kindled to them, and those who had come close had drowned in them.

As the years went by a mighty legend grew up around van Ryker and his woman. They became a part of Western culture—like fabled Henry Morgan who had sacked Panama and lived to be knighted and made a lieutenant governor of Jamaica. Only, van Ryker's story was more romantic, for he had been cut down at the height of his prowess and almost at the moment of his triumph. They are more glamorous who do not live to be old.

And if there were those who whispered in Tortuga that the *Sea Rover* still sailed the seas, if there were those in Port Royal and Spanish Town who claimed to have seen the fabled lovers, who claimed they anchored sometimes on a river in Carolina and sometimes in some unnamed Jamaica bay, they were not believed, for from that cliff in Cornwall Imogene and van Ryker had vanished into legend.

And so the story of this pair of lovers—changed and altered with each retelling—passed into legend and became part of the lore of the Western world. And on soft summer nights in the Scillies, with voices muted against the endless unchanging murmur of the sea, you may hear them tell again the story of van Ryker and his gold—and his woman.

Especially the woman.

> *The stories that men told of her*
> *Were very seldom true*
> *For all they really know of her*
> *Was that her eyes were blue....*

Watch for the thrilling sequel, bringing to a climax the tempestuous story of Imogene and her beautiful daughter Georgianna as Georgianna's dramatic love story unfolds in **Rich Radiant Love**, coming soon from Warner Books.

More From
Valerie Sherwood...